P9-CFU-181

RAINBOW
MARS

TOR BOOKS BY LARRY NIVEN

N-Space
Playgrounds of the Mind
Destiny's Road

WITH STEVEN BARNES
Achilles' Choice
The Descent of Anansi

WITH JERRY POURNELLE AND STEVEN BARNES
Beowulf's Children

RAINBOW MARS

LARRY NIVEN

TOR®

A TOM DOHERTY ASSOCIATES BOOK
NEW YORK

This is a work of fiction. All the characters and events portrayed in this novel are either fictitious or are used fictitiously.

RAINBOW MARS

Copyright © 1999 by Larry Niven

All rights reserved, including the right to reproduce this book, or portions thereof, in any form.

"Rainbow Mars," copyright © 1999 by Larry Niven; "The Flight of the Horse," copyright © 1969 by Mercury Press, Inc.; "Leviathan!" copyright © 1970 by *Playboy*; "Bird in the Hand," copyright © 1970 by Mercury Press, Inc.; "There's a Wolf in My Time Machine," copyright © 1971 by Mercury Press, Inc.; "Death in a Cage," copyright © 1973 by Larry Niven.

A Tor Book
Published by Tom Doherty Associates, Inc.
175 Fifth Avenue
New York, NY 10010

Tor Books on the World Wide Web:
http://www.tor.com

Tor® is a registered trademark of Tom Doherty Associates, Inc.

Book design by Lisa Pifher

ISBN 0-312-86777-8

Printed in the United States of America

This is for Marilyn,
who won't read fantasy unless I write it.

CONTENTS

Another major advance in our understanding of Mars has come from analysis of the MOLA topographic data. Although relative topographic variations have been known since 1972 from Mariner 9 data, the detailed topography needed to understand many of the features on Mars is only now being provided by MGS. Even with the present elliptical orbit, MOLA is providing vertical resolutions of about 30 cm with horizontal resolutions of 300 to 400 m. MOLA has been able to provide detailed topographic information about individual features such as impact craters, volcanoes, fractures, channels, and polar deposits. One discovery is that some of the channels, including Ares Valles in whose outwash area Mars Pathfinder landed, are deeper than previously thought, indicating more water has flowed through the channels than earlier suspected. In addition, MOLA has revealed that the northern plains of Mars are extremely flat, as smooth as the Earth's oceanic abyssal plains. The smoothness of the northern plains supports the theory that they are sediments deposited in a vast ocean which once covered this area.

"Revealing the Secrets of Mars" by Nadine G. Barlow
Ad Astra—the magazine of the National Space Society
July/August 1998

RAINBOW MARS

1

+390 *Atomic Era*. Svetz was nearly home, but the snake was waking up.

Gravity pulled outward from the center of the extension cage as it was pulled toward present time. The view through the wall was a jitter of color and motion. Svetz lay on his back and looked up at the snake. A filter helmet showed only as a faint golden glow around its head. It wouldn't strangle on post-Industrial air, and it couldn't bite him through the inflated bubble.

A ripple ran down the feathers along its spine, a gaudy flurry of color, nine meters from head to tip of tail. It seemed to take forever. Tiny rainbow-colored wings fluttered at its neck. Its eyes opened.

The natives of −550 Atomic Era would have carved his heart out without losing that same look of dispassionate arrogance.

Svetz raised the needle rifle.

A loop of it shimmied aside as he fired. The anesthetic crystal needle shattered on the wall. The shimmy ran down the tail, while Svetz fired again and missed again. Then the tailtip snapped down and flicked the needle gun out of his hands.

Svetz cringed back.

The rainbow-feathered head lifted to study him.

+1108 Atomic Era. Watery colors around the cage took on shapes. For an instant Svetz saw startled techs, and Ra Chen yelling. Then the snake fell over him in coils, knocking the breath out of him. Coils constricted around his torso. He wriggled an arm free and reached for the needle gun, but a loop of tail coiled around his wrist.

Immobile, he looked into the ophidian face.

The hatch opened. Techs played sonic handguns along the snake's length. It went limp. Hillary Weng-Fa and Wilt Miller pulled Svetz out of the X-cage and looked him over. Other techs coiled the torpid snake on a lifter platform for transport to the Secretary-General's Vivarium.

Wrona pushed past Chairman Ra Chen to lick Svetz's face. Svetz hugged her. The touch of fur was a comfort.

"Feathers," Ra Chen said. "Futz. Are *you* all right?"

"Fine. Sir, I think it *decided* not to kill me. Treat it right."

"The picture book didn't show feathers."

"There must be more than one kind of snake," Svetz said. "The locals worshipped this one. I'll bet the SecGen loves it."

"They'll find something else to worship. Svetz—" Ra Chen's words stuck in his throat.

"Sir?"

"Waldemar the Tenth is dead."

"Long live the Secretary-General." Then his fatigue-blurred mind caught up. "Wait, now. The natives were ready to cut my *heart* out for that snake, and now we don't need it?"

Ra Chen sighed. Svetz babbled, "Or do we? Who's the next Secretary-General? Does he like animals?"

"That's being settled, I don't doubt. Take Wrona home. Get some sleep. Everything goes to hell when power changes hands."

PART
ONE

"If only we had a time machine!"

2

Willy Gorky's coming was announced. The Institute for Temporal Research had two hours to prepare.

The atmosphere as Svetz arrived was low-intensity frantic. Hum of techspeak, hum of power, three techs swearing quietly over yellow lights on a display. Some looked up from the Guide Pit as he and Wrona passed. Nobody particularly wanted to talk to Hanville Svetz, but Wrona was still a curiosity.

The Director saw Svetz in a corner quietly eating a bowl of dole yeast. He said, "Get the dog out."

Svetz nodded and stood. He rubbed Wrona between her ears. "Home," he told her, and turned back toward the door. She laughed with her tongue lolling.

"Home, my ass," Ra Chen bellowed. "I need you here!"

"Make a decision, Boss."

Ra Chen took two seconds to think. Wilt and Hillary both got along with Wrona, but Svetz could see both techs on duty in the Pit. *They* couldn't take her. The Zoo dogs fought with her.

"The dog stays. Good idea anyway. We'll have something to show Gorky."

"Yes sir. Why are we showing off for Willy Gorky?"

Ra Chen looked toward the Guide Pit. It looked impressive, and busy. He said, "Waldemar the Tenth liked extinct animals. Waldemar the Eleventh likes planets and stars, they say, and he's not a mental deficient."

Svetz flinched. Nobody would have dared to use that term when Waldemar the Tenth was Secretary-General!

A whisper of wind from outside: limousines setting down in the drive.

"The Institute for Temporal Research has been transferred from Bureau of History to Bureau of the Sky Domains—that's the new title for Space Bureau. Willy Gorky's the Director. He's our new boss. Are you ready for that?"

Svetz smiled sourly. "Time will tell."

Four Space Bureau guards flitted through the Center examining everything. One of them appeared ready to shoot Wrona. As Svetz stepped in front of her he found Ra Chen and Zeera at his elbows.

The guard listened to Svetz's assurances, but he was looking at Wrona. Wrona looked back. On command she sat, then lay down, snout on paws.

"Tie her up," the bodyguard said, and turned away.

"We will do no such thing," Ra Chen said.

The guard froze, then kept moving. Discussion must have taken place outside.

Willy Gorky entered with three more of his entourage. He was Svetz's height, centimeters shorter than Ra Chen, but thick through the torso, arms and legs. He was half again Svetz's weight.

"Ra Chen, a pleasure to see you again! Lovely pond," he said.

He meant the rectangular pool outside. Ra Chen said, "It's not an extravagance. When we're pulling an X-cage home we need somewhere to dump the heat. Otherwise expensive parts melt."

Svetz's impression was that Gorky barely heard him. He bestowed a wonderful smile on one and all and shook their hands. Svetz felt bone-breaking strength held dormant.

Wrona offered her paw. Gorky didn't notice. He was looking into the Guide Pit.

The Guide Pit was inside a knee-high wooden wall, symbol rather than barrier. There was room for five to sit and work the instruments that guided extension cages into the past. From here the Institute could run both X-cages at once, though that was rare. Gorky must have heard descriptions. It was the heart of the Institute, and now it was his.

Two men with him wore tech uniforms, white coats lined with a score of bulging pockets, scanner sets on their heads. The woman wore something else, a loose one-piece, brilliantly patterned and covered with zipped pockets. She was an inch shorter than Svetz, and slender, topped with two centimeters of ash-blond fuzz.

She came straight to Svetz, or maybe to Wrona. None of Bureau of the Sky Domains seemed to know how to treat Wrona. They'd never seen a dog.

"I'm Miya Thorsven," she said, smiling at them both.

"Hanville Svetz, pleased to meet you. You're an astronaut?"

"Yes. And your . . . companion is a visitor from the past?"

"Somebody else's past. Wrona's people evolved from wolves. The X-cages sometimes veer sideways in time when they're coming home. It's a quantum mechanical thing," Svetz said as if he understood it.

"Why does she look so much like Dog?"

"You've been in the Vivarium?"

"Not yet. There's a web site that has holograms." Miya looked wistful. "Your achievements are wonderful."

Svetz had captured most of the Vivarium's animals. He preened.

She asked again. "Dog?"

"Dogs never went extinct. They're contemporary. If you think of a dog as a wolf that's been civilized, then intelligent beings civilize each other. Intelligent wolves must have done that too."

Miya nodded happily, and Svetz thought how strange it was to be lecturing an astronaut on nonhuman intelligence. He asked, "Have you met aliens?"

"No," she said.

"How far have you been?"

"Mars."

"Only Mars?"

Space Bureau techs were examining the Center and talking to the Institute techs on duty. The ITR techs were reluctant to answer. They looked to Ra Chen. Ra Chen and Willy Gorky ignored them all.

They were both hand wavers. Svetz saw Ra Chen's arms sweep around him to include the entire Center. Gorky stopped talking then. So did Miya Thorsven. She looked to her boss, and her worry mirrored his.

Gorky spoke briefly, gathered his entourage and left.

The Center's personnel gathered around Ra Chen.

"Good news and bad," he said. "The Center really could be shut down. Gorky wants to save us, he says—" Ra Chen ignored the collective cynical sigh. "His ass is on the line too. He wants to talk. He'll bring a man, I'll bring a man."

"*You*, Svetz. Don't bring Wrona. Zeera, can you keep things going here?"

Zeera Southworth scratched Wrona behind the ears. "You and me," she told the dog.

3

I always knew that I would see the first man on the Moon. I never dreamed that I would see the last.
　　　　　　—Dr. Jerry Pournelle

Waldemar the Fourth had liked flowers. Green Resources Bureau had saved him a few for the garden path that led to the World Globe.

Chair Gorky walked with Miya Thorsven, a few meters ahead of Ra Chen and Svetz. Their voices were relaxed tones too low to make out.

Six kinds of orchids lived on vertical slabs of plant nutrient. Labels floated beside them, and followed where the wind moved the flowers: holograms projected into a visitor's eyes. The roses weren't doing well, but mutations made for marvelous variety. *Broccoli, Brussels sprouts, Artichoke*: virtual labels said that some had considered these plants edible—

"Svetz!"

Thorsven and Gorky had reached the World Dome; but Svetz delayed. He'd never had a chance to linger here. "Boss, do you *want* to convey your sense of urgency to Chair Gorky?"

"Your point?"

"You told me once, never negotiate under a deadline. We're the masters of Time."

Ra Chen's head jerked once: *yes*. "What are you looking at?"

Svetz was watching minuscule motion on a leaf. *Caterpillar*, the virtual label said. It had too many legs to count. Svetz watched it bend double to cross from one side of a tattered leaf to the other.

The World Globe was new: Waldemar the Tenth's last construction project. The whole Earth was projected onto the interior of a globe, updated every few minutes with data from myriads of weather satellites. A walk with no railings led through the Globe. It was large enough that Svetz couldn't tell its size.

Miya Thorsven and Willy Gorky walked ahead of them. Miya glanced back. "Point out something interesting," Ra Chen said, "or else get *moving*."

"It's like looking at the Earth from inside, isn't it? Boss, have you spent a lot of time in the garden and the Globe? *I* never took enough advantage of the perks. This could be our last chance."

"It could, couldn't it?"

Miya dropped back and engaged Svetz in conversation. Ra Chen took it as a hint and caught up with Gorky. Oddly lit by the white glare of ice caps above and below, and a whorl of hurricane over the Pacific, the Heads of Space and Time walked ahead of their aides. They talked like old friends who hadn't met in some time: cordial and a little cautious.

Svetz heard a little of that. Gorky speaking: "I've always been sure that the Earth will need to be terraformed. More nuclear power, or orbiting solar power arrays—"

"Too late, Willy. Those forms of power don't leave residues, not even oxides of nitrogen and carbon. You stop putting that stuff in the atmosphere, people will stop breathing!"

"Do it earlier? Time machine . . ."

The World Globe was *big*. Svetz looked down at Antarctica and wondered how far he would fall. The height didn't bother Miya. He suppressed a sigh when he and Miya reached the far end.

The Zoo—Vivarium—had been a favorite place to Waldemar the Tenth, forty-first Secretary-General to the United Nations. Of course it was supervised. Bureau of History cameras were hidden everywhere. But any spy or media camera found here would carry a death penalty.

The Heads would have privacy from all but their own people.

Gorky noticed nothing but the dominance game he was playing with Ra Chen. Miya's eyes danced left, right, further, back. *Owl. Horse.* Snake watched Svetz pass. Svetz bowed. Snake nodded its regal, brilliantly feathered head.

Here a cage was torn open as if some monstrous bird had hatched from it. Two down was another, its shredded roof bowed inward. *Ostrich. Elephant.*

Horse's head came up when Miya walked past. It glared at Svetz along its fearsome spiral horn, and Svetz stepped away from Miya Thorsven without quite knowing why.

Gorky asked, "Have you done anything about replacing Elephant?"

He knew what the torn cages meant!

Ra Chen answered, "We had a pickup mission planned. Sir, what's our budget like?"

"Call me Willy."

"In public too?" asked Ra Chen.

"Please. Now, I can keep us going for a year, Bureau of the

Sky Domains and anything connected with Space. You can have anything you can convince me you need. Saving money won't help us. Keeping the time machine in repair, that would be normal maintenance. Another elephant, another ostrich . . . well, *why*?"

"Elephant can wait," Ra Chen agreed, and Svetz smiled. He had not looked forward to trying to get another elephant into the big X-cage.

"My thought is, extinct life-forms can wait! They aren't going anywhere," Gorky said. "On a legitimate mission, sure, bring home anything you like. *We* decide what's a legitimate mission."

Ra Chen said, "Waldemar the Ninth wanted videos of Jack the Ripper, John F. Kennedy, Ted Bundy—"

"Who?"

"Crime scenes. Executions. We hadn't built the extension cages yet. We mounted a vidcamera on the end of a boom and pushed it far enough into the past to record the Nicole Simpson murder. *Gah!* We can record anything we have *exact* time and location for. We got some famous riots. Then the machinery glitched up and we were off-line for two years. Waldemar Nine would have shut us down if he hadn't died first.

"Waldemar Ten wanted animals. Waldemar the Eleventh wants planets and stars, they say . . . ?" Ra Chen waited for Gorky's nod. "Willy, I don't know how a time machine can give you that."

"I thought I did." Gorky turned the sudden force of his glare on Svetz. "Hanville Svetz, isn't it? Svetz, none of this is to be spread around. Do you know what I mean by FTL?"

Svetz thought he did. "You need to go faster than light to reach any star while any one SecGen is in power."

"Faster-than-light is fiction."

"Fiction." *Huh?*

"Waldemar the Tenth was like a bright child. I said I could get us to the stars, and he believed it. Ra Chen, those books you rescued from California saved our butts. We used the science fiction as source material. We mocked up computer-generated landscapes and cities from other worlds, and aliens too. He believed all of it. But Waldemar the Eleventh won't. Our real power is pitiable."

Ra Chen could have dismantled the Bureau of the Sky Domains if he'd known that a year ago. A time machine could fix that! Svetz saw all that in Ra Chen's eyes, and saw him shrug it off. Ra Chen said, "Beware of wishes granted, Willy."

"I *know*. A bright SecGen who really wants stars! I thought I could use the Institute to get him that," Gorky said.

Miya Thorsven half whispered to Svetz, "Dominance games."

"I've watched a lot of this," Svetz said.

"Director Gorky swallowed up Ra Chen's department. Would Ra Chen help him justify that?"

Svetz told her what he thought Ra Chen would want her to hear. "If Ra Chen couldn't protect what he had, there's no point in asking for it back. If Gorky loses, the SecGen is likely to dismantle Time and Space and start over with relatives as his Chairs."

Gorky was saying, "We haven't sent anything bigger than a bedsheet to the stars, but we've had the planets for a long time. Hibernation and an ion-fission drive took a crew of five to Jupiter. That technique would take us anywhere, given time. We could build another Jupiter ship and fire it at Four-four, if we had the *time*."

"Four-four?"

"51 Pegasi 4-4, fourth moon of the fourth planet, is as close as we can find to another Earth for hundreds of light-years. Only, it's early Earth. Reducing atmosphere. We've never found an oxygen world.

"So. Send a drone package to 51 Pegasi. Move back in time by as long as it takes. A thousand years? A billion?" Gorky brushed aside their attempts to interrupt. "Algae in the atmosphere starts the terraforming process. Add higher life-forms before anything competitive can evolve.

"Now launch a manned ship. A hundred years to 51 Pegasi, we can manage that. We find Earth's twin waiting for us! Drop a hundred and eight years into the past. Phone home. The laser takes eight years to reach Earth from Four-four. It gets there a month after the ship leaves, or a *week*. Ra Chen, I take it that won't work."

Ra Chen was openly laughing. "I'd be *all day* telling you what's wrong with that. Willy, did you ever think of asking?"

"I thought you'd wind up owning *me* if I asked favors from the Institute for Temporal Research," Gorky said.

Svetz thought he was probably right, but Ra Chen chortled. "You see it, Svetz? He thought the extension cages were the time machines!"

"Ah." Svetz told Gorky, "No sir. The time machine is under the Center. The whole Center is just the top, like a lid on a jar, with a twisty folded-over quark accelerator underneath. The X-cage is only the part that moves."

Gorky asked, "What's its mass?"

Svetz didn't know.

"Three million eight hundred thousand tons," Ra Chen said with some satisfaction. "Under Waldemar Eight and Nine we built it all as a laboratory. After we got it working we built over it to make the Center."

"How much *could* you shrink it? Unlimited budget. We're only talking, now."

"How much mass can you put into orbit, Willy?"

"With the new heavy lifters, four thousand tonnes each flight."

"Forget *that*," Ra Chen said.

"You've been running a gigantic hoax," Svetz said. He missed Gorky's fury and Ra Chen's disapproval while he chewed new data. "What *have* you got? Willy, sir, what have you *really* got? Cities on the Moon? Mars? Asteroids?"

"Moon and Mars," Miya said. "Mars is just twenty people. Luna City is two thousand, I think, but buried, not much to see. The glass domes we showed Waldemar Ten came out of a computer."

"Anything on the asteroids?"

"Some automated mining projects that broke down. One day we'll get it right," Miya said. "Mine the asteroids for metal. Put all the factories in orbit—"

Svetz waved it off. "Heavy lifter?"

Gorky said, "We're building it. We're building four. I could ask for forty now, but I'd have to justify the expense eventually."

"Will the Secretary-General wait?"

Gorky's jaw set hard. "He'll wait for Divine Image. A year at least. Do you know what a Von Neumann device is?"

Both men shook their heads. Miya Thorsven lit up. "It's a machine no bigger than your two hands that makes more of itself! It's called *Michelangelo*. I worked on the Divine Image Project. Michelangelo mines the Moon and makes more Michelangelos and piles the slag along the Earth twilight rim. The numbers double over and over. In a year and a bit we'll have trillions of Michelangelos! They're carving the near face of the Moon into an image of Waldemar the Eleventh!"

Svetz gaped. Gorky murmured, "Resculpted from Waldemar Tenth, of course."

Ra Chen said, "Ambitious. If you're processing that much Moon, you could bake oxygen out of the slag too. You'd wind up with an atmosphere."

Gorky laughed and clapped a big hand on Ra Chen's shoulder, hard. "Right. Right!"

"Doubling rate?"

"Week and a bit—"

"But you get all your action near the end, don't you? For this next year there's nothing to be seen from anywhere on Earth . . . ? Just videos of any number of your little mining things crawling over Moon rock."

"Yes."

"He bought it?"

"He did."

Miya was looking at Gorky in shocked disappointment. Gorky said, "I'm sorry, Miya. After you came back to Earth, some of the Michelangelos were chewing rock in the wrong places. Others got blocked up, or made junk, or just quit. We'll keep fiddling."

He turned back to Ra Chen. "But a year from now we'll have to show the little buggers operating, or else have *something* to show him, or else I'd better retire to the Moon. That's real. There's been a city in Clavius Crater since before there were Waldemars. Six hundred years."

Svetz said, "Moon and Mars. Anything else?"

"Rovers! We've got toy boxes crawling over every planet and moon in the solar system, hundreds of asteroids and scores of comets, taking pictures and samples. We've sent Forward probes past more than forty stars, with more on the way, Svetz, but the Forward devices are just silver blankets made of computer elements and launched by light pressure. Enough laser power to cremate a city in ten minutes," Gorky said, watching to see if Ra Chen would flinch. "Firing for ten weeks."

"The lasers, they're on the Moon?"

"Yes."

"So you've got the Moon, and everything else is smoke and mirrors?"

"There's Mars Base One. Twenty men and women and some VR sets to control a thousand Rovers, Pilgrim model. I built it on the equator. I was hoping we could experiment with advanced lifting systems. Orbital towers. Maybe a Pinwheel. We never got that far. Too expensive. Even life support for cosmonauts is too expensive."

Ra Chen said, "But now you've got a time machine."

"And if I can't use the Institute, I'll have to break you up and sell the parts for what I can get."

Ra Chen didn't seem surprised. "You'd get nothing but scrap prices."

"How much do you spend just keeping the Center going? I'd save *that* much. It wouldn't save either of us, of course."

4

On the other side of its glass wall, fifty feet of short-legged lizard half uncoiled, lifted its head high above them, and spat fire along the glass. Gorky and Ra Chen didn't appear to notice. Miya stared up at the beast in awe and wonder.

"We should change the label on this," Svetz said, "now that Waldemar the Tenth is dead."

"Isn't it a Gila monster?"

"No. I found him in another picture book, after I caught him. Dragon!"

"*You* caught—"

She cut herself off because Gorky was speaking. "You can change the past."

"That's scary stuff, Willy! We've done that once or twice by accident," Ra Chen said. "Anyway, what would you change?"

"Right after the first use of a thermonuclear bomb, there were experiments with thermonuclear rocket motors in North America Sector. We've *got* nuke rockets now. We could leave designs on some lab table in the Industrial Age for the locals to copy."

"Why bother? Like you said, you've got them already."

"But they had the *wealth*. Ra Chen, if they'd had nuke rockets then, they could have built an orbital solar power system for what they spent on cosmetics! With ten years to work, and for no more than the price of perfumes and lip goo and stuff to shape their hair into topiary, they'd have had free power from the sky and a fleet of spacecraft left over at the end!

"*Now* we're living too close to the edge. Too much farmland turned to dust and blew into the sea over the centuries. Too little sunlight gets down to us through the industrial goo. Today that same price would buy about ten million lives. People starve, or they freeze in the dark, when Bureaus divert power from the cities. We lose thousands of lives when we launch a Forward probe, and those are *cheap*. The Industrial Age, *then* was when we should have moved. They put twelve men on the Moon and then went home for four hundred years!"

"I know considerable about the Industrial Age," said Ra Chen. "I've been *in* it. Hundreds of millions of people with thousands of insanely different lifestyles, all of 'em eleven hundred years dead. You'd have to get that kind of a mob moving all in one direction to persuade them to put a permanent base on the Moon instead of using perfume and lip goo and soap . . . and sunblock, which isn't just a cosmetic. Are you really that persuasive, Willy? Go ahead, persuade me. But tell me this first. If you did change the past, how would you get the credit? The SecGen's memory would change too. You'd have nothing to show but a huge bill for electricity."

"You thought of it too?"

Ra Chen barked laughter. "Everyone *thinks* of changing the

past! If it weren't for temporal inertia we'd have exterminated ourselves once already, remember, Svetz? And maybe other times he never told me about."

Miya was gaping, and Svetz grinned at her. Gorky must know the story already, if he knew about the torn cages.

Ra Chen said, "Willy, eleven hundred years ago you had thousands of ancestors. What if you do something to separate any two of them at the wrong time? You might edit yourself out. Or edit *me* out and find yourself stranded in the past."

Gorky said nothing.

"The new Secretary-General wants the solar system. You *know* it could be worse. Any slip you make anywhere in the past, you could wind up with no time machine and a SecGen who collects torture devices."

"All right," Gorky said, "no changes."

They walked in silence for a bit.

"Everything interesting happened eleven hundred years ago," Willy Gorky said. "Industry exploded across the world. Human numbers went into the billions. Highways and railroads and airlines webbed the planet. All the feeble life-forms went extinct, but ideas boiled! There was every kind of scheme for the conquest of Space. Antimatter rocket engines, antigravity, solar sails, hundreds of tether designs, the Forward probes, Orion spacecraft, and a thousand things that *didn't* work but aren't *generically* impossible."

Ra Chen mused. "Lost secrets?"

"Why not? The space elevator, *that* notion came from a country that was still medieval!"

"Space elev—?"

"You know what I'd like to do with Mars? Use the planet as a test bed. Terraforming experiments, of course. Build a space elevator too. Build *all* of the skyhook launch schemes, *all* the ways of getting to orbit without rockets. They all have that much in common. They're all dangerous! *Huge* potential energies involved. You could build them all cheaper, in miniature, because Mars has low mass and a high spin. Try them on Mars, where they can't hurt anyone!

"The Industrial Age is over, the world isn't rich anymore, and we can't afford to experiment. But what have we forgotten? What miracles could we find by raiding old libraries? If you search through two thousand years of the past you're bound to find *something*."

"Finding it is the problem," Ra Chen agreed. "I built the big X-cage to raid the Library of Alexandria before Julius Caesar torched it. It turns out that we can't reach back that far. But we got to the Beverly Hills Library in plus-sixty-eight Atomic Era! We scooped it all up just before the quake and the wave. Why don't you set some of your people searching through those old books?"

"I will. What about the Pentagon or the Kremlin? *They* must have had interesting stuff—"

"Secrets. Locked up, hidden and guarded. Willy, it's a mistake to think of armed men as dead."

The albino whale in its huge tank turned sideways to focus one tiny eye on Svetz. Whale looked better than he had after the capture. The broken harpoons were gone, scars starting to heal.

Gorky rubbed his eyes. "I'm just getting used to thinking in terms of time. We're still just talking, right?"

"R—"

"Aliens, I promised aliens to Waldemar Ten. Waldemar Eleven expects them too. Can your time machines find weirder animals than this?"

"Amazing beast," Ra Chen said. Whale's eye turned to look at him.

"We *could* have billed it as alien. From Europa, maybe."

"Willy, is there a chance at real aliens?"

"We haven't found life anywhere."

"Mars?"

"Long ago. There's fossil bacteria in Martian rocks dating from half a billion years ago. It's very primitive stuff, Ra Chen. Mars had seas and a reasonable atmosphere for less than a billion years, and maybe what we found evolved then. Or maybe it all evolved on Earth and got to Mars embedded in a meteor. Not an alien at all."

"Mars had life later than that," Miya said.

They turned toward her. Svetz caught Gorky's indulgent smile. Miya didn't. "There was life on Mars. There was civilization!

We have sketches made from telescope observations and descriptions from old astronomers, Schiaparelli and Lowell and Burroughs. *Hundreds* saw channels running across Mars, too straight to be anything but artificial!

"And it all disappeared over the next sixty years, before the first probes reached Mars. The probes found river valleys, but they were dry. Craters everywhere. Almost no atmosphere, nothing left of the water system. Nothing left of the water. High cirrus, and frost at the poles."

Willy Gorky told her gently, "A lot of these discoveries were made through the Lowell telescope in Arizona. Have you ever *looked* through a telescope at Mars?"

Miya shook her head. "I've never looked through a telescope."

"Most astronomers don't. Miya, dear, Lowell's telescope didn't have camera attachments. Eyeballs! Everything was a blur. That was the period when they decided Mercury was like the Moon, one face always to the Sun. They were drawing one face of the planet onto the other and didn't notice! Those canals—" He was talking to the back of her head now. "Tired eyes want to connect the dots. We've never found anything on Mars."

Watching her defeated expression, Svetz asked, "What if she's right?"

Willy Gorky laughed out loud. "Svetz, what do you know about other planets? Miya, you dug in those old river valleys! What did you find? Microscopic traces that might have been bacteria? Nothing else?"

"No, nothing," Miya admitted. Her cheeks flamed. Her grip on Svetz's hand felt like desperation. "But we haven't searched the thousandth part of Mars!"

Svetz said, "We've found some amazing surprises in the past. Miya? Did this all disappear just as we were going into the Industrial Age?"

"That's right."

Svetz threw up his hands. "If only we had a time machine!"

5

Single-minded as a spider, Lowell built his own
observatory to map them and spun a whole theory from
the web of lines that he created.
—William K. Hartmann, *Mars Underground,* 1997

It should have been just that simple.

"I want to see martian civilization at its height," Willy Gorky told them. "No, futz, we could get pictures like that from a computer! Ra Chen, show me video of Martians holding a funeral, then I'll send a team there to dig up the tomb in present time. If you're right, Miya. If there's a civilization. But if you could find *anything* alive . . . *anything* alien would get the SecGen off our backs for a long time. Svetz, a martian tool would do, or an animal. We've brought back soil samples from every large body in the solar system."

To the left of the armory door was a cluster of chairs and little tables, and a drink and dole yeast dispenser. Svetz sipped coffee and waited . . . but Ra Chen had developed the habit of letting Svetz deliver bad news.

So be it. Svetz told Willy Gorky, "We can't move an extension cage to Mars. The reach isn't there. There's no way to match velocities either."

Willy said, "We can use Rovers and Orbiters. Where *can* you put an extension cage? Anywhere on Earth?"

Ra Chen said, "Northern Hemisphere and some of the Southern. Beyond that, the Earth's mass—"

"Orbit?"

"Haven't tried. We build the cages like spacecraft, though. It's all Space Bureau hardware. They'll stand up to vacuum."

"Whale fitted into the big X-cage, didn't he? We can fit a module in there—"

"But not a launcher."

"*Yes*, Miya. Ra Chen, didn't I see antigravity beamers on the large X-cage?"

"Yes."

"Range?"

"How heavy is your probe module?"

"Pilgrims mass one hundred fifty tonnes, rocket and all. Twenty-two meters long, twelve meters diameter. I can assemble them in three months if you want them."

"That's tiny compared to Whale."

Gorky nodded. "I'll work out how many modules we want. We'll push the small X-cage back to before the Lowell observations—"

"Willy, will you settle for −550 AE? Seventeen hundred years ago, around five hundred years before Lowell."

"Middle Ages. Why?"

"It's when Svetz picked up Snake. Before the American continents got into the history books. Nobody local will bother us if we operate over the open Pacific. The time machine wouldn't have to be reset. That saves us a week, and funding too, Willy. You build your Pilgrims right, they'll just sit on Mars with their cameras running, right through the Lowell and Mariner periods."

"All right. The large X-cage homes on the small one? Good. Once you're in orbit you're halfway to anywhere."

Organization was a skill Svetz had never tried to learn. It wasn't enough that things happen. They must happen in the proper order. Rocket motors must appear before a hull could be closed. Fuel couldn't just sit in a tank; compressors must be ready to produce it at the right time. Why was timing so difficult for the Institute for Temporal Research?

Svetz sat in on endless discussions—

"Now, here's the tricky part," Ra Chen told Willy Gorky. "We launch the first load, then pull the big cage back empty. We load your next module inside, and we can take our sweet time doing it. Days, weeks, a year if there's a budget cut. Then we send it back to Miya and Svetz in the moment following the first launch. Launch again the same way. Or send it back to ten hours later, give them a sleep break."

"You can *do* that?"

Ra Chen smiled a fat ruddy smile. "Time travel is wonderful, isn't it?"

Three months stretched to four, and wouldn't stretch further because the Secretary-General's annoyance was becoming overt. And one morning they were ready.

6

The new extension cage was transparent nearly to invisibility. It was no smaller than the old extension cage, which had once held Svetz and an angry Horse. But Svetz and Miya were nestled in the bottom of a spherical shell, and that might have felt cramped—

"Cozy," Miya said. "Why isn't one of us in the control chair?"

Svetz smiled. "You'll see when we get moving."

She nudged Svetz's bag with her foot. "What did you bring?"

"Food, medical, and the trade kit. You?" He waved at the upper curve, where bubble helmets and the pelts of two rubber men were splayed out on stickstrips. "I haven't trained with pressure suits."

"If we have to go EVA, I'll take you through it slow and thorough. Trust me."

They lay foot-to-head, waiting while the Center milled around them. Svetz had become very comfortable with Miya. Her head was pillowed on his foot. He felt his own long, wispy hair brushing her ankle. He'd considered suggesting greater intimacy, but—as often in his life—he was afraid of losing what he had.

Through the open hatch he heard a murmur of techs and hum of the motors, and:

Gorky: "There never were canals on Mars. Miya's always been a bit flaky about canals."

Ra Chen: "Willy, you should have done this years ago! Pick up some Martians and you'll never have a problem with the SecGen again. You'd have Martians voting your ticket in the UN! Futz, you'd want to know what they knew about terraforming, too! Mars wasn't supposed to stay habitable that long, was it?"

Gorky: "We should look at Saturn's rings too. They're recent."

Ra Chen: "How recent?"

Gorky: "A few . . . hundred thousand years. Never mind. This is already costing too much! Antigravity, pfah!"

Ra Chen: "Antigravity beamers came from Space Bureau. Don't you always launch by antigravity?"

Gorky: "Oh, no. It costs four hundred a kilogram to launch with rockets. It costs a *thousand* to lift the same kilogram with antigrav. When Svetz lifted Whale into the big extension cage, that must have killed around three thousand people."

Ra Chen: "You said that before. Killed *how*, Willy?"

Gorky: "Lights brown out in an operating theater. Food half spoils but someone eats it anyway. Somebody can't afford to repair his floater, but he has to get to work. A construction company buys cheaper supporting girders for a new arcology. The money runs out on building a nuclear fission plant, but the power has to come from somewhere, so they burn coal. Soot winds up in a hundred million lungs, and there's more rads in it than they'd get from the fission plant.

"When wealth goes down the death rate goes up, even if you don't have a unique corpse to identify. Poverty kills. Most politicians have no idea what things cost. It's a United Nations tradition. But Waldemar Eleven, he's *very* aware of that. When a bureau diverts power and resources, people die. What he *really* wants, even more than that futzed portrait—"

"What's in the trade kit?" Miya asked Svetz.

Svetz withdrew his attention from the talking Heads. "It turns heavy metals to gold. It's easier to carry than gold. Look, you just enclose something in this superconducting net part and seal it—"

"What's making you so twitchy?"

Svetz tried to relax. Tried to *look* relaxed. "I can't see why all this took four months."

"You know, you can wait two years for a trip to Mars. Earth and Mars have to be placed right, and they don't move at your convenience. If you miss your window, you wait."

Svetz said, "The last trip I made, they pulled me out of bed at just past midnight. By five I was on my way. Waldemar the Tenth wanted a spotted owl. He wanted it *now*."

"Did he get it?"

"Miya, if the Industrial Age lists it as a protected species, we can't *find* it, unless it's a bison or a passenger pigeon. I was lucky to find *any* owl. It was somebody's pet, and she had some spooky weapons, *really* high tech. Someone from our future, I think."

"I'd love to think we have a future."

The pale-skinned tech named Zat Forsman lowered the big curved door and sealed them in.

Svetz said, "So we spray-painted spots on the owl—"

Everything went blurry. There was a flow of colors and textures, but no detail came through the glass. Miya started to ask a question, then trailed off as gravity changed.

They floated at the center of the sphere.

"If you were in the chair, you'd be hanging head down," Svetz said. "It's reversed when you're coming home."

"How long before we stop?"

"Mmm? Two hours. You were at the briefing."

Miya asked, "Who were the first human beings to have sex while traveling in time?"

"Nobody, I think. No, wait, there haven't *been* any mixed couples. *Nobody*."

"Great!" Her hands moved into his clothing.

Svetz had never had an offer that straightforward. He asked, "We're going for a record?"

"Hanny, dear, Captain Thale and I weren't the first in free fall by a thousand years!"

They hung their clothing on the inverted chair. Internal gravity pulled them together and held them. Miya fitted them together as if she'd done this before, and that left them at right angles in midair, hip to hip and laughing like loons.

7

That was different."

"Isn't this just like free fall?"

"In free fall you just float."

"Oh."

"Are we being recorded?"

"Hadn't thought of it. We can ask," said Svetz.

The four months' wait hadn't been wasted. High-tech devices from Space Bureau had been adapted for the extension cages. They had a voice link now, but no video. Svetz pulled himself up to the control board, opened the talker and said, "Svetz here, in transit, nothing to report. Testing—"

He heard Willy Gorky's voice. "Good."

"Sir, are you video-recording us?"

"Video and medical, but we'll get the data later. The talker only carries audio. You have to tell us everything."

"*Ex*cellent!" Miya caroled, and switched off.

"So. You've got your record."

"Look at me."

Svetz looked.

"Four months and you never touched me."

"*Sure* I touched you—"

"Never this. Never anything. Zeera keeps her distance from other men, so I wondered, but she doesn't brush up against you either. I wondered if you had something esoteric going with Wrona—"

"Hey."

"What kept you, Hanny? You could have had me in a *bed*."

"A bed? Ooo."

"Think of all the practice we missed."

"We did pretty well."

They were floating apart. Svetz said, "Grab something," and grabbed at the chair. Miya grabbed Svetz, and then they were sliding down the glass curve of the cage in roaring darkness. Sudden sputtering light illuminated a wilderness of whirling cloud.

Svetz crawled up into the chair and jabbed the talker. "We're here," he told listeners in the far future. "Nothing to see. We're in a hurricane, typhoon, whatever."

Willy Gorky said, "That was quick."

Svetz heard strangled laughter and rapid explanations. He saw Miya's lifted eyebrow and said, "Far as they're concerned, we just left. I'm taking us up now."

They couldn't feel the cage lifting. Texture in the darkness streamed past them, then the Moon blazed above a mountain of cloud, lightning flickering within.

The storm dropped away. The sun flashed over a horizon now curved. Miya said, "Wow."

"Eight hundred klicks and no problems. Thousand. Twelve hundred," Svetz said. "Don't look at the sun, Miya!"

"*I* know that!"

The Earth was a blazing crescent. "Fifteen hundred klicks. How high do you want me?"

Ra Chen's voice: "Are they high enough?"

Gorky: "No. Can you get at least to geosynchronous? That's 35,700 klicks."

Svetz: "I'll try." He waited, watching the altimeter. Minutes passed.

"I'm at 35,700. Stop here?"

Ra Chen: "Just because you can get higher doesn't mean the *big* X-cage can. Svetz, stop there. We're sending the large extension cage."

A great glass sphere hovered beside them in the instant Ra Chen finished speaking. Miya flinched, then said, "What took so long?"

"It's here," Svetz told his listeners. The first probe module nestled inside the big transparent shell. He tap-tapped, and the shell opened like a flower. "Look it over, Miya."

"It's the Orbiter. We want it in a pole-to-pole orbit around Mars." She reached past him and activated the launch.

The probe lifted. In seconds it was gone from sight, but Svetz could see the large extension cage shuddering, the antigrav beamers turning to follow it.

*   *   *

"We're pulling the large X-cage home," Ra Chen said.

"Good," said Svetz, and the great mass was gone.

Miya broke a small dark brick and handed half to Svetz. "Ration bar." She bit into her half. She saw his distrust and said, "It's dried dole yeast. I've got twenty flavors here."

He bit. "Not bad."

The link chimed. Gorky's voice: "Miya? We're *go* for the next load. Ready?"

"Boss, how did you . . . never mind," she said, and laughed.

Willy Gorky laughed too. "Quick enough for you? Took us three weeks to assemble the Collector module and get it aboard. Shall we send it now? Or give you some nap time?"

"Now," she said, and the large extension cage hovered beside them with the Collector and fission rocket booster inside.

The Collector was a low-built tractor with a chemically fueled rocket in its belly, mechanical arms and a pressure storage bin. They launched it, then took a break before launching the third and fourth. Miya kept up a running commentary.

The Orbiter would go pole-to-pole above Mars and relay messages from Pilgrim probes on the surface.

When the Collector returned a cargo to orbit, the Orbiter would carry it back to archaic Earth and a waiting X-cage.

The third probe held twelve toy-sized Pilgrims. Those would wander out in twelve directions from the martian equator. Their senses would watch and listen and taste the soil and the wind— "Hanny, I'm not getting enough thrust here. The Pilgrims mass too much."

"I can't keep the large X-cage. Ra Chen, pull it back."

"We need"—the large extension cage vanished—"more thrust!" Her small fist whacked his shoulder.

Svetz said, "Talk to her, Boss."

"Miya?" Ra Chen's voice. "We'll put the large cage through maintenance and send it right back."

"The Pilgrims will be *gone* in a—oh, here it is again." She watched the great sphere's antigravity beamers turn toward the third probe—carrying the Pilgrims, now far beyond sight—to boost it into course for Mars. "I could get used to this."

The Collector would need fuel for takeoff. The fourth probe, the Tanker, would land near the peak of Mons Olympus and use its nuclear power plant to convert martian atmosphere and six tonnes of liquid hydrogen into ninety-six tonnes of methane and liquid oxygen. Martians weren't likely to bother it there—

"Why not?"

"Life on Mars—*even* Mars—probably evolved in water. Mons Olympus pokes right out of the atmosphere. Okay, Hanny, it's on its way. Jump us."

Earth and stars blurred like paint in water as the extension cage entered time. Gravity was outward, away from the sphere's center, as they were pulled toward the present. Miya looked at him speculatively across the width of the extension cage.

Svetz grinned. "No time." He watched the inertial calendar for a few moments longer, then pushed the Interrupt. "We'll have longer going home. Yes?"

"Yes, my hopeful swain."

Swain?

The hurricane was gone. From fifteen hundred klicks' altitude the Earth's broad crescent was otherwise unchanged.

Miya took the controls. The antenna pattern painted across the surface of the X-cage shimmered as it called across three hundred and fifty million klicks to machines that had been crawling across Mars for three long years.

"That's done. Mars is about twenty minutes away at lightspeed. Forty minutes before we get a signal. Can you jump us?"

"No. We'll have to wait."

"Fine."

"We're nowhere near that accurate, Miya. We can't place a cage within a *year* unless it's matching locus with another cage."

Forty minutes later . . . all Svetz saw was the shimmer in the antennae, and Miya's hands moving. Miya called the Center. She got Gorky.

"Chair, we have message bursts from all four probes."

"Bring them home."

"The probes are all waiting for new instructions."

"Miya, we'll have to decide what to tell them first. Come home."

8

The Norse mythological world tree, Yggdrasil is an
evergreen ash tree which overshadows the whole universe.
—"The Ash Tree," from Mattiol's *Commentaires,*
Lyons, 1579

The whole of the Bureau of History and nearly as many from Bureau of the Sky Domains were crowded into the viewing room. There weren't enough seats. A crowd sat cross-legged ahead of the front row.

The Orbiter view showed red Mars strung with threads of gray-green six to eight klicks in width. Spectra showed lines of chlorophyll and water. Gorky protested, "They're too *narrow*. How could any optical telescope have seen *that*? Those old astronomers must have been going on nothing but intuition!"

"They got it right, though," Miya said. "Shall we call the SecGen?"

"Not yet." Willy Gorky shifted to the refueling module, the Tanker. They watched the mountain's vast crater come up (*flash!*) and past. The Tanker settled onto a wide ledge. The fission plant trundled out on an array of skeletal wheels, trailing cable, and stopped eighty meters away.

Gorky studied the readings. "Full tanks. Now we know we can bring something home. Forsman, replay that flash."

Instruments on the Tanker module had looked into the crater during descent. A white flash washed out everything, and then the audience saw a skeletal structure of metal tubes and mirrors occupying part of the central crater. Spidery strutwork supported curved mirror surfaces hundreds of meters across.

"Sculpture? Artificial, anyway," Miya said. "You've got your aliens."

"Good."

"Boss, do you see that?"

A floating flat *something* moved into view, distant enough to look tiny until Gorky zoomed. Then . . . an open flying vehicle with eight crew, possibly man-shaped, moving around the upper deck. "Pressure suits," Gorky said. "No wonder at this altitude, but what holds it up? Lighter-than-air craft don't fly without air."

They watched it glide over the crater rim.

"I wonder if they saw the Tanker come down."

Ra Chen asked, "We want to talk to them anyway, don't we?"

"Bring a few home. Ambassadors to the United Nations!"

"Kidnap?"

"We know what happened to Mars. Anyone we can bring out is *rescued*! Can you rebuild a Vivarium cage to house Martians?"

"Futz, yes. Just fiddle with the programs. It's already set to make breathable atmosphere for pre-Industrial plants and animals."

"*Ex*cellent. What's the opposite of genocide?"

Ra Chen laughed. "Nobody's ever needed one."

"Ra Chen, I'm wondering what we'd find if I sent a team to Mons Olympus in present time."

"Is it an active volcano? That could wipe out any traces . . . Willy, don't do it. Knowing what's there today would restrict our options in the past. What else have we got?"

Pilgrim One gave them a breathless run across ochre deserts at high speed. A glimpse of something in flight. More desert.

Pilgrim Two: ochre sand, a claustrophobic run through a sandstorm, then more sand and a line of gray-green. Miya's breath caught. Ra Chen slowed the view to real time.

Alien greenery, so flat that the low-built Pilgrim could look straight across six klicks' width of dry-looking vines. A row of small triangular heads peeped out of the web of dusty-green fiber to watch the Pilgrim pass. Infrared showed the heads as red dots: warm-blooded.

The plants showed spectra of chlorophyll and water. If there was free-running water, it must run beneath the plants.

"Mars has . . . *had* gigatons of water. Where did it all go?" Miya wondered.

Gorky said, "The Orbiter only found a few small seas. Most of the water must be already in the canals."

One of the animals pulled free and charged the Pilgrim. Body like a ten-legged weasel, face like nightmare, all teeth and hunger.

"I'll call," Willy Gorky said. To leave the viewing room must have been like pulling his own teeth, and he surely heard Ra Chen's chuckle, but he hurried. Nobody else could be allowed to break this news to the Secretary-General!

And the rest settled back to watch the show.

Pilgrim Two ran fast-forward alongside the canal with ten-legged weasels biting at it, then turned suddenly. Ra Chen slowed again to examine a slender arc of freestanding bridge, ornately carved. Pilgrim Two crossed, watched impassively by an inhumanly tall and slender woman in a golden mask, and rolled on into red desert.

Ra Chen began flashing from one Pilgrim to another. He was trying to pull too much data too fast:

Pilgrim Three rolled into thick ice at the south pole, and froze up.

Pilgrim Four was approaching dwellings when creatures on riding beasts attacked and disabled it with swords. Ra Chen froze the frame on dwellings like clusters of crystal pillars, elegant and fragile and ancient. Then on the attackers. Weapons in three hands out of four; bipedal; green skin; faces like overgrown insects.

"Two species! Unbelievable. We'll have to . . ." Ra Chen trailed off. No telling what might be needed at this point, or what he would have for resources.

Pilgrim Seven was crossing a web of valleys. Running the record at high speed made everyone seasick; Ra Chen had to stop. Up, down, up, down. "Valles Marineris," Miya said. "It was bad enough when it wasn't choked with greenery."

Gorky was back. He said, "Seven's not getting anywhere. Leave it."

Pilgrim Eleven rolled out of a sandstorm and found a smooth stone wall. It rolled placidly along the wall, seeing nothing.

Pilgrim Eight rolled among low red hills toward cloudless blue sky. A dark vertical line appeared intermittently when the Pilgrim was looking up. Some flaw in the camera? Ra Chen went into fast-forward and they bore the motion sickness as Pilgrim Eight rolled out of the hills and down toward intersecting canals. A town looked to have grown up around the base of what was no longer a vertical thread, but a slender pillar in pale brown.

"It's a tree," Svetz said.

The Heads turned full around. Ra Chen barked, "Svetz, are you sure?"

"I've *seen* trees."

And so had any of the few allowed into Waldemar Eight's Garden, but Svetz had seen them by hundreds and thousands, dozens of *kinds* of trees—"Most of them branch out like a family lineage diagram, you know? But a few just keep going up and up. Ash does that. Redwoods . . . you can't hold it in your head. It's like they're holding up the sky. Can you make the Pilgrim look straight up? How tall *is* that thing?"

Miya's grip was a vise on Svetz's wrist. "Hanny! Not *just* a tree. *Willy!*"

Noises outside: limousines. Then chaos rolled into the theater and everything came to a stop. Gorky's guards were followed by twenty conspicuously armed giants in United Nations Security uniforms. They searched the viewing room and strip-searched its occupants and threw half of them out before they let the Secretary-General enter.

Svetz saw a crown or headdress rising above the guards. It was all Svetz could see of the Secretary-General. The middle of the front row was a kind of throne, and the space in front of it had been cleared.

Waldemar the Eleventh sat down. His voice held absolute confidence and a bit of a stutter. "Willy, s-show me what you've got."

> *Its roots, trunk and branches bind together Heaven,*
> *Earth and the Netherworld.*
> —"The Ash Tree," from Mattioli's *Commentaires,*
> Lyons, 1579

Pilgrim Eleven rolled along a wall painted with nightmare figures faded to ominous shadows. The wall curved away; glass towers poked above its rim, barely glimpsed as the Pilgrim rolled into wilderness.

Pilgrim Four's last moments showed alien shapes on alien riding beasts, and hacking silver blades. United Nations guards shrank closer around Waldemar the Eleventh.

A slender vertical thread became an impossibly tall pillar, the center of a township of tall, spindly towers. Pilgrim Eight rolled past, many klicks wide of the town and the great pillar. Ra Chen froze the frame.

Waldemar the Eleventh asked, "How tall is that?"

Gorky relayed the order down. "Ra Chen, we need a better view of that."

Ra Chen said, "Formulate your instructions for the Pilgrims and we'll send 'em. Do you know what to tell the Collector probe? Do you know what samples you want sent back to Earth?"

Gorky said, "We need a view *up*. I'd think we want seeds, if it makes seeds, and a *lot* more information." His eyes flicked toward the Secretary-General. He would speak on any subject the SecGen raised first.

Pilgrim Eight ran straight to a canal, paused, then rolled in. Finding no easy way out, it followed the canal, sending out its light-enhanced viewpoint. Eyeless things fled from motion or the taste of metal. Queer near-human skeletons in skimpy armor, and far-from-human exoskeletons enhanced with miniature frescoes and artificial ribbing, lay intermingled along more than a klick of canal bottom.

Pilgrim Nine reached the northern ice and froze up. Gorky felt Ra Chen's eyes on him and said, "We weren't expecting significant ice."

Pilgrim Ten rolled northeast until a canal blocked its path. It followed the canal to a crossing canal; rotated, and found a free-standing arched bridge, fantastically long and slender. It rolled onto the bridge and into a city. Family groups stopped to watch it pass. Men, women and children, they seemed of an unknown human race, with scarlet skins and narrow lips and noses. In martian cold they dressed in little more than weapon belts and jewels. Armed nudists, looking very mammalian.

Miya whispered into a recorder. "Look for antifreeze in their blood."

Two women pushed a carriage like the cart for a dole beer keg. "Freeze that," Willy Gorky snapped. "Zoom."

It was rounded, the reddish-brown of martian sand, about a liter in size: an egg nested in fluffy cloth.

The Secretary-General spoke, and all other sound chopped off. "Well, Willy, you d-did it. Aliens. Alien civilization. What next? How big is your Collector d-device? Can you bring me an ambassador?"

"Ultimately I can bring a whole family, Mr. Secretary"— Gorky's eyes flicked to Ra Chen and saw his nod—"and house them in the Vivarium, but it might take years."

"Egg of a Martian, then. Something *soon*," Waldemar Eleven said, and Svetz thought: *In time for the coronation.*

Gorky said, "I don't know how to keep an egg alive. Easier with an adult Martian, I think. Mr. Secretary, I'd rather get some seeds from that tree."

They had seen only one object that might be called a tree. The SecGen didn't ask *which*. "Why?"

It was a strange conversation, Svetz thought. One did not speak to the Secretary-General without invitation. Gorky daren't even volunteer information, and that meant that the SecGen himself had to ask all the right questions. A rare skill.

"I want a look up," Willy said. "Mr. Secretary, I think that tree is an orbital tower, a Beanstalk. If it is, we'll take the whole solar system for no more than the budget we were getting from Waldemar the Tenth. Square klicks of orbital powersats. Asteroid mines. We'll set colonies on Mars and Europa and floating in the atmospheres of Jupiter and Saturn and Venus. We'd need to plant one of these on Earth. We'd need seeds—"

"Can you even f-find it again? It looked thin as a d-dream," the SecGen said. "Willy, I've been trying to find the mmm, outlines of Syrtis Major and I can't. The canals and vegetation change everything."

"Measure from Mons Olympus, Mr. Secretary. The tree's at twenty-seven degrees two minutes longitude, *zero* latitude," said Willy Gorky.

"Can your Collector device climb a tree?"

"No. Maybe we'll find seeds near the base."

"What's this going to cost me?" asked the SecGen.

"At least two more probes. Use of the time machine three times, maybe more. Maybe a manned expedition. Ra Chen?"

They talked money.

Svetz tuned it out. "Miya, we've found cities on Mars, and all they're talking about is that tree!"

"It might be, it just *might* be a Beanstalk. How else could it stand up at all?"

"Don't understand the question."

She started to answer, but the SecGen was departing. In their mania for order, his guards were turning all into chaos.

10

Jesse's rod (stem). The animating and energizing force
or light of Jesse; a genealogical tree; a phallus.
Sometimes represented by a vine, thus equating with the
beanstalk, Jacob's ladder, or Lugh's chain.
—Dictionary of Mythology, Folklore and Symbols,
by Gertrude Jobes

A man in Space Bureau uniform lectured the Institute people. "Geosynchronous orbit is 35,700 klicks above the Earth. Whatever you set in orbit at that height will circle the Earth in exactly a day. It's a privileged position, because the Earth circles itself in exactly a day . . ."

Svetz got lost. So he tracked down Miya afterward and asked her.

"Hanny, it's a *wonderful* notion. You know what synchronous orbit is? It's where we put the weather satellites."

"No."

"Um. Suppose you're orbiting just outside the atmosphere. You go 'round the Earth in an hour and a half, right? Higher, it's a bigger circle and you'd move slower. Takes longer. As high as the Moon, it takes almost a *month* to go around. Right?"

"Right."

"Somewhere in between is where it takes just twenty-four hours. For the Earth it's 35,700 km up. That's synchronous orbit. The Earth is spinning as fast as you're moving, so you stay above the same point."

"Okay."

"I take a coil of good strong rope. I set it moving above the equator with its center of mass at synchronous orbit. Now the coil stays just over a point on the equator, right?"

"Right."

"Now I reel the rope out until one end is on the ground and the other end is *way* out there for balance."

"That's your orbital tower?"

"Right. Now I run an elevator up and down the rope. I use it to lift cargo for the price of electric current plus any profit I can get away with. If I go past the synchronous point and then let something slide *up* along the rope, it'll fly off the far end with enough velocity to reach the asteroids."

"It's a tree, but it's *hanging from the sky*?"

"Yes, exactly!"

Svetz rubbed his eyes. He said, "That would cost . . . I can't imagine what it would cost. And you think you've *found* such a thing?"

"Hanny, what made you say it was a tree?"

"It . . . reminded me of a redwood. It went up and never seemed to stop."

"Like Yggdrasil! Like the world-tree from Norse legend!"

"But no tree could be strong enough! *Steel* wouldn't be strong enough—"

"No, Hanny, hold on. An orbital tower has to be strong, right. If you build it around Mars, you get high rotation *and* a lower mass, much lower, so it doesn't have to be *as* long or *as* strong. Picture it a hundred thousand klicks long, and the only thing strong enough is still carbon crystal fibers or fullerine tubules, and those are carbon too.

"I think you were right. We can't make such a thing, we don't have anything to make it *out* of, so why can't it be a tree? Life is carbon based. Trees are *good* at manipulating carbon. And if we had *seeds*, we would go to the planets for nothing more than electricity!"

Svetz, Miya, Zeera, and most of the techs slept on air cots in the Center while a composite team of Sky Domains and History Bureau wrote instructions for the probes on archaic Mars.

In the morning they were back in the small extension cage.

Gravity shifted. They floated toward each other, bumped skewed, and pulled themselves around. The clothing they stripped off kept floating back like intrusive ghosts. They made a game of batting garments away.

"Hanny! How many times do we have to do this before I'm a virgin again?"

Svetz laughed. "I've never gotten less hungry on any trip."

And later he asked, "Are we going for a record this time?"

"Mmm. Duration? Number? Intensity?"

"Not unless I get some rest."

"Someday I'm going to get you in a bed."

Svetz didn't answer. Miya asked, "What's the matter?"

"I had this notion once. Miya, we're going back to before time travel was even a concept. Once it was fantasy, fairy-tale stuff. In the late Industrial Age, Thorne and Tipler and some other top mathematicians showed that time travel was *theoretically* possible and did some designs. The Institute for Temporal Research came out of those. What if everything we collect from before plus-thirty Atomic Era is fantasy?"

"Hard to picture Whale as a fantasy! He's too big," Miya said. "Too scarred, too detailed. When you pulled him in, wasn't there a one-legged sailor still tangled in the lines and harpoons along his flank? That's gritty realism, that is!"

Svetz smiled. "Gila Monster would have *charred* me if I'd thought he was a fantasy. Horse tried to spear me like a wine cork."

"So."

"You're an adolescent's daydream," he told Miya. She purred into his throat, and he said, "And here we are, but we've never made love after plus-thirty AE. Maybe you're *my* fantasy."

"Am I? Great. Are you ticklish? Is *this* real? Is it?"

In the old days they had used the time machine to set a two-milligram test mass alongside itself. The experiment ate energy equivalent to the test mass times lightspeed squared. Bringing an X-cage to a spacetime it had already occupied would cause a surge in energy consumption. That was how it could return to its point of departure.

The small X-cage emerged just too late to watch itself vanish.

This mission would be cheap. They were only messengers, the messages already written.

To the Orbiter module: a burn to put it in a higher orbit.

"Excuse me?"

"It's in low Mars orbit now, Hanny. We don't want it hitting the tree. It's only luck that hasn't happened yet!" Miya kept working. "Of course the current Collector module won't be able to fly that high. We'll instruct the Orbiter to dive down and get it, and I hope somebody's writing *that* program."

The Tanker was already fully fueled and awaiting the arrival of a loaded Collector. No message needed.

To the Pilgrims: *converge on the skyhook tree at twenty-seven degrees two minutes longitude, zero latitude. Pan up and down. Focus every instrument on the tree.*

To the Collector: *follow the Pilgrims. Where they converge, find a high point and watch them. Defend against molesters.*

"We've already lost four Pilgrims. We can afford that, but we can't lose the Collector. All right, Hanny. Jump us by a year and we'll collect what they get."

Svetz dipped them into time, watched, tripped the interrupt. They'd jumped over two years. Miya sent the instructions. "Mars is close. Only about eighteen minutes this time," she said.

"Miya, doesn't Mars have two moons? Why haven't they chewed up the tree?"

Miya chewed her underlip. She turned to the control board.

"Miya?"

"I'm looking! The top of the tree doesn't taper off; it ends in a knob. Deimos is further out than that, but Phobos . . . Phobos is *below* synchronous orbit, it has to be, it goes around more than twice a day! Orbit's a little skewed, but it crosses the equator. It *can't* just keep missing!"

"Doesn't sound like your space elevator has been in place very long at all."

Miya said, "Yesss. Hanny, you have a knack for . . . ah, penetrating fantasies. It would have had to grow very fast, wouldn't it?"

"Or arrive already grown."

Message bursts from archaic Mars were streaming in. Miya checked to see that they were recording, and then Svetz set them moving forward through time to the present.

11

Lugh's chain. *The Milky Way, chain by which Lugh raised men to heaven . . . Equated with Bifrost, Jacob's ladder, the stem of Jesse, Watling Street.*
—Celtic mythology, *Dictionary of Mythology, Folklore and Symbols*, by Gertrude Jobes

1108 AE. It's a tree. In proportion it's as slender as an ash tree— no, more! But near the ground it bifurcates and spreads. Scores of near-vertical roots sink deep. The sixty-fingered hand covers the green breadth of a canal and a square klick of ochre desert on each side. Wreckage of a bridge rides high in the tangle of roots. Other, newer bridges in slender martian style stretch around and between other roots.

Wait now, that wrecked bridge was *lifted*, as if the tree's roots rose from the ground. How could a tree grow from the ground to orbit? Nothing could be *that* strong!

Paired silver lines rise along a vertical root and far up along the trunk. Look up: the tree rises out of sight. Silver lines continue as far as the eye can see.

The Secretary-General said, "This is hurting my eyes."

Svetz's eyes tried to twist as he followed Pilgrim One's viewpoint. Odd perspective here—

"The trunk gets thicker as you go higher," Gorky said in haste. "We were expecting that. Your normal tree is wider near the base. It wants compression strength, you see? It doesn't *hang*. This skyhook tree is tapered so that less weight is hanging below any given cross-section. That makes it stronger."

It looked infinitely tall.

The Pilgrim probes were close, near the roots and among them. Pilgrim One's viewpoint zoomed up along the pale brown line of the tree, into a dark fringe that began almost at the edge of sight, scores of klicks high. A ragged collar of foliage, already above the atmosphere, continued up the trunk as a vertical fringe, like the mane on Horse. Hard to see anything at all in there. Not dark green. Black!

The SecGen asked, "You wanted seeds?"

The Heads took it as an invitation. "If there are seeds, I'd expect them to fall into the canal," Ra Chen speculated.

"From that high up, they'd come down like little meteors," Gorky said, "shielded against reentry. Punch their way through the weed surface into the canal. We can't go there, Ra Chen."

"We could."

"There's a *town* built up where the canals intersect. The skyhook tree is *in* it. You're not thinking of a full-scale invasion of Mars, are you?"

"No, just send Pilgrims to search underwater."

"Oh. Good. Give me some time to study these records. I want to know if there are seeds higher up the tree. I'd like to search the black fringe."

"You didn't design the Collector to climb trees, did you, Willy?"

Miya leaned forward in the near dark, jaw set, her nails sinking into Svetz's shoulder. He asked, softly, "What?"

She whispered, "They'll have to use cosmonauts!"

Willy Gorky himself briefed them the next day.

"Ra Chen and I can't work out how to tell a computer program what a skyhook seed looks like. We don't know ourselves. Miya, Svetz, you'll send instructions as usual, then pick up return signals from the Mars Pilgrims. We'll send six Pilgrims underwater. They should be safe from the locals, at any rate."

Ra Chen said, "We'll mount a viewer in the small X-cage so you can scan whatever they find. We should have done that a year ago! Svetz, you've seen every kind of tree, you must have seen every kind of seed." He overrode Svetz's attempt to interrupt. "Our best hope is that you'll know a seed when you see it. Then tell the Collector module to go get it."

12

Eleven hundred years of development had shaped the Rovers. Early versions had explored Mars and the Moon. They had become smaller, lighter, cheaper, more clever. Later models roved the surfaces of every interesting body in the solar system. Some climbed like spiders. Some rolled as spheres with unbalanced weights in them. On worlds with no surface at all, Rovers floated or sank.

On archaic Mars, six Rovers (Pilgrim model) explored beneath the black waters of a canal. They found soft mud, and organic substances subsiding into softness, and things that tried to eat them. They had been told little. They examined discreet solid objects and discarded things that were too large or too small. They sought shapes that repeated as seeds would. When the command came, they crawled out of the muck to beam their findings to the Orbiter for relay to a point above the Earth.

Miya and Svetz ran through the murky footage. Many hours later Miya said, "This is boring."

Svetz stopped the display and lifted tired eyes. He said, "Best duty I've ever had."

"Really?"

"I've been chewed. I've been scorched. I've been almost eaten, almost fried, almost perforated, over and over. I go alone, because there has to be room for whatever I bring back. There's never been anyone to guard me or rescue me, or talk to, or love." There, he'd said it. "Every other trip, I've been hunting something with teeth. I *hate* . . . used to hate animals. Wrona seems to have talked me out of that. I am having a wonderful time."

Miya sighed and went back to work

The X-cage had come to meet itself. Now it hovered above the same fat blue-and-white crescent they'd left behind two trips running. Only the pattern of stars had shifted. The cage was hovering, after all; it wasn't in an orbit.

Svetz picked out an orange spark among the stars of Taurus near the western horizon. That was a *world*. He couldn't see it as more than a point.

If the Pilgrims couldn't find seeds, someone would have to go to Mars and look.

Miya pointed into the projection from Pilgrim One. "Look, Hanny, we keep seeing this shape. It's pottery, isn't it?"

Sunlight rippled across it: it was near the surface of the canal. "Vase. You can see the pattern. This symbol, it's that ten-legged toothy thing that tried to chew up Pilgrim Four."

"Not quite the same. A bigger relative. Hanny, I'm tired." Miya curled up in the curve of the floor.

Svetz called the Center. Hillary Weng-Fa answered. She went to wake Ra Chen.

"No seeds," Svetz said.

"How sure are you?"

"We get pottery, we get eggs. Bones look like each other, so the Pilgrims show us a lot of those. Once we got a mob of Reds in battle gear. They all looked alike. They were even walking in some kind of regular array. Pilgrim Six went right up to examine them. We've lost Pilgrim Six."

"Better tell Willy."

No telling how much time had passed in the present. Here, only an instant passed while the phone went dead, then live. He heard, "Miya?"

"Sleeping, Willy."

"Chairman Ra Chen tells me you can't find anything like a seed."

"We've typed fifteen styles of pottery. We find broken furniture. Not much garbage. Maybe there's a famine. We *did* find a heap of spiky seeds, fist-sized, but we searched through the rotten fruit around it, which wasn't pleasant, Willy, and it had more of the same seeds in it. There are skeletons of at least three biped species. Most of them look human. Some were wearing armor. The big four-armed ones grow their own. It's not as if they have wars, more like they fight in the streets every night. We've found big eggs. They're not seeds, they're eggs, and in fact they're humanoids' eggs, red and pale and black, all a little different. Mars's answer to population control. Willy, we're both exhausted."

"Get some sleep. Call me when you wake up. We're sending you to Mars."

"Willy—"

"We can refit a Moon Minim spacecraft and get it into the large X-cage. If it doesn't fit, we'll fit *something*. We'll brief Zeera. I don't see any way to get seeds off that tree except to go up it."

"Wait wait wait! I'm not a cosmonaut!"

Pause. "A chance to see Mars when it was alive? At United Nations expense?"

"Willy, we spent fifteen hours searching for your seeds, and six Pilgrims spent a year gathering the data. If there were seeds, they'd have fallen. If they'd fallen, we'd have found them. This tree is sterile, and aside from all that, I, Hanville Svetz, am not a cosmonaut!"

There was a brief pause . . . and Miya was watching him.

Willy Gorky said, "Twenty years ago I'd have killed you to steal your seat on that ship."

Ra Chen's voice: "Never mind, Svetz. Drop it, Willy. We'll send Miya and Zeera. You come home in the small X-cage."

Miya's eyes closed. Svetz curled up next to her and let it all drift away.

13

He woke to Miya's voice.

He was looking at a bullet-shaped spacecraft backlit against dark Earth and marked with riding lights. He knew what to look for: a faint halo around the ship, fading into nothing at one rim, was the shell of the large X-cage.

"You're awake? Good." Miya was already wearing a skintight in brilliant yellow patterns. "Svetz, this is a pressure suit. The helmet unlocks and flops back if you're where you can breathe. Flops forward to close, *lock it* or it's explosive decompression. Unzip everything before you get in. No, wait, strip first. . . ."

She watched, clinically detached, as Svetz zipped himself into the pressure suit. Stickstrips held it open against the wall, and it was still difficult. Limb by limb, then torso; lock each zip. From shoulder to waist, the back of the suit was a shell ten centimeters thick: enough to enclose circuitry and an air and water recycler. The bubble helmet locked against it when open. The rest of the suit was very flexible, very thin. It fitted him like skin on a dieter, just a little loose. He smoothed out some wrinkles. He pulled the big bubble down over his head, wiggled it into lock, and set the air going.

Miya guided his fingers to sensors under his chin. "This is your voicclink," her voice boomed, receded. "This zooms your helmet." Miya's face expanded enormously. "The other way—" The room pulled in around her. "Fisheye."

Looking down at himself he saw the patterns of a brilliant green lizard. Miya's skintight was yellow and orange flames, like a bird he'd once glimpsed and lost. Waldemar Ten would have loved it, but he'd asked for a spotted owl....

Above Earth's black night side, a half-seen circle opened like a flower and puffed a haze of ice crystals. Spacecraft and circle separated. In a haze of frost a tiny pressure suit moved toward them.

Stickstrips held an elastic belt twenty centimeters wide, with Space Bureau insignia on an even wider buckle, and a hooded silver cloak. Svetz left the cloak but donned the belt. Miya nodded and reached for a handle.

Svetz was used to changing gravity. He had a grip on the chair before the hatch opened. Air roared out; Svetz stayed put. The suit shrank in vacuum. Now it fitted him like skin on a sausage.

Vacuum outside, pressure in his helmet. The suit put pressure on his skin, but air still *pulled* itself into his lungs. He had to pull the belt tight around his belly before he could exhale.

Miya had placed herself near the hatch to catch him, but only now did she look back. His heart leapt. The skintight had shrunk around her. She seemed to be wearing nothing but yellow and orange paint.

Zeera Southworth pulled herself inside and moored her flight stick. Zeera in a zebra-striped skintight was a marvelous sight. Her gaze brushed his crotch, which may have showed signs of his interest, and he saw a swallowed laugh. "Svetz. Want to see a rocket ship?"

"Yes."

"Take the cloak," Miya advised him.

A flight stick was lift field generator and power source built into a meter and a half of pole, with a control ring at one end and a brush discharge at the other. Spinoff from Space Bureau, of course. The women bracketed him as they crossed to the large extension cage. They needn't have worried. Svetz knew flight sticks . . . though this one felt underpowered. A lift field wasn't a rocket. The Earth it pushed against was too far below.

He wrapped the cloak around himself. The Earth had rotated into somebody else's midnight as it turned beneath the hovering X-cages. Mars and the stars of Taurus hadn't moved.

They flew alongside a spacecraft like a bullet standing upright, and took their turns in the airlock. Lifted by antigravity beamers on the large X-cage, Svetz entered free fall.

14

The Minim was big. Three reclined chairs faced up into a transparent nose cone. Behind those was considerable cargo space. Svetz noted a rolled-up net, and a door in the hull big enough to admit a van.

"Roomy," he said.

Zeera said, "We don't really know what kind of seeds a tree this size makes—"

"They've got to stand up to reentry," Miya said, "at worlds maybe bigger than Earth—"

"A seed *could* be as big as that door," Zeera said. "If it's bigger, we'll have to strap it to the hull."

Tools were mounted around the cylinder wall. Svetz noted

stickstrips for three pressure skintights and three flight sticks. He waved at devices mounted in sleeves—

Zeera pointed. "Sonic stunners. Long-range blasters. Translators."

Three of everything. Wide stickstrips along the wall, to tether three crew for sleep. *We can refit a Moon Minim spacecraft*, Ra Chen had said. Svetz had refused to go to Mars, and *then* they'd built for three.

Miya had heard his refusal. He could lose her! Willy Gorky was manipulating him, but it wasn't as if he had a choice.

"Zeera, can this ship talk to the Center?"

Zeera tapped a device like the talker in the small X-cage. "Get me either Chairman," she ordered.

"Wait one," a tech said.

Gorky's voice. "Ready?"

"Zeera Southworth here. No showstoppers. Hanny Svetz wants to talk."

Svetz said, "Willy, this ship will clearly support three. I want to go to Mars, if it's all right with Chairman Ra Chen."

Silence crawled. Then Ra Chen asked, "Svetz, are you in free fall now?"

"Yes."

"How do you feel?"

"No problems." No motion sickness.

Gorky's voice. "I don't know what the small X-cage will do. Can we pull it back without a pilot?"

Ra Chen: "Yes."

Gorky: "Glad to have you, Hanny."

Miya broke in. "Willy, that changes the ship's mass by . . . ?" Her eyes questioned him.

"Sixty-one kilos," Svetz told her.

"Miya, you oppose this?"

Miya locked eyes with him and said, "No, Willy, I'm for it, but rewrite the instructions for boost."

Gorky: "Have to pull the cage back anyway. Our twenty minutes are up."

The large X-cage blinked, gone and back again. Miya snapped,

"Seat webs *now!*" and didn't watch Svetz's initial clumsiness. A ruddy dot above the Earth's limb waited.

He felt no thrust. The large X-cage shrank out of sight. A few minutes later the Earth was flowing past and the daylit crescent was narrowing.

Zeera watched her instruments. "Willy's pulled back the large X-cage again," she said. "Boost One accomplished. We're in orbit at eight KPS."

Svetz said, "Orbit? I thought we were on our way."

"We'll close-approach the Earth. Then the X-cage pops back and the antigravity beamers hit us again. This ship's too heavy to get into Mars intercept in one boost."

Miya nodded as if she understood, so Svetz did too. He moved about the cabin, testing his agility. He looked over the gear that hung on stickstrips along the cylinder wall. "Zeera? A translator for *Martian*?"

Miya answered. "Hanny, these have been used in United Nations sessions for near a thousand years. They can translate thieves' cant and old recordings of dolphin and whale song."

"We have a *live* whale!"

"Yes . . . hadn't occurred to me. Anyway, these things certainly don't have Martian on file. You and the Martians will have to talk until the translator can correlate some of your words."

Svetz unrolled a screen to cover the cylinder wall. Now it was just another floor.

The Earth turned full.

It came to him that being trapped in a tiny spacecraft with Miya Thorsven for two years wouldn't be half bad. Two more years returning, if Mars didn't kill them. He looked around the cabin, wondering how they could get privacy. Zeera had never shown interest in any man or woman . . . which reminded him. "Zeera. How's Wrona?"

"I brought her to the Center. She can go home with Hillary if the mission lasts overnight."

Overnight? . . . Oh. "Zeera, do you like Space better than Time?"

"I never told you, did I? When I was a little girl I wanted to *live* with Martians. We should've merged the two Bureaus then instead of waiting."

"Another fantasy fulfilled?"

Miya snapped, "Oh, get off that, Hanny!"

"Here's another," he said. "Marooned with two beautiful women, millions of klicks from planet Earth, for . . . four years, Zeera?"

She laughed. "Four years without Wrona, doesn't that bother you?"

"It's not four years for *her*."

"Won't bother us either. Have a look at this." She showed him what Ra Chen had built into what would have been storage space for provisions. "It's an advance on the temporal interrupt that we've been using to stop the X-cages. We call it Fast Forward or FFD."

15

Eight klicks per second is fast. Svetz never saw the large X-cage return. Telltales in front of Zeera told him when it came, how hard it pushed, and when it was gone. He only saw the Earth shrinking behind, and Mars like a glowing heart in Taurus.

Zeera said, "Miya, you'll appreciate this next move." She engaged the Fast Forward.

Svetz trusted the machines of the Institute for Temporal Research without understanding them. He simply enjoyed the show.

The slowly dwindling Earth shrank abruptly to a bright point. The sun itself was shrinking. The pink pinpoint that was Mars grew brighter . . . grew conspicuous. . . .

"I wondered where all the provisions were," Miya said lightly, but she had a death grip on her armrests. "This is time travel too, isn't it?"

"Minimally. We have to put ourselves in the right path before we engage, and then the vehicle just follows the path, the geodesic. We can't change course or dodge, or fight either, I suppose, but we're hard to hurt. The Heads say that if we hit an asteroid, it's good odds we'll go right through it."

Svetz asked, "Which Head?"

"Both. Grinning like fools," said Zeera. She was working at the keyboard. Pictures scrolled across one of the displays. "Svetz, have you seen these?"

In the display screen, Mars came up fast. An edge of horizon became a shield volcano of awesome size.

"It's the view from the Tanker?"

"Yeah. Watch."

The viewpoint dropped toward a vast crater, its bottom a glittering asterisk of mirrors; dropped past the rim, slowed above a rocky ledge . . . but lines and tiny numbers overlay everything he saw. Zeera said, "The Tanker, the Pilgrims, all the pictures that came back, Ra Chen and Gorky have been turning it all into maps. We can't get lost."

She wasn't looking at him. Svetz realized he was missing the view.

The bright orange point had become a disk. Not a disk now: a whirling sphere expanding much too fast. "That's close enough," Zeera said, and Mars jarred to a stop, as large as a full Earth seen from the Moon.

Thus far the trip had cost them forty minutes ship time.

"We still have to match orbit with Mars. Anything threatens us, we just go past. We've got fuel to abort and return. Miya, take the copilot slot." Zeera sounded edgy, and well she might. They were rubbing up against an alien civilization. They had examined little more than its garbage, but all the corpses wore wounds.

The *Minim* slowed at a tenth of a gee, spiraling in toward Mars. The planet waned to a shrinking crescent, then a great black hole in the stars.

They were moving inward of Deimos' orbit, and Mars was a spreading crescent, when Svetz found the tree.

It was foreshortened, pointing almost at the ship. The orbital tower looked like a giant's club. They were passing just above the massive, rounded upper end.

"Interestingly phallic," Miya said. "Or is that just me? *Hanny!*" as a diseased potato thirty klicks long came straight at them. Zeera screamed.

The hurtling moon missed them by . . . Watching it recede made it seem that Deimos had missed by two klicks or more, still much too close for comfort.

Miya came out from behind her arms. She looked at Svetz for a heartbeat, her face too pale. Then she turned her attention to the planet.

Mars was still distant by hundreds of klicks, but the *Minim*'s zoom display was good. Mars' crescent grew gibbous, then full. Canal patterns laced the deserts, knotted into cities at the intersections. There was a wide white northern ice cap. Miya swore monotonously. "That region has to be Syrtis Major, but there's nothing left of the shape! Valles Marineris is all gray-green . . . there, where all those minor canals converge. Zeera, every feature I know has changed. I'm feeling very lost. Wait, that's Mons Olympus, with greenery crawling up the sides. That's Aeolis coming over the horizon, and the tree growing out of it."

Craters thickened east of Aeolis. Canals crossed a few of those, the ones that held water. Mars covered half the sky. Features raced beneath the *Minim*, expanding. "Aeria," Miya said, "I think."

"Better be," Zeera said.

Svetz asked, "Zeera, are you going to land us?"

"No. Aerobrake."

"What's it mean?"

"You'll love it. Are you webbed in?"

The hull began to sing. A landscape of mottled ochre desert and ragged canyons and narrow gray-green lines hurled itself directly at his face, close enough to touch. Svetz clutched the arms of his chair and felt heat radiating from the window. He never thought to look at his companions. He heard Miya murmur, "Xanthe," and saw a monstrous crater pass beneath them.

Then the singing tapered off, but Zeera whooped and whacked his bony back. "Hell of a ride!"

Svetz began the process of relaxing his hands.

"This next part's tricky," she said.

Thrust built up against their backs. Mars was a shrinking crescent. A hint of a vertical line was growing ahead.

Zeera's mind was on her flying. She talked in staggered half
sentences. "Chairman Gorky's been seven . . . months rebuilding
the *Minim*. We missed the coronation, of course. We had time to
run your travelogues to *death* . . . but we just weren't seeing
enough . . . enough of the tree. It's Beanstalk seeds we're after.
Willy Gorky thinks the . . . SecGen is losing patience . . . but it's
really Willy."

"We're not on a rescue mission?"

"No, Hanny. If we can save some Martians, that's in order. But
first, where are the seeds?"

"Not *if?*"

"Hanny, we *assume* there are seeds. Seeds are wanted. Where
would you want to drop seeds if you were a skyhook tree?"

Svetz shrugged. "Deep water, for a plant that tall. The canal.
An ocean, if there was one."

"But you looked."

"They aren't there."

Miya said, "Hide seeds in the black fringe. Grow a cannon. *Spit*
them over the horizon at other canals."

Zeera said, "The fringe runs . . . along the mid-trunk for more
than twenty thousand klicks. You want to search all that?"

"Make us a better offer."

"The fringe is like leaves on a tree, Hanny. It makes sugar.
Spectrum off a laser flash showed us the chemical that does photosynthesis. It's *not* chlorophyll. A separate line of evolution. It's
probably from another solar system."

Alien.

"The fringe could make seeds too, I guess. You want to look
in the fringes? That's the plan, then. I've got us in synchronous
orbit. We can study the mid-trunk before I go down." Zeera cut the
thrust and they floated.

The trunk had grown huge. Svetz guessed it at five hundred
meters thick and a couple of klicks distant. He asked Zeera, "Do
we have to go down at all?"

Miya exclaimed, "Hanny! That's *Mars* down there!"

"I like to know my options."

Zeera sighed. "We've already used up too much fuel to get home. We'll need to land at Mons Olympus and refuel. *Now* make a choice. Do you want to go *down* the tree or *up* the tree? You've got flight sticks. I could let you off at the midpoint, then go on to refuel while you work your way down. Or you can ride down with me, maybe talk to some Martians, then fly to the tree and climb."

They spent a few minutes talking it over. Svetz wished they could call the Center and give the decision to someone else. No go: the talker would reach through time, but not through an interplanetary gravity gradient. They were out of contact until they could return to Earth.

Ultimately Miya said, "Let's get the job done first. Zeera, let us off here. We'll work our way down and join you at Mons Olympus."

Miya left her seat. In one-tenth gee she fished out three transparent bags and handed two to Svetz and Zeera. "Do you both know how to use these?"

Grinning, Svetz said, "This may never come up—"

"You can't breathe pre-Industrial air!" Zeera laughed. "It nearly killed Svetz on his first trip."

"Nearly killed us all once," Svetz said.

"My fault," Zeera said. "I gave steam cars the edge at the beginning of the Industrial Age."

"The change shock hit us and everyone stopped breathing and fainted. I got us into filter helmets—"

"If it wasn't for temporal inertia, we couldn't have fixed anything. There wouldn't have been an Institute *or* a time machine."

"See, Miya, you've got to have certain substances in your blood," Svetz said, "or your body forgets to breathe. Carbon dioxide, nitrogen oxides, sulfur compounds. You need other industrial by-products too."

Miya asked, "Why didn't you change too?"

Svetz and Zeera looked at each other. Zeera said, "You mean humans."

"Of course I mean humans! When the air changed, why didn't every human being on Earth change over to breathing pre-Industrial air?"

"The change shock moves at different rates," Zeera said. "We might all have suffocated waiting. Or strangled, if we changed before the air did."

"*All* right," Miya said. "We need filter helmets to breathe martian air at ground level. These aren't stock issue, they're altered for Mars. Note the insignia—" A thumbtip-sized orange dot on the forehead. "On Mars they have to concentrate oxygen and hold carbon dioxide and monoxide *out*. Don't try to climb with just these. In vacuum you need a full pressure suit. But keep them handy."

Svetz and Miya donned their pressure gear and tested the voicelink. Miya showed Svetz how to back into a rocket pack, set it and lock it to his back plate.

Nozzles faced back, up, down. Nozzles poked past his short ribs, facing forward. He was wearing high explosives on his back, and he'd known this was coming. They were in balance between Mars gravity and centrifugal force. A flight stick would push *up*: no help.

Miya affixed a flight stick to Svetz's back for use when they got lower; then a blaster. "Want this too?"

She was holding the needle gun. Svetz said, "Yes."

"You sure?"

"Habit. We don't use blasters on any normal mission. We don't want to kill anything in the past."

She turned and let him stickstrip a flight stick and blaster to her back, careful to keep it all clear of rocket nozzles.

Miya went out first.

The skyhook tree was fat in the middle, wider than any redwood. The black foliage only began much lower down.

"Let's do it," Miya said. Facing the tree, she fired her rocket pack. Svetz fired his a moment later. It kicked him toward the tree. When her flame died, he cut his off too.

16

. . . But most women, when they feel free to experiment
with life, will go straight to the witches' Sabbath. I myself
respect them for it, and do not think that I could ever
really love a woman who had not, at some time or other,
been up on a broomstick.
—Isak Dinesen, "The Old Chevalier,"
from *Seven Gothic Tales*

The mid-trunk was glossy, void of detail but for a glittering silver thread. Svetz used his helmet to zoom on it. The thread split into two parallel lines.

"Miya?"

"I see it. The Martians have built a lift. That's what you *do* with a Beanstalk."

Svetz asked, "They'd have used it to explore the solar system, wouldn't they?"

"Time is your thing, not mine. There are lots of little moons in the outer system, some almost as big as Mars. If Martians had been there, we'd have found *something*. Mars must have been just starting to reach out when something interrupted. Some disaster."

Svetz reset his helmet view. Unzoomed, the trunk was still coming close. Far around the curve was a creasing of the . . . bark? It stretched for several klicks, as if a silver-gray wing were folded along the trunk.

"Ready for retrothrust?"

"I haven't taken my fingers off those switches since you showed them to me." The bark was *very* close.

"Good. Hold off, though, Hanny. You see anything scary?"

"Lift cables. We've got Martians above and below. Those folds: you see them? I want a better look at those."

"Retrothrust," Miya said. He didn't see her fire, but he toggled switches with four fingertips. Nozzles poking past his ribs fired.

His back plate pulled him backward. The trunk came softly up to meet him.

There was nothing to cling to.

Zeera's voice: "Are you on the tree?"

Miya: "Phoenix has landed. Hanny?"

Svetz: "Snake is on the tree. Zeera, how's your view?"

Zeera: "I have views through both your helmet cameras. I will call you from Mons Olympus."

Blue flame puffed. The *Minim* spacecraft receded and was gone.

17

Beanstalk. *Universe tree of fairy tales; ladder or road to the heavens? . . . The rope trick of India is related to the belief in a stairway to heaven.*
—Dictionary of Mythology, Folklore and Symbols,
by Gertrude Jobes

Svetz followed Miya around the trunk. The sun shown directly on them. Svetz deployed his silver cloak like a parasol, but he was still sweating. The porous pressure suit let his own sweat cool him. Otherwise he'd have steamed himself to death.

He asked, "Should we be wearing sunblock?"

"The suits block UV," Miya said.

He drifted alongside the silver-gray crease. "Blanket big enough to cover a city. Square klicks of it," he reported, for Miya and a later audience. He touched it. "Flimsy stuff." He crawled under a fold of tissue-thin leaf and turned his headlamp on. He was instantly dazzled. "Yow! It's a hall of mirrors in here."

"A skyhook tree could use light-sails to maneuver. Grow them like leaves."

They crawled around under the silver-gray leaf without finding anything but bark and mirror.

They followed the metal rails down to a switching arrangement. "Willy would have used a maglev track, not a box on rails," Miya said. "This must be deadly slow. *Building* it must have been deadly slow."

"Maybe they live longer. Now what?"

"Down," Miya said. She fired rockets and was off down the trunk. Svetz followed.

She was nearly out of sight, but her voice remained clear. "Cut your thrust *now*. Hanny, use the flight stick when it's time to decelerate. We've got gravity now. If you see anything on the trunk, tell me."

"Nothing but the cable." He was falling. Free fall hadn't bothered him at the midpoint. This was different. He fell alongside the tree as if he'd jumped from an arcology's roof, falling too fast and dead already.

"I see another silver wrinkle, another light-sail leaf. Don't get too close to the trunk, Hanny."

Svetz didn't intend to.

"Big box on one of the cables. It's just an open cage, barred, lots of boxes inside, some troops too. Hanny, *duck*."

"Duck what?" he asked. He still hadn't seen the barred box she spoke of, but he fired a puff of rocket exhaust to push him sideways.

"I'm just being cautious," Miya said.

There: a barred box on the rail. He zoomed his view, and saw a metalwork cage sculpted into a festival tent. Sparks lit the cage, puffs of flame from a dozen tubes. A flicker tugged at his peripheral vision: bits of metal passing silently through the space he'd vacated.

Miya had gone past the lift before they could react. They must be shooting at Svetz.

Carefully rather than quickly, Svetz pulled the flight stick from its tape and set it between his legs. It surged and lifted him away from another volley of what must be kinetic weapons. Faceplate magnification gave him shapes within the grillwork, just for an instant, as he hurtled past.

He'd seen at least five species of manlike and alien creatures among the fifteen or so. Some looked like humans in gaudily decorated armor, or in plain armor but with oversized misshapen heads; some were bigger, with too many limbs; four clung to the bars, all limbs, like Octopus, who shared Whale's cage. One was standing apart, weaponless, but he felt its regard: a cream-colored creature three meters tall, a skeletally gaunt giant fitted with great goblin ears stuffed into a fishbowl helmet.

"Missed me twice," Svetz told Miya.

"Any damage?"

"No. I'm losing you, though. Not f-falling as fast." His teeth were starting to chatter with reaction. He'd better stop talking.

Gravity had grown strong. The trunk slid past him ever faster, minute by minute. The band of dark foliage was still below him, but rising. Something on the trunk—

"Miya? That row of loose struts?"

"I see it. Artificial?"

"No, I think that would be stems for light-sail leaves. The leaf material's gone. Martians might have harvested it, like a farm for mirrors."

Miya said, "I'm going into the forest."

"East side, foliage strip, aye. Decelerating." He'd never had a partner on a mission. He'd never had to coordinate every futzy move with someone else.

The flight stick thrust up against Mars' pull, but it gave him maneuvering range too. He needed it. He'd drifted too close to the trunk.

He heard, "Hanny, I misjudged. I'll be landing five or six klicks below the top."

"Want me to go in higher up?"

"Do that."

The flight stick was steady under him. The trunk slid past, slowing. He dropped alongside black foliage, sparse at first, then thick and dense.

Miya: "I'm on. I'm inside. Yeee!"

"Miya!"

"Something jumped at me. I had to shoot it. These blasters don't leave much. Svetz, are you in?"

"At, not in." Svetz hovered, looking into a wall of black forest. The fluffy surface looked no more substantial than a dandelion ready to blow. He had no real wish to go inside, and no way to avoid it. Something in there had tried to kill Miya.

He fished out the blaster and fired into the black wall, angled down.

Foliage flared white. There was no recoil. The blast speared straight through until the tunnel showed red Mars at its far end.

Things swarmed out. Gravity and momentum pulled them away before he could see much of them.

He tracked a lens-shaped creature as big as a bungalow, the last in a whole fleet. Maybe Zeera could get more detail from the recording.

Coils of cable fell thrashing, then stretched out, klicks and klicks of it, reaching. Svetz used the zoom feature to track it. One end brushed the tree, dragged along it, caught more, loop after loop . . . thick cable marked with a black-on-milk diamond pattern . . . that was a wedge-shaped *head*.

Yes indeed, there *was* more than one kind of snake.

"I've fired a hole right through the forest. Things came out. Now I'm going straight in," he reported.

"Futz of a way to explore," Miya said.

"We're not exploring. We're looking for seeds. Seeds on a thing this size ought to be immense. Unmistakable."

"We can hope."

He coasted in. Coming out of the sun had him nearly blind despite his headlamp. When his eyes adjusted a bit, he jetted down the channel.

Whatever might consider him edible must have died or fled. Twenty minutes later he let himself fall into sunlight.

"Miya, I'm out. Have you moved?"

"Still inside. I'm not finding anything."

"I'll drop past your position by . . . oh, fifty klicks and go in again." Svetz was already falling, his flight stick providing just a touch of lift.

Miya sounded tired. "Hanny, it's too big a job."

"I know. We're missing something. We need to know where to look, but I just don't see the right pattern yet. Zeera, are you with us?"

No.

"Miya, if you were a tree, you'd want to drop your seeds in water, wouldn't you? The tree did that. Sank roots where two canals crossed."

"So?"

"This band of foliage ends, what, a hundred klicks up? If seeds dropped from the bottom, they'd fall at a slant. Coriolis effect would pull them . . . two or three klicks east?"

"We'll look."

A twinkling overhead. The Martians' lift cage was in view, much lower than it had been. It must be nearly falling, and it was flashing light.

"Miya? They're coming down."

"Can you find cover?"

"I can put foliage between me and them. I'm falling faster than they are. We could talk to them if your translators worked in vacuum."

Two hundred klicks lower, the fringe of black foliage had swollen to become a match for any forest still on Earth. Svetz charred out another tunnel.

Again a swarm of creatures fled his blaster beam. A nightmare shape took an interest in Svetz. His blaster dissolved it, but he'd attracted attention. Four rippling silver sheets with eyes in the middle drifted near, studying him. Living light-sails: *not* the light-sail leaves that grew on the tree, but maybe part of the same evolutionary line.

Svetz *knew* that if he fired on ambulatory mirrors, his own beam would come back at him. He jetted into the tunnel. They didn't follow.

He slowed midway to look around.

Limbs became branches became little branches became twigs. Growth here was fractal, like a fern or a tree. He saw nothing like flowers or fruit or seeds or pinecones.

Miya was taking more time to explore, but she was making bigger jumps. He stopped another hundred klicks down and dipped in again. Tree parasites had grown sparse. Nothing else had changed.

The upper tree was a line of winking lights when he emerged. Pretty. Svetz zoomed his view. Lights twinkled all along the trunk to the far tip. Signals. . . . "Miya, they're talking about us."

The edge in her voice matched his own. "I see it. Mirrors. They can chop huge mirrors out of those light-sails. What the futz is that?"

Something ghastly bright was coming at them out of the night. The breath froze in Svetz's throat. Something like an eroded gray mountain came straight toward the tree, turning massively as it came. The flicker of mirror-speech stopped as it moved on them, growing, growing, gone past with several klicks' clearance.

Fear made Miya's voice ragged. "Missed. Hanny? Talk to me!"

"I'm okay, but that was disturbing. Phobos? It must scare the Martians into fits every time it comes by."

"It and the tree must be in a resonance pattern. Ha! We can *hope*. What else have you found?"

"Look up," he said. Her suit was badly chosen, too like the colors of Mars, but he'd spotted her. "I found *you*."

He dropped past her and slowed, keeping his distance. She eased alongside him. Two flight sticks fell together along the narrowing trunk. Dawn was crawling down the tree toward Mars. A broad crescent of dawn crawled across black land toward the base of the tree.

Not *black* land. He saw lines of light, brighter where they crossed. Cities formed where canals met. There were more cities, arcs of light like little crescent moons on the darkness. Directly below was a cruciform glow. But none of those lights were blinking.

"Up here they're talking with reflected sunlight," Miya said. "Talking about strangers on the tree. They'll get answers as soon as it's daylight below us, and then the whole planet will know all about us. Maybe it's time to talk to some Martians."

Svetz agreed. "Offer them refuge. Tell them what's going to happen."

"We don't exactly *know* what happened, Hanny."

"Makes us less persuasive. And from everything I can tell," Svetz said, "Martians would rather open fire than conversation."

There were lights flickering below, not *on* Mars, but—

"Duck," he said. Another open cage was rising toward them, flashing with reflections and tiny puffs of fire. Futz, there were crabs crawling all over the outside! Crabs as big as Wrona, with human faces, it looked like. Human shapes inside the cage were doing the shooting.

He glided sideways to put forest between him and what he'd seen.

"Futz!"

"What?"

"Something hit my helmet," Miya said.

"Futz! Pull into the foliage, let me look at you!"

"I'm fine. My ears are ringing a little."

Still falling, braking with their flight sticks, they eased around the narrowing curve of the tree. Svetz heard Miya cursing softly before he spotted it.

Above them on a second pair of silver tracks, a wooden raft hung vertically. A cargo lift, rising. Things were tied to it: a boxcar-sized bulb with a door in one end, and several smaller boxes. Man-shapes were clinging to the web of lines.

Something struck his back-shell, *not* from the cargo lift. Svetz yelped and lifted on the flight stick. But that would take him too close to the guns on the cargo lift! Around the trunk, then, with bullets trying to follow him, and then turn off the flight stick and fall!

"Where are you?" Miya asked.

"Falling. West side."

"The trunk below us is swarming! Hanny, let's go with your guess. Go in at the bottom end of the black forest. Hide in there. Hope we see seeds. Zeera, are you reading us?"

The shadow of dawn had crept down the trunk to its base. Half of Mars was alight, and all of the skyhook tree. Svetz squinted down into a coruscation of blinking lights. Sunlight and mirrors: Mars was talking back to the tree. But stare into the blaze and you saw more.

Aircraft too high to be aircraft.

He zoomed his faceplate, and saw thousands of flying vehicles around the base of the tree. Higher up, mere hundreds, all (it seemed) trying to dock against the trunk. But that high, they must be in vacuum!

The Pilgrim probes had videotaped what seemed to be hard-shelled dirigibles. Could Mars have a lighter-than-vacuum gas? What *was* he up against here?

Some of the sparkling was weaponry: puffs of fire and a glitter of projectiles falling short. But some of the weaponry wasn't aimed at them. The natives were fighting each other.

Miya said, "Zeera's over the horizon, and the Orbiter doesn't seem to be in position to relay. Still with us, Hanny?"

"Still intact and on course for the bottom of the forest. Miya, I may have used flight sticks as often as you have. Just not in Mars gravity while trying to move inside a sausage skin."

"Very good. Anything goes wrong, yell for me. Don't think it over first."

18

Jacob's ladder. *Typifies a soul's approach to perfection. A universal axis or World Tree. Equates with Ama-no-Hashidate, the Beanstalk, Lugh's chain, stem of Jesse, Yggdrasil.*
—Dictionary of Mythology, Folklore and Symbols,
by Gertrude Jobes

A flyer ruptured and began to sink in a scattered cloud of men.

Mars still pulled like a planet. The flight stick was lifting at maximum, but Svetz's belly still thought he was sliding down a smooth glass hill. But the treescape slowed, slowed . . . until the black forest was a world-sized bulge above him and he was starting to float back up.

Miya drifted alongside. Below them the trunk was infested.

Svetz had barely heard of termites. He had to picture something like Von Neumann nanotech machines turning living wood into more of themselves until there was nothing left but the machines. It looked like that, just a haze of motion, until he turned up the zoom.

He had not anticipated that the wealth and power of Mars, five hundred and fifty years before Earth's first atomic bomb, could match the wealth of the United Nations of 1108 AE. But armor and manpower of that order was crawling up the tree at them.

The twinkling wasn't all mirrors. Close below them, slender man-shapes were fighting green-clad six-limbed giants. Faceplates winked like silver mirrors. Here and there were twinkling blades. Stick-figure shapes, improbably tall, moved about the trunk undisturbed, observing the fighting like hundreds of wandering referees.

Svetz said, speculating, "It's a technology race, like the First Cold War. Somebody saw us using tools that no Martian has. They can't let anyone else get to us first. We came to rob them. They're all swarming up the tree to be first to rob *us*."

One of the factions was getting too close. Svetz saw puffs of gunfire. Swords or not, they still had kinetic projectiles.

"Let's get into cover," Miya said. The forest flared briefly and left a charred tunnel. Miya jetted into it. Svetz fired rockets and followed.

It was soft, cushiony. Wriggle through, wriggle down. "That's me behind you, so don't shoot."

"Good. I don't see any parasites," Miya said. "Or seeds."

Even seeds of Earth could take *any* shape. Pinecones, spiky peach pits, smooth almonds, great melons with tiny seeds, avocados, acorns, sesame.

Whatever their form, skyhook seeds would look all alike. They might be armored against reentry heat. Otherwise Svetz had no idea what to look for, and Miya of Space Bureau had even less. He was seeing nothing but foliage—

"Have a look here," Miya said.

He saw her below, by pink Marslight. He wriggled down beside her. They'd left most of the tree above them now, and Mars was close below. They peered down through a hole in the sky.

The lower sixty klicks of tree was swarming with troop carriers and cargo vehicles. Miya said, "I'm wondering—"

The tree shuddered. They had that instant's warning, and then the trunk lashed like a whip.

It was worse than any earthquake. Svetz was totally disoriented. His arms and legs strangled a black branch that was trying to fling him into the sky. His grip was being shaken loose.

Eerily calm was Miya's voice. "Hanny, I've lost my flight stick. Can you come and get me?"

"What was that?" The tree was shuddering still. Miya was nowhere in sight.

"Don't know. Don't care yet. Come and get me."

She was falling!

Stop a moment. Think. "Was it lifting?"

"My flight stick? No. Maybe it stayed in the tree."

Svetz saw it wedged in branches. He reached, and the tree shook it and him out like overripe fruit. He was spinning down, dizzy and disoriented, with his own flight stick in one hand and the other falling with him.

A flare of rockets sent him close enough to grab.

"I've got them both. Wait one." He wrapped himself around his flight stick, gripped the other in an armpit, and barely stopped himself from twisting the lift throttle. He'd lose her if he lifted!

"Miya, you've got your rocket pack. Find me and come get your flight stick. Do it before we both burn up."

"Understood. Can you see me?"

"No! You're the same color as Mars! Who picks your wardrobe? Look for me; I'm green and I'm turning on my blinks."

"Blinks, aye aye."

"We'll make great targets. Oh, *futz*!" He screamed in terror as the tree ripped loose.

Whatever was happening below was half hidden in a cloud of chaff. Some of that chaff was vehicles and men. The tree's lateral surge must have shaken most of its parasites loose. The torn base of the rising tree trailed wood chaff and artifacts: twisted silver rails, pressure suits of human and nonhuman shape, falling sky ships. A falling lift cage: men and green giants and big crabs were swarming out and over it, and what they hoped to accomplish was beyond Svetz.

Svetz's emergency suit lights were scintillating in preprogrammed panic. He was a clear and vivid target. Maybe Miya—

"I see you, Hanny."

—Maybe Miya would get to him before anyone else. And there she was, a flickering orange flare rising past him. Svetz twisted the flight stick throttle hard over. "Do *not* make your burn. I'm chasing you," he called.

She was there again, coming down, and he twisted again to kill the lift, rockets too close. "Let me do the docking—"

"Just give me the flight stick!" she screamed. He hadn't guessed how frightened she was. She snatched at the brush discharge with both hands, and had it.

The tree's torn base rose past them, big as a wooden moon. He glimpsed Miya again, high above him on the flight stick, and lost her. They were falling fast. Already he could hear a whisper of wind. They'd burn as meteors if they couldn't kill their velocity.

It was not a time to worry about staying together.

Her voice was clear, almost calm. "Too much weight on the tree. They overloaded it."

"Are you all right?"

"Decelerating. I lost it for a moment there, Hanny. Look out overhead, there's a lot of futz falling at us."

He looked up at men falling silent in vacuum.

A sky ship dropped past him, slowed and rose again.

His hand scrabbled at his back. He must have dropped the blaster, but he was instinctively reaching for the needle gun, and he found that.

The vessel was alongside him. It might have been a dirigible balloon with wooden decking along the top. Men swarmed out of an interior well, anchored themselves, and hurled something. It unfurled as it came: a net.

Svetz twisted the throttle *off* and dropped under the net. They pulled it back and prepared to throw again.

Something ripped the vessel wide open. For an instant Svetz could see into a tank running bow to stern, filled with gas glowing by the light of a vermilion laser. Then the glowing gas puffed out and the vessel dropped away.

Wind sang a reedy melody, pulled at his helmet, set up a tremor in his flight stick.

Martian vehicles dropped past him. Nobody seemed to be firing at Svetz. Some fired at each other. None tried to match the lifting power of Svetz's flight stick.

And then one did. A sky yacht was floating down toward him.

He shifted laterally. So did the yacht, matching his lift. It was brick shaped, covered with masts and nets with no regard for streamlining.

"Miya, a flying yacht tried to net me, and now I've got another," he said. He looked for a target. He could glimpse men, but they were under hatches, firing through slits.

Miya said, "I'm clear. I can get to you, but not fast. I'm already in the atmosphere."

They must have recognized his needle gun as a weapon. The ship rose above him. A net flew. He dodged. They pulled it back and threw again. He dodged.

Air sang past him. He could feel heat on his shoes, the backs of his legs, his forearms.

The sky yacht's crew tired of trying to net him. He saw puffs of flame from covered slits, and tiny metal missiles whacked the back of his flight stick. The brush discharge sputtered blue lightning and he fell.

Nothing had hit *him*. He was falling with a dead stick between his legs, but he wasn't dead yet. He twisted every control. The stick only sputtered puffs of lightning. He kicked it away from him.

The sky yacht was falling alongside him. The net came down again, and this time, rocket pack or not, Svetz didn't dodge. The net swept him in, and the flight stick too, and pulled him toward a wooden deck.

Svetz fished out the flight stick and threw it overside.

The deck knocked the wind out of him. He felt it surge under him, the yacht pulling upward. "They've got me," he said.

19

In one respect at least the Martians are a happy people;
they have no lawyers.
—"A Princess of Mars," by Edgar Rice Burroughs

Describe the vessel," Miya instructed.

"Seventeen meters by seven, fitted out like a boat, no keel, no aerodynamic surfaces. Two long tanks with a narrow cabin between. I'm not guessing about that; I saw a tank ripped open on another craft. There are firing points forward, kinetic energy weapons, a motor aft and a deck across the whole top. I'm lying on the deck." And he looked up at a row of silver masks.

They wound the net around Svetz to immobilize him. Svetz said, "They look like men, what I can see. Except . . . one."

"Don't leave me hanging."

"It's just watching. Squatting with its knees *way* higher than its head. Bubble helmet isn't quite big enough for its ears. It's wearing just the helmet. It's covered with white . . . feathers! Bird ancestry."

"Hanny, it wouldn't be related to anything from Earth."

The crew fished his needle gun out and gathered 'round to study that. One crewman fired at something as it fell past. When he saw no result, he fired a crystal into a wooden post. It left a tiny streak of white powder. He was not impressed. He kept the needle gun.

Several crew picked Svetz up and turned him for inspection.

They reached through the net and opened buckles until they had freed the rocket pack and could slide it off his back. They must have recognized the bell-shapes as rocket nozzles. They were careful with it, bracing it against the deck before they tried to fire it. They couldn't make it work.

They'd find the safety override soon enough.

Svetz spoke while they were playing with the rocket pack. "Miya, they're built like basketball players. Their pressure suits are not quite skintights. They're quilted and painted in camouflage, all reds, and they wear bracelets and toques over the suits. They're wearing silver masks. The masks are pictures of human faces, like death masks. Little windows for eyes. Gems in some of the masks. I won't be able to use my translator until we've got air. *Talk* to me, Miya."

"I'm here, Hanny."

"The decks are wood. The fittings are wood. There's some metal, maybe iron and gold, but I'm surrounded by literally tonnes of wood!"

"Enjoy. I've found seeds."

"Tell me."

She had flown over the city. "Graceful towers that go up and up. Those slender arched bridges. Streets wind high up between the towers with no support but a few arches thin as an afterthought. Everything looks fragile. They build like they've forgotten gravity, Hanny. The tree's been dropping all kinds of heavy stuff; it'll knock down half the city before the day's over. Nobody was going to notice me in all that.

"I came down east of the city. I found thousands of craters all in a line, all sizes—stuff that fell off the tree over the years—except that a lot of little craters were just the same size, two meters across. I dug seeds out of the centers of those. They look like big yellow apples."

"Mission accomplished."

"Yes! But, Hanny, I still can't get Zeera. I can't even get readings from the Orbiter."

He'd been hoping for better news. The time machine couldn't reach Mars. The Orbiter was to carry them back to Earth orbit. Without the Orbiter . . . ? "Don't kill anyone from now on, all right, Miya? Without the Orbiter, what we are is immigrants."

"Hanny, the blaster is the only weapon I've got. How do I rescue you without killing anyone?" She sounded brittle.

"They haven't hurt me yet. When we get air I'll try to talk my way out."

Miya said, "I'm looking over the . . . you called them roots, but I don't think so, Hanny. They're anchors. Some of them have fallen over. They all fell eastward. The ones still standing are already sprouting black fuzz at their torn ends. I think I know what's going on here."

"Yes. Yes. Futz, Miya, that's awesome. Should we be looking for two kinds of seeds?"

"I think so. Hanny, are you glad you came?"

"Let's wait on that."

"These flying yachts keep nosing around. I can dodge them, but there are too many now, and they're shooting at each other, and I just think I'll get out of town. Any idea where you're likely to land?"

"I'll ask the captain when we get some air. Maybe you'd better check in with Zeera."

"That would take days. I'll hide and wait. Keep in touch."

There were big holes in the city, big enough to see from a hundred klicks high: fallen towers and fallen anchor trees, and fires spreading unchecked. Open water glittered where a fallen tree had blocked a canal. These trees had seemed mere roots when the main trunk was in place. Now they seemed immense, bigger than any building.

The ship had fallen far. Svetz could feel an honest wind blowing now, and hear the rumble of a motor. The vessel didn't hover long over the city. It chugged toward where a vertical thread hung from the sky.

"Miya. We're following the skyhook tree. That's west, isn't it?" *Freed of the mass of its anchor trees, the tree rises. The orbit expands. Moving west-to-east with the planet's rotation, the tree lags and falls behind.* "There's nothing west of us but desert."

"I'll follow. Keep me posted."

His captors took off their helmets and sucked air like they'd never tasted it before. Martian suit recyclers didn't seem to be as good as Space Bureau's. Their features were narrow and their heads were long, with pointed chins, but they seemed quite human. One crewman reached down and fumbled around Svetz's head until he found how to open his bubble.

Svetz couldn't move his entangled hands. "I'm going to faint now," he said.

The man didn't understand, of course. He spoke a few words. Svetz said, "My translator must hear you speak before it can help us."

The man spoke at length.

Svetz talked with the Martian, and breathed whenever he remembered. The Martian taught Svetz one word at a time. *Eyes. Fingers. Grasp. Breathe. Fall. Matth from Noblegas*, the Martian who was teaching him, *Sailor middle rank. Svetz*, himself. *Skyrunner*, this dirigible yacht beneath them. The orbiting space elevator still drifting ahead of *Skyrunner*, with its far end sprouting silver flowers, was the *Hangtree*. Aft was *Hangtree City....*

The air was pre-Industrial, and thin. *Breathe!* But there wasn't enough carbon dioxide in his blood. *Breathe . . .*

He revived because they'd closed his helmet and Miya was shouting in his ear. "Hanny! Answer!"

"I've been unconscious." His arms were still bound. His translator had a pickup outside the helmet. It must have heard whatever was said, storing the sounds without understanding. "I'm having one of those days," Svetz said.

Miya said, "Ride it out."

Matth was answering too. The translator hiccuped and said, "Why do Svetz throw the—?"

Svetz guessed, and bellowed his answer to get it through the bubble. "Why did I throw the flight stick?"

"Yes. Buy your life with it?"

"You hurt my flight stick. I thought it would hurt us. I bought all our lives."

Another Martian shouted, "Matth? I tried to net it." He displayed a net with a black hole burned through it. "The flare would have killed many of us."

Matth nodded. "Svetz, did you make that happen?"

"No!"

Miya: "I'm turning down the volume."

Matth said, "You are slave to the ship now. Your life you must give for the safety of *Skyrunner*." There was no question in his voice, and no doubt. Did Martians become slaves that easily? It would explain why he had been rescued, not killed.

"Why did you sleep?" Matth asked.

"You opened my helmet and left me with not enough breath."

Matth made an intuitive leap. "You come from where the air is different. Another world! Earth?"

"Yes."

"From *Earth*?"

Svetz was growing hoarse. "Matth, free my hands! I can make my voice loud."

"With your *hands*?" Matth considered. "Swear not to attack us or *Skyrunner*."

"I swear."

"Swear for your friends."

He couldn't really vouch for Miya, and Zeera had a bloodthirsty streak. He said it anyway. "I swear."

Matth freed him. Svetz stood up. He twiddled the volume control and asked, "Can you hear me?"

"Yes," said Matth and Miya.

"Good."

The deck surged with little gusts of wind, just enough to throw his balance off. Lower gravity seemed to make it worse. There were handholds all about him and a rope along the deck's rim. Svetz wobbled forward, handhold to handhold, seeking a better view.

He said, "I see other sky ships."

Matth said, "Those are enemies."

Svetz lowered his helmet over his head and zoomed. "The closest is bigger than *Skyrunner*. The next two are about our size, and one of them has big crabs all over the deck."

"They are part of the—" Something wasn't translated.

"The ships further back are too slow. They won't catch us. Some of them look like the lens of an eye. I can't tell how big they are. I count fifteen total."

"You have good eyes."

"You said the crabs are part of . . . something?"

"Several kinds of men gathered to make Hangtree City. The"— the translator hesitated—"Allied Peoples. There is a prophecy, Svetz. The world will dry and die. We hoped to use the Hangtree to lift ourselves to space."

"When did the Hangtree come?"

"When Lord Pfee was a child. Lord Pfee?"

A Martian answered from a higher platform. "Matth, I have a vessel to fight!"

Matth went to join him. The two spoke. Presently Lord Pfee bellowed a string of orders, then came with Matth to join Svetz. Lord Pfee asked, "Can you see great distances?"

"Yes. What do you want to know?"

"Tell me what you see?"

"Ahead, nothing but desert." Svetz zoomed his view. "Some right-angle patterns just at the horizon, right by a few degrees. Might be foundations for a city. Behind us, two ships our size and one twice as long and more flat, all at about our altitude. They're pacing each other now, and they're all closer than they were."

"The markings?"

"Where would I look for them? Never mind, I see what you

mean. It's a hand, fingers spread, painted across the bow. All three ships."

"Flags?"

Miya misread his hesitation. "Brightly painted cloth on a mast or pole."

Svetz knew that! "I see them. They're flapping, I can't read them at all. Blue on the big one, the same pattern on a little one, and the other one is yellow and red." Svetz looked up. The banner flapping above him was yellow and black. "None like yours. One of the lens shapes is catching up."

Lord Pfee asked, "Weapons?"

"I don't know what to look for. The ships all have little holes in front. The big ship has two, and there are tubes on deck that look like they can turn."

Lord Pfee nodded. He barked rapid orders to Matth. Matth left.

Svetz asked, "Tell me how the Hangtree came."

Lord Pfee peered at him suspiciously. "If I take this glass thing off you, you die?"

"Yes." It might take an hour, but he'd be unconscious, unable to save himself.

"What you threw away, wasn't it to keep a secret from us?"

"I thought it might explode and kill me. Weren't you told?"

"Yes. What of this?" The rocket pack. "For flight on the tree?"

"Yes." Svetz wobbled across deck to where they'd mounted it. He showed Lord Pfee how to work the rockets.

"And this?"

"Needle gun. These needle crystals dissolve in blood. It puts animals to sleep. Enemies too, but only from close."

"Not a useful thing."

"Tell me how the Hangtree came."

"I do have a ship to fight, Svetz. Still . . . come." Lord Pfee led him up a ladder to a railed balcony. "I can command from here. You can use your far-vision to keep me informed. What is your interest in the Hangtree?"

"We hope to lift vessels into the sky, to the other planets."

"Yes, the Allied Peoples thought so too. . . ."

20

Lord Feshk ruled a city of many thousands where two canals crossed. "I was his fourth son out of fourteen," Lord Pfee said. "Few of us are left."

A city of a hundred thousand or more, Svetz decided as he listened, and hundreds of klicks of canals bordered by farming land. Lord Pfee wasn't counting slaves, children, women, elderly, or maimed: only men who could fight.

When Lord Pfee was three, peculiar black-headed plants were found growing around the edge of a canal.

Ten years later they were a mighty grove that partly blocked the canal. They threatened a bridge of great age and beauty. Lord Feshk ordered them cut down.

Beneath woody silver-brown bark, they were stronger than any metal made on Mars. Uprooting them would have involved digging out a canal. Lord Feshk didn't order that. He thought he had something valuable.

He built a fortress twenty manheights above the ground with the alien grove as his pillars.

When Lord Pfee was seven, a black string floated down from the sky. Children watched it wavering through the grove, blown by winds but always returning. "We chased it for days. I was still young enough to enjoy climbing." Ultimately it got tangled in the black trees, and there it clung.

No man could see how high it led. Over years, the trees bowed inward, crumpling Lord Feshk's fortress, until the tops of every tree in the clump had grown into a single knot around the dangling string. That grew to a thick silver-gray vine. Children were told not to pull on it. They did that anyway, and it held their weight.

A century passed.

"Lord Pfee, do you mean a hundred martian years?"

"Yes. I was married and a landholder and had four girls by then." And what had been a black string hanging from the sky grew thick and thicker, until it and the anchor grove merged into one vast trunk. The black tufts became a ragged black collar that rose to the edge of space with the growing of the anchor grove. More black foliage ran up the Hangtree's silver-brown flank.

Savants came from all over Mars to study the Hangtree. Lord Feshk didn't like them. He taxed those who came, and restricted their movements, until the races of Mars allied and attacked his city.

"We were killed or scattered, Lord Feshk's children. My sisters married. They're safe, and they know my secret. I and my few remaining brothers and our children rule homes buried in a desert."

"But we found you on the tree. Did you join this Allied Peoples?"

Lord Pfee spoke with the reluctance of a criminal confessing. "We scavenged a city abandoned when its water source dried up. We found wealth to build a few airships and modify them for vacuum. We unburied their gate, marked in ancient runes whose meaning was madness. Green Cross, on a featureless desert! We scavenged the name too, and joined the Allied Peoples as Green Cross.

"But I wear Lord Feshk's face." Lord Pfee tapped his silver mask, now tilted back on his head. "We all wear our ancestors' faces. We have not forgotten who killed our father. When word came that creatures had crossed from another world, we sensed opportunity—"

A man shouted. Lord Pfee left him abruptly.

There was a mast. Svetz zoomed on its peak to find an observer tending a mounted tube. Lord Fesk was bellowing thinly, gesturing widely at men tending a similar tube on a rigid mounting. They were playing with objects (*zoom*) feeding small pointed cylinders into a feed belt for the tube.

Lord Pfee returned and spoke as if they had never been interrupted. "Allied Peoples comprises five tool-building species including the insect giants, the Tunnel Crabs and their mindless symbiote carriers, the Smiths and the Softfingers and ourselves. Most of Mars accepts the prophecy that the world will dry and die. The High Folk counsel us to accept our fate. But the Allied Peoples would change that future. Some factions babble of settling Earth. Svetz, would you give them help or war?"

Svetz said, "It wouldn't matter. You couldn't stand or walk or fight under the pull of the Earth."

"I've heard that too. And some babble of siphoning water from a large ice-shelled moon of"—the translator hiccuped—"Saturn. When I was a child we had no notion that that world had moons or rings!"

Miya broke in. "Europa is lighter than Mars. It's water under an ice shell. Hanny, you could position a tether with its center of mass in the second Lagrange point, with Europa between it and Jupiter. Europa's tide-locked, so you'd still have an orbital tower."

Svetz relayed most of that. "And people of your world could move around there too."

"Their plan is not mad?"

"No. I'm worried about your sky ships, though. How do you lift?"

"We use a gas that pulls up when irradiated with the sixth kind of light. Inert, the gas is still lighter than air."

"That is weird," Svetz said. "Bizarre! But if it works by lifting away from the mass of a planet, then you can't get to Europa. Between the worlds you'd be adrift."

"The Softfingers use something else, something secret."

"Rockets?"

"Do you mean like the recoil of a gun? Is that what you use? Can you teach us?"

Svetz said, "I can do that. Lord Pfee, is that one of the High Folk?" Indicating the skeletal giant on the mast.

"Yes. Ignore him. He is with *Skyrunner* but not of it, with the Allied Peoples but not of it. Man, when we fought to reach you on the Hangtree, we hoped for more from you than a weapon that puts animals to sleep if they're close enough! What would your people pay for your life?"

"Ransom?" He heard the gap: the translator didn't have that martian word.

Pfee spoke, and "Ransom," the translator agreed. "Weapons or wealth or ideas, power to take back Hangtree City! We must command the Hangtree itself, I suppose, to hold the city. We might rule in tandem, my people and your men of Earth. But have you anything to offer?"

"Rockets, eventually, but maybe I can buy my way free now." It might be worth his life. "Lord Pfee, give me some object you don't need anymore."

Lord Pfee spoke to a warrior.

The enemy ships—"They're rising," Svetz said.

Lord Pfee laughed. "Why, so they are!" And he went below deck.

What happened then looked like group madness. Twelve men boiled out from below deck, all wearing pressure suits like golden armor. They replaced men at various stations. Those disappeared below. The ship surged upward.

Smoke and fire puffed from the nose of one of the enemy ships. Railing along the leftward side of *Skyrunner* splintered. Then the other ships fired too. The big tubes made a guttural drumbeat *boom*. Some of the crew fired devices that were more like needle guns; Svetz heard their higher-pitched *snap*, and a flurry of *snap*s from oncoming ships. It all sounded distant, harmless. Near vacuum was eating the sound.

But impact weapons chewed the rails and the masts. The crewman who was carrying Svetz's needle gun sprayed red mist and screamed a diminuendo behind the calm of his silver mask.

The skeletal alien clung to a mast and watched.

Lord Pfee emerged with his mask closed. He shouted through it. "They're trying to get above *Skyrunner*. Fools! We can rise higher than they. We're stripped to leave the air entirely!" He handed Svetz a double handful of vertebrae as big as a man's. "A *terwheeel* was our dinner two days back. Will these do?"

Svetz ignored Lord Pfee's evident amusement. "Yes. You should not see what I do next."

"It nibbles *my* mind that I should not leave you alone, Svetz!"

Svetz shrugged. "You'll have to fight your ship. Set me a guard you can trust with wealth."

"I do not have even one man to spare," Lord Pfee decided. He closed his silver mask and began moving about the sky ship, giving his commands in sign language. He stopped briefly beside the High Folk observer.

Svetz felt his suit contracting in near vacuum.

As for the following ships, two had fallen away. The largest was spraying vermilion. But a ship marked with yellow and red lifted to keep pace while its crew threw mass overboard, and one of the lens-shapes had come much nearer.

Svetz opened his trade kit, and suddenly realized that the observer was squatting beside him, all bones inside a heat-insulating fluff of tiny white feathers, its knees higher than its head. It made no signs and didn't try to speak.

As instructed, Svetz ignored him. He fished out the superconducting net and wrapped it around the bones from dinner and sealed the edge. He started the conversion sequence.

Skyrunner tilted far forward. Svetz squealed and rescued the trade kit without releasing his scissors-lock on a mast.

Miya: "What was *that*?"

Svetz said, "We're in a battle. I'd better tie myself down." He still had the net.

"I've been following your ship, Hanny, but you've gone way above me. Keep me posted."

"Miya, they haven't briefed me on their plans!"

Skyrunner's nose gun fired. The sound was almost lost to vacuum, but Svetz felt the deck jump. The ships below were firing, but their missiles were fighting gravity. *Skyrunner* fired again, and again. The big ship sprayed vermilion and sank.

A missile struck *Skyrunner*'s side.

The trade kit had finished its work. Svetz took the altered vertebrae out and stowed the kit. Two ships below *Skyrunner* were both falling. Altitude was a major advantage here. But the red-and-yellow-marked ship was pacing *Skyrunner*. The lens had come in range too. It looked like two silver woks set edge to edge, with a small glass dome on the upper surface.

Skyrunner rocked to another hit.

Sailor-Second Matth crossed the deck at a run-and-climb, making full use of every handhold. Matth stopped by Svetz. From his bellow the translator picked out, "Weapon . . . buy your life and freedom . . . ?"

Svetz handed him an altered vertebra. It hadn't gained mass. It was porous gold now; it would melt down into a much smaller ingot.

"Gold." Matth turned it in his hands; twisted it and broke it. "What shall we do with this? Push it down their throats?" He flipped the pieces overboard. "Mars has all the gold we need." He was off at a half run, half climb, sprinting from handhold to handhold.

Svetz caught a flicker and turned in time to see what happened next.

The silver lens jetted a tight column of flame, very like Miya's blasters. Flame grazed the right side of *Skyrunner* and ripped it from bow to stern. *Skyrunner* shuddered and was the center of a luminous vermilion cloud. The lurch and roll caught Sailor-Second Matth off balance, and then Matth was in flight, flapping wildly.

"Miya, I'll be down shortly," Svetz murmured. He felt the right side of the ship, his side, sink.

"No hurry." Miya caught something in his voice. "Hanny?"

Once upon a time it had begun to bother him that all of the people he met in the past were *dead*. When he told Zeera his problem, her take was quite different. "They're not dead, Hanny. Nobody's dead. If you don't believe me, go back and talk to them!"

"Hanny! What's happening?"

He told her. He was hanging from a horizontal mast that projected from the vertical deck of a ship. The ship was falling toward noonday Mars with red desert below. One tank was still lifting. It wasn't enough. In a few minutes he was going to be dead.

The crackle of gunfire paused, then became a continuous rattle. The remaining sailors were those who had found handholds. Now they saw no reason to reserve ammunition. *Skyrunner* lurched to two quick impacts from the big guns of the red-and-yellow sky ship.

Skyrunner was falling . . . and then it was *really* falling.

Svetz released the net that bound him and cast it as a line for climbing. Those hours on the tree were all the experience he'd had in free fall, and he'd better use them *now*. Too soon, *Skyrunner* would be in the winds.

Martian sailors watched him. Two, then three began crawling up the vertical deck.

Svetz reached his rocket pack.

The three didn't like that. They moved toward him a little less timidly, a little faster, as he wiggled into the harness.

The rocket pack was built to maneuver in free fall, not to fly. It would thrust at half an Earth gravity. It must be almost empty. Svetz burnt another teaspoon of fuel jetting *down* to pluck his needle gun from a dead Martian tethered to the underside railing.

For an instant he might have gone further. Where was Matth? Svetz zoomed his view of a hundred falling dots scattered across red Mars. Some were debris. Some were men, and several of those were flailing.

Skyrunner had not lost lift quite soon enough for Matth. He would reach Mars ahead of *Skyrunner*. Svetz could never have reached him.

The sky ship was slowly tumbling. Crew were crawling up the vertical deck to tether themselves along the railing. Svetz clung where he was, but he didn't tie himself. "Miya? Mind if I talk this out?"

"Brief me! *Always* talk it out."

"I'm high enough to be in vacuum in a ship that has a tank of some light gas along either side. The gas lifts if it's irradiated with what sounds like a laser. It's antigravity, not our version. Now the right tank's ruptured. Left side isn't lifting either. If *that* tank's been shot open too, then we're just another crater."

"What do the Martians think of all this?"

Svetz watched a crewman tying himself in place. They were all lined up along the left railing. Many of the silver masks were turned toward Svetz. Some had guns, but all wore swords.

"They've all tied themselves in place against the crash. I've been rescuing my belongings. They haven't decided what to think of that."

Lord Pfee was still belowdecks, where the controls must be.

Miya asked, "Where are you planning to hit?"

Planning? "Well, there's something below us. A crater showing under the sand, with markings around the rim like the blueprints for a city. Maybe it's a buried city. You might not see it from ground level."

"I'll watch."

"O futz futz *futz—*"

"Hanny?"

He shouted in joy. "We're lifting! I *knew* it! Ships were shooting at us. Lord Pfee dropped us away from them. Now he's turned on the lift again. It's just one side, we'll still crash. That's why they're all clustered along what's going to be the top. I don't think that'll save them."

The dead men watched him, fascinated: an alien talking to himself, in vacuum and moments from death.

He watched the desert come up at him, and when it was very close, Svetz fired the rocket pack and jumped. He balanced face-down as flame roared past his ribs. A Martian snatched at his ankle as he went by, and missed. The man drew his firearm and sent a quick shot after Svetz. Then he was rising above *Skyrunner*, but Mars was rising faster.

21

He couldn't see.

He could hear, though. A voice yammered in his ear. "Hanny! I saw you come down but I can't find you. *Hanny!*"

He was bruised everywhere. His back hurt. Something hot was burning his elbow. He tried to push away from it. That pulled his face out of the sand, and then he saw sunset light.

In the triumph of the moment he bellowed, "I still live!"

"Where?"

The sun was high. Right on the too-close horizon were the sunset colors he'd seen, below a navy blue sky. Closer yet, *Sky-*

runner looked like a glass bottle dropped on pavement. A big bird (*zoom*) flight stick and orange rider were circling the wreck.

"Miya, I'm not in the sky yacht."

"Oh. Good!"

"It was getting *some* lift, but near the end I used the rocket pack. I think I ran dry. I hit like a bomb, but . . . not as hard as they did."

Svetz stood up, testing, taking his time. That hurt. In reasonable gravity he'd never have made it. But broken bones would be a deeper hurt, and what had burned his elbow was a rocket nozzle.

"*There* you are. Can you walk?"

"Worth a try." He took a few tentative steps. "I can walk."

"That's good, because we only have one flight stick." She hovered above him. "I thought you were dead, Hanny. *They're* all dead."

"I'm not surprised. Are you all right?"

"I didn't learn anything in . . . Hangtree Town? You got lucky. This Allied Peoples sounds like something we want to join."

"Why?"

"They've been exploring the tree for a century! They must know where to find seeds! And it's not as if we're protecting Earth, Hanny. A Martian couldn't stand up in Earth gravity."

And these people were cosmonauts, like Miya. Still—"They take ransom. Slaves too. Don't trust them until we have to."

She looked at him doubtfully. "Are you always this distrustful?"

"Maybe."

She changed the subject. "I think you were right about a buried city. It's ten klicks west of here, so it's on the way. Let's give it a look."

He limped across a crescent dune. Then another, watched by Miya hovering left and above. Then a wide arc of rough-edged rock. "Miya? Meteor crater?"

"Right. Mars has a lot of these."

He favored his left ankle. There might be cracked ribs among all the other aches and bruises. Fatigue softened the sensations and martian gravity softened the load. He stagger-danced, light-headed and light-bodied, feeling a bit drunk.

Above a horizon that was knife-sharp and too close, the tip of the skyhook tree still showed as a spray of silver blossoms. A small crescent rode above it.

A line of gourds faced the sun, each as tall as a small man. Something odd about them, or about the lighting, or just their presence on a lifeless desert. It was out of their path, but Svetz turned toward them.

Miya was amused. "You've got energy to spare?"

"Curiosity. Curiosity to spare," Svetz said.

No wonder they looked funny. They were black where they faced the sun. In the shade they were pale. Chameleons evolved to conserve heat.

He was moving too slowly for Miya, so she zipped over to see the grove for herself. The grove lurched into motion, scattering at turtle speed. Startled, Miya almost plowed into a dune.

She returned and settled ahead of him. "Just animals. Hanny, what's *our* interest? Here, you ride for a while." She handed him her flight stick.

There was a bag tied to the shaft. Svetz hefted it. Heavy. "Seeds?" He zipped the bag open.

She'd collected five yellow globes, big as a fist and heavier than Earthly fruit. Their rinds felt like ceramic. They had an apple's dimple and the melted stump of a stem.

She said, "Now all we have to do is get home."

He climbed onto the flight stick. Why hadn't she put him on the flight stick first? Assessing her partner's fitness? Or attitude?

Miya walked briskly, with a disconcerting bounce in her step that she brought under control by leaning forward. Svetz floated above her. She leaned farther, her feet pushing back, and farther, until she was running almost parallel to the sand. He had to speed up. He could hear her huffing breath, but the skintight suit slowed her not at all. The dust-puffs of her footfalls were two meters apart.

She ran up the slope of a dune that blocked her path, crossed the lip and was airborne for more than a second. Her laughter rang in his helmet, and he joined in.

"You're wonderful to watch," he said. "Practice?"

"Two years! Get some rest . . . then I'll teach you."

Another crescent moon rose behind the slender trunk. In a few minutes it emerged from behind the trunk and hurtled up the sky.

"Miya?"

"I've been watching."

"Well, those moons are *both* bigger than the pair of wasted little captured asteroids we've been living with."

"I know, Hanny." She slowed to talk. "They don't look like that on present-day Mars. Maybe it's an atmospheric effect, some kind of optical illusion. Moonlight filtered through stratospheric ice crystals. Has anyone ever figured out why Earth's moon looks bigger when it's close to the horizon?"

"No."

"We were right about the solar sails, though. The Hangtree is trying to steer itself. I wonder where it wants to go."

"It left a set of roots at Hangtree City," Svetz said, "and seeds for more."

"But that's where it got hurt. Maybe it'll drop seeds in some safer place, or just move out and away."

"Back where it came from?"

"It's built to settle planets. I think we're looking at a piece of genetic engineering by a race with techniques way ahead of ours. But Mars is ideal for an orbital tower. Low gravity, high spin, means the tree doesn't have to be as long or as strong. It won't find anything else that good in the solar system. It must have come from some other star, Hanny."

"What's its second-best choice?"

"Earth." Miya began to run again.

The horizon was a symphony of reds. A vertical black line crossed a hot white point: the sun near setting.

They did not at first realize that they were running through a city. Nothing showed in the billows of sand and harder dirt beneath. But the path of least resistance was a lowlands that ran straight as an arrow. Then Miya's foot plunged through the surface, past her knee, and her chest hit the ground hard.

Svetz settled. He would have leapt off the flight stick to help her, but he could barely move. "Miya?" Thinking of trap-door spiders, he worked the needle gun off his back.

She wiggled her leg loose; stretched it and bent it. Then she looked into the hole. "It's eaten out under the surface," she said. "Only water does that. Hanny, there was water here." Her hand felt around in the hole, then came out with black refuse. "Feels like old dry leaves or moss." She stamped. Again. Turf collapsed under her heel, and fine sand flowed in like oil, hiding all evidence.

He asked, "Want to fly for a while?"

"No, I'm fine." She began to run again.

Svetz limped along on foot, leaning on the floating flight stick for support, not trying to keep up. His cramping began to ease up. He wasn't trying to prove anything, just getting the feel of what was around him. It had worked for him in Earth's past. Here, stuck in a sausage skin—

"Miya, how's your recycler doing?"

"No problems."

All in one motion, Svetz threw back his bubble helmet (*poof!*), took a limp transparent bag from an inner pocket and pulled it over his head. He sealed it around his neck, tasting of just the least whiff of alien air.

The filter helmet inflated. The air tasted fine, with proper traces of carbon oxides, nitrogen oxides and petrochemicals. Something martian was still seeping through the semipermeable membrane. Meteor dust, dust of alien plants, and aeons of time. A bit too heavy on the carbon compounds. Now he could hear a thin wind brushing over low dunes and crater rims: a lonely sound.

"You all right?" Miya asked.

"Fine."

"Then what's the point?"

"Nothing lasts forever. I don't know where the flaws are in these pressure suit recyclers. I trust a filter helmet."

"Makes sense." Miya imitated him. Now they walked with their bubble helmets thrown back.

Svetz's footfalls jarred echoes from below him. He'd heard that sound a few minutes ago and not quite noticed. Now—"I think we're walking on a roof," he said.

"Is *that* what you were expecting?"

"Don't know."

Miya shrugged. She drew her blaster. Svetz backed up a dune slope to give her room.

At a touch of the trigger, sand exploded outward, then flowed into a conical hole. The dune flowed downhill into it. They backed away as the cone deepened. Then the flow eased, and yellow light was shining out of the sand.

Svetz wondered, "Troglodytes?"

"Clavius Base is like this. They could be human. Hold up," Miya said.

They waited for angry Martians to come boiling out. When that didn't happen, Svetz said, "I want a look."

"Here, take the blaster. Wait, the backblast—"

"No. Needles."

"Get your helmet up! It'll stop a bullet."

Svetz poked his helmet and needle gun into the hole. "Nobody home. The floor's five meters down. I guess they didn't like bumping their heads." Some of the walls were transparent. He was near one of those. There was a silver pool below him, like quicksilver or molten silver, as big as a baby's bassinet. "I don't want to go straight down," he said. "You don't either. Are you carrying line?"

"Yes. Here."

He went in feet first with a line in his hand. He swung back and forth, then dropped onto bare floor between a pair of small couches.

22

They had a house of crystal pillars on the planet Mars by the edge of an empty sea . . .
—*The Martian Chronicles*, by Ray Bradbury, 1946

Their counters were clicking, but there weren't enough rads to hurt them. Miya traced the radiation to lights that glowed in the walls and ceiling. She looked them over and said, "Hanny, there's no way to replace these bulbs."

He speculated. "They're supposed to last as long as the house."

Miya kicked a wall of pink stone. It was meters thick. "That could be forever! Look where the corners are rounded on the stairs . . . and the walls, *there* where people would brush against them. Futz, they weren't *ever* expecting a new brand of lightbulb!"

Light gleamed off pink sand beyond a glass wall.

They climbed into a red stone tower via a spiral stair. Its peak was just above the sand. Tall, narrow windows around the top faced in seven directions. Time had etched the glass.

"Arrow slits. I don't think they worried about lasers."

They looked in vain for an escape tunnel or an airlock to keep sand out. The desert had come unexpectedly. Then again, there were no bones.

Miya took the temperature of the pool of silver lava: 190°C. "Hanny, it's a stove! That's a perfect cooking temperature!"

"And still hot? Check for rads."

"It is radioactive. Stay clear."

"Still think it's a stove?"

"Cosmic rays and thinner air. Martians might not be afraid of radiation."

"Wrap the food in foil—"

"Or just dip it and let the hot metal drip off. I don't see any spatulas or forks. Would they just pick cooked food out of that with their fingers?"

*　　*　　*

Clearly there was no householder to attack them.

They never found anything like a toilet. Maybe the sand had buried an outhouse.

Opaque walls surrounded the back of the house. Here were two closet-sized rooms, doorless, separated by a mirror wall. In its center, a frieze of two spindly human shapes. . . . "Wrestling?"

"Having sex," Miya said, "in masks," and touched the frieze with her fingertips. The wall turned transparent. Another touch opaqued it. "Privacy. They could take it or leave it."

"Where are the beds?" Svetz wondered.

Miya shrugged. *They took the beds with them, or they disintegrated, or there weren't any because Mars gravity is so light. . . .*

Svetz found a touch plate.

Gray fog seeped from the floor. They backed out fast. Fog filled the room to half a meter deep. At the doorless doorway it hovered like a breaking wave.

Svetz watched for a time, then reached into it. It sagged under his hand, congealed into foam like a too-soft mattress. He threw himself into it. It held his weight.

He cried, "Miya! Is this or is this not a bed?"

"Hanny, we have a mission. We've learned as much as we can here."

There was a snap in her voice. He looked at her face to see if she meant it. She did. Chagrined, he rolled out. *There's certainly something we haven't learned. . . .*

Before they left he got the other room to generate another bed of semisolid fog. Twin bedrooms, no doors. No closets. He would have liked to ask. . . .

They climbed out the way they came.

"Teach me to run," Svetz said.

"Are you up to that?"

"I can always stop."

"Start by walking. Now you're bouncing too high. Feel it? You want to stay closer to the ground. *Reach out* with your feet. Lean forward a little. Now start pushing back with your toes. . . ."

He tried to keep his run level, following curves to avoid up-and-down, leaning *way* over to take a curve. Miya flew alongside. His knee and back and ribs were easing up. They still hurt. He'd get medical attention when they reached Mons Olympus.

They kept to the heights. They'd seen that the old canal was treacherous footing.

Thin air had him gasping, but he ran for half an hour before he had to stop. Then Miya walked alongside him, not using the flight stick. Presently she asked, "What are you singing?"

"Don't know." A tune was running through his head. The music was there, and the thoughts, but the words didn't quite fit.

" ' . . . float past all our days,' " he sang, and reached farther, and found only:

> *We dare not face the ocean's loss,*
> > *A change already come.*
> *The world's long death must never harm*
> > *This stove, these lights, our home.*
> *We build to hide ourselves from Time*
> > *a stone and crystal wall*
> *And Time will float past all our days*
> > *along the Grand Canal.*

"Doggerel."

"It's not quite right yet."

"*Ocean?* Never mind that. *Why* are you singing?"

"I'm happy." It was true: a grin was pulling his face out of shape. He let it have its way.

"Why?"

The gravity made every few footsteps a dance. "I fell twenty thousand klicks and I'm alive, I'm healing, I'm on *Mars*."

"You don't care about Mars, Hanny. I talked to Zeera. You're ITR's best operative, but you're afraid all the time. You're no explorer. You tried to back out!"

"Why *am* I singing, then? Hey—"

"How would *I* know?"

"But I *do*! Miya, was that or was that not the last native martian bed you will ever see in your life?"

"And?"

"It wasn't any kind of a record you wanted. It was *me*."

"That was then."

"*You* could have said something. You didn't have to wait until we were moving through time."

"That was *then*."

The song still played through his head, lyrics writhing around a theme. Yes, things change, but she *had* loved him.

"How big a town was this, do you think?" Svetz pointed down toward the dry canal. "The canals that cross at Hangtree City weren't any bigger than this. Look: smooth, then rectilinear lumps on the far side. Buried buildings. That shallow bulge. City Hall?"

"Hanny, do you regard yourself as mission oriented?"

"Is that a cosmonaut's term?" He thought about it. "History isn't like astronomy. Miya, my briefings tend to be totally futzed. I've had to rethink my goal on every mission. Even this one. We've got the seeds that grow the anchor trees, right? Are we still looking for the seeds that grow the Hangtree?"

"Not on the martian surface, I wouldn't think."

"And you don't think that big bulge could be a granary? Or a library?"

She didn't answer.

"We don't know how to find Hangtree seeds, what they look like, or even if the Allied Peoples have a billion of them in storehouses ready to launch at Europa."

Her voice was turning brittle again. "We can't read Martian, Hanny."

"It's not a library anyway. Likely it's something we don't have a word for. But you have to *look*, Miya. You don't find anything if you don't look."

"We searched the Hangtree!"

"First you dream. Then you look in a hundred wrong places. Maybe one of those buried buildings is your library, and somewhere there are picture books or comic books, and in one of those you find pictures of the Hangtree and some seed clusters and a close-up of a seed. Or maybe you find something you never expected at all."

"A seed storehouse?"

"No, not that. Why store them at all? Let the tree deal with them. We were probably looking at the wrong end."

"What?"

"Think like a tree, now. You're anchored deep in the watery soil of Mars. You grew an anchor grove and then linked to it, and now it's a part of you. Your roots close on the bedrock, way down. You grow more anchor trees in case you lose your anchor and have to reattach. You make Hangtree seeds too, orbiter seeds, because Willy Gorky needs them. But are you putting them in orbit? *Why?* You already *have* Mars. Why do you want competition? You want your children on *other* worlds—"

"Yes."

"It's what you were *made* for. So you drop your orbiter seeds from the upper end. The far tip is swinging 'round at better than escape velocity. It flings them at the stars."

A long moment passed. They were both panting. Then, "How long have you been thinking like this, Hanny?"

"Only just. It always feels like I should have known right away, but it can take forever. I have to go down all these blind alleys first. I . . . eventually . . . get it."

"All right. I'm starting to see what Zeera meant."

Svetz was starting to wish he'd heard that conversation.

"All we'd need to do is go get them," Miya said. "Take up position beyond the high end of the Hangtree and catch what falls. Hanny, what's wrong with this picture?"

"You tell me."

"It feels wrong. Throw seeds all over the sky? It's a strategy that works on Earth, works on a planet, but, Hanny, the sky is bigger than that."

"Futz, Miya, you can't steer a seed."

"Ahh," Miya drew it out, a long sigh. "Willy and his seeds. We're hung up on seeds. All right. We still need to get to Mons Olympus. Four thousand klicks across Amazonis, but we can do it. I don't know our fuel situation. Maybe Zeera's already taken care of that." And she would say no more.

*   *   *

They'd been following the crests of three interlocked craters. The broad, dusty road that had been a canal cut through two of them, and time had worn them near to nothing. But the largest and latest impact had fallen on the canal itself. Svetz thought to find water backed up behind the blockage, but it was dry on both sides.

"Hanny, why didn't we go look under that bulge?"

"Because we don't split up, and this is a space mission, and you've been on Mars and I haven't."

They walked for a time. Then she said, "Hanny, I didn't realize you were taking my orders. This is an ITR mission too. If you think about it, you've seen more aliens than I have. Pre-Industrial humanity isn't *like* us. They're closer to nature. They're surrounded by ten thousand times as many species as we've managed—"

"You want me in charge, Miya?"

No answer.

"I think Zeera's the official Head of Mission. Thing is, you *clearly* weren't taking *my* orders, so—"

"Hanny." She pointed.

Beyond the next dune was another. Something slid over its crest like a caterpillar crossing the edge of a leaf. It had far too many legs. It was gone before he could see more.

"Something alive," he said. "Big."

"What? Really? I meant the house."

House? Where she pointed . . . where the crater rim abruptly ended, chopped through to make a canal, stood a clump of crystals. Two were of smoky transparency, two were the color of brick, and the nearest was black. Not much like a house, those structures. But now he could see the shadows of rooms, and—

"I *did* see something stalking us, Miya. It looks like a caterpillar dreaming it's a tiger."

The blaster was in her hands. Svetz cradled his needle gun. They eased casually toward a peak—the high ground—and waited.

"Doesn't have to be a predator," Miya said. "What would it eat out here?"

"What would it eat if it isn't?"

"Mmm. Something living below the sand?"

"There," he said as it came over the crest of the nearest dune.

For an instant he saw why such a creature might want ten legs in Mars gravity. The beast didn't charge off the crest and maroon itself in the air and wait to be pulled down. It flowed over and down in a minimal shower of sand, bending like a caterpillar, its legs hugging the contours of the dune, and was already *much* too close.

Over the dunecrest and down to the flat and up the side of the crater, it came *fast*. It had a huge head in a collar of red fur, several rows of teeth, and four little tongues splayed like flower petals near the back. Svetz fired anesthetic needles into the thing's huge and gaping mouth. In the last instant he twisted and leapt away.

The creature whipped around to follow, and stumbled. It tripped over its multitude of feet, and one side went down and it rolled. It rolled over Svetz. Svetz, half crushed, caught its weight on both feet and *kicked*.

The beast snapped at what it felt under it. Svetz yelled as he felt teeth close on his ribs. They slid off the slippery skintight and snapped shut on his silver cloak. That ripped like tissue.

He was alive. He lay as he'd fallen, taking stock. No blood, no torn flesh. He'd look at bruises later.

The needle gun didn't look broken.

The ten-legged predator lay twisted on itself and glassy-eyed. Miya?

Miya hovered on her flight stick, looking down. "Hanny?"

He tried sitting up. "Fine."

She had pulled her helmet over her head. "I saw another one."

"Why didn't you use the blaster?"

"Hanny, it was too close. I lofted the flight stick and climbed on after I was up, because I d-didn't want to come down, after all, and by then it was on you."

"Use it now." Svetz set his own helmet in place and looked around. He would have to *find* a target before he could zoom on it. "See anything?"

"No."

"My bruises have bruises on them." He started walking. He could still do that.

"Anything we do with a blaster could mark us for any aircraft," Miya said.

"Right. Will you look at this?"

They stood like quartz crystals thirty-odd meters tall, almost vertical but leaning a bit at odd angles. Two crystals might have been made of cut pink brick. Two were of smoky glass. It still looked like a geological outcropping, but within the glass Svetz could see rooms and spiral stairs.

The near side of this nearest structure was a black wall painted with blurred pink silhouettes. One, high up, had the shape of a bird or big insect. Three could have been human athletes, a child and two adults, if one adult was wearing a helmet or had a head the size of a watermelon. The big-headed one was holding a weapon or baseball mitt or Jai-alai basket. And the fifth silhouette was a black circle, a ball or discus in flight. The bird was diving on it.

"Energy weapon," Miya said.

"Might be just paint." Svetz touched the child's silhouette and felt the raised edge. "Nope. The flying woks have energy weapons that could have done this."

"They fought for the last of the water. Bet on it. Hanny, let's be careful. People who fight like this might set traps too."

"We should be on the roof."

"No, we just don't use the door." Miya fired at a transparent wall and stepped through the hole.

Svetz backed after her. No ten-legged tigers followed them.

Here was another pool of silver lava. Miya took its temperature: 190°C. "Same as the other one. I was right, it's for cooking. Up the stairs, those little staggered platforms are where they ate."

"Let's stay here. The beasts won't come into a house."

"Hanny, is that your expert opinion?"

Would he stand behind that? He would. "Anything that thinks like a ten-legged tiger won't trap itself in this maze of rooms. Furthermore, it's my expert opinion that I need rest. I don't know where you're getting your strength, Miya. I've run out."

He didn't wait for an answer. The sleeping rooms must be in one of the opaque towers. He borrowed the blaster and shot a hole in a wall. Up the spiral stair were two matched cubicles bigger than closets, and a glass wall with a faded obscene frieze on the glass.

The touch point in one room got him nothing.

The other deployed gray smoke that half-congealed to a springy bed. He heard Miya behind him, and he said, "Mine."

"One of us should stay on guard," she said. "Me?"

"My mind's foggy. Do it. Wake me up when you can't stand it anymore." He started to strip off his pressure suit. Just opening zips was enough to tell him that the air was martian-cold. He kept it on. The gray foam accepted him and he slept.

He woke.

Miya was on the stair with her back to him.

He rolled out of the foam. He touched her shoulder and she jumped. "Four hours," she said. "It's still dark out. Nothing threatening. The moons—well, look for yourself. How's the bed?"

"You're going to love it," he said.

She nodded. She crawled into the foam.

Feeling the need to stretch, he went downstairs. He felt elated. Maybe that was only the bouncy feel of Mars gravity. There were no windows upstairs or down. The only light came from the forever bulbs. He armed himself before he stepped out.

Behind the sharp, close horizon was a silver flower, the Hangtree with solar sails deployed. That would be west, then. The Hangtree in its higher, slower orbit must be near setting.

Above the Hangtree, one of the hurtling moons was a glowing disk smaller than Luna but still too large. He watched it for an hour or so while he stretched against yesterday's kinks and injuries. The moon rose up the western sky. It was pale and featureless . . . but it was changing phase, from full to a fat crescent.

Maybe Miya had guessed right: that was moonlight on stratospheric ice crystals.

The corner of his eye caught motion.

He jumped straight backward through the doorway. The dark shape resolved, all teeth and too many legs, and slammed into the jamb while Svetz completed a backward somersault and jumped again, straight up three meters of stairwell. The beast roared like a high-pitched jackhammer and pushed through into the house. It was as big as the door.

Still in flight, Svetz screamed back, "Miya!" in case the beast's roar hadn't wakened her. The curve of the stairwell caught him. Now that his feet had some purchase, Svetz reached for the needle gun on his back.

Too slow! The beast flowed up the stairs and Svetz had to jump again. Its roar froze him and he landed badly. Miya must have heard the roar—

Miya was in the bedroom door with the blaster in her hands.

He stumbled past her, snatched at the doorway, turned with needle gun in hand. Too late. Miya fired downward. Her backhand slapped his chest, sending him into the other bedroom as the blast roared back up at them.

He waited until he couldn't hear anything before he crawled out.

The beast was gone. Below the upper landing, both lower landings and half the stair were gone. Shrapnel had spattered the living space below.

Miya said, "What a rush!"

"My hero," he said. He craned his neck to see if the flight stick had survived. It looked untouched.

Miya said, "There, there, my pretty one, no danger shall harm you."

Svetz said, "We're doing this all wrong."

"It's dead. We're alive. Sorry about the stair."

"No, hear me out. We can't walk a quarter of the way around the planet! We've got one flight stick. I stay here. You take the flight stick to Mons Olympus. Debrief Zeera and vice versa, then come back here with Zeera's flight stick and we'll fly back."

Miya thought it over. Presently she nodded. She said, "You're the boss."

"I don't know how to give orders. I was alone on every mission."

"There has to be a boss." She looked over the landing's fractured edge. "Long way down."

"Nah." Mars gravity. He jumped.

She caught him by his backpack frame and lifted him. "You'd just have to come back up," she said.

"That's right, you've only had an hour's sleep."

"Never mind that. Take off your skintight."

"Why? . . . oh. Miya, I'm getting whiplash here."

"What do you mean?"

"I thought you'd made yourself pretty clear, so I gave you up. I'm not sure how often I can do that."

She sat down on the edge of the landing and swung her legs, not looking at him. "You work for the ITR. I work for Space Bureau. Most of the time we wouldn't be in the same time *or* place."

"I hadn't thought that far." He sat down beside her.

"Had you thought of transferring?"

"We could ask. X-cages don't generally carry two crew. Me, I'm not a cosmonaut. But we could ask."

She sighed.

He asked, "You want your hero's reward anyway?"

"Sure." She moved to kiss him through two filter helmets, and caught herself. She began opening zips instead.

Svetz watched her nakedness emerge while he dealt with his own. He didn't know where the zips were on a skintight pressure suit. It slowed him. Miya opened a score of zippers in a few seconds' time, then started helping Svetz with his. Suddenly she yelped, "It's *cold*!"

Svetz grinned. "I wondered!"

"Well, how the futz—" She saw the only answer. She zipped, zipped, and pulled, and Svetz leapt naked into the sleeping room with Miya on his tail.

She was the only warmth in the world. The congealed gray fog wrapped itself partly around them and held some of their heat. "It's still futzy cold," she said.

"Well, try to remember why you slept in your pressure suit."

"Oh, was that it? I thought I was too tired to take it off. Or maybe I just hadn't decided, Hanny. But a thought finally plods across my sluggish mind. *Zeera never saw you on a mission*."

"No, of course not."

They had to keep the filter helmets. They still couldn't kiss. The gray foam impeded their lovemaking. It tangled them. Svetz finally got enough of his arm free to reach a touch point. The fog softened to mist and seeped into the floor. Miya pulled them together in frantic reaction to the cold, and they connected.

And presently broke free and sprinted for the skintights.

"How the futz did Martians do this?" Miya asked, and went back into the room to look at the frieze. "Hanny—"

"Did it without the bed, didn't they?"

"Right. Kneeling."

"The bed's only for sleeping, bet on it. If Martians had seen us they'd have laughed themselves sick."

"Well." They grinned at each other. Then . . . skintights weren't good for coitus, but they were fine for cuddling.

"I was furious with you," she said.

"That's what I thought, but I couldn't see why."

"For letting me think you were dead."

"Miya, I couldn't tell the difference myself!"

"How are you feeling now?"

"Beaten. There are places where I don't hurt. Miya, what's your fantasy Hanville Svetz like? Is he taller? Brawnier?"

"Braver than Zeera thinks you are. Agile. Nonlinear thinker. Heals fast."

"Does he negotiate or give orders?"

"Depends. You talk it out when there's time. Hanny, I'm describing what I see."

"If you see that when we get home—"

"If Wrona will have me."

23

> . . . across the gulf of space . . . intellects vast and
> cool and unsympathetic, regarded this earth
> with envious eyes. . . .
> —The War of the Worlds, H. G. Wells

After she was gone, Svetz tried to guess how long the flight would take. Moving at high altitude through Mars' already thin air,

Miya could make a hundred and fifty klicks per hour. Mons Olympus was four thousand and a bit, far around the curve of the planet, but with no chance of getting lost. Mons Olympus would loom like a piece of the sky.

Twenty-five hours. Give them an hour to debrief. Twenty-five coming back.

He stayed in the Martian house, that first day. His injuries had stiffened up.

By noon of the second day he was beginning to starve.

The suit would conserve water—as the filter helmet would not—but it wouldn't feed him. He had to distract himself somehow.

He went exploring. He stayed on the bare rock crest and kept his needle gun in his hands.

They might have been a pack of wild dogs, all hunger and teeth, in the moment he glimpsed them. They flowed up the rock slope in a surge that was like so many maglev trains. He fired carefully into their mouths. The nearest fell at his feet.

They were miniatures of the ten-legged killers, no taller than Wrona but three times as long. They were dead. The anesthetic had shut down their breathing.

He dragged two back to the house.

Svetz dissected one, talking his way through it for the record. He learned little. They had the wet red interiors of mammals. He could identify a single longitudinal lung. A stomach segued smoothly into an intestine that coiled neatly down the abdomen.

He cut up the second adolescent and dropped the legs into hot silver metal. He had read of this: that men and women had killed animals for food. He didn't believe it until he lifted his filter helmet to free his mouth. Then the smell hit him. He did not decide to eat; he found himself tearing meat from the bone with his teeth.

It was good! He nearly broke a tooth, he had to learn to chew around the bone, and the meat was tough, but he was ravenous. He made himself stop, appalled at himself, and waited to see if he'd get sick. A hour later, he gorged.

He deep-fried the rest of the legs and several strips of what he thought was muscle, zipped it all into sample bags and set it outside where the martian cold would keep it.

Night. The Hangtree was below the horizon, not even a silver highlight now.

Noon of the third day: now he could begin to worry.
Miya didn't answer the beam.
He waited through the fourth day.

In the afternoon there came a dust plume on the horizon. Svetz zoomed on a spidery crucifix moving across the desert. It resolved into a low-built vehicle.
The helmet said, "Hello, Hanny!"
"Is that you? West of me, on the ground?"
"Yes. I couldn't get to Zeera. We've only got the one flight stick, but I found this."
Miya was sailing along the dry canal. There was a wheel under the open cabin and four more wheels on long springy booms, and sails splayed on a mast and the booms.
He ran down to meet her.
"Get aboard," she said. "I don't want to stop in one spot. We might sink."
Svetz tossed his burden in and climbed after it.
"What's that?"
"You hungry?"
"Don't ask."
"Here."
"What *is* it?"
"Don't ask."
"Take the wheel." She examined the leg briefly, then ate as he'd showed her, helmet back, filter helmet on. Lift the edge of the filter helmet, bite, close it.
"Just keep us pointed west. Stick to the canal," she said. "It's light enough, it won't break through the crust. Hanny, this is *good*. Are you going to tell me—?"
He told her. She asked for more.

*   *   *

Zeera was pinned down with monsters all around her. Miya couldn't get near her. They'd talked by beam.

"Is she hurt?"

"No," Miya said, "but she's given up. I had trouble getting her to talk at all."

The crater in Mons Olympus was an observatory. Zeera had looked down into a vastness of telescope mirrors. Square klicks of mirrors and framework still didn't fill much of that tremendous crater.

The Tanker was half hidden in a tangle of structures, two klicks northeast of the crater rim. A laboratory and army bivouac had grown up around the Tanker. When Zeera hove into view, they fired on her.

She flew out of their range and uphill before she brought the *Minim* down.

"Did they damage the *Minim*?"

"Not then and not after, but Zeera says they could, any time," Miya said. "Now the *Minim*'s surrounded too. Zeera's safe in the cabin, but they shot at me as soon as I got close."

"Projectiles?"

"No, they've got blasters! Big heat beam projectors! Did you know the outer hull of the *Minim* is a heat superconductor? Makes reentry easier, but it also means a blast of heat won't melt holes in it."

"Did you try your blaster on them?"

"Hanny, I thought I'd better get you first."

Instead of leaving him four thousand klicks away, without air, food, water, or transport. "Good. I'm still catching up here. They've got a whole laboratory around the Tanker, right? And it's been there for years? We're lucky if they haven't taken the Tanker apart. Did it look all right?"

After long silence Miya asked, "Hanny, how the futz would *I* know if they drained the tank?"

Svetz said, "Get some sleep."

Driving a sailcar was fun. He'd had days to grow used to the screaming wind; it lost force now because they were racing ahead of it. The car was rolling too fast to sink through the dried dust. The canal was so wide that he couldn't see both rims at the same time. It would be hard to hit anything.

A line of big birds, needle-nosed and wingless, chased them for three or four klicks and never quite caught up. Svetz wondered if they were his dinner, then if they were chasing their own dinner. They looked to be just having fun. But the nearest one seemed to be wearing—

"Miya, give me a sanity check."

She wriggled around to look where he was pointing. Zoomed her faceplate. "That thing is wearing a belt. Or maybe it's a collar. With tools hanging on it."

"Matth said there are five sapient species in their funny alliance, plus the observers. This would make seven intelligent species, right? How could this many all evolve together?"

"Can't," Miya said.

"They could evolve separately," Svetz mused. "It's another quantum mechanical thing."

"I'm tired, Hanny. What are you talking about? Time lines merging?"

"Yes, just before everything ends for this whole world. Like virtual particles, no investigator is supposed to see this."

"But we're seeing it."

"Maybe we're not supposed to be here either."

But Miya was asleep. In the morning she remembered nothing of big needle-nosed birds wearing tool belts.

Come night, Miya wanted to keep moving.

They mounted her flashlight on the roof, pointing straight up. She hovered above him on the flight stick, in the beam, while Svetz sailed.

At midnight they switched. Miya made him take the blaster. He showed her how to use the needle gun.

At dawn Miya slept again. She didn't wake until near sunset. Svetz got an hour's sleep before night fell, and then they both had to be awake to drive.

After two days of driving she was caught up on sleep.

Dawn: he flew above dark green canyons cutting through red desert. Far ahead was a row of . . . something repetitive. He took his time descending.

Pyramids. The row began above the canal, and the first was no bigger than a fist. Each that followed was larger, and each had been broken open. The row descended to the canal floor as if the architects had mindlessly followed the disappearing water.

The line continued. Built on the floor of what had been a canal, these last could hardly be ancient tombs. More like row houses.

The last was as big as a mansion, and the peak was missing. They gave it a wide and wary berth. They were already past when Svetz saw a skinny arm emerge from the pyramid with a rounded brick in its hand.

Midnight. Miya brought the flight stick down to the aft boom, tied it, walked forward. They traded places at the wheel. Svetz crawled back along the boom. He didn't have Miya's balance, and it was very dark.

Svetz flew high. The tiny flashlight on the sailcar was a bright pinprick on black land. A moon ghosted overhead, west to east: Phobos, a featureless pale lamp much larger than any tiny captured asteroid. Stratospheric ice crystals? Its light illuminated nothing until he'd flown for hours, until his night vision began to adjust.

Below, wide to the left and far aft, motion reflected the moonlight.

Svetz moved out of the sailcar's flashlight beam. He could still see the light as a wobbly line of lesser darkness in his peripheral vision. An intruder in the sky was catching up with them, their paths slowly converging.

"Miya?"

"How you doing, Hanny?"

"We have company. Turn the flashlight *off*." Already the intruder was an enemy. Strangers met during his trips to Earth's past had usually been suspicious, jumpy, ready to kill a man who didn't dress like they did.

He used his faceplate to zoom on the intruder. He got a jittery image of a smooth-surfaced silver lens. "One ship. Big, I think. Flying double-wok, rounded, with no decks. Not the same style as *Skyrunner* was. Some other race."

What had Matth called them? *Skyrunner* had been destroyed by a ship like this, armed with a heat cannon.

The intruder was nearly alongside Svetz, but far to the left. Svetz dropped the zoom. At once he saw the second ship, flying even higher than Svetz and just above the larger ship, tending it.

He watched it for some time before he saw it swing right, abandoning its post for something more interesting. The second intruder had seen Miya.

Svetz saw the lens-ship tilt nearly to vertical. Saw an aperture open in the rim, and that was enough.

"It's after you," he said. He'd been keeping the blaster in a zipped pocket. He drew it carefully, knowing how much he didn't want to drop it.

"Shoot it!" Miya demanded.

He fired. "Way ahead of you."

The smaller ship rocked in the jet of flame. It fired a wild actinic jet of its own. Not a laser, it spread too much, but it didn't spread like a rocket exhaust. Maybe a plasma jet held together by its own magnetic fields.

For an instant it held, and then the flying wok flared. Svetz saw the ship shred itself inside a dying fireball.

He lifted. He could do that by touch. There was nothing solid above him. Eyes aboard the large intruder might have seen him when he fired, as the point on a line of white plasma; but now he would be only a dark dot on the sky.

"Hanny, report! I saw—"

"I got the little ship. The big one *had* to have seen me. I'm lifting. They'll try to chase me. There's no chance they'll find you until dawn if you'll just turn off that futzy flashlight!"

"I did. Why not just shoot them down?"

"I blinded myself."

She didn't say anything.

"There's nothing that can hurt me this high," he said. "I'll just wait for my sight to come back."

"Good plan." Miya sounded jittery. "Look, if you don't find me then, just keep west to Mons Olympus. Get to the *Minim*."

"Right."

He couldn't see. It was chilly without his cloak, but no worse than chilly. The flight stick flew on, altitude unknown.

Miya called not much later. "I saw where the wreck hit. I'm going to look it over."

"Bad idea," Svetz said.

"In and out quick, trust me."

It felt like hours passed before she spoke again. "What did your rebels call them? Softfingers? I've found parts of at least four bodies. They look like dry-skinned octopuses. They've got ten arms with no bones in them. They're bigger than men. Oversized heads with an external skull, and big bulging eyes.

"The undersurfaces of the tentacles are thick with callus right up to the . . . shoulder. The underside of the pressure suit is a curved plate, a skid. I pried one up. It's covering the air supply. The mouth is on the bottom." Pause. "Hanny, do you remember Gorky's maps?"

From footage taken by the descending Tanker, Gorky had made maps of every size. They'd all studied them so that they could find the Tanker.

"Remember a white rock formation on Mons Olympus? It looked chopped, sculpted, but no special shape? Well, that was a Softfingers skull."

"Charming."

"Hanny, I found rolls of mirror cloth. It's solar sail material harvested from the skyhook tree's leaves."

"An innocent cargo ship? They had one futz of an energy weapon."

"Aye aye, but I sure hope we know what we're doing."

"Miya, get out of there before they come to bury their dead."

"*You* don't know they . . . right."

*   *   *

Something blurred and bright floated in his sight. Joy flooded through him: his sight was returning. He watched it for a time, trying to guess its size and distance.

"Miya? Is it still night where you are?"

"Sure. How high are you?"

"I can see the curve of the planet." An arc of light, without detail. "And I can see Mons Olympus." The crater's rim was aflame with dawn. No mistaking it now, though his sight was still blurry.

"Go for it."

24

He said, "Zeera?" and waited.

These were the foothills of Mons Olympus. The mountain looked like a tilted continent from this close. Zeera should be in line of sight.

"Hanville Svetz calling Zeera Southworth for the Institute for Temporal Research. Zeera, answer."

"Svetz?"

"Hi, Zeera. What's happening?"

"They shoot at me when I try to take off. If I try to work the airlock, they shoot. Sometimes when I look out."

"How many? Where are they? Can you see them?"

"They shoot at me when I look! They've got things like blasters, but big!"

"How much damage have you taken?"

"I can't tell. Maybe none. The blaster only shoots heat beams, I think, and it recharges in ten minutes. There are two at least. The *Minim*'s hull superconducts heat, it can take that much energy and radiate it away before they can fire again, but my engines overheat and shut down and I fall about a meter! I did it twice more. I thought you'd need the data."

"*I'd* need—?"

"You, Miya, *somebody!*"

He heard the edge of hysteria in her voice. She wanted rescue! He said, "Well, I'm here."

"Just stay away. You'll go like an ice cube in coffee."

"I can't leave things the way they are. We'll starve. You've got all the food. Zeera, did the Tanker look ruptured?"

"Not ruptured, but they took off one of the landing motors and tested it," Zeera said, "and they built a kind of token wall around the nuclear pile. Radiation must have made someone sick."

"They didn't cut the cable?"

"No, they're letting it run."

"Who am I fighting?"

"I started a war, coming down. The people around the Tanker were human. These things with all the arms and no bones, they're astronomers. I'm not guessing, Svetz. They use radio. I tuned in and used the translator. There was some kind of long-term truce. The men had the Tanker and the . . . astronomers—"

"Softfingers."

"—Softfingers had the telescopes, but they both saw the *Minim* come down, and that set things off. I heard them fighting over me."

"Sanity check," Svetz said. "You hovered above the crater because you wanted to see the telescope setup. The Softfingers saw you then. Then you went into a landing pattern over the Tanker. They fired on you?"

"Yes, the men. They had impact weapons. I put some mountain between me and them, fast, but I could see the astronomer ships coming down at me. They've got aircraft like two saucers set lip to lip. They were blasting the camp around the Lander when I got out of sight. One came after me. He got me with a heat cannon. My engines started to shut down. I hit the override and got down as fast as I could, and I've been here since."

"Okay. Stay put. I'm on it."

"The astronomers killed most of the people and kept the rest as . . . the translator says *slaves.* Hanny, what are you going to do?"

"Maybe I shouldn't tell you. If you heard them, they could listen to us." Svetz didn't believe they could translate, but he didn't have a plan, either.

*   *   *

He was well up Mons Olympus now, just a few klicks high, though that still put him above where a man could breathe. He might still be too small to notice, but as soon as he fired a blaster, they'd be after him

The Tanker had taken pictures all the way down. Gorky had maps of every size, and Svetz had studied them for months. He didn't expect to have trouble finding the Tanker. But where was it?

He *could not* keep circling forever in hope that something would look familiar.

Wait now . . . he *knew* that white rock formation from Gorky's maps. Miya had dissected a Softfinger, and she said this was the shape of its skull. So the Tanker should be . . . there. Svetz looked for a compact silver bullet shape. The Tanker was Moon-built motors, turbines, compressors and the nuclear pile to power them, but most of its volume would be tanks.

It was there. It was nearly hidden in a maze made up of ladders and pipes and flattened spheres, a long silver line of cable that led to the nuclear power source on its tractor treads, a dismounted rocket motor braced against a hillside, and a score of little buildings too pretty to be prefabs, too hastily built to be houses . . . martian work in the style of Hangtree Town . . . and two bigger structures that looked more like beehives.

Still, he could not imagine how he'd missed the Tanker. It sat on the highest flat spot the Tanker's computer could find. Space Bureau wouldn't *hide* the fuel it would take to get their samples home!

"Zeera, I have the Tanker in view. Tell me again how you get them to shoot at you."

"Any time I try to take off. Any time the airlock door wiggles. Sometimes if they see me in the flight dome, they blast a granite outcropping. I'm right under it."

"So the rocks around you would be covered with scorch marks, would they?"

"Yeah! Look for kind of a big rounded granite skull. They shoot it any time I poke my head into the flight dome. They shot the eyeholes first. Now they're shooting just over my head and making gaps for teeth. *Human* skull."

He'd found another little beehive high above the Tanker, beside what might be a heat cannon, though he'd never seen a weapon like that one. A line ran down to a patch of black cloth or paint. Heat radiator?

He flew wide around.

Zeera couldn't have flown very far . . . and she hadn't. The human brain is configured to turn random patterns into faces. The moment he glimpsed a skull carved into the granite cliff, he dropped, then eased the flight stick uphill.

He was rising up an arc of ridge, maybe part of an old meteoroid impact. Mountains weren't immune. The ridge might hide him. He eased up the slope, then veered away fast. At the crest was another beehive-shaped building.

He followed the ridge around and came up at the other end.

The *Minim* was in a shallow dish, the impact point of that old meteor strike. It was about the same size as the Tanker. Most of the *Minim* must be tanks too: he knew how cramped the skimpy cabin was. The cone at the top was the flight dome. He'd expected to see Zeera inside, but he didn't.

The beehive hut had the *Minim* in full view, and a good view of the blasted cliff. Through a door—one meter tall, two meters wide—he could see a small telescope pointed at the *Minim*. The heat cannon was a big tube on a massive swivel. What must be a control chair was mounted in the swivel, behind the tube. A black strip—not a cable, more like a line of paint—led to a broad black patch on the slope below.

Fine. "Zeera?"

"Hanny?"

"Wiggle the airlock door for me."

"Why—" She chopped it off.

Svetz didn't watch the *Minim*. He wasn't looking straight at the gun either: he'd been blinded once already. He watched for the line of flame that speared down from the granite skull and bathed the *Minim*.

Svetz said, "Wait it out, then stand up in the dome. Eyes closed."

The flame died. He looked up the granite mountainside, past the crudely blasted skull pattern, and found the wok ship perched above the eye sockets. A point on its rim was glowing orange, brighter than sunlight. "Now. Stand up. Wave," he said. If Zeera was right, the wok ship couldn't fire again.

There was no second blast.

"Good. Thank you, Zeera," Svetz said, measuring angles with his eye. Two guns, she'd said. They'd held the second in reserve, and that *had* to mean that there wasn't a third. Right?

He took careful aim on the wok ship, and fired.

Immediately he lifted and dropped below the ridge, swept around the curve and rose on the blind side of the beehive hut. Fired and held his aim. The hut flared into a rising fireball, and behind the fireball was the heat cannon glowing orange and red, and flame colors streaming from the control chair where there had been a Softfinger gunner.

The wreckage of the wok ship was still rolling downhill. Svetz rose into full view, held the pose for a long moment, lifted at two Earth gee, looped and dove behind the ridge again, circled far around and rose, making himself a target.

Nothing.

"Open the airlock," he said, already diving. "And get me a ration bar!" At the last moment he veered hard, looped—*still* no heat blast—settled into the airlock and punched the cycle point. He was aiming through the outer door until it had actually closed.

He'd done it.

The inner door opened. Zeera gaped at him from one of the command chairs.

He was gasping for air that wasn't getting through the filter helmet fast enough. He pulled it off and took the ration bar out of her hand.

He went through them as fast as possible, the things he'd planned if he got this far:

Eat! Stuff more ration bars in his pockets for himself and Miya. He ate steadily, and talked through a full mouth.

"Zeera, find the maps the Tanker made coming down."

Zeera nodded. Where he'd been expecting joy and gratitude, she only looked exhausted. But she set to work. Presently she had the display he remembered, complete with Willy Gorky's overlaid contour lines and notes. "*Yes*. Now, Zeera, what did you see coming in? Sketch it for me."

She looked up. "There's more."

Put the needle gun back on the wall. Fat lot of use it would be on Mons Olympus, where every friend and enemy wore an armored pressure suit! Plug the blaster into the wall for a recharge. Take down the other, freshly charged blaster. He was fizzing with energy. It would be dreadful if he forgot something crucial, and they couldn't have very much time.

Take a sonic too. There was still enough air to transmit sound. Blasters made noise, but the sonic stunners were too shrill for human ears. What kind of ears did Softfingers have?

Why was she still looking at him? "Zeera? There's more than what?"

"Svetz, they've shot down the Orbiter."

"What?"

"I was linked up and recording. Multiscreen, orthogonal views and a window for data. I thought I could learn something more before I landed. The Orbiter was crossing over the tree, and then something came up from the Mars direction and hit me between the eyes and everything just went! It's gone, Hanny. We can't go back to Earth."

He absorbed that. "No wonder you're a little twitchy. A week ago? Trapped here with nobody to talk to and nobody to help. Have you been eating?"

"Eating? Yes. Sleeping, no."

"There are things we have to deal with *now*. Maybe none of the Softfingers saw me burn this place out and nobody got a message off, but that can't hold forever. We should be out of here. Can you expand this map?"

"They'll kill us."

"They will if they find us still here. They've got more than heat cannon, Zeera. They took projectile weapons off the humanoids. We need to move. I want you to rescue Miya."

"I'm low on fuel."

"How low?"

"I saved some, actually. The *Minim* wasn't as massive coming down, because you and Miya weren't in it." Her hands moved. Displays changed: she'd set the *Minim*'s pile to warming. Then the map shrank and all of Mons Olympus was in view. "Where is she?"

"We've been following this dry canal. I don't know what she'll do when she gets close, and I don't want to lose her. You take off, you follow the canal until you see a car with pale blue sails."

Unexpectedly Zeera giggled. "Right, so I can tell it from all the other sailboats running around Mars. Svetz, it sounds like fun!"

"We've been starving."

"H—"

"It *was* fun."

"Svetz, what if they follow me?"

"You're on a ballistic parabola. These martian ships are dirigibles. They *can't* follow you, but they'll try. Anything that lifts off, I shoot it."

"Shoot it?"

"I burned down a wok ship last night. I'm armed and maneuverable and too small to see."

"You start a war and they'll wreck the Tanker!"

"The Tanker has the same superconducting shell that saved you."

"They stripped off some of it. Didn't I say?"

Futz! Svetz said, "Zeera, they still can't *kill* us. The *Minim*'s safe. They can only trap us again. So in a few minutes I'll take my flight stick out and bring the war to them."

She nodded. "Bring the war to them," she repeated. "War? I don't expect they'll worry much about one man on a flying stick! And if you kill everyone on the mountain, we still can't get home!"

"Zeera, it's not as bad as that. We can use your FFD to move us."

"Say again?"

He'd hated the use of initials all his life, and now they had him doing it! "The Institute's Fast Forward device that got us here in the first place. Turn it on and ride it to present time. Base One is buried, so we can't find it without Miya, but she knows the codes that'll get us into the Base. Of course Willy will want our heads."

"Fast Forward. I never thought of that," Zeera said.

Good! "One more thing." Svetz took the bag from Miya's flight stick and spilled five golden globes. "We've got seeds. We both think we only got the seeds that grow into roots to anchor the big one, but Willy can't scream *too* loud if we cut the expedition short."

"Oh, Hanny, that's great!" She picked one up. "Futz, it's heavy."

"Storage?"

"There."

While Svetz put the seeds away, Zeera was at work. "Hanny, I've got the *Minim* on a ballistic trajectory down to *here,* where the flats meet the foothills. It's where the canal peters out. I'll phone her once I'm out of these rocks. It looks like I've got fuel to get back up, but I can't hover at all. Up and down and unless I spot her in time, she'll have to come to me. And the *Minim* can't fight. You'll have to do that."

25

Svetz went out the airlock, over the ridge and down and around and up the mountain, following the route he'd marked using Zeera's map. By now it felt like he'd been born riding a flight stick. He was moving fast as he rose into view of the Tanker and the laboratory facilities around it.

The *Minim* lifted into view. The flame of its exhaust wasn't much brighter than the daylit mountain.

There were octopoids everywhere. Several were sunning themselves on the hill. What looked like an open cafeteria served several more. A few wore what must be pressure suits, star-shaped with a glass dome in the center. He wasn't trying to count, and he'd miss some anyway. Twenty in view?

Big eyes bulged beneath the skullcap shells. A few had noticed the tiny *Minim*. Svetz was rising fast, and now he couldn't tell if any had seen *him*. Nobody was shooting at him.

He hadn't seen any wok ships on his first pass. He didn't see anything in the air now. He did find two beehive-shaped huts and the heat cannon mounted beside them, looking down from the edge of a mesa.

The *Minim*'s rocket flame went out and he lost it.

Svetz and Miya must have been shot at by every kind of Martian who ever stalked the nightmares of primitive Man. Even so, the danger Svetz feared most was Zeera Southworth.

Zeera was on a short fuse, and that put Svetz on a time limit. If she was really as desperate as she'd seemed, then all she had to do was abandon her crew, turn on the Fast Forward device and ride to the present. Find Base One—which was buried, but surely they'd mark it with paint! No need for Miya's codes if Zeera could talk her way in.

Svetz and Miya would be left as involuntary colonists on a doomed world.

He'd done what he could. If everything went right, Miya would be with Zeera, safe until Svetz could join them both. The trick was to move *fast*.

He rose level with the mesa. It was painted with a gigantic ten-pointed asterisk. There was a bigger beehive building at the edge. He pegged it as a broad landing field with warehousing, and no aircraft currently in residence. Where was the big wok ship?

If he'd seen a ship he'd have had to go after it. Seeing no ship, he had a problem. He'd seen a big wok ship last night, coming here. By now it should have reached Mons Olympus crater.

He was rising fast. The wind blew straight down, battering at his bubble helmet. Then glare-white plasma blew past him from below and he knew he'd been seen.

It missed him by a fair distance. He'd left the asterisk far below. The lip of Mons Olympus crater was near, and he turned off his lift and coasted upward.

Radio messages must be alerting the observatory even now.

He'd hoped to reach the observatory without giving warning. Too bad. They might be expecting him, but they couldn't expect what he was about to do.

The crater in Mons Olympus would have held all of the Hawaiian islands.

Dots of sunlight glare ran in rays along the bottom, tremendous sheets of mirror in a far larger array. Two or three square klicks of landing field had been marked off with another asterisk. As Svetz dropped closer, he could pick out a hexagon of beehives, and then the big double wok ship. A score of octopoid astronomers were unloading cargo from a big hatch under the rim.

If everything else works out, Svetz thought, the *Minim* will still have to be refueled. There must be nobody to attack the Tanker while we do that. Best to take out everything that can fly, *now*.

He tried not to think how many Softfingers he would have to kill. He was not used to killing people.

Svetz dropped toward the ship, took aim beneath the hatch and fired.

In daylight the light didn't blind him. He played the flame against the ground, bouncing the backwash into the ship. Bearers who weren't caught in the flame dropped their burdens and fled into the shadow of a mirror. With all their rubbery limbs functioning as legs, they looked like so many pinwheels. But he'd killed ten in less than ten seconds.

Then the big double wok lurched into the air and turned with its hatch closing, and Svetz was falling too fast. If he didn't lift quick he'd be nothing but a smear.

Lift and thrust. The flight stick pulled out of its swoop, and Svetz ran beneath several acres of mirror, slowing, slowing. He didn't want to ram the framework! No hurry. Softfinger astronomers would flinch from firing on their own mirrors.

They flinched, maybe, but they fired. He saw flame wash around the mirror's edge, and he turned away. There were big arcs and pillars under the mirror fabric to shape the paraboloid. He could see well enough to dodge.

He emerged into sunlight and immediately veered under another mirror just ahead of a blast from above. And emerged again, almost under the big ship's belly.

The ship flew tilted, but the aperture in the rim wasn't looking at *him* yet. He lifted hard, firing at the ship's belly, and rose past the rim and fired down. The disc was spinning on its vertical axis, heat cannon coming around, and his blast hadn't hurt the belly at all. Why would it? That must be its reentry shield! But he kept rising, and veered and rose again, playing his fire against the upper surface.

The blaster was searing his hand through the glove—waste heat—but he'd melted a hole. He held his fire on it.

Something puffed fire from inside the ship. It lurched. Its heat cannon was coming around, and Svetz veered hard. Plasma washed past him once and again. This ship had two cannons!

With a flight stick, the only way to dive was to turn off the lift and let feeble Mars gravity have its way. He had lateral thrust, but if he wanted to change his path quick, the only way to go was up.

Svetz went up.

More fire was coming down at him from four heat cannons on the crater's vast rim. The astronomers had gotten organized. But only the big wok ship was in flight. He had cut them a new rocket nozzle, and that was blowing flame.

He was rising fast now, spiraling to avoid the mounted heat cannon. He was above them now. He saw no point in attacking fixed installations or astronomers in general.

The big ship ripped through a line of mirrors.

Svetz kept rising.

"Zeera? Miya?"

He should have them in line of sight now. He'd risen into near vacuum. His suit was tight around him and he'd tightened the belly band so he could breathe. The planet's wimpy gravity was pulling him down toward what seemed a fuzzy white dot from this height. He'd placed it in relation to the octopoid's skullcap.

"Svetz calling—"

They both cut in at once. "Hanny!" "Svetz!"

"Are you all right? Are you together?"

Miya laughed. "Yes and no—"

Zeera: "I'm down. I saw the sailcar too late to do anything about it. I set down in shadow, over against the south edge of the canal."

"Tell Miya where you are!"

Miya: "It's all *right*, Hanny, I have the *Minim* in sight. The wind's died on me, but sailing is still faster than running. Ten minutes. How are you doing?"

Svetz said, "I went up to the Observatory and shot down everything that flies. Now I'll take out whatever's around the Tanker." He was giving it *way* more confidence than he felt.

Zeera said, "You *won*?"

"So far. There's still the Tanker. Now, if you'll work up a ballistic course to the Lander—"

"Already done, Svetz! I'm just waiting for Miya!"

Miya cried, "Hanny. Hanny, I can see two flying woks coming from the east!"

"Oh, *futz*! East?"

"Everything that flies, eh?" Zeera.

"Futz. I should have . . . it wouldn't have made a difference. Miya, how close are they?"

"Just two dots if I don't zoom. I only just sighted them. They're not very close, and I don't know how fast they are."

Svetz mulled it through. He'd shot down the little escort ship. The big cargo craft must have told the Observatory: *Our escort was shot down by an unseen enemy somewhere along the old canal.* They'd sent two ships to search for the bandit, and here they were coming back.

A blurred dot had become an asterisk: the landing pad above the Lander.

"Miya, I'd say they flew right past your old sailing craft without finding it interesting." Which meant . . . "Zeera, if the wok ships get too close, take off. Take off without Miya. Miya, they'll *have* to follow Zeera. They don't know what she'll do, they don't know what she *can* do, and some hysterical Softfinger astronomer is telling them about *me* right now. Zeera, I'll clean out the area around the Lander before you get here."

Miya said, "Hanny, the big cargo ship—"

"I shot it down. There was a wok ship overlooking the *Minim* and I blew that up too. I couldn't find any others. Just gun emplacements."

He was decelerating hard. The asterisk came up. Big flat area. Why hadn't the Lander come down *here* six years ago? He saw the answer in fused rock. Astronomers found the Lander, then used those heat cannon to melt a bigger landing field above it.

A cannon swiveled to look at him. He blasted it, then the other, then played his flame over the big beehive storage shed.

The explosion was actinic white, less like dynamite than lightning. He hugged the flight stick. The shock sent him spinning. He got straightened out before he hit anything, and watched a fireball rise where the storage shed had been.

So much for stealth.

Then again . . . Svetz lifted and coasted around and down with not much to hide him. There might *be* no more defenses. He dropped below the level of the Lander, around and up.

He was looking into man-built prefab houses. Twenty . . . more like thirty octopoids were in view, most of them in motion. A few were struggling into pressure armor that had arms like a drain-cleaning device and a centered transparent dome like Svetz's own bubble helmet.

Nobody saw him. Every Softfinger was looking up at the landing field and its dissipating cloud.

Svetz felled two dozen octopoids with his sonic, dropped and swung 'round the slope and came up again nearby. More houses. Had anyone heard anything? How would he tell? They weren't agile, these octopoids: they didn't run about screaming incoherently. They *did* have eyes beneath the skullcap shell.

He circled, pouring silent sleep on the Softfingers, then floated into a street between two rows of houses. Several octopoids saw him and pointed before they slumped. One must have reached a phone.

He dipped between two houses and plasma flame lashed out behind him.

He hadn't seen where it came from. He was reluctant to make himself a target, but he didn't see a choice.

He popped up just above the roofs. There were only two beehive buildings down here, and Svetz fired on the one in view. Dropped back and scooted. The return blast almost fried him, but he saw a general direction.

Not from the octopoid-built beehives. From one of the houses.

Svetz ran down the line of houses, firing. Another blast placed the right house. He flew toward it, lifting, firing. The house melted out from around the gun. The gunner must have melted too, or fled.

He could see octopoids fleeing downhill like so many wheels with no rims, skidding and catching themselves, their low center of gravity compensating for their clumsiness. He let them go. But he took the time to blast every dwelling. No hidden thing would emerge later.

He floated high. There were no octopoids in sight. Was there anything he'd missed? *Oops.* "Zeera?"

"Coming down, Svetz. Two minutes."

"I don't think they left you a landing spot."

"Blast me one!"

He opened up with the blaster again. The half-cremated beehive he'd taken for a lab blazed again and slumped further. Ash remained, and something solid and massive, one of the Lander's rocket nozzles. He poured fired onto it at close range. It slumped and was gone . . . and something hot and bright was coming down at him.

He zipped away from under the falling *Minim*. It settled gently in the ash pit, not far from the Lander.

26

Where's Miya?"

Zeera descended from the *Minim* in a long jump. "I left her a flight stick."

Miya spoke in his helmet. "I'm on my way. Altitude twenty klicks. I have you in sight. I've lost one of the wok ships. The other's following me, but it's slow, hasn't caught up yet. Shall I try to lead it to the Observatory?"

Zeera ordered, "Stay and protect the Tanker."

Softfinger astronomers had dismounted two of the motors, one to disassemble, one to test fire. They'd disjointed a landing leg. The Tanker sat tilted, too low and wide to fall over. They'd ripped off a sheet of the superconducting reentry shroud. They'd opened every hatch cover. They'd pulled hoses out in long coils, and spilled methane and liquid oxygen (Svetz could see where puddles had turned martian dust to patches of dried mud) and let the compressors replace it (the readouts read FULL.) Then they'd tied off the hoses and cut off the nozzles and taken them somewhere.

"Could be worse. We'll have to make nozzles," Zeera said.

Svetz held a severed tube in each hand. He felt somewhat emasculated. "What's it take?"

"Not much. Anything watertight. We'll use the spare pressure suit. That and some stickstrips."

"Here comes the wok ship," Miya reported.

Zeera said, "We're busy. Can you hold?"

Miya said, "I'll get above them and hit them before they get here."

"I'll send Svetz up when I can."

He helped Zeera lift the methane hose into place and wrap the join. It sprayed fluid, but most of it was going in. Svetz took to the air.

Eastward was a flying silver button. He saw something fluttering around it. He said, "Miya, don't bother shooting at the underside. That's a reentry shield."

"Thanks," Miya said. A tiny shape darted and flickered around the wok ship . . . and he dared not watch. Where was the other ship? If Miya was patrolling high, he'd go low.

The *Minim* and Lander made good targets. They'd shed Soft-finger heat rays without harm, but spilled fuel would burn.

Zeera's voice: "Svetz, give me some help. I need to change hoses."

"Miya can't fight two ships, Zeera."

"I'm disconnecting the fuel. Why isn't the other ship in your face right now?"

"Don't know." They split up, he thought. One ship to track and kill Miya. She's riding a flight stick; they must think she's me. The other ship went to the Observatory to protect what's left.

He could help Miya now. They'd kill that first one quick, then double-team the second. But if he was wrong?

He hovered low above the Tanker and *Minim*.

Fire speared down, its origin too high to see. Above and about the *Minim*, a thin mix of fuel and martian air puffed and tried to catch.

Svetz lifted. He'd been lucky. Miya couldn't hold off two! But the second ship had spotted him instead. While the other's heat cannon recharged, he could act.

Here it was, lower than he'd guessed.

Svetz fired up at its belly, just to make the Softfingers wary, and drew nearer. The aperture came around. He swerved, fired, swerved out of the fringe of their return blast and fired again. The wok ship couldn't turn fast enough. He played his blaster on its upper sur-face and saw a runnel form, and then the wok ship was rising, try-ing to disappear in the sky. Svetz followed, up, up, above the wok ship and holding the trigger down hard, but his blaster was dead.

"I'm unarmed," he reported. "I can buzz around them until you get here, Miya."

Zeera shouted, "Get down here and help me pump oxygen!"

Miya said, "My target's falling. Zeera, take cover. It'll hit near you. Hanny, I can't see your target yet."

"I'll get them to shoot."

The second ship would fire on him no matter what he did! He

dropped wide of the Lander on a wiggly path. Make them choose their target. The thing he must *not* do was hover.

Flame seared past him. He cursed reflexively.

"I see it! Hanny, go help Zeera."

He set down next to the *Minim*. There was no problem matching the severed oxygen hose to its intake, then wrapping it with the spare suit and then with stickstripping. It only took four hands. They started the pump and watched oxygen boil out around the join.

Svetz asked, "Was the leak this bad . . . ?"

"Don't *worry*. We were supposed to have extra for exploring."

They watched the sky.

A bright star appeared, and drifted down.

They both began shouting at once, and Miya had to bellow into her suit mike. "Got them! Futz, they nearly fried me! You hurt them, Hanny, I only finished it. I'm coming down. How are you doing?"

"Near done," Zeera said.

The voice from the sky said, "Feed me!" An instant later Miya dropped beside them.

They *had* to get out of the pressure suits. Then Zeera laughed and waved a hand in front of her nose, and the *Minim*'s air system howled. It was futile to think about baths.

Miya's mouth was full, and Zeera was trying to tell her about Svetz's suggestion. "It's so easy! We just turn on the Fast Forward and wait!"

Miya swallowed deliberately. "You're for this, Hanny?"

"I'm not for it. I just haven't thought of anything better."

"We'd be aborting the mission. We only have seeds for the anchor grove."

Zeera exclaimed, "It's something to show Ra Chen and Willy!"

"We don't have what it takes to grow an orbital tower. That is what we came for!"

Svetz asked Zeera, "Think that tank is full?"

She glanced at her board and nodded. They went outside,

pulled the oxygen hose loose and sealed up the *Minim*, all in silence.

"Ready to launch," Zeera said, "if we can figure out where to go."

Svetz said, "We have options. Go back to Hangtree Town. Stay and be natives. There are things we can teach them, if we find someone who wants to be taught. We might learn something too. How to grow a Hangtree."

Miya's voice in their helmets: "You favor *this*?"

"No. I'm just thrashing around."

"Well, *I've* got a plan," Miya said.

"Leader, speak to us!"

"Trust me? Come in and button up the *Minim*. I'll show you."

27

Dead of night. The stars were ablaze, seen through no trace of cloud and only the barest trace of atmosphere. The Hangtree had fallen below the horizon days ago.

"FFD," said Miya. *"On."*

Sunlight blasted their eyes.

Day and night strobed. Zeera cursed and clenched her eyelids tight. Miya looked out, grim and squinting. Svetz pulled his helmet into place.

Now the sun was a dark spot hurtling east to west, over and over, but the light-dark-light landscape was still uncomfortable. Pressure tents and vehicles appeared in a pattern not quite centered on the spot where the *Minim* moved through time, all built in the fashion of the red humanoids. The Tanker disappeared in sections. A few minutes later all the activity on the plateau went away. The temp housing began to decay and collapse.

Miya switched off on a day in late afternoon.

The Hangtree was high in the sky, east by south. Bouquets of tremendous silver flowers bloomed at both ends. The splintered bottom end had healed: it was pointed like a stem emerging from a silver corsage, ten thousand klicks above Mars.

Miya asked, "How far did we come?"

"There's no gauge for the FFD," Zeera said. "Just an on-off switch."

"Futz! Give me a guess, then. Three years or so? The Martains must think we just disappeared. Now the tree's higher, but it took forever to get there. So the Hangtree is leaving Mars, but it's taking its sweet time—"

"Miya, what's your *plan*?" Zeera demanded.

"Launch."

"We can't reach Earth!"

"Rendezvous with the Hangtree. It's not in geosynchronous orbit anymore, it's higher than that, but we can still reach the midpoint. The midpoint will still be in free fall."

"We can do all that," Zeera said carefully, "but why do we want to?"

"Launch us. I'll tell you on the way."

"Are we in a hurry? Miya, what you need is sleep!"

"I want to get *moving*. Hanny, get into your suit. You too, Zeera. If I'm wrong I want to *know* it."

"Midpoint of the tree, aye aye," Zeera said. "Check my work."

They were pilots, he wasn't. Svetz watched them, and presently said, "The telescopes in the crater may be up again. When they see us in flight, the party's over."

Miya murmured, "Launches are finicky, Hanny."

Zeera said, "I've got the *Minim* in low orbit. We circle half around the planet and do a second burn—"

Svetz reclined his chair and watched for double-wok ships in a navy blue sky.

He snapped out of a sound sleep when the floor roared at him and gravity doubled. The ship rolled. The biggest mountain in the solar system dwindled behind them.

The motors went quiet. Zeera said, "We'll make another burn to close with the tree. Twenty-five minutes. Miya, are you planning to moor us to the trunk?"

"Right. I think I've worked out the Hangtree life cycle." Miya closed her eyes and said, "We don't have fuel to reach Earth, right? But we can get on the Hangtree and ride it. Anchor to the tree. We'll get there with a reserve of fuel. Then Fast Forward until we see where it's going. If I'm wrong, we abort. Reentry and Fast Forward, land at Mars Base One and call Willy. Start over."

Mars was a vast black curve beneath black sky. Fuzzy light was just peeping over the horizon: not the sun, but the Hangtree's upper cluster of mirrors.

Zeera started her second burn.

Svetz was able to make out a vertical line, almost invisible against the black sky, motionless and infinitely distant. It didn't look threatening.

"What's that?" he asked, and it was suddenly far too close. Zeera yelled and fired attitude jets. The *Minim* twisted viciously and surged.

The intruder whipped past. They craned around to see it recede: a silver-brown cable hanging unsupported in space, there for an instant more, then gone.

Miya said quietly, "The Hangtree's dropped a sapling."

A juvenile Hangtree? "That's good, isn't it?"

"Might mean I'm not crazy."

Zeera said, "I'm correcting course now. That cost us some fuel."

The parent Hangtree rose; become large; vast; a world in its own right, coming up too fast as Zeera turned the *Minim* for a final burn. Thrust pulled them into their seats, then eased. A vertical bar on the displays stretched, lit up in red, kept stretching, turned yellow.

Svetz asked, "What's that?"

"Hull temperature," Zeera said. She turned the *Minim*, and they looked into a hot pink glare.

"Heat rays. Futz 'em," Zeera muttered. "Did either of you see any kind of projections on the mid-trunk?"

"Sail struts," Svetz said. "Down the trunk by no more than twenty klicks. Sail material harvested, struts still in place." The glare of Softfinger heat rays washed out all detail, but he'd seen. "We can moor to those. Zeera, what about the heat cannon?"

"Can't hurt us, but projectiles can. I need to moor us *now*." Another puff of thrust sent them downward, still closing with the trunk.

The heat rays touched wood. Red fog boiled out of the bark and closed around the *Minim* before the Softfingers turned their weapons off. Svetz looked for double-wok shapes in the red murk. What he saw was a man-built dirigible airship moored below them, much too close.

A final tiny push and they were up against bark, in a ring of light-sail stumps. Miya was already in the airlock. Svetz followed her through, his flesh shrinking from unseen high-velocity bits of metal.

Slowly, carefully, Miya showed him how to make knots that would come apart at a pull. They wound cables around the huge stumps, moored the *Minim* tight, then climbed back inside. The airlock held them both, intimately, as something like a rainstorm began: bullets ticking against the hull.

The sky lurched into motion.

The inner door opened. Miya moved briskly to her chair.

Svetz blocked the sun's flickering arc with his forearm. He watched stars whirling around him, the brighter twinkling of clustered light-sails, whirling Mars sinking away. A wooden structure built itself on one side of the *Minim*, and continued to flicker with motion.

"Studying *us*," Svetz guessed. "They saw us disappear here. Zeera, could they detect us?"

"How would I know?"

Mars was a ruddy dot, not even a half-moon anymore. The sun was fixed, a glare among the mirrors at one end of the tree.

Svetz asked, "Miya, you had a plan. Are we still on track?"

"Me? Plan?" Miya laughed, then sobered. "All right. I'm trying to think like an orbital tower here, like a *tree*, Hanny. Where does a Hangtree want to go? It must have crossed interstellar space to get here. Why didn't it go straight to Earth?"

"Low gravity, high spin. Mars, not Earth." *She'd* told him that.

"But Mars is mostly desert. Earth is mostly ocean. Why wouldn't a Hangtree want to zero in on the richest water-and-oxygen spectrum in the sky? Our problem is we got hung up on *seeds*," Miya said. "A plant can bundle tiny bits of information into a million seeds. A Hangtree can't do anything that simple. Interstellar space is just too big to *find* anything by accident. Even a seed that got lucky wouldn't be anything more than a bit of meteor.

"It must have crossed space as a tether, already a hundred thousand klicks long and festooned with solar sails, all ready to move into place and take over a planet." She looked at them. "Right?"

Svetz was reserving judgment.

"Ten thousand years on route, getting energy from starlight but using up its reserves of mass, getting more like a dried-out dead tree all the time. It leaves fat and arrives lean. Anything that migrates does that," Miya said. "It finds a world and takes up orbit, maneuvering with the sails. Drops seeds. An anchor grove grows. The Hangtree drops a root. The grove sends up water and soil nutrients. The Hangtree sends down sugar sap. They feed each other. They grow.

"It picked Mars because Mars is easy. Earth makes a better garden, but two and a half times the gravity means a tree has to be longer and stronger. *Now* it's strong enough. It was almost ready to tear loose from Mars. Then we got here and war came swarming up the tree. All that dead weight tore it loose, or maybe it was just *ready*.

"It's going to Earth."

28

When it became clear that nothing was going to happen fast, Zeera and Miya went to sleep, leaving Svetz on watch.

* * *

The tree had made accommodation with the prevailing tide. Its down branch was pointed into the sun. Constellations streamed past, conveying a sense of progress, marking a year for every circuit.

There was motion on the tree.

The dulled silver elevator track was being stressed, stretched, pulled apart. Anchor points popped. Torn ends slithered away from each other, up and down the trunk. Then a wave of repair ran down the rail and left it intact and shining silver and flickering with traffic.

Mirrors at the tree's end points flickered endlessly. Bubble domes sprang up along the tree's up branch, then were replaced by more angular, more solid structures. Svetz could see their mutating silhouettes against the glare of mirrors at the up end.

Beehives formed along the down branch. Plumbing began to grow along the bark. Suddenly the pipes were shattered and most of the beehives became charred craters in the bark. It all began to grow again, like mushrooms.

Svetz tried to guess how many Martians, how many martian races, were still on the Hangtree. It seemed they'd built vertical cities, fought, then reached an accommodation.

The tree was maneuvering, going somewhere: the flicker of light-sails told him that. The *Minim*'s instruments might have told him more if he'd learned to read them.

New light-sails were beginning to unfold on the old stumps around the *Minim*.

The elevator track wriggled restlessly, now crooked, now straightening. Torn again, repaired again . . . ?

Hours passed in the *Minim*. Svetz had lost count of the years passing outside. Sixty? Seventy?

Light glinted from Miya's eyes. She was awake.

He spoke his fear, lightly. "We *are* going to Earth, aren't we?"

"I'm sure it's what the tree wants." Sleep made her voice gravelly.

"Maybe it's ready to cross to another star."

Miya wasn't looking at him. Her fingertips glided over her instrument display.

Svetz said, "We've been between planets for something near a century. Whatever Martians are still with us must have made their peace with the tree—"

"They're here if they want to be. Any Martian would have had time to get back down to Mars."

"What if they learn to steer the tree?"

"*There's* a nice thought." Miya laughed. "They could take the tree to Europa. Let it pick up gigatons of water, bring it back to Mars, cut into the trunk and let sap bleed out. Fill up those canals! *We'd* end up at Europa with no fuel and nothing to eat. Pass me a dole brick, Hanny."

He did that. Miya said, "Now, the FFD completely futzes up our inertial guidance, and the computer can't find our location because nobody thought to tell it about changes in the constellations. But I've graphed our insolation—that's the light that's been falling on us since we left Mars. Here." *Tap.* Svetz's display changed. Sure enough, that was a graph. "Curve looks choppy, doesn't it? Sunlight should be more steady. Maybe all the mirrors screw it up. But see for yourself, Hanny, we're getting *twice* the sunlight now. We're going in toward the sun, not out. Anyway, the Earth-Moon system went past while you were talking, and here it comes again. See it?"

Svetz never could find anything that someone else had to point at. He said, "I'll take your word."

"Are you awake?"

"I want some sleep, if you can take over."

"Go ahead."

Still asleep, or trying, he let both arms drift up to block a bluewhite strobe. It almost worked. A fitful glare lit up his eyelids anyway.

When he opened his eyes, the *Minim* was in a bouquet of rippling mirrors.

The mirrors shifted languidly. Edges parted and closed again. He caught partial views of glare-white clouds forming and swirling and dissolving frenetically on a whirling blue background. A black shadow swept across . . .

Zeera saw that he was awake. "We haven't moved for a while. We thought you should be up when we turn off the FFD."

"Should think so. Martians all around us." Svetz loosed himself from the web. He was groggy. Free fall made him clumsy. "Good call, Miya. Earth. Did the tree touch down yet?"

"Not yet. It's dropped seeds. Showers of seeds, a dozen times in a dozen places. I think it must be waiting to see which anchor trees come up. We've been here two years and a fraction. We're not in geosynchronous orbit; we're drifting."

"Can we finally check in with the Institute?"

"The talker doesn't work in Fast Forward. We'll have to drop out." Zeera's forefinger reached.

"*Hold* it!"

Miya spoke soothingly. "Hanny, we're fine. We programmed the *Minim* for reentry. Those light-sail stumps weren't dead after all, so we're pretty well hidden from any Martians. We drop out, we use the talker to call present time—"

"Cut the *Minim* loose first! Miya, *we* can't see *them*. Take translators and blasters too. Are we all going out?"

Zeera laughed. "Translators? In vacuum?"

"If you find yourself wound in a net in some Softfinger pressure dome, Zeera, you will be glad you have a translator."

"*All* right, Hanny. You and Miya do that. I'll phone home."

29

The spinning Earth jarred to a stop. Svetz went out first into a forest of mirrors. Yes, it was fun to squeeze in next to Miya, but they'd be too confined to fight!

He worked fast. Reality rippled bewilderingly, showing him an army of brilliant green bulb-headed lizards. Now came a forest of companions in a yellow pattern, and Miya was beside him, helping. Now came larger distorted shapes in silver-brown—

Svetz whirled and lashed out. He couldn't remember snatching out the heavy blaster. Blaster handle and fist whacked hard into protruding glass goggles in a bronze mask as big as his whole chest. Glass shattered and sprayed.

A meter of sharp silver lashed out. Svetz ducked under the backhand stroke as a long-barreled weapon spat fire past him. Then both weapons were wheeling through space while the intruder covered its face with both arms, trying to hold in the air. While Svetz gaped, a third appendage reached far out and closed like a vise around his leg.

If he'd seen the intruder first, he'd have frozen in terror. It was four meters long. It had six limbs like an insect, but no thorax or tail. And Miya was on its back, her fingers working to pull its upper arms loose.

Fog puffed out. The intruder went limp.

Svetz wriggled out of the loosening grip on his knee. He barked, "Zeera, did you cover all that? Do you see more of them?"

"Just the one, but *futz*!"

"I want to bring it in. Don't vent the air, *pump* it." A live prisoner would be nice ... vacuum doesn't kill instantly ... but a corpse would do, and they'd *want* that air.

Miya disengaged herself from the monster and pulled it around to look at it. She couldn't have seen much inside the hard-shelled suit. She wrestled the helmet off. "Come see these eyes," she said.

Svetz shuddered.

Had he disappointed her? She said, "I used to envy you. The weird, wild creatures you've seen and touched. Come on, Hanny. Look at the way the eyes are placed, so it can see to both sides at once. It could almost be an herbivore—"

He let her pull him close.

The skin was yellow-green. The eyes were closed under lids that might have been cut from tennis balls. They were too far apart, vulnerable-looking at the edges of a squarish head. The Martian would see forward too. Hands opened and closed reflexively at Miya's touch. The middle pair were thick and clumsy, with a callused heel.

The *Minim*'s great cargo door opened to the sky in a trace of icy fog. Svetz and Miya pulled the creature inside.

"Some erg counter has me on *hold*," Zeera said. "Shall I close up and pressurize?"

"Right," said Miya.

They pulled a cargo net over the alien. The *Minim* had just become a lot smaller. Zeera said, "I wish we could bag that. When it starts to rot—"

Miya said, "We can look it over first."

Svetz didn't want to be involved in *that*. "I'll finish up out there. I want us loose," he told Miya. "No, wait." He fished his blaster out and put it back on the wall. "If we'd fired these deathtraps in that house of mirrors, we'd be nothing but ash!"

"Oh, futz! But, Hanny, what if there are more?"

"It's a risk."

Svetz took his time, methodically pulling tethers loose and coiling them and stowing them under hatches on the hull.

Any creature this big had to be something of a loner, just to find enough to eat! If a squad of green giants had found the *Minim*, they would hardly let Svetz smash their man's visor and kidnap him, would they? They couldn't be *that* different.

If these lines got tangled, the *Minim* couldn't reenter.

But, methodically pulling cables loose and stowing them, he kept spinning around to look for intruders.

Miya's radio voice said, "It's not breathing. How are you doing?"

"Near finished."

"I've got its suit off. There's flexible tubing down the insides of the suit. It's got a backpack too."

The *Minim* was free.

"There aren't any fingernails or toenails. Its ancestors may have had an exoskeleton, but there are only a few plates left, like it was born wearing armor. The tusks are bone, and there are bones and joints in the limbs . . . no ribs . . . still, a well-developed endoskeleton. That middle pair is legs and arms both. I can almost see how the shoulders rotate. Mph?"

"What?"

"Oh, *now* I see. Hanny, you're going to love this."

"I'm coming in."

Miya's arms were around the green giant, compressing its torso, releasing. "It still isn't breathing."

Too much to hope for, wasn't it, that an alien captive would be built like Earth's life-forms? Still—"Insects don't have lungs. Check for openings along its sides."

"That's what I *meant*, but spiracles still have to be pumped!"

Zeera shouted, "Futz it, will you both strap in? I might have to launch—"

The cheery voice of Willy Gorky barked, "Zeera! How's it going?"

Zeera's arms waved frantically, summoning Miya and Svetz to their seats. "That's a long story, Willy, but we've got everything you wanted."

The voice from the other end of time said, "Great!"

They took turns talking. "We saw at least five kinds of tool user. I'm pretty sure they weren't all intelligent."

"Miya's collected some seeds—"

"—big, heavy golden spheroids with a texture like foamed ceramic for a reentry shell. But those only make the anchor trees, Willy—"

"—we think."

Descriptions of the last leg of the flight had to come from the women, while Svetz's eyes peered between the mirror blossoms, up and down the trunk.

"The tree still has some drift to it," Miya said. "It's been dropping seeds. It prefers targets on the equator—"

"Strips of seeds fifty klicks long, generally crossing a shoreline."

"You'll remember that the grove on Mars was partly on a canal."

"Boss, we don't exactly know what to do *now*. The tree won't bud a sapling until it's ready to move on. If it locks to Earth and we leave it in place, will it still be here in present time?"

That was a serious question. Ra Chen and Gorky held rapid discussion with techs and time travelers, irritatingly half audible. Willy Gorky said, "We certainly want to watch the tree link up."

"That could take years," Svetz said.

"Not for us."

"Willy!"

There was whispering at the other end of time. Then Willy Gorky said, "You've got the FFD, Zeera. Use it. And the Secretary-General wants to see some Martians. Have they made any attempt to contact you?"

"Yes and no—"

"We had a prisoner, sir, but we th—"

"It moved," Svetz said.

Miya loosed herself and went to look.

Without the pressure suit it still looked armored. Dark green back, pale yellow face and belly. Jeweled ornaments were riveted to exoskeletal plates, and holsters for tools including tube weapons and knives. Nasty little spines of polished metal jutted from its mid-limb wrists. There were rows of holes along its flanks.

Thick eyelids suddenly rolled open. Bulging eyes wobbled independently as they scanned the *Minim*, making Svetz's own eyes hurt, then both centered on Miya.

The hull rattled. Svetz turned to see shapes like spindly frogs bounding among the mirrors. Tubes in their hands spat fire. He saw three six-limbed giants wrestling a much bigger tube into place. It poked out through the silver petals, looking straight at him, and he yelled, "Launch! Launch now!" Turned to scream, "Miya—"

Tether yourself! died on his lips. Miya had been distracted. Six limbs wrapped themselves around her and pulled her close. Her fists and heels pounded against the creature's shell.

"Launching *now*," Zeera said.

The intruder sighed and sagged limp under nearly Earth's gravity of thrust. Miya rolled clear.

Dead aft, the big tube was looking right at the *Minim*.

"We have a live prisoner." Zeera spoke crisply above the rocket's muted scream.

"Great!" said Willy Gorky. "But you launched? To Earth? *Of course* to Earth, sorry, I'm still catching up, but Zeera, we want those Martians! The SecGen—"

"They were firing on us!"

The burn ended. The big tube spat orange flame. Attitude jets puffed as the *Minim* slewed sideways: automatics avoiding a meteor. Something massive *tacked* the hull anyway.

The mid-trunk dwindled. It was still huge, a world in itself. Was it more slender than it had been at Mars? Earth's Hangtree must be longer because geosynchronous orbit was higher. *Of course* it must have grown longer year after year, and more slender too, and *that* was why the rails had ripped!

Miya still wasn't in her command chair. Svetz looked back. Miya was moored to the wall by sleeping tethers, just beyond the monster's reach. She was talking, the monster was talking, and the translator was talking too.

Svetz always hated learning a new language.

He said, "Willy, the only Martians *I* talked to did all their talking after I was a helpless prisoner. Maybe we've done exactly the right thing."

From the other end of time Gorky said, "Ah . . . maybe. Where are you coming down?"

Zeera said, "South America, northern edge of what became Brazil, right on the equator and just at the shoreline. It's where the anchor trees seem to be having the most success."

"Good luck."

"Wait! Sir, how do you expect to get us back?"

Willy Gorky said, "We'll send the small X-cage for you. Call us when you get down and give us decent coordinates."

"How?" Zeera cried. The inertial calendars on the X-cages weren't that accurate, the *Minim* didn't have one, and Willy Gorky didn't see the problem at all.

Ra Chen broke in. "You gave us your location in space. Brazil, equator, shoreline. Get there on foot if you have to, but get us a *date*. Ask a local."

Gorky: "Would a primitive have a dating system?"

Ra Chen: "Mayans and Incas did, but . . . hmm . . . we couldn't read them. Zeera, what you really want is a Spanish invader. Look for metal armor. Get Christian dates."

"We'll try that."

30

On the night side of Earth was no trace of city light. The planet was *black*. Nearly uninhabited. Population . . . a few millions? And now they must search among savage locals for a savage Spaniard halfway round the world from Spain. For a Spanish *conquistador*, as likely as any Martian to kill a stranger on sight.

But *that* problem might never arise. "Zeera, these motors wouldn't even *lift* us. They weren't built to land on Earth."

"Yes, Svetz, they were. Minims launch from Earth and refuel in orbit. This one was *re*built for Mars, heavier, with an expanded cabin, but it's pretty much the same. Most of the volume is tanks. We fall motors-down. What's under us is a fuel tank that's supposed to collapse if we hit too hard. It takes the shock. We don't."

"You've been thinking about this too."

"Oh, yes. And about that impact weapon that might have torn up our reentry shielding."

From aft Miya called, "I've been telling Thaxir about Mars. About what's going to happen. She wants to talk to us."

Thaxir? *She? Us?*

"I was born on the tree," the green giant said. "I know only what my mother told me of those days when the tree broke loose. We were royalty, and I am a princess in Memnonia. My age is near thirteen, I think. We have clocks to keep the time our ancestors kept by sun and dark."

Really, Thaxir's speech was as interesting as what the translator was saying. Her mouth wasn't insectile, but the mouth and lips of a mammal, though tusks as long as Svetz's forearm would make her speech mushy even if it were shaped by lungs.

But Thaxir breathed through spiracles. Svetz saw what Miya was trying to tell him: tubes ran down the inside of her pressure suit to feed two rows of holes along her sides. She spoke in a prolonged belch, and swallowed air to keep it going.

The translator said, "Our nature is conquest, but the tree is too fragile for war. The Allied Peoples have not made war in thirty years. We live with the Hangtree and the Hangtree is our life. I have tried to learn why we should want to leave. Miya cannot tell me."

"I told her about Mars," Miya said to Svetz.

"The world was to dry and die. My parents knew the prophecy," said Thaxir. "When the Hangtree broke loose, they could have gone home to their children and grandchildren. They chose the tree."

"To their. . . . ?"

Miya told Svetz, "They live a long time."

Her parents already had grandchildren forty years ago, Mars time: seventy-five Earth years. "And you're under thirteen?" Twenty-four and a half in Earth years, among beings who might reach a thousand.

"Futz, Miya, we've kidnapped a little girl."

"You have made me slave, and I remain slave," Thaxir said with composure, "until my warriors can rescue me. But my heart is with the tree."

"The tree's intent may not be the same as yours," Miya told the Martian. "The Hangtree crosses between stars. It only stops at worlds to take nourishment, to make itself strong for the crossing."

The green giant's lips pulled back from her tusks: a terrifying sight. "Another star! Yes, we hoped."

"You won't have a sun for thousands of years. Understand? The bark of the tree, you know how thick it is. It's insulation! The core of the tree won't freeze, only the outside. Only you and your people."

Thaxir snorted. "We survive! Vacuum sucks air and water from our bodies, but we build pressure tents and then walls. Other kinds attack us for our position on the tree. We fight them until they must make peace. The tree stretches and tears our rails, locks each group of us away from what we need elsewhere, but we build again. If the sun is distant, we will use solar mirrors to gather the light. Have we survived vacuum and starvation and war to be stopped by cold?"

Miya considered. She asked, "You don't live together, all of your species, do you?"

"No. Mother says we are distributed by what we can defend. There was more of fighting for turf before the Hangtree settled in above this cloudy world. My father died in the war. Now—" Thaxir stopped talking.

Miya asked, "Secrets?"

"I cannot tell you how we defend ourselves! You may not demand. There are laws for treatment of slaves!"

"We're going down to Earth. Our vessel won't lift again. We have no way at all to attack any part of the Hangtree."

Thaxir thought that over. "No way to return me? Even for high ransom?"

"If we find a way, we'll return you. You can carry our message. Some of you must want to leave the tree before it freezes you."

A stubborn silence . . . though Thaxir's face was hard to read. Where her nose would have been was a flat plate with a stylized pictograph carved into it.

Miya asked, "What do you eat?"

"The tree bears bountiful life. There is fungus. We make a paste from the starchy roots of a parasitic plant. There are animal forms big enough to feed an army for a week." She wriggled. "If I may reach my pack?"

Miya reached through the net to release the little pack on the green giant's back and moved it around to her arms. Thaxir pulled out a flask, then a big shapeless lump of something wrapped in mirror leaf, then a beautiful golden arch set with gems, the frame for a score of taut parallel strings.

Svetz asked, "Musical instrument?"

"Yes, a windstorm-minor. Listen." Thaxir played a tune of strange intervals, all sharps and flats. It seemed to Svetz that she was trying to duplicate some pattern already known . . . like a computer . . . yet there was charm in the moment's uniqueness.

Miya spoke, unaware that she interrupted. "A crossing between stars would take thousands of years. There won't be sunlight. No source of energy for anything that lives on the bark. It will all die, and so will all of you, and even if you could survive, *you*, Thaxir, would never live to see another star."

The pack had disgorged a slate and stick, and Thaxir was draw-ing. She said, "After all, what choice have we?"

"Some of you who want to accept our offer could gather at the tree midpoint, where there is no gravity. We'll send you the large extension cage. We'd like some from each of the Allied Peoples if possible. The large cage would hold—Hanny?"

Svetz thought it over. Going forward in time, gravity would plate them across the interior of the shell. "You could lay them out around the whole inner surface. Twenty of these green giants, or a hundred Softfingers or eighty red humanoids . . . I never saw the crab things close up."

Miya asked, "There are more of you than that, aren't there?"

"Of the species from the south, the Fishers and High Folk stayed to share the planet's fate. Only the Smiths chose to ride the Tree. Five kinds. A million warriors."

It didn't matter if Thaxir was inflating the numbers. Miya said, "So we can't take you all. Think, now. If some of you stay and some go with us, it's much more likely you won't *all* die."

"You argue as a gambler?" Thaxir was amused.

"Probabilities."

"It may be some mathematicians will go with you."

"Do your people live at the Hangtree's midpoint?"

"Softfingers hold that region. They're all arms, you know. Freely falling, they are more dexterous than we. We"—the trans-lator hiccuped, then—"green giants, we hold the tree from its far end to forty thousand klicks inward. There we have nearly the same weight as on Mars. It's the best part of the tree."

The translator helped them get their measurements straight-ened out. Reds held a stretch along the inner branch, from 18,000 to 23,000 klicks altitude. That was roughly martian gravity: they could fight species that were less strong but more dexterous. Thaxir was not reluctant to describe the locations of rival species, but she avoided any mention of their defenses.

What was she doing in Softfinger turf? "We repay a debt. Eleven of us lend our muscle to help the Softfingers extend their city. Other species are involved too. I thought to use the sunflower stalks as anchor points for some preliminary construction. And there you were. And *you*"—looking at Svetz—"you smashed my face before I could so much as scream."

"I was frightened," Svetz said.

"Is there such a thing as a mirror in this place?"

Miya said, "No. Thaxir, your face is fine. The carvings, they aren't touched."

"What is that whistling?"

"Earth's air, slowing us. Don't be frightened." Miya plucked the netting around the green giant. It was taut. She pushed the windstorm-minor under it. "You'll be fine. Hanny, *we* should strap down."

She and Svetz made their way forward. The sun was a sudden flame ahead of them, bisected by a flat black horizon. The sound of a harp joined the thin wailing. Air screamed around heat shielding intended for Mars, not Earth, and Thaxir was playing a weird and lovely counterpoint.

Through the flame colors Svetz couldn't tell what was below them. He wouldn't have known the geography anyway. The hull's scream had a warble in it now, and Zeera, who knew this ship better than Svetz, wasn't looking happy at all.

Wisps of cirrus went past. Svetz could make himself believe they were slowing. His weight was easing. The *Minim* was falling almost vertically, and what was below was hard to make out, but . . . "Zeera?"

"Let the computer handle it, Svetz. Look, those trees off there must be the anchor grove. Ten, fifteen klicks away. We came pretty close."

"That's water, isn't it?"

Miya said, "Cosmonauts always fire too early. It costs fuel. We learned to just let the program handle it."

The motors fired. The *Minim* tilted hard over. Ocean below, shoreline where the nose pointed, and slender trees tipped with black.

There wasn't enough thrust. They'd *known* that, and now the motors were firing horizontally, not slowing their fall.

The *Minim* tilted to vertical, then a bit farther. Svetz heard the hull rattle and hoped it was landing legs deploying.

The ground came up much too fast.

31

Baba Yaga or Baba Jaga. *A female supernatural of Russian folklore . . . a cannibalistic ogress. . . . Her abode is a little hut constantly spinning around on fowls' legs in a clearing in the distant forest; this is surrounded by a picket fence topped with skulls. The Baba Yaga rides through the air in an iron kettle stirring up tempests, or in a mortar which she moves by a pestle as she sweeps her traces from the air with a broom . . .*
—*Funk & Wagnall's Standard Dictionary of Folklore, Mythology and Legend*

Svetz cautiously tested his neck—*not* broken—and his back, before he looked around. "Is everyone alive?"

"Fine," Miya said dubiously.

Zeera said, "Svetz, it wasn't *that* bad a landing, considering we came down on two legs!"

Svetz asked, "Didn't *that* used to be *there*?"

The intertemporal speaking device, torn from its mounting, lay next to the Martian's head. They scrambled down to look.

The green giant lay as if dead, but air was going in and out of her spiracles. The talker had missed her head. It looked partly crushed. There was nothing to try: it only had one switch.

"Futz! The talker's dead. *Look* at it! We're cut off."

Svetz pulled a filter helmet over his head and went out.

He came back in much faster, pulling it off, gasping, "Zeera! Have we got filter helmets for Earth atmosphere?"

"Yes, Svetz. Ra Chen won't let us go into the past without them.

He made sure the drawers are *labeled*, see, so if you can read the ITR logo—"

"*Thank* you, Zeera. We all get one. Miya, you can't breathe what's out there—"

"You told me, Hanny." She was cautiously prodding Thaxir. "Nothing broken, I think, unless it's under one of these plates. Gravity's going to bother her, and I can't guess what she eats."

The outer door was now a horizontal platform. The sand was twelve meters down. There should have been a ladder. There was only a pulley system, not yet deployed.

Svetz and Miya rose on flight sticks and circled the *Minim*.

It was hot! And humid! They were wearing loose ship's clothing cinched at wrists and ankles. In seconds they were soaked through.

Two of the *Minim*'s legs were still retracted. The remaining pair had plunged through a meter of water, deep into sand. If the *Minim* hadn't come down hard, it would have toppled over. The tide had withdrawn now.

The *Minim* stood upright on two slender legs. The burned gouge along its flank ran almost through into the oxygen tank.

"Company," Zeera said softly.

"I don't see—"

"In the trees onshore. Use infrared."

Trees as slender as wands stood just offshore, growing out of the sea, tufted with black: the anchor grove. A forest of tangled greenery and shadows grew densely inland: the opposing life of Earth. Svetz turned a pair of mag specs on those.

Mag specs were almost as good as a pressure suit's fishbowl. By infrared Svetz picked out hot spots five feet tall. Now he could zoom them in normal light: a dozen or more short dark people standing perfectly still within the shade of the Earthly forest. Men and women both, though they looked so odd—poor diet?—that Svetz identified the women only by their breasts.

Zeera said, "I'd say they don't want to talk."

"Fine by me," Svetz said.

"Let's talk about our orders," Miya said. "The talker's dead.

That makes it moot whether we need a Spaniard to tell us what time it is. Do we still want to watch the Hangtree link up?"

East of them the Hangtree hung above the ocean, almost fading into the blue sky. Hard to judge how far away it was, but at least several hundred klicks, several degrees of the Earth's circumference. The bottom faded into horizon haze.

Svetz said, "Maybe it *is* linked up."

Miya gave him a look of disgust.

"The Fast Forward," Zeera's radio voice reported, "is futzed."

"That too? How bad?"

"Ten centimeters of superconducting wire would fix what I can see. I just can't seem to find it. I'm looking where it should have been packed."

Svetz knew better than to try to help Zeera find something, and *she'd* packed the *Minim*. He said, "Miya, let's look around."

"What's the point?" Then Miya said, "Yes, Hanny. We're in no real hurry, are we, Zeera?"

Zeera sounded distracted. "Not until I find—well, and *food!* Sooner or later we'll need a way to feed ourselves. Hold up . . . we've got dole bricks for a long time, two months anyway. No, no hurry."

They went back in and came out wearing only shorts. Shoes would have had to come off the pressure suits: big bulky things they both rejected.

They flew among anchor trees no thicker than Miya's waist but scores of meters tall. The tip of the tallest was a black puffball five or six meters through. Miya hovered close up against it. "Notice anything interesting, Hanny?"

"No. It's fluffy, like black cotton."

"Cotton?"

She was drifting down the slender length of the anchor tree, and Svetz followed. He said, "It's a plant. People used to wear it."

"So we're looking around where we don't even know what the questions are. You need curiosity to solve puzzles, *you* told me that, and there are always puzzles to solve, because all of your missions go wrong, right, Hanny?"

The water was wonderfully clear. The slender trunks went straight down through the water and into the sand. Any roots must have begun spreading out far beneath the sand, reaching into bedrock, forming a network to anchor what would presently attach itself: a mass greater than any mountain, pulling *up*.

Svetz said a bit defensively, "We accomplished the mission this time, didn't we? But landing a Mars Minim on Earth wasn't part of any plan *I* helped make."

Miya let him see her turn off the radio link to the *Minim*. "That black cotton looked very soft and cushiony. Would you like to make love in a tree from the stars?"

"Well, futz. I didn't plan that either."

They drifted back up. They'd be hidden from the *Minim* . . . but a fall from this height would kill them. Svetz suggested, "Let's moor some lines."

Miya swam into the foliage; Svetz stayed aloft. He'd catch her if . . .

"There's branches all through this. I can anchor us. Come on in."

The puffball material had some of the hampering effect of a martian "bed," but not as bad. It cradled them, held them together. Cuddling afterward, they lifted their filter helmets to kiss, and Miya tasted Earth's air.

She was instantly in love with it. Svetz had to pull her filter helmet into place when she started to pass out.

Then, still tethered, Miya crawled down through the tuft to look through the underside. Svetz wasn't going to bother, but he heard Miya's radio whisper. "Come see this!"

Svetz swam through the foliage and stuck his head out of the bottom.

A man was on the beach, looking up at them. He was pale-skinned and dirty, shelled like a Green Martian, but in rusted metal.

Miya said, "We've found Ra Chen's conquistador."

32

They didn't want to be seen flying. They locked their flight sticks, then dropped them to the ground and slid down the smooth trunk. They planted the flight sticks in a conspicuous green bush, the brush discharges sticking up like strange golden blossoms.

"Hold it, Hanny."

"What?"

"When the sun's right behind you there's a ring of light around your head. It's the filter helmet. We don't want the sun behind us when we approach a local."

The shelled man was no taller than Svetz or Miya. He looked pale and ill. He wore weapons, but he didn't try to reach them. Tilted against a supporting tree, he watched them descend as if they might be hallucinations.

Then he drew himself up before them in yoga tree position and said, *"Yo soy John de Castores del Camoes . . ."* and continued at some length.

"I am Jack," said the translator.

In Earth gravity Jack wore armor around his torso and carried heavy baggage too. No wonder he seemed bowed beneath the weight. He looked amazingly dirty. His beard and hair were scraggly and matted and overgrown. He carried his helmet, and Svetz wondered if his overgrown hair would still fit into it.

The United Nations translator recognized the language: not Spanish, but Portuguese. It had that in storage. It learned the archaic forms much faster than it had learned martian speech.

Jack wanted food. He was here to fish, he explained. Beneath these very strange trees—?

Svetz said, "Orbital tether," and heard the silence: the translator didn't have that term yet. "Hangtree roots. Beanstalk?"

The translator spoke. Jack thought that over, then said politely, "Beneath these beanstalk roots the fish and shellfish thrive. But Dinis and I, we are sick of fish!"

Miya offered him a dole yeast bar. Jack bit into it and looked dubious. Then he offered them a dark strip of . . . something.

Svetz took it because he couldn't guess how Miya would react. He lifted his filter helmet and caught a wave of smells. Some of that must be coming from Jack. He put the dark strip in his mouth. It was hard enough to break teeth.

Saliva softened it, and then it tasted like . . . strange, like . . . ancient messages crawling up from his primitive brain. *Corruption*, and *meat*, and *fire*.

"Jerked meat," the translator called it, "with these you locals call *chilis* for flavor."

"Meat. From a beast?"

"From some local creature I do not know, which Dinis shot. But the animals become wary and our bullets run low. Sir, my companion Dinis is hurt. Do you know local herbs to help him?"

Before they could admit to knowing nothing of the locality— which Svetz had already decided not to do—Jack had spilled his pack on the sand.

Blanket. Knives. A bottle and a small bag, both made of something like Naugahyde. Gear for mending a boot. An ornate religious thing, cross-shaped. Jack showed them leaves and roots wrapped in cloth, half a dozen varieties. This root they had cooked and eaten and liked. This helped constipation. These leaves they had spread on Dinis' wound; it hadn't done much good—

"And your *do 'yeesbar*. God ordains that true medicine must have an evil taste, and truly I feel better. Where does it grow?"

"In another country." Svetz handed Jack another bar, for he'd finished the first. "We must hoard them," he said.

Miya picked up a small, heavy bag. "What's this?"

Jack took it quickly. "Silver coins. All I have. Would that they were gold. We hoped to find gold in this place, but—" He shrugged. "Will you come and look at my sick friend Dinis?"

Jack told his tale as he led them through the jungle.

The shipwreck had left twelve. Attacks by primitives out of jungle shadows, snakes bigger than a madman's nightmares, fever, starvation, rumors of gold, greed and madness among their officers, had winnowed them down to two.

The jungle had nearly strangled a small stepped pyramid built of huge stone blocks. Jack led them nearly to the top and through a great doorway.

The room wasn't large. Amid a junkyard of primitive tools and elegant stoneware, Dinis lay on a dais beside rusted armor. Dinis looked much like Jack; they even dressed alike. All the same, Dinis had been dead for hours.

Jack asked hopefully, "Is it possible . . . ?"

Did he really expect dole yeast to restore a man to life? Svetz didn't laugh. He said, "We cannot help this man."

"Were we fools to lodge in this alien temple? Ah, Dinis! But we had not strength to build shelter."

Svetz said, "Jack, our mission leader tells us that nobody is ever truly dead."

Go back and talk to them, Zeera would have added—

Jack seemed to relax. "You are Christian!" he marveled. "And Svetz is your name? Russian?"

Svetz let that stand. "Jack, what is the year?"

"We left Portugal in the year of our Lord fifteen sixty. Since then I too have lost count. Two years, I think. In this place one cannot even guess when Christmas might come!"

Jack announced that he must bury his friend Dinis Alvares de Albuquerque y . . . another name of considerable length. Miya explained that they must report to their mission leader. Svetz saw Jack's disappointment before Jack turned away to dig in the earth with his blunted sword.

Miya was right: they *could not* help with Dinis' funeral. Jack would see that they didn't know the rites!

Still—

Translator *off*, suit radio *on*. "Zeera, people made coins out of gold, didn't they?"

"For a while. Then they went to paper and plastic."

"If I found you a little silver, could you make wire?"

"Superconductor would be better . . . oh, all right, Svetz. Silver's ductile, I can pound it."

Miya whispered, "Hanny—"

"Go on ahead, Miya. I'm right behind you."

Svetz went back to where Jack was digging in the earth with his blunted sword. Translator *on*. "Jack, give me your silver for a few minutes and I'll give you gold coins back."

Jack stared, then laughed. "Truly, I hear the sounds of my home! Why would you do this?"

"Because I need silver." *Because I've evaded helping you with a friend's death rites.*

Curiosity warred with distrust, and Jack handed Svetz his pouch.

Svetz went into the trees, out of sight. He took the largest coin out of the pouch, then dropped the pouch into the superconducting net of his trade kit. The conversion took a few minutes.

Svetz realized his mistake when he picked up the pouch. It too had become gold . . . and that would tell Jack more than Svetz wanted told. He fished out a zipped sample bag and poured the coins into that. He brought that to Jack.

Jack poured the coins from hand to hand, then bit one. "Where did you get these, Master Svetz? And *this*?"

The clear plastic pouch. Futz! Svetz said, "That's a secret, Jack."

He took a coin and bit it, but it didn't have any taste at all.

The woman had taken the net off Thaxir. As Svetz watched, the green giant rolled over onto her side, then her belly, then lifted herself on all sixes. "Very good," Miya said. "You'll stay healthier if you can exercise. Hello, Hanny."

Careful of her balance, Thaxir slid a middle arm toward her pack. She saw Svetz go tense. "Hungry," she said. She fished in the pack and came out with a lump wrapped in a patch of Hangtree mirror. What was inside might have been white cheese.

She ate half of it in two bites. Then, "Will you taste?"

Miya broke off a crumb and (ignoring Zeera's horror) put it in her mouth. "There's almost no taste," she said. "Like tofu. Thaxir, I think you could eat dole yeast. Try this."

Still on all sixes, Thaxir let Miya put a chunk of dole yeast in her mouth.

Her eyes squeezed shut. They heard her voice muffled. "Your food tastes like canal scum. My weight holds me paralyzed, and the tree hangs above us, taunting. So much for worlds. Miya, will you help me to lie down again? I don't want to fall."

Svetz helped Miya ease the Martian down. He could feel Thaxir's strength. Her problem was fear.

He asked, "Do you eat meat?"

"Some meat. Most plants. To choose too carefully is to starve."

"I'll find you something. Zeera—" He showed her Jack's silver coin.

"Counterfeit," Zeera said after testing it. "Only part silver. Not very conductive at all."

"Is gold conductive?"

"Why? *Oh!* Wait, now, Svetz, silver's ductile. I'll hammer this into shape and *then* we'll change it."

"About the green giant," Svetz said. "Why not put her in water? Let her float."

Zeera took the charge out of a blaster and began to pound on the silver coin with the butt. "She's an alien, Svetz. What would salt water do to her? She might dissolve! Or anything! How did you get this?"

Svetz told her.

"This Jack knows you can make gold?"

"I handed him a bag of gold. He doesn't know where I got it. He's the last of his crew. Who would he tell? And what if he does? There were tales of people who could make gold. They were called alchemists. That's why we made the trade kit, Zeera!"

Zeera belly-laughed. "*You* might have started that story, right here!"

"Why not?" Svetz reclined his chair and went to sleep. His dreams were shaped by the tapping of a blaster butt on a silver coin, and Zeera's monotonous swearing.

The pounding stopped.

What Zeera had was a narrow little bar, not quite a wire, to replace a mere whisker of superconductor. "All right, Svetz, turn it into gold. Miya, we want to videotape straight up."

And all of that was the work of a few minutes.

Miya went to help Thaxir roll over again. "Thaxir, do you understand all this? We're going into the future—"

"Where my companions and my consort-by-contract are all grown old or dead, but the tree is linked to Earth. Good."

Zeera glared at them. "Last chance. Did any of you leave scraps of high tech underwear for some archeologist?"

Miya made a show of patting herself. "Nope."

"Anything conspicuous in some unlikely place?"

"Jack," Svetz said. They were leaving an ally.

Miya shrugged. Zeera flipped the FDD switch. The sun dropped like a giant meteoroid and plunged them into the dark.

33

They shared a meal and took turns in the bath bag, and drifted through half a year, while the Hangtree drifted up the sky. When Zeera judged it straight overhead, she turned off the FFD.

Night again. The tree loomed huge and weightless. Silver blossoms blazed down, but not so many as there had been. A tiny moon was tangled among the blossoms.

Miya said, "It's still not connected."

"Well, it's in position," Zeera said. "Hit it again."

"We *do not* want to miss this. *Wait*." Miya took her time, lolling in her reclined chair with her mag specs pointed straight up. She said, "I can see the taproot and it's still fifty klicks too high. Zeera, hit it."

Day and night strobed. Svetz had found nothing, but he kept his mag specs pointed. *There* it was, thrashing like a string in a hurricane.

In real time, what was happening? A root descended through ferocious stratospheric winds. Weighted at the end? Light-sails unfurled to move the tree's position against the wind below, to drag the line along a strip of anchor grove until—

Miya hit the cutoff. The strobe ended just past dawn. They'd jumped by twenty days.

Harder to see now that it wasn't moving, a silver thread descended from heaven. Its end was tangled in the black tops of the anchor grove. The winds might still be vibrating it, but it was under tension now. The tree was in place; its light-sail leaves were furled; its mass was pulling *up*.

"I want a better look at that," Svetz said.

He and Miya drifted among the black treetops. A silver line no thicker than coarse wire rose from one of the tufts. It was tangled through the black cotton of this and two other anchor trees.

Miya collected vegetation for Thaxir to try. Black anchor-tree foliage; green leaves and stems and a dug-up root; lichen and mushrooms; seaweed.

Thaxir liked lichen and certain leaves.

They jumped the *Minim* four days.

Zeera was getting cabin fever. She and Svetz went out while Miya stayed with Thaxir.

Three anchor trees had merged. The root line reached straight out of the common tuft. All the other trees, that had once stood straight, now leaned toward the trees that had caught the dangling line.

Zeera was clumsy on a flight stick. She hovered above while Svetz drifted among the black treetops.

Earth's ecology was adapting to the alien grove. Seaweed grew among the trunks, and seabirds hunted fish. A bird had made a nest in the black foliage and laid eight small blue eggs. Svetz collected the eggs for Ra Chen.

"They'll rot," Zeera objected. "We'll be months getting home with the FFD."

"Doesn't the *Minim* have a cold box?"

"Have you *seen* one? Wait now, maybe the Vivarium only needs to study the interior structure. If we don't expect eggs to *hatch*—"

So Svetz put them in the trade kit and turned them to gold.

*   *   *

Another six-day jump made it clear that many of the anchor trees were going to merge. The root line had grown thicker, as thick as Svetz's little finger.

They jumped another ten days, and studied the anchor grove through the *Minim* dome. The grove was merging into a single mass. Anchor trees farther away had fallen on their sides. Their trunks grew along the ground. Some merged head to tail. Only those closest to the Hangtree root still stood, and those leaned, growing into one conical stalk. The collar of black foliage was growing ragged.

Svetz and Miya geared up and went through the inner door. Miya's hand stopped him on the launch platform.

Below the launch platform, a ring of men in metal shells was converging on the *Minim*. A sailing ship built like an ornately carved bathtub lay at anchor nearby.

Miya dropped her flight stick. "We can't go down to meet them. No ladder. Better not fly either."

"Right." Svetz thumbed his translator on. "Jack!"

A soldier stepped forward. They all looked alike, and Svetz had to guess he was looking at Jack. Jack was clean. He had shaved.

Svetz shouted down, "What's—"

His own voice carried, but the translation didn't. Svetz turned up the volume on the device, pointed it down and asked in a normal voice, "What's happened while we've been away, Jack?" Let the translator do his shouting.

Jack shouted back. "A great wonder! This—you called these beanstalk roots? This monstrous beanstalk sprang from them overnight! It happened while I was in delirium from fever." He moved like a healthy man now. Dole yeast might have cured a vitamin deficiency.

"But, another great wonder! The *Saint Mercurius* has arrived! Please make the acquaintance of Captain Magalhaes, Major Pereira, Father De Castro . . ."

"Look at her!" "Wouldn't you like to—" "So beautiful!" "Shame-

free barbarian devils!" Other voices were intruding. Miya flushed and stepped back out of sight.

The translator wasn't picking up just the shouts. It caught several near whispers and translated them all.

"The one in the window, I wonder if she bares her breasts too?"

"To have two such wives—"

"But they are dark."

"He gave Jack gold. He must have much more, to treat it so lightly."

"Why does he not invite us in? What might this wizard be hiding inside?"

Svetz tried to answer only the shouts from Jack and Captain Magalhaes. "A pleasure to meet you . . . so far from home . . . little chance to explore . . . the weather seems most pleasant in the morning . . . yes, some of us have learned to eat fish . . . what is the date?"

"I must ask the navigator." Captain Magalhaes lowered his voice, not to a whisper but to a softer authoritative bark. *"Three mongrels of a dark, strange race, a man with two wives who claims to be Christian and Russian. Father De Castro, is this a Christian? Is this a Russian?"*

"I have met Russians. Their skin is whiter than mine. Whiter than my father's I should say, given what this fierce sun has done to my complexion. Their ceremonies are queer, and their beliefs are strange. Jack, I do not see what you trusted in this Svetz. Did you see his dwelling?"

"From a distance, sir, and then it was gone."

"And now returned."

"It stands on two chicken legs." This from Father De Castro. *"I think this man may be a kind of Russian sorcerer."*

From Jack: *"Sir, I believe he saved my life. I know his generosity."*

"Well, Jack, perhaps you are too trusting." Captain Magalhaes raised his voice. "Master Svetz, the year is fifteen sixty-four in the month of April, and we are ten days from celebrating Easter. We hope you will join us."

Miya touched his arm. "Keep it cool here? I have an urge to cover up."

"Sure," Svetz said, and he stepped forward smiling as Miya stepped inside. "Thank you, Captain. Jack, look what I found!"

He tossed down a handful of gold eggs.

Jack caught two of the eight. The others fell and lay like golden eyes looking up from the mud. The shelled men stared, for less than a heartbeat.

Then Jack reached to pick up another egg—and so did every other man except Captain Magalhaes. The priest got one. Jack had three; he stepped out of the scuffle and handed one of the eggs to Captain Magalhaes for inspection.

Miya stepped out wearing a ship's blouse. She saw the knot of excitement and asked, "Hanny, what did you do?"

"Who, me?"

"Hanny!"

"They've been waiting for me to invite them in. Miya, they must think we have an invisible door down there where there's nothing but hydrogen tank. Not showing them my home makes me an ill-mannered barbarian, right? So I distracted them—"

"You gave them golden eggs and watched them fight!"

"Right," said Svetz, and he waved and grinned widely and went back inside. "Zeera, let's jump a few days. I can't think of anything more we want to learn from these . . . savages."

"We'll miss their holy day. They'll be *sure* we're sorcerers."

"Aren't we?"

They counted ten strobes and dropped out at midnight. Miya and Svetz went out with mag specs.

The Portuguese ship was still at anchor. A glare on shore near the ship was the remains of a cookfire. Oblong wooden structures reflected infrared light.

Nothing interesting had happened to the Hangtree, so Zeera jumped them again.

Miya stayed to tend Thaxir. Svetz and Zeera went out.

The line from the sky was no thicker, but for a swelling several meters above the tuft. Zeera found another lump six meters higher, and another, and another.

"Pumps," she said. "You can't get fluid very high with just capillary action."

"Look, Zeera, those little bulges are *crawling*. Moving up the line. Not pumps. More like little cargo vessels."

"Svetz, we're going to have to stay and watch this."

They dipped into the green forest to collect a variety of leaves for the Martian. Svetz asked, "Zeera, what about Thaxir? She could float if you put her in a pressure suit."

"Well, yes, if her faceplate wasn't smashed!"

Svetz lifted again for another look at the swellings on the cable. "Thirty to forty meters apart. A tablespoon of water each. Hey, Zeera, what's wrong with this picture?"

"Maybe they pull apart as they climb. You know, accelerating."

"They'd better. Otherwise . . . add it up and it's enough mass to pull the tree down."

"Is that what happened at Mars?"

"A million tonnes of war fleet. If the center of mass of an orbital tether drops below geosynchronous orbit, something's got to fall."

Zeera said, "Maybe we can fix that faceplate."

That part turned out to be easy. Zeera cut two lenses out of a fishbowl helmet and embedded them in a meteor patch, size large. That fit across Thaxir's pressure suit mask.

They waited for night and high tide.

Thaxir watched on the airlock platform while her captors worked at putting the pulley system together. Then, suddenly losing patience, she began climbing down the pulley ropes.

Svetz found it a startling sight. Thaxir had been sloughing her exercise, but now she was a tremendous insect climbing head down, all six appendages gripping the ropes. Despite Earth's gravity, six limbs were enough.

There were hot spots in the jungle. Svetz wondered what the soldiers thought they saw.

Thaxir descended into the surf. "Zzz," she said, and the translator said, "Pleasure."

Svetz and Miya swam around Thaxir. She seemed to be comfortable for the first time since her capture. She asked for her pouch, with her food and her harp, and they dropped that down to her.

Times had become too interesting for the locals. They were gone, leaving time travelers and Portuguese in possession.

Miya and Zeera went to pick leaves for Thaxir in the forest. They took the trade kit; after all, they might meet Portuguese.

The *Minim*'s cameras were mounted to watch the black knot where all the anchor trees now merged, where the root trailing from the Hangtree was now thick as Miya's calf.

The cameras found several Portuguese sailors on a climbing expedition. The near-horizontal trunks were easy going, but climbers were stalled near the peak. Still, why had he assumed that sailors couldn't climb? They must spend half their lives in the rigging of sails!

So Svetz might have gone with the women, but he stayed to watch.

He had thought the Portuguese might approach him. They had seen golden coins, then golden eggs, and now they must have glimpsed a sea creature moving about the *Minim*. But nobody had come. Perhaps their religious father figure had warned them away from wizards.

The women returned at sunset. They took turns cleaning up in the *Minim* before they would talk to Svetz.

"We met some conquistadors in the woods," Miya told him.

"Learn anything?"

"Don't talk to strange men," Zeera snapped.

Miya said, "We did some teaching too." The women wouldn't meet his eyes, nor each other's.

Svetz let it go. Eventually he'd get the story.

34

Thaxir had slept floating. This morning she played in the water, getting her exercise without fighting gravity. Svetz sat on the launch platform, watching.

He felt restless. They were wasting time, and there was no need.

How did a Hangtree grow? Could it survive to the present? Would it move on to some other star? What would kill it and what was its life span? The only things left to learn would all be learned using the Fast Forward device. With the FFD they would watch it all happen, wait for present time, and ultimately report it all to the Institute—

Thaxir! A breaking wave had caught her and was washing her toward shore!

A Martian might well find an ocean terrifying, and indeed she seemed paralyzed, borne headfirst toward the beach on her belly plates.

Svetz considered rescue. The tide was in. He could reach shore with a flight stick and risk being seen; or let the waves wash him in . . . but then he'd be stuck onshore for hours . . . though it might be the only way to help Thaxir.

Waves rolled her up the sand.

Wouldn't it be better to hail her, using the translator, and ask her to wait? Futz no, if the tide went out he'd have to roll her back to the water! But now she was on all sixes, crawling headfirst back into the waves.

And shelled men at the edge of the woods were shouting, gesticulating, then dropping to one knee and aiming their kinetic weapons tubes—

They fired into green water and foam. Thaxir was gone.

Miya and Zeera were both sleeping. Svetz caressed Miya's foot. She snapped alert in an instant.

"Portuguese onshore. I'm going to have to talk to them. Is there anything I'll have to apologize for?"

Behind his shoulder a chilled voice said, "Do not apologize for anything. That's an order, Svetz."

Miya said, "Believe it, Hanny."

"Anything to make *them* apologize for? No? Great. And what do I tell them about Thaxir? She was onshore. They saw her."

Miya said, "Let me sleep."

In the *sshh, hisss* of waves there was a music born of madness. Svetz tried to ignore it, but his mind ran away from him, chasing the beat.

The water was withdrawing from the land. Svetz glanced down to be sure, but yes, Thaxir was in the shadow of the *Minim*, safely hidden in floating weed. She was playing her windstorm-minor harp in time with the waves.

Svetz called a cheery good morning to six Portuguese.

The conversation that followed was all shouting over diminishing distance and hissing waves, but Svetz didn't have to do his own shouting.

The Captain was missing a man. Had Svetz or his wives seen Alfonso Nunes?

Svetz answered, "Well, but men in armor all look alike from a distance. Was there anything distinctive—?"

"Alfonso Nunes is short, Captain, very hairy, and lost his helmet long ago, so his face is dark." The translator was picking up normal voices again.

Captain Magalhaes shouted, "Six went out to the woods yesterday afternoon. Five returned. There was no blood on the survivors. They will not speak to any but the priest, and Father De Castro *will not* speak. I must not violate a covenant, but I must know. Has any soldier tried to rob you, Master Svetz?"

"Nobody has troubled us here."

"Not even the great sea creature? I saw it myself, Master Svetz. We fired on it to protect you."

"I think it harmless. I armed myself and swam with it yesterday, Captain, and it did not trouble me." Svetz was beginning to enjoy himself. Remembering Whale's undying hatred for its captors, he said, "Many large sea creatures enjoy the company of men."

"It is known that you and your women have gold. No?"

"We gave you what we had. Why would we need such stuff here?"

"He lies, Captain, let me try my surgical skills on his tongue—"

"Why, Peter, would you wade into the sea to shout your threats up at him on his platform? Peace, Peter. Patience. Master Svetz, where did you find these golden eggs?"

The Portuguese were growing hoarse. The shouting was wearing them down, and Thaxir's music, that might have been the sound of the sea hereabouts. They were losing subtlety; their greed showed through.

An antic whim took Svetz. Futz, they'd never trust him anyway, and now he was sure that they'd offended his women. He pointed straight up along the Hangtree.

"From up there. I got the coins there too, but I'm not wanted back."

By their questions he let them add their own details. Together they concocted a wild tale in which Svetz climbed to orbit, robbed a giant of coins, returned and captured a bird that laid golden eggs—who had escaped, and must be still at large in the jungle. "Maybe Jack saw it. Shall we talk to Jack?"

"Jack has gone exploring," said Captain Magalhaes. "We should join him, I think. I thank you for the suggestion." Captain Magalhaes turned away, but some of his soldiers were looking toward the green jungle, and others toward the Hangtree/Beanstalk rising to infinity. And the voices went on.

"Alvarez, you thieving son of a dog, tell me what that sorcerer's women will have told him! Will he kill us all with his magic?"

"Captain, they are not hurt. We only wanted to have our way with them."

"But they are hiding gold, you understand, Captain!"

"No, we would not have hurt them even if—"

"Alfonso threatened the dark woman. Truly, he might have hurt her, not just had his way with her, yes, Peter?"

"Peter Alvarez da Orta, if you lie to me now, God will never find your soul."

"They were not hurt! Sir, sir, they were not hurt! We blocked their way. Alfonso Nunes set the edge of his sword against the black woman's throat and spoke his threats, and then we all fell over and could not move. Evil was the day we came to this unholy place."

"But you could see and hear?"

"Yes, Captain."

"Two women. Six men. Pitiful. What happened to Alfonso Nunes? Did they drag him away?"

A pause. Then: *"Yes—"*

"No—"

"We didn't see—"

"Captain, Captain, no! Stay your hand! We will show you. Peter, we must." And they were among the trees, and their voices fuzzed out.

Thaxir was elated. She tried to describe the sensation of riding a rolling wall of water down onto powdered rock in two and a half Mars gravities, with all her limbs pulled against her body to make her into a great unstoppable missile. The translator was losing phrases. An epiphany, Svetz gathered.

How did she feel?

Her soul was complete!

But physically?

Water was her natural element! She could float, waking or sleeping, and rest, or she could swim against water's resistance and exercise her whole body.

"We need to be about our mission," Svetz said. "Will you come with us into the future?"

Thaxir was startled. She took some time to think, then, "Would you leave me behind if I asked?"

"Why not? But I don't think it's a good idea. Earth's gravity will kill you young, even if you could find a food supply. In the present we can levitate you. We'll take care of you in the Vivarium until Willy Gorky knows how to make Mars habitable again."

Thaxir asked for details: Vivarium? Levitate? Then she rolled on her back to look up at the *Minim.* "How will you get me back up there?"

"Do you think you can climb?"

"Well, let me try."

Svetz watched her climb the ropes of the half-completed pulley. She didn't have trouble until she was nearly free of the water. There she stalled. Miya came out on the platform to watch. Thaxir dropped back, and tried again, and failed again.

"We'll set up the pulleys," Miya said.

Thaxir disappeared underwater.

Svetz and Miya went to work. They weren't surprised when the green giant didn't surface at once. It might be her last chance to swim. The oceans of the thirty-second century were polluted to a green-and-black goo.

During a rest break he turned his mag specs on the Hangtree. There had been attrition, but he saw at least two climbers in the black tuft. The root that ran into the sky had become as thick as a man's leg. A third man was climbing it, eighty meters up. Another was pulling on the root.

He could hardly be needed to hold it steady. He too must intend to climb it.

The view through the *Minim* dome was the same as the camera's, almost straight up the anchor trunks, past the underside of the black tuft, and up into infinity. Anyone might be in the tuft.

Zeera came out. "What's this about?"

"Getting out of here, I thought." They'd been having trouble arranging the pulley system. It was new to them both. "Now I'm not sure. Zeera, did you kill someone in the woods?"

Silence. Miya ignored them both. Svetz said, "Alfonso Nunes. Short, very hairy, almost as dark as you. Didn't wear a helmet."

"Six of 'em thought they were going to rape us and torture us," Zeera said. "Miya stunned them down. We talked a little about what to do with them, but we couldn't move them without letting them wake up. Just putting them to sleep didn't seem like much of a lesson. Miya wanted to steal their pants and dye their, uh, pubic region."

"Not enough?"

"They think we've got gold. They would've tortured us to get it. Rape, that's just entertainment. Svetz, they take it as their *due*. A woman doesn't walk alone or speak to a man if she has a protector to speak for her. A woman alone is, is anyone's. They have to be taught, Svetz! And you'd *steal their pants*?"

"They're showing something to Captain Magalhaes right now." Svetz asked, "What is he going to see?"

Zeera turned away.

Miya answered. "They're going to take him to that temple Jack showed us. He's going to find a gold statue. Life-sized. Reclining. Obscene. Why didn't Thaxir toss us her pack?"

"Don't know." Right, the Martian had left her pack underwater when she tried to climb.

"Where is she?"

"Don't know. Am I being distracted, Miya? Always talk it out, remember? Let's talk about a gold statue. I take it you," turning to Zeera, "used the trade kit on Alfonso Nunes." Svetz looked into the forest, but the Portuguese were all gone. "Why him?"

Miya answered. "He had his pants off. He had Zeera down on that stone dais before I got to my stunner. Knife at her throat. I had to stun them both and then wait for Zeera to wake up. He stank like nothing I've ever smelled—"

"Like the ostrich cage after the roc broke loose," Zeera said. "And he was hard—"

"He had an *impressive* erection. Nunes could have had a great media career if he'd waited a few centuries, right, Zeera?"

"Right. You could have stopped me."

"Zeera, I had a different impression," Miya said coolly.

Svetz said, "They're showing that statue to Captain Magalhaes right now."

"Why'd they wait this long?" Miya wondered.

Zeera laughed. "Gold," she said, mocking. "They don't know how to move it or hide it or sell it, but they want it."

Miya said, "Hanny, we turned some of those stoneware things to gold too, and that row of knives. They might think it was all native work. Hide him in plain sight. What is it, Hanny?"

Svetz touched his mag specs. What he thought he'd seen—
"Thaxir."

Thaxir was out of the surf and almost to the trees. Her pack
was on her back. Six-limbed, Thaxir managed a fast crawl. "What's
she doing?" Miya wondered. "Escaping?"

"I *told* her we'd leave her here if she wanted," Svetz said.

She was into the forest, shouldering trees aside.

A Portuguese came running out. He ran down the beach,
southeastward, never slowing.

They made a meal while they talked it over.

"The default option is that we can leave her," Zeera said.
"Any objection? Willy Gorky wanted us to negotiate with her,
but she's not negotiating and she's not in contact with the tree
anyway."

"She'll starve," Miya said. "Hanny, don't you have an opinion?"

Svetz had been letting them run on while he watched the anchor grove. They were wasting time, but Svetz himself shied from
abandoning a story half finished.

Jack was on the Hangtree, a hundred and twenty meters above
the anchor grove. He'd left his metal shell below. This would not
be much like climbing rigging. Ropes would have some slack to
them, would run horizontal in spots. Still, he climbed on. Two men,
Portuguese but without their shells, waited below him in the black
foliage.

Thaxir was not to be seen.

Svetz said, "She knows what she can eat. You know, I've taken
a lot of prisoners in my time. I'm used to considering them property, but they don't *talk* to me. I'm inclined to consider that Thaxir
owns herself. I'm surprised at what she can do in Earth gravity.
Maybe she'll maim herself. Maybe she'll crawl back to the sea for
rest and sleep, and forage on land, or just eat seaweed. Maybe the
conquistadors will kill her, but she knows the risks as well as we
do or better! So the question is, how long will it be before she
needs rescue? Do we stay or go? Or Fast Forward by a year and
look again? *Hyah!*"

"*What?*"

"It's her!" A great yellow-green insectile shape poked itself above the black fluff. Jack's companions flung themselves away, out of the tuft, and how they fell was not to be known. The Martian began to climb, six limbs around a silver thread.

Miya was scrambling for mag specs; Zeera had hers. "There. She can *climb*. She was faking us out, sure as futz. How high can she expect to get?"

"Whatever. We can't do anything about it. The *Minim* won't fly and the flight sticks won't carry anything like that much weight."

Thaxir wasn't moving fast.

Jack was hardly moving at all.

"She's catching up. She'll have to get past him," Miya said.

Jack looked down and saw the monstrous shape coming up at him.

Zeera said, "Svetz, try your IR on the beach."

"Zeera, I want to see—" But he knew the sound of terror. Svetz obeyed: found the beach, looked for hot spots, and zoomed.

Where a Portuguese had burst from the forest forty minutes ago, nine were now wrestling with some massive tube.

"Zeera, get us ready for Fast Forward. I'll cut these lines." Svetz dropped to the cargo level and went out the airlock.

Within the shadows of the forest, shelled men were backing their big metal tube against a tree trunk. Svetz had a familiar view, straight down the axis.

He slashed away the never-tested pulley system. Most of it fell into the sea. He pulled what remained through the airlock, then stabbed virtual buttons. The airlock doors closed.

"Get us into FFD," he told Zeera, but she was already doing it.

The tube blinked fire. Clouds raced. The sun set and rose again.

"I wonder how that came out," Miya said.

Svetz said, "I'd say Jack is a doomed man. And isn't it a wonderful thing, to be able to leave all your mistakes behind? I'm just wondering, though, what will happen if those men go home with an obscene statue made of solid gold. They'll have all of Europe thinking that there's gold all over these continents, and the locals don't deserve to keep it."

There was silence and the flicker of time passing, until Miya asked, "Hanny, did you do anything with the talker?"

Talker? "No. Zeera?"

"Last I saw it, it was lying . . . lying right next to Thaxir's head. Do you suppose that was in her pack too?"

"It was broken. Beyond repair, wasn't it, Zeera?"

"Oh, yes."

"But that's still the answer," Svetz decided. "She took the talker. But *why*?"

35

During the opposition of 1894 a great light was seen on the illuminated part of the disk, first at the Lick Observatory, then by Parrotin of Nice, and then by other observers. English readers heard of it first in the issue of Nature *dated August 2. I am inclined to think that this blaze may have been the casting of the huge gun, in the vast pit sunk into their planet, from which their shots were fired at us.*
—*The War of the Worlds*, by H. G. Wells

The Portuguese ship lasted a minute or two, then zipped away.

They watched the anchor grove shed its black top. A knot remained where it had been, where anchor trees joined the root of the Hangtree; but it had grown a klick or two higher, and the marks of a join were fading. It was all one organism now.

Far above, where Earth's atmosphere no longer filtered the sunlight of naked space, photosynthesis stored energy as some form of sugar. Water and soil nutrients from below, sugar from above, and so the tree survived and grew.

They watched, and argued, and took turns reading notes into the record. They ate dole bricks and drank recycled water. They took turns sleeping. Svetz and Miya made love on the cargo net while Zeera slept above them, beneath a strobe made by the whirling sun. Years passed outside the *Minim*'s ruined hull.

More ships came. Wooden buildings sprang up. The green forest shrank back to reveal patchwork farmlands. Farm gave way to factories, then to city.

And the shore receded so gradually that Svetz hardly noticed, but now the *Minim* stood among six- and eight-story buildings. Was the land rising? Land did rise and fall . . . but the Hangtree only grew greater. Svetz could picture roots spread through the bedrock beneath this land, *lifting*.

Passing time began to wear on the *Minim*'s crew.

Well over a thousand years of development had shaped the *Minim*'s water-recycling system, but how well had it survived martian shellfire and a crash landing? Fast Forward itself was experimental. After several weeks aboard the *Minim*, in an environment that changed like dreams, it was easy to imagine that water had begun to taste of trace elements accumulating, that dole bricks had gone bad, that air was developing a stench.

Zeera developed an annoying cough.

Passing centuries swept them into a future that diverged from their own. The tree was grown vast. It cut the sun's arc like a storm cloud moored in place. Briefly, tall structures with glass faces rose in a crescent about the base of the Hangtree, using the trunk as a main support structure. But the tree was alive and its shape changed year by year. Glass slabs stretched and crumbled . . . and remained in place as slums. The ruined glass faces and the cracks were mended with stucco or concrete, over and over.

External sensors registered air becoming Post-Industrial.

Zeera's cough cleared up when she saw that. "They'll be burning coal in Europe. Running steam engines. Svetz, Miya, that stuff is almost breathable!"

"Read it again," Miya suggested.

Though factories had appeared even on this equatorial shoreline, readouts still showed too little carbon dioxide, too much oxygen. "We can't go out anyway," Miya said. "Futz, we're all going crazy in here! But we can't. First thing you know, we're under arrest for illegal parking."

"I don't get this," Zeera said. "We're assuming the Hangtree makes sugar, right? Even if chlorophyll isn't what it's using. Martians live on the sap! But it's being made outside the atmosphere, so where's all this oxygen coming from?"

Miya was willing to speculate. "CO_2 and water come up with the sap. Sugar and oxygen go down the same way, or maybe oxygen just diffuses through the bark and *drifts* down. What the *futz*—"

Miya's reactions were faster. She hit the FFD switch.

The sun stopped at high noon, tangled in mirror blossoms.

A metal structure as big as a ten-story building came out of the sea on a tripod of three-hundred-meter legs. It was walking toward the city, but now it turned ponderously, as if it had just seen the *Minim*. Svetz could almost make out what was inside the tiny dome . . . and then light brighter than a thousand suns flared at them.

Even a Softfinger plasma blast wouldn't have hurt the *Minim*'s superconducting hull. But the gouge over the oxygen tank flared and gave way in the instant before Miya stabbed the FFD switch.

Then everything strobed, but the *Minim* rang like a bell. Svetz's seat flung him forward and then back, cracking his neck like a whip. He saw flame backfiring through the break in the oxygen tank. An instant more and the *Minim* would have exploded like a car in a movie.

Seasons passed outside while the *Minim* creaked and toppled to a thirty-degree angle, and stuck there.

The three-legged thing was gone.

The city had been leveled. They watched it being rebuilt.

"I think those were Softfingers," Miya said.

Svetz said, "I didn't see. Even if it was Martians, were they from Mars or the Hangtree? We're deep into Industrial times, after all. Mars must be dying. Zeera, how long—?"

"Twelve hundred years to go."

*   *   *

Svetz was in the shower bag. The display flashed a radiation warning, and Svetz was about to yell when Zeera switched off the FFD.

He said, "I thought I saw—"

"Here." Zeera had the meteor sensor going in passive mode. A map of the Earth showed a swarm of red arrowheads. "We just passed the Year Zero, Hanny. First atomic bomb. Propeller planes. Anything that cracks the speed of sound *now* isn't local."

Arrowheads swarmed over the center of the North American continent, but others were on the equator just about . . . here? Svetz looked up. An overlay on the dome was blinking red arrowheads around little fast-moving dots.

"Those are Softfinger lens ships," Miya said. "They're invading Earth again. What do you think, are they looking for nuclear test grounds?"

Ten lens ships all wheeled to converge on the *Minim*. Svetz said, "I think we should punch out."

Miya hit the FFD. Plasma cannon blinked and were gone. Cityscape around the *Minim* showed craters and broken walls. They began to grow back.

"Futz. I'd have liked to know more about *that*," Miya said.

Zeera said, "Mars must be on its last breath by now. In twenty years we'll put our first probes around Mars, and not a drop of water or a whiff of oxygen left. They must be desperate. Anyway, we're halfway home."

They waited it out.

They detected a much bigger blast of radiation: another lens ship attack, or else they'd seen the One Race War, if time hadn't been bent too badly.

An earthquake shook the city, *blink*, and half the buildings were down. That must have been the shock from the Hammer of August falling offshore from Chili in 2391. Shoreline cities had washed away. Bureau of Space Resources had not been able to stop the minor asteroid; they didn't even have spacecraft to mount a pretense. The United Nations hierarchy took the blame for the destruction, and were executed. Waldemar the First took power.

Building styles changed: they were smaller, more graceful, with more land around them. Population was dwindling, partly due to UN planning, but not everyone could adjust to post-Industrial air. "We're right on track," Zeera said, and coughed.

"We don't know that."

"Time lines converge when they can. Changes we make are smoothed out. You've *seen* that, Svetz."

Miya usually sat out these discussions. She didn't know enough history to have an opinion. They mostly argued to convince Miya.

So Svetz said, "The time machine is too big to move itself. The extension cage goes out on an arm that can swing in four dimensions. Coming home, there's no *telling* where it might swing to. I've met someone from a culture that blasted the human race to extinction. Wrona came from one where wolves evolved instead of men. But I've always come back to the Institute time line. Because the extension arm is attached at both ends! But the Institute time line can change too, Zeera. You've seen that."

"And we put it back."

Miya was looking up through the dome.

The Hangtree filled the sky. The Moon and stars hung in its branches. The Moon was only one light among a hundred mirror blossoms. Mag specs could find strange architectures forming tiny cityscapes along the trunk.

She whispered, "What legends are being made about *that*? We don't have to wonder, do we? Yggdrasil. The axis runs through the Earth. A variety of heavens are in the branches. Hanny, how could we have had the legends before the tree was in place?"

"There were legends of werewolves before I ever found Wrona's time line," Svetz said. "Dreams and stories wander across the time lines."

"Well." Miya gestured upward. "You think it's so easy, then put *that* back the way it was."

"I thought you wanted it."

*   *   *

The black was very restful. Sleep had not favored Svetz for a long time, but now the darkness went on and on. He slept as if drugged.

In the sudden light he snapped awake and—

The sun sat on the ocean and wouldn't move.

Barricades and familiar UN police uniforms surrounded the *Minim*. Thousands of people surrounded the barricades. A few wandered inside the perimeter, acting like they knew what was going on.

Miya and Zeera were asleep in their command chairs. Svetz ate a dole brick while he watched and waited. Presently Miya stirred. Svetz asked her, "Did you turn off the Fast Forward?" and *then* he noticed a dribble of silver where Jack's coin had run molten.

Miya saw what surrounded them and jerked upright. "It's present time! Hanny, we need to find a vidphone."

36

*The stem spreads its branches over the entire sky; their
leaves are the clouds, their fruits the stars . . . The ash
tree* (Fraxinus) *itself is the Nordic Tree of Life, symbol of
strength and vigor. . . .*
—"The Ash Tree," from Mattioli's *Commentaires*,
Lyons, 1579

As a police Roton lifted them toward the sky, they saw a metropolis of eight to ten million spread beneath the vastness of the Hangtree. *Root Town*, the police pilot called it, and *World Tree.*

An hour later the Roton set them down at the Institute for Temporal Research in Angels City, west coast of North America Province, where the garden had been.

They took deep gulps of air flavored by cactus blooms. The roses and once-edibles were gone. Scores of varieties of cactus bloomed in dry earth and perfect crescent dunes. Was this some whim of the new Secretary-General?

And where was the ornamental pond? The pond was where they dumped the heat from a returning X-cage!

They were still enjoying the taste of post-Industrial air. Zeera's cough had come back during that last thousand years, and Svetz had caught it too. They'd been *sure* the *Minim*'s air was foul. The instruments were sure it wasn't.

A crowd wove its way through the cactus to meet them.

Willy Gorky shouldered between them. He had lost weight. "Miya, why didn't you call? How did you *get* here?"

"Fast Forward. What else was there?" she snapped. "Willy, why didn't you send us an X-cage?"

"We've only just finished resetting the small X-cage! That was no trivial problem, Miya. You never gave us a date."

Miya said, "But why would—"

"Got it," said Svetz. Ra Chen's disgusted look suggested that he'd seen it too. "How long has it been since our last call? Four hours?" Ra Chen shrugged his eyebrows: *Yes.* "Miya, we used Fast Forward, and that's why we didn't get rescued. Because we're already *here*."

Zeera was nodding. "The other end of the talker link, before the talker was smashed. *That* was present time. *That's* when the FFD burned out. These things won't go into the future. Four hours ago? If we'd been awake we'd have called you right back!"

"But why can't we still send—" Gorky stopped, seeing the way they all looked at him. "What would happen if we sent a rescue vehicle now? Would you pop like so many soap bubbles? Would I be looking at two of everyone?"

Nobody answered. Nobody knew.

The time machine was running on standby. The large and small X-cages looked ready to go, though none of the stations were manned.

A dozen techs were seated around the drinks dispenser, off

duty now that the time travelers had been returned. Svetz recognized dark Hillary Weng-Fa, pale Zat Forsman and ruddy Wilt Miller from his own past. The rest were strangers, though they knew *him*.

While the two Heads and three time travelers walked in and took seats, Zat and a stunning Eurafrican woman, tall and narrow as a soda straw, put coins in the dispenser without asking what anyone wanted, and brought them—water.

Clean water. Svetz savored the taste. People were acting peculiar; he would wait to learn why. And why the drinks dispenser had only two settings. And what *was* it about the way they all looked?

The time travelers must look like three rats turned loose from a dirty cage. Ra Chen was amused and not hiding it. He looked good: he too had lost weight.

He said, "We jiggered the inertial calendars on the X-cages. The intertemporal talker is a kind of a little X-cage, after all. Whatever travels in time needs more energy to co-exist with it. It's like hitting a bump: we can sense that."

Willy Gorky exclaimed, *"That's* what you were doing?"

Ra Chen laughed. "We never got a date, but there are tricks we can pull. We're all set to send the X-cages back toward minus 500 AE, which is just pre-Columbian, and pop out where the talker was ruined—when you landed, right, Zeera?—pick you up, leave an instrument package and come home.

"Still, we don't know everything about time. Zeera, did you learn anything about the squirrel?"

After a long moment Zeera said, "Squirrel?"

Ra Chen frowned. "Batatosk?" Zeera was still looking blank, as well she might. "Secretary-General Victor Four wants the giant squirrel that used to run up and down the World Tree. It was bigger than Whale, so he's got to have it. If it was a squirrel at all. Ole Romer, the ancient Danish astronomer, *he* saw it and thought it was a squirrel, but what it *was* . . ." Ra Chen felt their confusion. "What?"

"Sir, it seems we've changed the past a little," Svetz said. "What was our mission?"

"We know when it died, Svetz. The impact caused the tidal wave that washed away Rio de Janeiro! It might have been sick or old for longer than that. But, futz, the X-cage was already set for pre-Columbian. Batatosk must have been in its prime then. Locate it, send for the large X-cage, get the squirrel and bring it home."

"Nothing about Martians?"

"Martians?"

"Tree dwellers?"

"Legends. Fire giants, frost giants. If they were real, they've been extinct since . . . oh, before serious telescopes. Those were *Martians?"*

Willy Gorky looked at Ra Chen before he spoke. "I'd like to rescue some Martians. Did you have any contact with them?"

"Mostly hostile." Svetz saw body language he half understood. He asked, "Tell me about merging History Bureau and Bureau of the Sky Domains."

Willy said, briskly and without rancor, "Right, it's all History now. Victor Four likes strange animals, just like his brother. He's financed a Heavy Lift Extension Cage."

"We fulfilled our mission," Svetz said a bit belligerently. "We went to Mars for the seeds to grow *that*," and he gestured southeast. Far around the curve of the world, the Hangtree still owned the sky. "We didn't just grow seeds, we brought back the tree itself. With that we can own the sky!"

Willy Gorky said, "Not under Victor Four, I think. *Mars?* What's it like?"

Svetz swept up their plastic cups and went to the dispenser for refills. He came back cradling five cups, and set them down without spilling. He'd bought himself a few seconds to think.

The dispenser had only two settings: water and carbonated water. That seemed important.

He said, "Willy, we had a Martian too, but she's gone back up the tree—"

Bong.

Miya demanded, "What the futz was *that*?" But Svetz and Zeera were running toward the Guide Pit, and the Heads were just behind them.

"Talker," Svetz called back.

"But we can *see* all three extension cages!" Ra Chen shoved into the Guide Pit. He tapped the virtual display. "Head! Talk to me."

An inhuman voice spoke with the sound of a sustained belch.

"Translator!" Willy Gorky demanded.

Zeera beat them to the draw. "Let me *set* it, sir. *This* is Portuguese. *That's* Martian."

Ra Chen made way for Gorky. "Talk to me," Gorky said.

Syllables burbled. The UN translator said, "Such is our intent. Is Miya within sound of my voice, or Svetz, or Zeera?"

Miya pushed past. "Miya, here and now, 1109 AE. Thaxir?"

"Yes."

A tech was trying to fine-tune the talker, but Gorky was tending to that himself. Softly he asked, "Zeera, could this be *your* talker? The setting's changed. How badly—"

"It was *ruined*!"

Miya had been talking rapidly with the voice at the other end of time. She said over her shoulder, "Thaxir says—tell them yourself, Thaxir."

"I took the ruin of your talker. We studied that until we could build one ourselves. What you said of probabilities made sense to us, Miya. The love of adventure may take some of us to future Earth instead of the stars. What must we do?"

Ra Chen asked, "How many want to come?"

"Thaxir—?"

"We have travelers from all of the five races." The martian voice gave numbers. Four green giants, fourteen red humanoids, twenty Softfingers, three of the great crabs and six of their humanoid symbiotes. Of the Pious Ones, only the Smiths had settled on the tree; eleven would try Earth. "If you can give us low gravity, I will come too. I am too old to reach the stars, even if the tree would go, and I laid my last egg long since."

"Sir, I have the new setting," Hillary Weng-Fa said.

Gorky demanded, "We can call back? And get thence with the small X-cage?"

"Yes. They're calling from plus-eleven AE—"

"Miya, tell her we'll call back," Ra Chen said.

"Thaxir, we're switching off now, but we'll switch on again before you can draw breath. I know how strange that sounds, but it's true." Miya switched off. "They want rescue!"

"Svetz—"

Svetz had been adding it up. "One load in the large X-cage, but they'll be crowded. Setting up a cage in the Viv— . . . Bestiary is no problem. Whale's got all the room he needs. That many Martians will too. We can set shelves at different levels, and give them material to make houses—"

"The mission," Ra Chen said gently, "was to retrieve a *squirrel*."

Willy Gorky asked, "Just what kind of promise did you make, Miya?"

"Rescue as many as want to go. That was our mission, Willy! You wanted a Beanstalk, but Waldemar the Eleventh—"

"Miya," Willy said gently.

Walls have ears. Victor the Fourth was the Secretary-General, the *only* Secretary-General. "—wanted Martians," Miya said anyway.

"Willy," said Ra Chen, "we never really get used to the way time changes things around—"

"Martians," Willy Gorky said. "Ra Chen, does it strike you that Martians on the World Tree would know a lot about the squirrel? They've *lived* with it. If we can get the Martians first, we'll have their help in retrieving the squirrel."

"*Two* trips for the large extension cage. Twice the cost."

"Right. Absolutely. What settings are you using for his cage?"

"I—"

"Batatosk. What does he eat? Nuts the size of this dome? No, that can't be it, because if one of those ever fell, anytime in human history, we'd have records. So we don't know what to feed him. Don't know how much room he actually needs. It might be thousands of klicks. He might want a vertical treadmill with variable gravity, but I'm guessing there. If we take time to study him to see what he needs in the way of a cage environment, he'll probably die." Willy Gorky glared into Ra Chen's eyes at close range. "If only we had somebody to *ask*!"

"Point *taken*, Willy."

"There's lots of Martians. We can house *them*. We'll get readings for archaic Mars right out of the *Minim*. But we only get one shot at Batatosk. If *he* dies—"

"Yes."

Not liking it, Svetz asked, "Wouldn't we be giving the squirrel's cage to the Martians?"

Ra Chen brushed it off. "We built *six* of the big cages, when Waldemar Ten was SecGen and we had the funding. Whale in one, Roc in another—"

"*Roc* survived?"

"Used to be Ostrich? Anyway, Batatosk would have gone in one. If we ever get the Heavy Lift X-cage running we'll go after the Midgard Serpent, and if we can ever reach back far enough we can house a Brontosaur and a Tyrannosaurus Rex. Separately. No, housing's not a problem, and . . . yes, drown it, we'll get the Martians. Get 'em back for me, Miya."

37

UN officials were beaming the *Minim*'s records from Root Town to the Institute for Temporal Research in Angels City. It was a slow process.

"If you're near the tree, you can relay from the mirror sails, but we're not close enough for that. There are only a few orbital windows such that a relay satellite won't crash into the tree," Willy Gorky said. "You'd think geosynchronous orbit would be safe, but the mass of the tree only allows you two stable points, Lagrange Four and Five, just like the Moon. You can do twelve-hour pole-to-pole orbits. Not near the tree, of course."

"That must take lots of delta-V," Svetz said, and sipped his water. He'd barely heard the word, but he knew it was a measure of fuel consumption. Low Earth equatorial orbits were the easiest to reach.

"You're drowning right. You need so much delta-V for either set of orbits that you might as well go to the Moon for anything but weather satellites and signal relays. All these stations are too high. You lose signal definition." Willy's fist clenched on his glass. "Svetz? *You* could put anything you wanted in low Earth orbit without smashing into the World Tree. Right?"

"We could, right."

"Drown me! Even men?"

"Right."

"When?"

"First man went into orbit in plus sixteen AE."

"*Drown* me! *We* had to go straight to the Moon."

"Is that bad?"

"In the reign of Chaka Third, between plus one eighty and two hundred AE, we put a dozen men on the Moon, brought 'em back, and never went again for thirty years! The world had already used up too many resources. Svetz, without the tree we could have had a Moon colony by fifty AE! Our space program is a pitiable thing."

"You said that."

Willy looked up. "To you?"

"Wait." Svetz thought. "That was then. That was the other you, when the first man stepped on the Moon in 24 AE. *That* Willy wanted a Beanstalk!"

Aghast, Willy asked, "Why?"

Pitiable, Svetz thought. "Our idea," he said, "was to run elevators up the tree, or a linear accelerator. Get to orbit and beyond for whatever the electricity costs. Drop asteroid mining ships from the upper end." He drank the last few drops of water. Water was expensive; he hadn't noticed yesterday. "Nobody thought we'd have to fight seven kinds of Martians to do it."

"Vic Four wouldn't support it anyway."

"Willy, I'm starting to think that nobody really tries to get the stars for his grandchildren. Anyone who wants the stars must want them *now*. For eleven and a half centuries—"

"Sir." A tech was trying to get Willy Gorky's attention. Willy turned as if glad to escape.

"Sir. We have numbers for archaic Mars, air comp, temp, gravity and so forth—"

"We need to rework the large X-cage and furnish a cage in the Bestiary. Six hours, Svetz. Entertain yourself."

The dole yeast dispenser was empty.

Svetz brought Miya a cup of water. Miya had been talking to Martians for hours.

"The first invasion from Mars was a Softfinger fleet," she told him, "in minus fifty AE. We saw one of their walkers. Almost nobody came back. The Martians on the tree thought it was some disease of Earth that killed them all. We think it was gravity.

"Thaxir says the rebuilt talker has been ready for centuries. Nobody wanted to use it. All these centuries, the peoples of the tree must have thought they could invade Earth any time the tree failed them.

"When the first few atomic bombs went off in Year Zero, the Softfingers tried some reconnaissance missions. They were sure we'd use the bomb on the tree if they didn't hit us first. They wanted to know where the bombs were. Most of their wok ships never even set down, but when they got home, the pilots were dying. Earth's gravity breaks their internal membranes. I've been trying to tell Thaxir how antigravity in the Zoo works—"

"Make room." Svetz slid into place and said, "Svetz at 1109 AE calling Thaxir. Are you thence?"

"I am hence, Svetz."

"The antigravity the Sky Domains uses is expensive. We don't use that in the Zoo—which they seem to call the Bestiary now, Miya. Thaxir, we use a magnetic field that acts on the magnetic moment of hydrogen. We can float organic material. I saw them float a half-million-ton bubble of seawater into Whale's cage, then move Whale in without hurting him. Believe me, putting martian gravity in a Mars environment cage is the easy part."

"I will convey. Svetz, Miya tells me that there are none of us on the tree in your future."

"Our past. Your future. They tell me the same. They tell me some tremendous animal—"

"Yes, Miya spoke of that. A squirrel is a beast that run up and down trees? And your first telescopes saw something large running up and down the tree? Svetz, I have consulted with our storytellers. Long ago, red Martians invaded Crab territory during a border dispute. We think your Ole Romer saw their heavy war lift while they were ferrying troops and armaments."

The Secretary-General wasn't going to like that, Svetz thought. He said, "Get yourselves into place. When you're ready to be picked up, and not before, smash the talker. That brings us. We can't hold the large X-cage in the past for very long at all."

"Yes, Miya told me. Svetz, I need rest. I don't have your human stamina." And the ready light went out.

Miya looked exhausted, gaunt and drooping. Svetz told her, "*You* need sleep."

"And something to eat, and a bath. We both . . . all need baths, and nobody's offered us one."

"Let's check it out. Find Zeera too?"

"Good."

"Miya, it's present time. Do I still look good to you?"

She smiled, took his hands and squeezed hard. "You look like me, I bet. Tired. Half starved. Let's get something to eat and then bathe each other."

The large X-cage loomed over the middle of the dome. An extension arm behind it ran into the same metal housing from which a smaller arm led to the small X-cage, to the right of the Guide Pit.

Strangers were at work in the Pit, writing in the specs that had come from the *Minim*. More strangers were gluing a bin the size of a bungalow to the upper curve of the X-cage. Wilt Miller was supervising. He hailed them.

Svetz was relieved. Most techs were total strangers who had known him for years. That was disconcerting. Wilt was an exception, and easy to spot: skin that was always sunburn red, and flame-red hair.

Wilt gestured at a pile of hardware two men high. "Look it over. What part of this is garbage? What are you going to need for this mission?"

They discussed it.

Pressure suits, of course. They'd fill the X-cage with a Mars-style atmosphere and wear pressure suits themselves. No telling if refugees would bring enough oxygen. They'd want Gorky's special filter helmets for breathing Mars atmosphere.

"Lines. Hanny, you'll be maneuvering near sixty refugees in vacuum and free fall," Miya said. "You'll need stickstrips and fix-points and lines. I'll get those from Space Bureau, Wilt. Give me a man and a floater cart."

Bottled water. Medical equipment: what kind of accidents were likely to hurt or kill Martians during a rescue? Svetz listened, nodded, advised.

Then he asked Wilt about baths and showers.

Bath? Well, that was awkward. Gorky wanted the large X-cage off in five hours. Everyone was busy, so the bath was available, yes. The problem (Wilt was explaining as Miya returned) was in finding enough people to take a bath!

"Zeera won't like the conditions," Svetz told Miya.

"She'll be pissed if we don't invite her. Won't she?"

"Sure."

The lock on the bathroom was a guard program. They typed in an appointment, then went looking for a quorum.

They found Zeera and Ra Chen on cots in the sleep area. Ra Chen was snoring like a machine with a bad bearing. Zeera was awake. "Too hungry to sleep anymore," she said. "What's up?"

Svetz tried to explain what was going on. "The guard program isn't corruptible, or else I don't know the codes. There's a big dou-

ble door. It won't let in less than eight or more than twelve. One
tub, lots of towels, and a sonic for cleaning those."

"They're short of water," Zeera said.

"We noticed. Are you in?"

"I'm in." Zeera sounded tired. "I'd bathe with Elephant. I'd
bathe with Gila Monster. Futz, why not, he could dry me with his
breath. So I guess I'll bathe with you two."

Hillary Weng-Fa and Zat Forsman were loose, or else they took
pity on three bewildered time travelers, and they brought three
strangers. Eight was enough.

The bathroom was roomy. The tub was luxurious, finely carved
and ergonomically shaped, equipped with water jets and bubbles.
But it wasn't big.

Eight bathers sudsed each other before they took turns enter-
ing the tub. They rinsed each other, dried each other, and drifted
into communal sex so easily that Svetz never had a chance to be
startled.

Water was to be celebrated.

He was deeply involved with Hillary and trying to think of a
polite way to break loose until he saw Miya with Zat. That was
a relief of sorts. Sometime during all this he looked at Zeera—
up near the ceiling where the sauna heating was, laughing
down at them, naked as he had never seen her, dark and gaunt
as a wraith.

Zeera called down, "How important is Horse?"

Horse? "Why?"

"Svetz, even your weird fantasy theories don't claim that our
unique horned horse needs a virgin attendant *in 1109 AE*."

She'd been reading the old stories. "You're right. So?"

She said, *"Mart!"*

Mart Torgeson, a total stranger until today, was lolling in the
tub. He looked up brightly. "Change your mind? Azeera, I've been
chasing you so long—"

Azeera?

"And now you think it's going to be easy?" Zeera slid into the
tiny tub and whispered in his ear, and he jumped. And accepted
the challenge.

Svetz watched in awe and unease. *Zeera must think that the end of the world is coming.*

Most of them needed the tub again after all that activity. The water was *black*. They'd certainly burned up an hour and a half when a tech poked his head in and called, "If you're a time traveler, you're wanted."

They'd finished loading and programming the large X-cage. Willy Gorky and Wilt Miller waited. Willy said, "We've tagged Wilt to go back for the refugees on the tree, but we also want to send someone who's talked to a Martian. Zeera, you got some sleep, didn't you? If you're up to it—"

Zeera breezed past Svetz and Miya. "I'm in, Boss."

"Look it over. *All* of you. We may have missed something. We launch in ten minutes."

Wilt Miller, with his ruddy skin, might pass for a red Martian if he'd dyed his hair black and had cosmetic surgery to soften his jaw. Maybe that was why the Heads had chosen him.

Ra Chen came to join them.

Zeera and Wilt climbed into pressure suits and entered. They were lost inside the volume of the large X-cage. It would run on remote control from the small cage, but there was also a chair and horseshoe of controls. Zeera took the chair. Wilt set some fixpoints and anchored himself to them. Svetz closed the hatch on them and stepped back.

The sphere faded in an instant. The extension arm behind it faded away in a direction no human eye could follow. Now only instruments could record its progress toward the past.

Svetz was inclined to monitor.

He was thwarted. Ra Chen said, "Drown me! Willy, where are you going to put them?"

"Sir, I have men working on a cage in the Bestiary."

"Ah. Good. Willy, I'll take care of the mission here. Time is my turf, Mars is yours. Take Svetz and Miya along and look over that cage! Someone might have missed something."

They walked toward the entrance with Willy Gorky. "Hang on a second," Svetz said, and looked for the water dispenser.

There were the tables, left of the Armory, but where—? "Willy, I'm lost. Where's the water dispenser?"

"The what? Come on, Svetz, you're not any thirstier than anyone else."

38

Once there must have been a thousand kinds of cactus. Svetz hadn't known that, but he couldn't doubt it while surrounded by scores of surviving varieties. It bothered them that many of them seemed to be dying.

Miya whispered, "Hanny, the chairs and tables were there, but there's *nothing* between the Armory door and the Pit. What happened to the drinks dispenser?"

"I thought it was over. I thought we could adapt. The world. Our species," Svetz said. "All we had to do was wait."

"The drinks dispenser?"

Willy had left them behind. He waited impatiently at the bridge that led through the World Globe. He didn't look that strong, that energetic, until Svetz looked at Miya and then down at himself. The flesh hung on their bones. Their stomachs bulged with starvation.

He asked, "Willy, what happened to Victor's brother?"

"Waldemar? I liked him, Svetz. I tried to teach him about the stars. He died in childhood," Willy said, and coughed. "Lung troubles." And Willy led them into the World Globe.

Miya stopped in the middle. Svetz stopped too. There was no need to speak.

Again it was as if the skin of a world had been inverted, and they stood at the center. But this world was not their own. The oceans were small blue patches on a world gone mostly red. The continental shelves were dry land. A blue worm wriggled the length of the valley that had been the Mediterranean Sea.

Willy turned back. Misunderstanding, he pointed out a ridge

that stood up from what had been the seabed of the Atlantic Ocean. "Are you familiar with Atlantis? Some saltland farmers found the ruins in Waldemar Four's time. On your time line—"

"We didn't have technology to look that deep," Miya told him.

"Well, come on." Willy forged ahead.

Miya lingered. "Hanny, did you see? They've got canals."

Blue threads wriggled over the Earth. The largest followed the old rivers and the beds of the Baltic, Black, Caspian, and Red Seas, and the sites of the Great Lakes; but rectilinear networks branched out from tiny cubistic pumping stations on the old natural curves. Cities crowded around the remaining seas, hundreds of klicks below what had been coastlines.

Antarctica was a diminished ice cap on a greatly expanded continent. Highways wide enough to see from orbit led across dry seabeds to Australia, Africa, South America. Svetz pictured trucks as big as tanker ships laden with freshwater ice. . . .

They caught up to Willy Gorky near Whale's cage, which was more properly an aquarium. He shared it with crabs and a seaweed forest. Whale held Svetz's eye. *You made us extinct. Now it's your turn.*

"This is why we have to guard the Bestiary," Gorky told them. "Every so often someone tries to break in. All that water! They must think it's fresh, of course, but there's enough fresh water in the Bestiary to . . . to . . ."

Svetz turned around when Willy trailed off. Willy was on the ground. He looked dead.

Svetz said, "These locks are beyond me. Miya—" Miya looked dead too, an angry and desperate ghost. They must all be seconds from death. "Willy? Sir! Do you know a code to get us into the cages?"

Willy stirred. "Cages. Why?"

"We need water!"

"Ra Chen told me some of the codes. Which cage?"

Svetz looked about him. The door to Whale's cage was up a stairway. He didn't want salt water anyway. Snake's head lifted from his coils . . . Horse came to his feet, horn poised for murder . . . Rabbit seemed to be hiding, but Owl, housed in the same cage, watched from an artificial tree branch. Dog—

"Dog."

"Woof. State your name first." Willy's head flopped back.

They picked up Willy, one under each shoulder. Willy didn't weigh much.

Dogs crowded around the door, waiting eagerly to greet them, panting, laughing. They were of various sizes, colors, and breed mixtures. Miya shied back a bit, but Svetz felt no fear. He said, "Hanville Svetz. Woof!"

The double door unlocked and they went in. Three dogs swarmed him, and one was Wrona. Another was sniffing Miya, unsure. They walked Willy inside and set him down.

The air smelled *wet*. You could taste it on your skin: *wet*. A big dish of water stood half full and open to the air.

They scooped water with their hands until their thirst was quieted. Then they dribbled water into Willy's mouth, into his hair, into the collar of his shirt. He smiled and opened his eyes.

Sitting with a dog under each arm, Svetz asked, "Willy, have you any idea what Wrona is doing in *here*?"

"Dogs need water." Willy's voice was a bit slurred. "She has to be protected. What did you think, we'd send her home with you?"

Svetz scratched Wrona's ears. "We'll fix it," he said. She looked up at him in perfect confidence. "Willy, we're dying. Right?"

"We're holding on," Willy said. "The Antarctic ice isn't gone yet."

"But we changed the past, Willy. The change shock is still coming down the line. I thought fifteen hundred years of intense natural selection would have shaped us for the dryness, but it isn't going to be like that. When the time line adjusts, the human race will have been extinct for hundreds of years."

"Svetz . . . what did you *do*?"

"We brought the World Tree to Earth," he said. "It must have sucked up most of the water on Mars already. We busted it loose from Mars. It left a sapling behind in orbit. The sapling must have finished draining Mars. Meanwhile the Hangtree came to Earth and drained us."

"Wouldn't it have come anyway?"

Svetz was jolted. "Miya? Is he right?"

"I don't *know*." Miya was starting to cry. "Of course that's what a Hangtree would want, but . . . it wasn't finished. Didn't have *all* the water. On our time line the Hangtree must have waited too long at Mars. Something happened."

"What?"

"Oh . . . Phobos? I wondered if the Hangtree's trunk could oscillate in a harmonic rhythm with the inner moon's orbit. Every time the moon comes past, the trunk would be off to one side. Hanny, it would be easy to disturb such a system. Close approach from an asteroid, or a solar flare pushing on the mirror sails, or just chaos in action. Leaving Mars, it would have to be dodging *both* moons. But I'm guessing, Hanny. Another possibility—"

"Miya, Svetz," Willy Gorky said, "the question is what to do *now*."

"Chop down the tree," Svetz said.

"*That?*" Willy gestured southeast. Though the World Tree couldn't be seen from Dog's cage, it was there in their minds. To think of destroying such a thing was ludicrous. In Norse myth, Yggdrasil wasn't a part of the Earth. The world of mortals was a part of Yggdrasil.

"Earlier." Stubbornly Svetz went on. "When it first linked up, the trailing root wasn't any thicker than my finger. If only we had a *time machine*!"

Miya said, "Hanny, if you chop through the link, the tree's still in geosynch orbit. It dropped *lots* of anchor groves. It'll just link up again."

Svetz's mind began to run in little panicky circles. *When the Tree reached Earth it was already too late. We have to chop it before then, at Mars. Wait now, we* did *that. It came here. We can't get to Mars anyway, an X-cage won't reach that far, the* Minim *can't lift from Earth.* . . . Wrona's fur under his fingers, the perfect trust in her eyes, were anchors to reality; but whatever reality might be, he was losing it.

Willy said, "Chop off the top?"

Miya said, "Ah."

"Right, then. Chop it with what?"

Svetz said, "Wait. Would that work?" His mental mapping caught up and he said, "Of course it would *work*, you just have to chop off *enough*. Yes!"

"Let's have a look in the Armory," Miya suggested.

That got a quizzical look from Gorky, but Svetz felt he had his balance back. He said, "Of course all of this has to be done at a dead run. What's out there is not much different from current Mars. Too dry for humans."

Wrona held off the other dogs somehow while they drank deeply and splashed their collars and shirts and hair. The dogs didn't much like intruders at their water dish.

Willy asked, "What about the Martians on the tree?"

They looked at each other gravely. When nobody else spoke, Svetz said, "I can't see a way to save them."

Miya nodded. Willy Gorky stood up, a little wobbly, and said. "The small X-cage is set and ready to go. Are we? All right, *go*."

Somebody had brought in a big lifter platform. Good idea—Martians wouldn't be able to walk—but it was unattended. Ra Chen and three techs were all in the Guide Pit. One of the techs was on her back with her knees and head propped up.

Willy told the Armory door, "Willy Gorky, come to the arms of Victor Four."

A massive door opened. Svetz looked at what was inside the Armory. It was evidently a kinder, gentler age—

Willy said, "I don't know what you thought you'd find, Miya. We're ready for riots, and of course we're ready for big animals, but not a major deconstruction project."

—It was also an age in which rioters might invade the Secretary-General's Garden and Bestiary in search of water. The weapons locker held mostly sonic stunners: thirty or more handguns and six two-handed sonic crowd sprayers of a design Svetz had never seen. They looked to be heavily shielded against backstun.

The net sprayer was a bulky two-handed thing. It would tangle an ostrich or an elephant, or hundreds of rioters.

There was Space Bureau pressure suit armor for half a dozen. It too might double as riot gear.

There was nothing like the blasters they'd had aboard the *Minim*.

Svetz was used to a needle rifle. He took one. Miya and Gorky looked at him oddly, so he put it back.

And now he was right out of ideas.

"Incoming," Ra Chen called.

Routine announcement, but he wanted help. Svetz saw why. Another tech had passed out, leaving only Hillary Weng-Fa and Ra Chen himself.

Svetz slid into the Pit.

Nothing in the displays looked urgent. The large X-cage was being reeled in, passing minus two hundred AE, minus eighty, plus ten . . . Out on the floor, the extension arm faded a meter from the wall. At first glance you might mistake the end for a hologram washed out by sunlight. Keep looking and your eyes would try to . . . try to follow . . . Through long practice Svetz wrenched his eyes away.

Plus two ten. Three hundred.

Willy and Miya were at the Pit. Miya was holding a hand stunner. She said, "Hanny, we don't have anything to cut a Hangtree with."

"I know."

"Now what?"

Six hundred. Seven sixty.

"Man the lifter, Miya. We don't have anyone else. One thing at a time. That's a little fast, Hillary."

Eight thirty. Eight ninety.

"Too fast, Hillary!"

"Yes, but what do I *do*?"

Svetz showed her. The numbers slowed. Telltales showed that

the excess heat was being dealt with. Going . . . where? Not the pond; that was gone. A radiator fin somewhere?

Ten ninety. Eleven hundred.

"Incoming."

Eleven five—

The extension arm was blocked by a ghost, then a solid transparent shell.

A variety of Martians had been plated around the shell. They wore pressure suits as various as their shapes. In the instant the X-cage came home, they all fell toward the Earth's center. Now they were thrashing and trying to pick themselves up where gravity had dropped them. Svetz looked for Wilt and Zeera.

A froglike entity with a pointed face occupied the control chair. Svetz found Zeera and Wilt in a cluster of red Martians. Their hands—futz, they were prisoners! And what was *that* pointing down the axis of the X-cage?

Its size and placement made it hard to see—too big and too foreshortened—but only for that first instant. Under the big equipment bin in the ceiling, a tube of crystal and copper and silver ran nearly the length of the large X-cage. The back end was welded in place. It was a heat ray cannon longer than Whale, and the lens looked straight into the Guide Pit.

Svetz jumped over the wall and ran. They'd left the Armory open. Svetz snatched up a two-handed sonic and ran at the X-cage. He was out of the line of fire, but next to the great glass door, as the doors began to open like flower petals.

All the four- and six-limbed martian shapes were thrashing around trying to get to their feet, or trying to wave blades or long-barreled guns at the door. Bulge-eyed octopoids attended what must be the firing mechanism, which was a sort of cockpit. Svetz had no idea whether a heat ray would fire through the X-cage's door or wall, or reflect. He guessed that they didn't either. They waited.

Miya was on the other side of the opening door, her sonic handgun ready.

A green giant lurched into the bug-eyed cannoneers and sent them sprawling in a tangle of rubber limbs.

Miya forced her hand inside the doors and began spraying sound. Svetz had to wait. One full second, and then he could poke in both arms and the crowd sprayer. He sprayed everything in the way, aiming for the back of the cannon, where the controls seemed to be, and where another green giant was wrestling with the first.

The first must be Thaxir, but it didn't matter. The crowd sprayer was not selective. He sprayed them both, and the two Soft-finger octopoids who wriggled free of the wrestlers and were trying to reach the trigger cockpit. He was inside now, and he waded toward that, holding his aim on the cockpit. Alien hands and blades kept popping up in his face, but nothing around the cannon controls was moving anymore, and now he was there.

Zeera and Wilt had wriggled away from their captors. He fired bursts around them, and around Miya, and nothing else seemed to be moving in the cageful of Martians.

His arms were numb.

These Martians were still conscious, Svetz remembered. They just couldn't move, or answer, so he was talking to himself as he inspected the great weapon.

"All right, now we have a heat ray. How the futz does it work? Cockpit and big attitude jets. Built for free fall. More plasma weapon than laser. Maybe it'll cut the tree. *Maybe*. Futz, I think we can save the Martians! *Willy*—"

Ra Chen and Willy Gorky were in the X-cage. Willy was pulling a red Martian woman out. He'd set the edge of the floater against the doorway. Svetz cried, "Willy, stop!"

"What?"

"Put her back. We can save them. Just leave the Martians where they are."

"But we've *got* them—"

"And we want to *keep* them. We didn't send the large X-cage back far enough in time. Look, Willy, we're going to chop down the tree *before* they were rescued. The only way to *keep* them rescued is to take them back with us, because this time line is going to disappear."

Willy looked a bit sick, but he said, "Got it."

"Leave them in the large X-cage. We have to take that back anyway, because there's no easy way to dismount the cannon—"

Ra Chen said, "It's set for the wrong time. Sixteen AE."

"We'll have to reset it."

"That'll take hours. Svetz, I really don't think we have that long."

"I don't either. And *they* don't." Waving into the X-cage. Earth gravity killed Softfingers quick.

Ra Chen said, "Advise me then, drown you! *Think!*"

The silence was a rustling of Martians. Sonic weapons set muscles twitching at random.

"The small cage is set for the right time," Miya said, "isn't it?"

"Yes?"

"And you can set the large X-cage to meet the small one, can't you, Hanny? It's how you got Whale. Then—"

"Stet, got it, thanks." Ra Chen was on it. "Hillary, you and I can run the X-cages. Zeera, you take the small extension cage back. It's set to drop out where the *Minim*'s FFD disappeared around minus three fifty AE. That's where your team went into Fast Forward and came here. Then—"

Hillary Weng-Fa said, "Wait now, Boss. You're going to *kill everyone in the universe?*"

"You're dying now," Svetz told her. "When we've done our job you'll be restored to health."

"But it won't be me!"

"In a few hours it won't be anyone, Hillary."

"I'll take my chances! *You* think you'll save yourself—"

"Hillary."

"Boss?"

"Most people will be in better shape after we've done this. Millions of people won't be dead anymore. We're all near dead, even if you've got too much courage to admit it."

Nice phrasing, but Hillary Weng-Fa wasn't showing courage. "It won't be *me*! I, I can't help you do this."

"No, of course not. Go home, Hillary. Zeera, you and me. We'll be running two X-cages. We can send the large X-cage back to meet the small X-cage on manual, soon as it's in place. Are you up to it?"

"Certainly."

Hillary cried, "Zeera, you'll disappear along with the rest of this!"

"Willy, you'll take the small X-cage back," Ra Chen continued. "It's set for the right timespace. There are only two things you need to do." He stepped into the small X-cage and pulled Willy after him. "The chair swivels. This whole display on the left is remote controls for the large extension cage. On arrival, you punch *this*. It summons the large X-cage. If we didn't need someone to do that we'd send it empty. Then pull *this* in the middle. That's the go-home. I can't see any way you can get in trouble, and it's a futz of a ride."

"I'm in," Willy said.

"*Now*, Willy."

Willy climbed into the small X-cage. Zeera and Ra Chen took their places in the Pit. Svetz joined them, but he only watched. They were both better at this than he was. Willy watched them all with a look of wary anticipation.

The small X-cage disappeared. The extension arm led off in a direction the eye could not follow.

Ra Chen said, "Hillary, are you still here? Go home. Svetz, Miya, you take the large X-cage. What have I forgotten?"

Svetz said, "Thaxir. Get her apart from the rest before they ball up."

Martians had fallen all around the control chair. Miya found a green giant and swore that she was Thaxir. It took three of them to pull her up the slope of the wall, away from the others.

"What else?"

Miya said, "Pressure suits! Ra Chen, I think that's a plasma weapon. We'll examine it on the way, but we'll have to open the cage to use it. And question some Martians."

Zeera said, "Translators. The net gun and something to cut nets. More sonics. Net the trigger on the cannon and net the Martians and keep them apart, and spray a net over Thaxir. You want to keep them stunned, and you don't want them wriggling loose, and you don't want them to open the door or fire the cannon."

Ra Chen rubbed his temples. "Sounds like a lot. Anything else?"

Miya lifted her sonic handgun and fired. Hillary, reaching into the Armory door, dropped like loose bones.

"That's all I can think of," Miya said.

"Get that stuff and get aboard."

39

Svetz took the control chair. Miya tethered herself with the lines and fixpoints Zeera had abandoned. They watched Ra Chen and Zeera in the Guide Pit until all the colors went to chaos, and gravity shifted to the center of the shell.

A rustling of stunned Martians followed them into the past. Svetz and Miya hung head down. Svetz had done this before, and it didn't seem to bother Miya.

The Martians had all settled into a ball. Miya sprayed a net over them and tethered it to the curve that had been the ceiling. Thaxir hung in a net near her. Miya had already sprayed a fine net over the cannon's firing cockpit.

Every Martian was wearing some kind of pressure envelope. Softfinger, green giant and red Martian pressure suits were no surprise: Svetz had seen them before. The big crabs with their ogre-human faces, and their mock human mounts, wore separate pressure envelopes with sockets to join them. Inflated bubbles with attached bottles held red Martian children, spindly six-limbed dark green children as tall as a man, grinning pointy-faced frogs festooned with tools, tiny ogre crabs and infant crab-mounts. Other such bubbles held animals and plants in what looked like terrariums. Thaxir hadn't mentioned *that*.

The child-bubbles remained closed; but all the adults had opened their helmets or zippers. Earth's post-Industrial air couldn't be good for them, despite the high carbon dioxide content. Svetz asked, "Shall we switch to martian air?"

"I don't want to close my helmet. Did you bring—?"

Svetz held up a pair of clear bags: filter helmets labeled for Mars.

"They act like they're running out of air," he said. "They took enough to board the X-cage and enough more for the children. They must think we still have pre-Industrial air. Or—"

"What?"

"Or they're running out. What if the tree stopped giving them oxygen?"

Miya asked, "Why would it do that?"

"Parasite control? We can ask."

They donned filter helmets. Svetz adjusted the air monitors.

Miya spoke to the elderly green giant. "Is that why you called us, Thaxir?"

Thaxir couldn't answer, assuming this *was* Thaxir. The green of her shell was yellowed. The plates of her face bore a wonderful array of fine, delicate carvings, and an old crack that Svetz's blaster handle might have put there ages ago. She hung, twitching a bit.

Svetz said, "I wish I *really* knew how sonics affect a Martian."

"I'm tired," Miya said. "You?"

"Wiped."

"From the moment we hit the target date, we have to keep going for twenty minutes," Miya said. "That's right, isn't it? Then we can quit. We won or we didn't."

"Right."

"Go easy with the sonics. Don't knock them out again. They'll all want to close their helmets when we open that big door."

She turned back to the green giant. "The Hangtree is killing the Earth. It killed Mars too. We need to chop it down when it's young. I beg you to tell us how this weapon operates."

Thaxir twitched. Not just a tremor: she was trying to speak, and she was amused.

While they waited, Svetz opened the talker. "Ra Chen? Boss?"

"Problems?"

"Smooth as silk."

"Then get off now. Call when you're in place." *Click.*

He hadn't realized. The talker was using up Ra Chen's life span, and Zeera's too. They might have only minutes.

If a Martian got too restless, Miya stunned it on low. The species Svetz could recognize were men and women in equal numbers, a good many elders, a handful of older children. They had come as a colony even if their intent was conquest.

Thaxir was stirring. While Svetz monitored the telltales, Miya talked to her, believing she could hear.

Thaxir mumbled slurred martian gibberish. The UN translator adjusted in seconds. It said, "Wake cannon masters."

"Who?"

"Cannon masters know." They waited. Presently Thaxir said, "Softfingers made the cannon. Don't put Softfingers to sleep."

Martians were stirring.

Miya asked, "Which ones?"

"Softfingers all look alike." *Chuf chuf chuf*—a sound that came from Thaxir's sides, her spiracles. Laughter. Then, "Let them all wake."

The large X-cage moved steadily into the past toward where the small X-cage had popped out. Svetz wasn't needed at the controls. He let himself down on a tether to examine the weapon.

It had to be a weapon, didn't it? Svetz remembered that heat beams from a wok ship diverged more than a laser, and reflected less. Plasma gun! If they fired it inside the closed X-cage, they'd cremate everything in a moment.

Thaxir had said that twenty Softfingers would come. There might have been that many, but they were a tangled mass of tentacles, indistinguishable even by gender. Twenty awake would . . . would what? Try another mutiny?

He brushed a few wakeful Martians with the stunner on low. More and more were waking. Softfingers were stirring too. Svetz cut a hole in the net, pulled a Softfinger out—about his own weight, less than fifty kilograms now—lifted it to the shell and netted it in place. Then another, and another.

Miya was saying, "If the tree dies, Earth lives. If Earth lives, we can make Mars live again. It might take a long time, but we can. Thaxir, do you have a problem with that?"

"Trust me, Miya?"

"I haven't decided. What did you hope to gain at the Institute?"

"Softfingers outnumbered us. Fools we all were, not to bring more of us. They took our weapons. If they have a plan, they did not tell *me*. But many joined them. The promise was of a time machine, with a chance to change old mistakes."

The green Martian was ten times Miya's weight, and she was stirring again. Trust her? Miya had a stunner. So did Svetz.

"Why did you run from us?"

The Martian said, "Long time ago. You and the others told me this much, that your end of time and mine should talk. Told me more, but I believed that much. Then the landing smashed your talker. I knew that my people on the tree could build it again. I could not guess what else we would learn in learning how to do that. I did not know if you would share knowledge.

"I carried out your wish as you told it, but I did it my way. When we are made slave, obligations bind us. But to be slave does not kill our minds. Obligation runs two ways."

Svetz said, "We don't hold intelligent beings as property at all."

"Is that why you let me run?"

"Yes."

"I wondered. I serve you, Miya, and Svetz and Zeera too. You seek to destroy what destroyed my people's world. The scope of your ambition is a madness that excites my awe. The tree was our home, but you say it will destroy us, and I believe you."

"Thaxir? Why?"

"The sap that runs through the veins of the tree holds dissolved oxygen. We sink pipes. Always we have our air that way, and water and sugar too. Galls grow around the ends of the pipes and close them so that more must be drilled. But now the tree learns to close the pipes much faster. Faster every year."

"Can you tell us how to work the cannon?"

"No." *Chuf chuf chuf.*

"Can you tell us which Softfingers are the cannoneers?"

"No. I can tell you some that are not." *Chuf chuf chuf.* "Svetz, one you have chosen is gravid. It makes them clumsy. The cannoneers were not gravid."

Svetz had netted nine Softfingers in an arc around his control desk. It was heavy exercise. The inertial calendar read 160 AE, with no real accuracy, but the X-cage was halfway thence and nothing had burned out. He lowered the gravid Softfinger back to the net; moved her in, chose another—

"Too old. No, not the injured one either."

—Chose another, sprayed the net closed. His captive wrestled with him sluggishly as he moved it into place.

This mode of time travel was much faster than Fast Forward. But Fast Forward would have given them a view! Now ten Softfingers, and Thaxir, wriggled restlessly against a chaotic rainbow.

When would Thaxir ask to be freed?

Miya asked her, "Can you talk to Softfingers?"

"Yes. Miya, I remember how long it took for your device to learn my speech. Best if you let me translate."

"They have their own speech?"

"Yes. But Softfingers will never agree to destroy the tree."

This sounded suspiciously like the end of all their hopes. Svetz climbed back up to where Miya and Thaxir hung. He asked, "What if we make them slaves?"

"None are made slave except by agreement. Any may die if he will not be slave. Any may be silent if he will not speak to a captor. Any may refuse to act. Some are slaved by degrees. Do this, refrain from that, reveal knowledge, give up a weapon, justify details of living style to a lord's servant, bit by bit until free has become slave. It may take centuries or generations. I have seen it again and again," old Thaxir said. "Are you sure none of you are slave?"

Svetz didn't answer, nor did Miya.

"I chose to be your slave. These will not. They will not tell you how to harm the tree."

"We'll have to guess," Svetz said.

"Svetz, will you trust me? Miya?"

"If you have something in mind, see if you can describe it."

Chuf chuf chuf. "I intend a dance of words, too chancy, too variable, too strange to reach through a speaking device into alien minds. If I can make this work, I will make legends, but you must trust me."

"We'll trust you," Miya said. "What do you need from us?"

Thaxir said, "Leave your pressure suit helms thrown back. Move more Softfingers. Do not notice me."

Leathery bug-eyed octopuses, red-skinned humans, insectoid giants, froggy elves, near-headless humanoids and ogre crabs were all stirring in the net.

Thaxir began talking to the nearest Softfingers.

Miya and Svetz moved down the tethers to the wriggling mass of Martians. Most were conscious, and they wanted to talk. The UN translator knew Red Martian and Green Giant and was learning other speech too, and it tried to translate it all in a babble of white noise. Svetz turned his volume down. "Leave it this way," he said to Miya.

"We could get away from this—"

"We can hear everything that goes on. I don't know if Thaxir ever noticed that, but I don't think we want the octopoids to. If they know we can listen, Thaxir may have trouble. You trust her? Why?"

Miya shrugged. "We don't have to, really. Let's see what happens. Maybe Thaxir can get some instructions. We still have to guess if they're right, or else guess how to work these funny controls. Either way, do you feel lucky?" She pointed. "That one."

They extracted a Softfingers. They moved that one and another and netted them.

There was food and water in the storage bin. Not much. They ate ravenously, and talked of the past before they'd met, and watched the Martians.

Their translators were speaking again. Svetz could barely hear. He chose not to raise the volume. The incomplete translation stuttered.

"*—from Earth. Destroyed the sky watch station on Highest Mountain—*"

"*Horror! We are captive to these—?*"

"Think guile, plan revenge. They have not thought to close their pressure envelopes."

"Allies and infants would be left open to the empty. Must they die?"

"Guile. These were shaped by Earth's thick air. Shaped by Mars, we can live longer in the empty. But wait, a word makes them safe." Thaxir lowered her voice further and spoke a single emphatic syllable. The translator gave it as, *"Close your outer skin or burst like a sandgrape, witless child!"*

Miya said, "She told us to leave our suits open. Does she expect to open the door to vacuum?"

"Not without warning, I guess."

"But you can't *lock* the control board, right, Hanny?"

"What for, when I only moved animals?" Svetz had sometimes wondered. Owl had claws to pull and turn knobs and a beak to punch keys.

The light changed. Gravity changed. Martians wailed and peeped and gibbered as their net sagged toward the floor.

Just as matters were becoming interesting, they were back among the conquistadors. Twenty minutes to Ragnarok.

40

Three hundred meters northeast of the anchor grove, a Portuguese army was converging on nothing, becoming braver as it became clear that there was no enemy. The shallow sea showed not a trace of the *Minim* spacecraft that must have disappeared fifteen minutes ago.

Soldiers had finished reloading a cannon and, under the direction of a frantic officer, began inching its aim toward what must have been a puzzling target: a tight cloud of hundreds of human and alien shapes floating high above them, rising out of sight before anyone could quite be sure it was there.

Svetz said, "Futz!"

"What?"

Svetz's thumb was on the direction vector, pushing hard enough to break it. *Up, up, up.* "We should have had Willy go up the tree in the small X-cage! We could have met it there! He's got twenty hours to play with. Wc only havc twenty minutes. Futz!"

The large X-cage ghosted through a layer of cotton-ball clouds and kept rising. Svetz zoomed his mag specs and found a silver stalk rising straight up from the black head of the clustered anchor trees. He'd follow it up.

The man-shape on the stalk was Jack.

A great yellow-green insectile shape was climbing up below him.

Svetz was looking almost straight down along the root to the black tuft. He kept raising the magnification on his mag specs. He was tempted to delay, to see the end of it, but he dared not. The X-cage was rising fast, but it wasn't a rocket: it wasn't accelerating. The climb up the Hangtree was likely to eat most of their allotted time!

Tiny Jack fled from a yellow-green ogre with tusks and too many limbs. He climbed with hysterical strength in the only possible direction: *up.* And he had lost. The monster reached from below and plucked him up in two forward limbs.

Jack's knife slashed twice across the green giant's chest plates. Thaxir ignored it. With exquisite care she turned him around, then transferred Jack to her middle limbs, never losing her grip on the root nor on Jack.

In that position he couldn't reach the monster. He slashed at her pack. Something fell . . . and then young Thaxir set him against the stalk below her. Jack wrapped himself lovingly around the Hangtree root. Some glittering thing from Thaxir's pack was falling, and Jack's knife fell too.

At maximum zoom Svetz still couldn't see anymore. He called to Thaxir, "What *was* that?"

Old Thaxir said, "My windstorm-minor, curse that thief! An heirloom I will never see again."

"Thaxir, you must have been killing yourself climbing in Earth gravity. What did you think you'd find?"

"I expected that my folk would send the lift down as far as it could go. There, Svetz—"

The Hangtree was swollen to tree trunk size. Suddenly there was a silver rail, and a barred box at the bottom, sixty klicks above the Earth.

"Quite a climb."

"A record never to be matched. I was years recovering my strength."

"What if it hadn't been there?"

"It was."

Altitude: 40,000 klicks. The large X-cage was already above geosynchronous orbit. Svetz was staying alongside the tree, so the X-cage, moving at orbital speed, was back in free fall.

Svetz saw activity of some kind on the trunk as it sped past, but nothing flashed at them, nothing impacted. They were rising fast.

. . . And Jack was going home with a golden harp, an alien shape of gold set with jewels, that made an alien song. What would they make of that in ancient Portugal? Golden harp and golden eggs and a bag of golden coins. Doubtless the King of Portugal would take it all . . . kings did that, Svetz thought . . . unless Jack sailed into some foreign port, England maybe, and sold the loot there.

Would he tell his tale? How could he not? His companions would know it by heart before they reached port. They might have trouble describing John's absolute terror of a yellow-green four-armed monster with tusks who stands ten feet tall and swings a sword no man can pick up. As the legend spreads it might describe only a simple giant or ogre . . .

Better phone home!

Svetz activated the talker. "Boss? We are thence."

He heard a soft murmur that might have had words in it.

Creepy. The voice of a quantized, uncertain future. He switched off.

Thaxir spoke Softfinger sounds. The translator said, "See, they trust me." Then she called in green giant speech, apparently addressing another green giant, "Miya, go and look at the cannon!"

That individual's eyes swiveled, then came back, puzzled.

Svetz said, "You go, Miya. I'd better stay at the controls."

Miya held Svetz's eyes but asked Thaxir, "What shall I look for?"

"Look like you do not expect help from any Martian!"

The Hangtree had grown broad as a freeway, even in the stretched and slender form that had crossed interplanetary space to Earth. Svetz tried to keep the X-cage near it without crashing into it. Altitude: 60,000 klicks. A trace of gravity had returned, with a vast Earth overhead. The control chair was inverted.

Miya wedged her head and shoulders into the cannon's cockpit. It was too small for anything human. Svetz was tempted to laugh. She looked very awkward. She pulled and pushed and touched, and if she set something off they'd all be dead. Softfingers and other Martians were paying her considerable attention; two or three Smiths were either shouting instructions or cursing.

The phone rang.

That wasn't the intertemporal talker! It was the remote in the small extension cage. Svetz punched in and said, "Willy?"

"Futz of a ride, *yes!* Hello, Svetz. Are we still on track?"

"No showstoppers yet. Where are you? And why aren't you on your way home?"

"Svetz, I've getting great pictures. I suppose I'm pacing you, but you're too small, I haven't even glimpsed you. If you can bring this off, I want a record. I want to *watch*! If you can't . . . well . . . there won't be anything to go back to."

They talked further. Svetz was glad of the company.

At 90,000 klicks the tree had narrowed as much as it was going to, its diameter no more than a city block. Thirty thousand klicks farther out, he could see how the tree swelled into a knob. It looked like . . . If he could cut into that, would he find an encysted asteroid, swallowed for ballast?

No telling, ever.

He brought the rising X-cage to a stop. Now he had only about four minutes to play with. "Thaxir," he asked, "do you know how to work the cannon?"

Thaxir said, "Yes. Do you know better than to fire it against a closed door?"

Svetz didn't move. "Yes. What now?"

"Wait. Are you armed with your sleep-thing?"

He didn't reach or look. "Yes, both of us. Miya, are you tracking this?"

"Ready, Hanny."

Thaxir shouted a single syllable.

It galvanized the Martians. They began screwing down helmets and zipping zippers and stickstrips on themselves, their elders and children. The translator was saying, "Close your outer skin or burst—" Svetz pulled his own helmet closed and saw Miya do the same. He tapped the icon that would suck away the air in the shell.

A beam of white heat missed his forearm and plunged deep into the controls.

Svetz threw himself backward. A fireball blasted back out of the hole and somehow missed fusing his helmet as it puffed across the diameter of the X-cage. Svetz fired in the direction the beam had come from. Miya was firing too. Their sonics swept the Softfinger gunman and several others.

Elsewhere, another Softfinger loosed itself at Thaxir with a leap that spun it like a buzz saw. Its spin caressed the net-bound Thaxir, and Svetz held his aim and waited—dared not put Thaxir to sleep!—waited, and fired. The pinwheel octopoid spun away, slack and senseless. A knife spun free.

Thaxir lifted herself free of the slashed net. "If you can still open the door," she said, "do it." She closed her helmet.

The gunman's aim had been precise. The heat beam had put a hole in the left branch of the horseshoe control board. That array controlled air composition and pressure, lights, recorded warnings, and of course, the door.

Thaxir joined Miya at the trigger housing. The translator picked up her speech. "I persuaded some among the Softfingers that if they cut me loose, I could fire the cannon while the door was closed. We would die. The Earth would die. The tree would survive to carry the rest of our races to the stars, if we could change the future and survive the tree itself. In any case they would have their vengeance."

In the quantum-randomized future, Ra Chen was dead or never born; but his urgency (*Advise me, Svetz!*) lived on in Svetz's mind. (*Think!*)

"They revealed to me what weapons they still have," Thaxir said. "A knife to free me, a heat gun to ruin your door lock, both swallowed in sealed bags—"

"Swallowed?"

"To be disgorged at need, Miya. I alerted you and trusted your reactions. The rest was up to you."

There was vacuum inside and out. Martians of every description were shouting at each other in silence. The large X-cage had sucked the air back into its tanks.

Good enough. Svetz touched the remote. "Willy!"

Nothing. He remembered to plug the jack into his suit mike. "Willy!"

"How's it going?"

"Willy, you need to use the remote controls to open the door in the large extension cage. Do it now. Right now."

"Hanny, nobody showed me how."

"Don't panic. I've used these myself. Now, right in front of you, you should see . . ." He talked Willy through it. *We are the masters of time* . . .

The door opened like a flower.

More Softfingers had cut themselves free. Svetz shot them with sonics as they moved.

A thread of light burst from the cannon's mouth. It was searing-bright until it impacted the tree four or five klicks away. Then the intensity became intolerable.

Miya and Thaxir seemed to have the cannon under control. A halo of gas and particles surrounded the tree now, illuminating the plasma beam.

The tree tore apart.

The severed end was rising. Sap sprayed into space, boiling and freezing into a vast white plume. Nothing much seemed to be happening to the main body of the tree. "Turn it off," Svetz said into his suit mike.

"Hanny, we don't have instructions for that. Thaxir says that wasn't supposed to be needed."

"Well, if you don't turn it off we can't close the door, and then we can't go home, and the energy buildup will blow the Institute off the map, and us too. But we did it. We won. There will be a future."

The beam went off. "Got it," Miya said.

"Willy, are you still on? Close the door for us. Willy, stop filming and close the door on the large X-cage. Willy!"

The door closed. Willy Gorky said, "Patience is an underrated—" But Svetz pushed the go-home and the voice went away.

41

> PHAETHON n. Class. Myth, *a son of Helios who*
> *borrowed the chariot of the sun for one day and drove it*
> *so dangerously close to earth that Zeus struck him down*
> *with a thunderbolt to save the world from catching fire.*
> —*Random House Dictionary of the English Language*

The main dome was crowded to the teeth. Every face showed triumph . . . until they looked into the large X-cage.

Ra Chen barely flinched, but Svetz caught it. A few techs looked bewildered; a few were frightened; some gaped, then laughed. Of sixty or seventy present, half were wearing United Nations Security uniforms, and they showed no emotion at all.

Body language told Svetz what man was the Secretary-General. He and his guards were off to one side, and Ra Chen with him.

The Secretary-General was no bigger than Svetz. The crown of his head was bald. Otherwise he bore thick brown hair, eyebrows and beard. At sight of a crowd of Martians he started forward, wild with delight.

Security blocked him. Any attack on the SecGen would take Ra Chen too. An attack from the large X-cage would fall upon guards and techs first. The large extension cage had last come here as an act of war, but UN Security didn't know *that*. They were only being prudent.

And of course everyone was waiting for Svetz to open the door.

The noise the Martians were making died a little. They were fainting in Earth's gravity. Svetz and Miya set about cutting the nets.

The small extension cage faded into view. Svetz saw rage flash in Ra Chen's expression, but he covered by moving briskly to help Willy Gorky out.

Willy delayed for a moment at the controls.

The door unfolded like a great flower. *Thank you, Willy!* A door big enough to pass Whale allowed a dozen techs to swarm in. They came out carrying Martians.

Ra Chen must have assembled every lifter platform in the UN Research Complex. As quickly as they could, they got the Martians into low gravity, stripping them of weapons where they could. No doubt the Softfingers kept a few swallowed. Svetz and Miya helped, trying to keep species separate, setting infants in bubbles among their own folk. The techs didn't seem to think that was important, but it might be worth Thaxir's life.

The Secretary-General was bubbling with questions. The guards wouldn't let him near the Martians yet, so he made do with the Heads. Willy Gorky was just a bit diffident with the SecGen *and* Ra Chen. Ra Chen was cordial and brisk and gave way to both.

My time line, and it's really Waldemar the Eleventh, Svetz decided, *but the World Tree's Willy Gorky.* A dominance dance between the two Heads should be fun to watch, given that they *each* thought they'd lost to the other. Now Willy was pulling heavy golden spheres from a pouch and handing them ceremoniously to the Secretary-General. UN guards intercepted the seeds.

The last of the Martians, a six-generation family of reds, was being floated away.

Ra Chen eased free of the others. "Excellent work, Svetz! Those seeds will look really good in the Palace. Maybe we can grow a few trees." Ra Chen's grip closed like iron on Svetz's forearm. "We need to talk."

"Set guards for Thaxir, Boss," Svetz murmured, smiling. He was being pulled outside, through the front. "Guard the Martians. They'll kill our source if we just turn them loose in a Vivarium cage. Thaxir's one of the older green—"

"First things first, Svetz. How did you and Willy Gorky change places? And why?"

"What?"

The wonderful, elaborate drinks dispenser was back. Ra Chen pulled him past it and outside.

"We sent you back in the small X-cage. We needed to know if any of the Martians were setting us up for something. Willy Gorky just *had* to go back and rescue sixty Martians himself. His first trip through time, and nobody had the least idea what these creatures really have in mind. If anything happens to the Head of Sky Domains, we're finished," Ra Chen said. "And now you're back, but the Head of Sky Domains is in the small X-cage and you're in the big one! Svetz, is this another one of *those*?"

The reflecting pool was back too.

Svetz said, "Changes in the past. Other time lines. Those, *yes*, Boss, but let's just deal with the martian refugees first. Then I've got a great story and Willy's got visual aids to back us up."

The severed treetop rose like a comet, spraying a tremendous frosty comet-tail lit by raw sunlight. Long after the treetop itself was out of view, the trail of frost continued to expand.

Gorky had most of the tree in view in a wraparound shot that filled the display wall. Svetz could see it all.

At first the tree seemed unchanged. But its center of mass was below geosynchronous orbit. Left to itself it would have moved in a closer, faster orbit; but it couldn't. It was anchored. The mass pulled ahead of the rotating Earth, and the Earth pulled back, slowing it, lowering its orbit farther.

The bottom of the tree, the root, was still anchored to the earth more than an hour after Miya and Thaxir had severed the top. The Tree tilted forward, arcing toward horizontal. Then, deep in the bedrock of Brazil, roots ripped free. The tree pulled away, carrying away a disintegrating black clot of anchor grove.

Now tidal forces began to swing it back to vertical. The lower end dropped until the Hangtree's torn bottom was ripping through the atmosphere, blazing like the sun.

The bottom of the tree was a meteor trailing flame and smoke all around the Earth. Prairies and forests blazed in its wake, a noose of fire circling the planet. Above the atmosphere, Yggdrasil's mass pulled it along. The tree was burning at the bottom as it sank toward the Earth.

"The legend of Phaeton," Miya breathed.

"No, that happened way earlier," said Svetz.

"Why, Hanny, don't you believe in time travel?"

Futz.

No wonder the medieval world was afraid of comets. If such a mass had fallen all at once, at or near orbital speed . . . well, legends would have told that tale too.

Gorky, Ra Chen and the Secretary-General engaged in intense discussion within a horseshoe of guards.

They summoned Miya. Talk continued.

A UN guard went for refreshments, not to the ITR dispenser but to the limousines. They summoned Zeera. Svetz bought and ate a carton of dole yeast, then another.

They summoned Svetz.

He told the tale as if they hadn't heard it twice already. Prompted, he spoke of Martians left behind, the furred High Ones, the big birds who wore tool belts.

The Secretary-General didn't leave until midnight.

Then Svetz dared to eat what had been sitting untouched. He and Miya snatched food they didn't bother to identify, in a scrambling of hands. They fed each other bits of anything interesting, laughing at each other's greed, and belatedly thought to bring Zeera into the circle. But Zeera shied away.

Ra Chen was talking genially to Gorky. "You had your Beanstalk. You had the solar system. Wasn't as useful as you thought, was it, Head?"

"Ra Chen, I still have it. Hillary?—drown me, they've all gone home! I don't blame them." Willy raised his voice. "Who knows how to work the holo projector? I want just that first bit back."

"I can do that," Miya said.

Light blazed fiercely from the World Tree. Fog haloed the heat ray, and then the top of the World Tree ripped free. Thirty thousand klicks of severed end rose at escape velocity. Sap sprayed at the stars—

And again. Miya had looped the record. "This is what I meant," Willy Gorky said excitedly, and pointed with his laser. A red dot traced the flow of fluid and steam. "I need to show this to the Martians, *all* the Martians—"

"Tomorrow, Willy," Ra Chen said gently.

Willy sagged. This was the World Tree's Willy Gorky, half starved in a starving world, the Willy Gorky whose Bureau of the Sky Domains had been eaten by the Institute for Temporal Research. In this spacetime he was master, but he was tired.

"Go home," he said, "find beds. Tomorrow. If only I had a time machine!"

They set the holo projector up in the Vivarium, outside the cage that held five martian civilizations in miniature. Martians watched them, and discussed what they were seeing.

There were sound pickups in the Mars cage, as in all the cages—the sounds an animal made might be of interest—but no speakers. Techs linked speakers to UN translators programmed with what Svetz's translator had learned of Mars. Wilt Miller mounted them inside the Mars cage. Five varieties of Martian watched them do it.

As soon as they were out, the froglike Martians—the Smiths— swarmed over the devices and took them apart before Gorky could begin speaking.

Willy Gorky waited with amazing patience. They waited with

Willy, until Zeera lost patience and went four cages down to tend Horse. The rest stayed.

Horse seemed glad of the attention.

In present time, one need not credit a children's story.

But Svetz knew that they had lost the Zeera of the baths, the Zeera who turned a conquistador into gold, *that* Zeera who had stayed with *that* Ra Chen in another time line so that they could destroy it. *That* Zeera would not be petting Horse.

When the Smiths had reassembled the translators, Willy Gorky told them, "I can restore your planet."

No Martian spoke. Svetz's eye found Thaxir among the green giants. He was relieved: she sat dignified and straight among her kin.

Willy said, "What I need from you is transportation. I know you didn't bring any kind of spacecraft, but you *know* things. I want to know how your wok ships work. I need to know how to make a gas lighter than nothing. Anything that helps me reach the planets is worth having.

"Think about it. Tonight I will show you *how*."

Daylight would have washed out Willy Gorky's hologram recordings. They had to wait for night.

Zeera still had seeds: heavy golden spheres hardened against reentry. It took jeweler's equipment to open them. Inside they were built like pomes. The laboratory's first attempt at a DNA scan failed. It must be some other genetic molecule that reproduced a Beanstalk anchor tree. They'd find it.

Willy worked with the Bureau of the Sky Domains' astronomers. They knew what to look for now. The world's telescopes were turned on Europa. Data began flowing back.

The Vivarium, nightfall:

The severed ends of the World Tree came apart, trailing oceans of water in a wide frosty comet tail. The blood of the tree sprayed across the sky.

Willy Gorky spoke for the translators in the Martians' housing. "It goes on and on. Gigatons of sap, mostly water infused with oxygen and some interesting nutrients—I zapped it with a laser to get a spectroanalysis—"

An elderly Smith had come forward. "Our world's water," he said. "Other species stayed to share the fate of our dying world. The tree was our destiny."

Willy didn't miss a beat. "Our fate too, but we sidestepped. Your world's water, yes. Now I'll show you how to get it back."

And he showed them.

A sapling left at Mars fifteen hundred years ago had sucked away that world's remaining life. What it sensed of its parent's fate was unknowable. How do trees communicate? But on *this* time line, the Hangtree had been chopped down and killed at Earth.

When its sapling child had as much water as Mars had to give, it had moved, still feeble, *outward*.

The sapling was at Europa. Given that the ancient Mariner probe had found no Hangtree at Mars, it must have been at Europa for at least a thousand years.

In the holo view it was a mere silver thread, as thin as imagination, but it was long. Its center of mass stood well out from Europa, in the stable L2 point made by Europa and Jupiter.

"Did you learn *anything* about guiding the Hangtree?" Willy looked hopefully up at the rows of alien faces. "Europa is a water ocean under a shell of ice. That thing is sucking it up. All we need to do is guide it back to Mars. Then chop away the root and bleed its veins dry, let the sap drain into the old canals and ocean beds. Oceans of water. Sugar and nutrients for fertilizer. You'll have a world again."

Willy's voice rang. "But we can't get there from here. Earth's gravity is greater, our space program is a pitiable thing, our rockets can barely lift themselves. But with those and your antigravity dirigibles or your wok ships to lift them free of Earth's gravity, we can get there. We can get anywhere.

"We'll make Mars live again. Will you help me?"

He had them. Without being able to read alien faces, Svetz still knew: he had them.

*   *   *

"It's not what I really wanted," Willy Gorky admitted later. "It's a thousand years too late. I wanted to take the planets while the Earth was still rich."

Ra Chen had formed his attitude long ago. *Thou shalt not change the past. Not by accident, not deliberately. Disaster and chaos will result.*

He said, "Willy, you'd have roughly ten productive years if you marooned yourself in the twentieth century. No conspicuous technology means no modern medicine and no UN translators. We could train you in their language, but you'll still have an accent nobody can define—"

"Like Werner Von Braun!" Willy said.

"Whatever. And now you think you can talk an insular and defensive agency of an ancient government into doing your will? And still compete with any other branch that might want their funding?"

Willy Gorky didn't answer.

"Willy, it's just a fantasy."

"I know that, Ra Chen. We'll *still* have the stars. The past is dead. I'll build from here. From now."

THE REFERENCE DIRECTOR SPEAKS:

The humanoids and green giants and their cultures, guns and swords and negative-gravity dirigibles, all derive from Edgar Rice Burroughs, except for the houses and stoves, which belong to Ray Bradbury, and those slender towers that probably belong to Robert Heinlein more than anyone. The crabs, and the headless near-humanoid servants that carry them, are also from Burroughs.

Schiapareli and Lowell and a host of other astronomers of the early twentieth century saw and described the canals.

The flightless bird (Tweel) is from Stanley Weinbaum's "A Martian Odyssey." So is the pyramid builder.

Of the C. S. Lewis Martians, Fishers and High Folk (observers, called High Folk because they live on the heights, turf nobody else wants) and Smiths, only the Smiths left Mars for the tree. They liked the challenge. Yellow-faced, hairless, pointed, shabby-looking, built like a frog.

Lewis' *eldils* are missing, and so are Heinlein's Martians and many others, because they were more powerful than the author.

The sailcar came from Flash Gordon Sunday comics.

The Hangtree or Beanstalk, in its earliest form, was the creation of a schoolteacher who served the Czar. A host of fine minds have elaborated the original concept of an orbital tether.

The tentacled astronomers derive (loosely) from H. G. Wells, *The War of the Worlds*. One appeared *as* an astronomer in "Old Faithful," by Gallun. Their lens-shaped craft were a familiar sight over the Midwest in the 1950s.

The Tanker module—which carries a nuclear reactor and six tonnes of liquid hydrogen, to make ninety-six tonnes of methane and liquid oxygen from the martian atmosphere, was evolved from plans outlined in *Mars Direct*, by Robert Zubrin.

Ole Romer, Danish astronomer, was brought to France by Christiaen Huygens. He invented the transit instrument. He measured the speed of light using eclipses of Jupiter and the timing of Jovian lunar orbits. On the Hangtree time line, he'd have had a telescope and an excellent view of Yggdrasil.

SVETZ'S TIME LINE

The first story of Svetz of the ITR is set in +1100 Atomic Era (AE) and −750 AE. Horse was intended for the SecGen's twenty-eighth birthday.

The picture book of animals dates, from 10 AE = 1955.

1108 AE June: death of the Secretary-General, Waldemar the Tenth.

+1108 AE November: back in time to

−550 AE = +1395 AD: missiles to Mars carrying probes. Interrupt takes them to

−545 AE: retrieve data, return to

+1108 AE November. Process data. First sight of the Mars Beanstalk. Mount the second expedition to

−545AE=+1400 AD: send new orders to the Mars probes. Interrupt takes the X-cage to

−543AE=+1402 AD: Collect the results. Return to

+1108 AE November. Involve the SecGen. Mount third expedition.

−543 AE=+1402 AD: the rescue aspect is abandoned in the search for skyhook tree seeds.

Ten months pass in the present, and the Coronation takes place without announcements regarding Mars, while *Minim* spacecraft and support systems are prepared and Zeera is trained as pilot. Subsequent talker contact is with

+1109 AE September.

−541 AE=+1404 AD: arrival at Mars using Fast Forward. Exploration of Mars and the Beanstalk/ Hangtree ends with the *Minim* moored to the Mars Beanstalk in flight. Engage Fast Forward . . .

−375 AE=+1570 AD: the Mars Beanstalk settles into Earth orbit. The *Minim* lands in northern Brazil.

−375 to −374 AE: Svetz and company witness the

Portuguese encroachment in jumps, using the FFD. Everything subsequent is seen in longer jumps.

−48 AE = +1897 AD: Svetz hits the interrupt because something massive buzzes him in the X-cage. He's picked up some serious energy discharges: pods making hard landings, dropping from the tree: the H. G. Wells invasion.

~+10 AE = ~+1955 AD: Softfinger ships over the American Midwest.

+1109 AE October: HOME. Successful mission. But the tree is on the horizon, grown huge. Everybody is getting very thirsty, very desiccated. RETURN TO

−374 AE=+1572 AD: Chop down the tree. Brave the havoc and go home to +1109 AE.

THE FLIGHT OF THE HORSE

The year was 750AA (AnteAtomic) or 1200 AD (Anno Domini), approximately. Hanville Svetz stepped out of the extension cage and looked about him.

To Svetz the atomic bomb was eleven hundred years old and the horse was a thousand years dead. It was his first trip into the past. His training didn't count; it had not included actual time travel, which cost several million commercials a shot. Svetz was groggy from the peculiar gravitational side effects of time travel. He was high on pre–Industrial Age air, and drunk on his own sense of destiny; while at the same time he was not really convinced that he had *gone* anywhere. Or anywhen. Trade joke.

He was not carrying the anaesthetic rifle. He had come to get a horse; he had not expected to meet one at the door. How big was a horse? Where were horses found? Consider what the Institute had had to go on: a few pictures in a salvaged children's book, and an old legend, not to be trusted, that the horse had once been used as a kind of animated vehicle!

In an empty land beneath an overcast sky, Svetz braced himself with one hand on the curved flank of the extension cage. His head was spinning. It took him several seconds to realize that he was looking at a horse.

It stood fifteen yards away, regarding Svetz with large intelligent brown eyes. It was much larger than he had expected. Further, the horse in the picture book had had a glossy brown pelt with a short mane, while the beast now facing Svetz was pure white, with a mane that flowed like a woman's long hair. There were other differences . . . but no matter, the beast matched the book too well to be anything but a horse.

To Svetz it seemed that the horse watched him, waited for him to realize what was happening. Then, while Svetz wasted more time wondering why he wasn't holding a rifle, the horse laughed, turned, and departed. It disappeared with astonishing speed.

Svetz began to shiver. Nobody had warned him that the horse might have been sentient! Yet the beast's mocking laugh had sounded far too human.

Now he knew. He was deep, deep in the past.

Not even the horse was as convincing as the emptiness the horse had left behind. No reaching apartment towers clawed the horizon. No contrails scratched the sky. The world was trees and flowers and rolling grassland, innocent of men.

The silence—It was as if Svetz had gone deaf. He had heard no sound since the laughter of the horse. In the year 1100 Post-Atomic, such silence could have been found nowhere on Earth. Listening, Svetz knew at last that he had reached the British Isles before the coming of civilization. He had traveled in time.

The extension cage was the part of the time machine that did the traveling. It had its own air supply, and needed it while being pushed through time. But not here. Not before civilization's dawn; not when the air had never been polluted by fission wastes and the combustion of coal, hydrocarbons, tobaccos, wood, et al.

Now, retreating in panic from that world of the past to the world of the extension cage, Svetz nonetheless left the door open behind him.

He felt better inside the cage. Outside was an unexplored planet, made dangerous by ignorance. Inside the cage it was no different from a training mission. Svetz had spent hundreds of hours in a detailed mockup of this cage, with a computer running the dials. There had even been artificial gravity to simulate the peculiar side effects of motion in time.

By now the horse would have escaped. But he now knew its size, and he knew there were horses in the area. To business, then . . .

Svetz took the anaesthetic rifle from where it was clamped to the wall. He loaded it with what he guessed was the right size of soluble crystalline anaesthetic needle. The box held several different sizes, the smallest of which would knock a shrew harmlessly unconscious, the largest of which would do the same for an elephant. He slung the rifle and stood up.

The world turned gray. Svetz caught a wall clamp to stop himself from falling.

The cage had stopped moving twenty minutes ago. He shouldn't still be dizzy!—But it had been a long trip. Never before had the Institute for Temporal Research pushed a cage beyond zero PA. A long trip and a strange one, with gravity pulling Svetz's mass uniformly toward Svetz's navel . . .

When his head cleared, he turned to where other equipment was clamped to a wall.

The flight stick was a lift field generator and power source built into five feet of pole, with a control ring at one end, a brush discharge at the other, and a bucket seat and seat belt in the middle. Compact even for Svetz's age, the flight stick was a spinoff from the spaceflight industries.

But it still weighed thirty pounds with the motor off. Getting it out of the clamps took all his strength. Svetz felt queasy, very queasy.

He bent to pick up the flight stick, and abruptly realized that he was about to faint.

He hit the door button and fainted.

*   *   *

"We don't know where on Earth you'll wind up," Ra Chen had told him. Ra Chen was the Director of the Institute for Temporal Research, a large round man with gross, exaggerated features and a permanent air of disapproval. "That's because we can't focus on a particular time of day—or on a particular year, for that matter. You won't appear underground or inside anything because of energy considerations. If you come out a thousand feet in the air, the cage won't fall; it'll settle slowly, using up energy with a profligate disregard for our budget . . ."

And Svetz had dreamed that night, vividly. Over and over his extension cage appeared inside solid rock, exploded with a roar and a blinding flash.

"Officially the horse is for the Bureau of History," Ra Chen had said. "In practice it's for the Secretary-General, for his twenty-eight birthday. Mentally he's about six years old, you know. The royal family's getting a bit inbred these days. We managed to send him a picture book we picked up in 130 PA, and now the lad wants a horse . . ."

Svetz had seen himself being shot for treason, for the crime of listening to such talk.

". . . Otherwise we'd never have gotten the appropriation for this trip. It's in a good cause. We'll do some cloning from the horse before we send the original to the UN. Then—well, genes are a code, and codes can be broken. Get us a male, and we'll make all the horses anyone could want."

But why would anyone want even one horse? Svetz had studied a computer duplicate of the child's picture book that an agent had pulled from a ruined house a thousand years ago. The horse did not impress him.

Ra Chen, however, terrified him.

"We've never sent anyone this far back," Ra Chen had told him the night before the mission, when it was too late to back out with honor. "Keep that in mind. If something goes wrong, don't count on the rule book. Don't count on your instruments. Use your head. Your head, Svetz. Gods know it's little enough to depend on . . ."

Svetz had not slept in the hours before departure.

"You're scared stiff," Ra Chen had commented just before Svetz entered the extension cage. "And you can hide it, Svetz. I think I'm the only one who's noticed. That's why I picked you, because you can be terrified and go ahead anyway. Don't come back without a horse . . ."

The Director's voice grew louder. "Not without a horse, Svetz. Your *head*, Svetz, your HEAD . . ."

Svetz sat up convulsively. The air! Slow death if he didn't close the door! But the door was closed, and Svetz was sitting on the floor holding his head, which hurt.

The air system had been transplanted intact, complete with dials, from a martian sandboat. The dials read normally, of course, since the cage was sealed.

Svetz nerved himself to open the door. As the sweet, rich air of twelfth-century Britain rushed in, Svetz held his breath and watched the dials change. Presently he closed the door and waited, sweating, while the air system replaced the heady poison with its own safe, breathable mixture.

When next he left the extension cage, carrying the flight stick, Svetz was wearing another spinoff from the interstellar exploration industries. It was a balloon, and he wore it over his head. It was also a selectively permeable membrane, intended to pass certain gasses in and others out, to make a breathing-air mixture inside.

It was nearly invisible except at the rim. There, where light was refracted most severely, the balloon showed as a narrow golden circle enclosing Svetz's head. The effect was not unlike a halo as shown in medieval paintings. But Svetz didn't know about medieval paintings.

He wore also a simple white robe, undecorated, constricted at the waist, otherwise falling in loose folds. The Institute thought that such a garment was least likely to violate taboos of sex or custom. The trade kit dangled loose from his sash: a heat-and-pressure gadget, a pouch of corundum, small phials of additives for color.

Lastly he wore a hurt and baffled look. How was it that he could not breathe the clean air of his own past?

The air of the cage was the air of Svetz's time, and was nearly four percent carbon dioxide. The air of 750 AnteAtomic held barely a tenth of that. Man was a rare animal here and now. He had breathed little air, he had destroyed few green forests, he had burnt scant fuel since the dawn of time.

But industrial civilization meant combustion. Combustion meant carbon dioxide thickening in the atmosphere many times faster than the green plants could turn it back to oxygen. Svetz was at the far end of two thousand years of adaptation to air rich in CO_2.

It takes a concentration of carbon dioxide to trigger the autonomic nerves in the lymph glands in a man's left armpit. Svetz had fainted because he wasn't breathing.

So now he wore a balloon, and felt rejected.

He straddled the flight stick and twisted the control knob on the fore end. The stick lifted under him, and he wriggled into place on the bucket seat. He twisted the knob further.

He drifted upward like a toy balloon.

He floated over a lovely land, green and untenanted, beneath a pearl-gray sky empty of contrails. Presently he found a crumbling wall. He turned to follow it.

He would follow the wall until he found a settlement. If the old legend was true—and, Svetz reflected, the horse had certainly been *big* enough to drag a vehicle—then he would find horses wherever he found men.

Presently it became obvious that a road ran along the wall. There the dirt was flat and bare and consistently wide enough for a walking man; whereas elsewhere the land rose and dipped and tilted. Hard dirt did not a freeway make; but Svetz got the point.

He followed the road, floating at a height of ten meters.

There was a man in worn brown garments. Hooded and barefoot, he walked the road with patient exhaustion, propping himself with a staff. His back was to Svetz.

Svetz thought to dip toward him to ask concerning horses. He refrained. With no way to know where the cage would alight, he had learned no ancient languages at all.

He thought of the trade kit he carried, intended not for communication, but instead of communication. It had never been field-tested. In any case it was not for casual encounters. The pouch of corundum was too small.

Svetz heard a yell from below. He looked down in time to see the man in brown running like the wind, his staff forgotten, his fatigue likewise.

"Something scared him," Svetz decided. But he could see nothing fearful. Something small but deadly, then.

The Institute estimated that man had exterminated more than a thousand species of mammal and bird and insect—some casually, some with malice—between now and the distant present. In this time and place there was no telling what might be a threat. Svetz shuddered. The brown man with the hairy face might well have run from a stinging thing destined to kill Hanville Svetz.

Impatiently Svetz upped the speed of his flight stick. The mission was taking far too long. Who would have guessed that centers of population would have been so far apart?

Half an hour later, shielded from the wind by a paraboloid force field, Svetz was streaking down the road at sixty miles per hour.

His luck had been incredibly bad. Wherever he had chanced across a human being, that person had been just leaving the vicinity. And he had found no centers of population.

Once he had noticed an unnatural stone outcropping high on a hill. No law of geology known to Svetz could have produced such an angular, flat-sided monstrosity. Curious, he had circled above it—and had abruptly realized that the thing was hollow, riddled with rectangular holes.

A dwelling for men? He didn't want to believe it. Living within the hollows of such a thing would be like living underground. But men tend to build at right angles, and this thing was *all* right angles.

Below the hollowed stone structure were rounded, hairy-looking hummocks of dried grass, each with a man-sized door. Obviously they must be nests for very large insects. Svetz had left that place quickly.

The road rounded a swelling green hill ahead of him. Svetz followed, slowing.

A hilltop spring sent a stream bubbling downhill to break the road. Something large was drinking at the stream.

Svetz jerked to a stop in midair. *Open water: deadly poison.* He would have been hard put to say which had startled him more: the horse, or the fact that it had just committed suicide.

The horse looked up and saw him.

It was the same horse. White as milk, with a flowing abundance of snowy mane and tail, it almost had to be the horse that had laughed at Svetz and run. Svetz recognized the malignance in its eyes, in the moment before it turned its back.

But how could it have arrived so fast?

Svetz was reaching for the gun when the situation turned upside down.

The girl was young, surely no more than sixteen. Her hair was long and dark and plaited in complex fashion. Her dress, of strangely stiff blue fabric, reached from her neck to her ankles. She was seated in the shadow of a tree, on dark cloth spread over the dark earth. Svetz had not noticed her, might never have noticed her . . .

But the horse walked up to her, folded its legs in alternate pairs, and laid its ferocious head in her lap.

The girl had not yet seen Svetz.

The horse obviously belonged to the girl. He could not simply shoot it and take it. It would have to be purchased . . . somehow.

He needed time to think! And there was no time, for the girl might look up at any moment. Baleful brown eyes watched him as he dithered . . .

He dared waste no more time searching the countryside for a wild horse. There was an uncertainty, a Finagle factor in the math of time travel. It manifested itself as an uncertainty in the energy of a returning extension cage, and it increased with time. Let Svetz linger too long, and he could be roasted alive in the returning cage.

Moreover, the horse had drunk open water. It would die, and

soon, unless Svetz could return it to 1100 PostAtomic. Thus the beast's removal from this time could not change the history of Svetz's own world. It was a good choice . . . if he could conquer his fear of the beast.

The horse was tame. Young and slight as she was, the girl had no trouble controlling it. What was there to fear?

But there was its natural weaponry . . . of which Ra Chen's treacherous picture book had shown no sign. Svetz surmised that later generations routinely removed it before the animals were old enough to be dangerous. He should have come a few centuries later . . .

And there was the look in its eye. The horse hated Svetz, and it knew Svetz was afraid.

Could he shoot it from ambush?

No. The girl would worry if her pet collapsed without reason. She would be unable to concentrate on what Svetz was trying to tell her.

He would have to work with the animal watching him. If the girl couldn't control it—or if he lost her trust—Svetz had little doubt that the horse would kill him.

The horse looked up as Svetz approached, but made no other move. The girl watched too, her eyes round with wonder. She called something that must have been a question.

Svetz smiled back and continued his approach. He was a foot above the ground, and gliding at dead slow. Riding the world's only flying machine, he looked impressive as all hell, and knew it.

The girl did not smile back. She watched warily. Svetz was within yards of her when she scrambled to her feet.

He stopped the flight stick at once and let it settle. Smiling placatorily, he removed the heat-and-pressure device from his sash. He moved with care. The girl was on the verge of running.

The trade kit was a pouch of corundum, Al_2O_3, several phials of additives, and the heat-and-pressure gadget. Svetz poured corundum into the chamber, added a dash of chromic oxide, and used the plunger. The cylinder grew warm. Presently Svetz dropped a pigeon's-blood star ruby into his fingers, held it to the sun. It was red as dark blood, with a blazing white six-pointed star.

It was almost too hot to hold.

Stupid! Svetz held his smile rigid. Ra Chen should have warned him! What would she think when she felt the gem's unnatural heat? What trickery would she suspect?

But he had to chance it. The trade kit was all he had.

He bent and rolled the gem to her across the damp ground.

She stooped to pick it up. One hand remained on the horse's neck, calming it. Svetz noticed the rings of yellow metal around her wrist; and he also noticed the dirt.

She held the gem high, looked into its deep red fire.

"Ooooh," she breathed. She smiled at Svetz in wonder and delight. Svetz smiled back, moved two steps nearer, and rolled her a yellow sapphire.

How had he twice chanced on the same horse? Svetz never knew. But he soon knew how it had arrived before him . . .

He had given the girl three gems. He held three more in his hand while he beckoned her onto the flight stick. She shook her head; she would not go. Instead she mounted the animal.

She and the horse, they watched Svetz for his next move.

Svetz capitulated. He had expected the horse to follow the girl while the girl rode behind him on the flight stick. But if they both followed Svetz it would be the same.

The horse stayed to one side and a little behind Svetz's flight stick. It did not seem inconvenienced by the girl's weight. Why should it be? It must have been bred for the task. Svetz notched his speed higher, to find how fast he could conveniently move.

Faster he flew, and faster. The horse must have a limit . . .

He was up to eighty before he quit. The girl lay flat along the animal's back, hugging its neck to protect her face from the wind. But the horse ran on, daring Svetz with its eyes.

How to describe such motion? Svetz had never seen ballet. He knew how machinery moved, and this wasn't it. All he could think of was a man and a woman making love. Slippery-smooth rhythmic motion, absolute single-minded purpose, motion for the pleasure of motion. It was terrible in its beauty, the flight of the horse.

The word for such running must have died with the horse itself.

The horse would never have tired, but the girl did. She tugged on the animal's mane, and it stopped. Svetz gave her the jewels he held, made four more and gave her one.

She was crying from the wind, crying and smiling as she took the jewels. Was she smiling for the jewels, or for the joy of the ride? Exhausted, panting, she lay with her back against the warm, pulsing flank of the resting animal. Only her hand moved, as she ran her fingers repeatedly through its silver mane. The horse watched Svetz with malevolent brown eyes.

The girl was homely. It wasn't just the jarring lack of makeup. There was evidence of vitamin starvation. She was short, less than five feet in height, and thin. There were marks of childhood disease. But happiness glowed behind her homely face, and it made her almost passable, as she clutched the corundum stones.

When she seemed rested, Svetz remounted. They went on.

He was almost out of corundum when they reached the extension cage. There it was that he ran into trouble.

The girl had been awed by Svetz's jewels, and by Svetz himself, possibly because of his height or his ability to fly. But the extension cage scared her. Svetz couldn't blame her. The side with the door in it was no trouble: just a seamless spherical mirror. But the other side blurred away in a direction men could not visualize. It had scared Svetz spitless the first time he saw the time machine in action.

He could buy the horse from her, shoot it here and pull it inside, using the flight stick to float it. But it would be so much easier if . . .

It was worth a try. Svetz used the rest of his corundum. Then he walked into the extension cage, leaving a trail of colored corundum beads behind him.

He had worried because the heat-and-pressure device would not produce facets. The stones all came out shaped like miniature hen's-eggs. But he was able to vary the color, using chromic oxide for red and ferric oxide for yellow and titanium for blue; and he could vary the pressure planes, to produce cat's-eyes or star gems at will. He left a trail of small stones, red and yellow and blue . . .

And the girl followed, frightened, but unable to resist the bait. By now she had nearly filled a handkerchief with the stones. The horse followed her into the extension cage.

Inside, she looked at the four stones in Svetz's hand: one of each color, red and yellow and light blue and black, the largest he could make. He pointed to the horse, then to the stones.

The girl agonized. Svetz perspired. She didn't want to give up the horse . . . and Svetz was out of corundum . . .

She nodded, one swift jerk of her chin. Quickly, before she could change her mind, Svetz poured the stones into her hand. She clutched the hoard to her bosom and ran out of the cage, sobbing.

The horse stood up to follow.

Svetz swung the rifle and shot it. A bead of blood appeared on the animal's neck. It shied back, then sighted on Svetz along its natural bayonet.

Poor kid, Svetz thought as he turned to the door. But she'd have lost the horse anyway. It had sucked polluted water from an open stream. Now he need only load the flight stick aboard . . .

Motion caught the corner of his eye.

A false assumption can be deadly. Svetz had not waited for the horse to fall. It was with something of a shock that he realized the truth. The beast wasn't about to fall. It was about to spear him like a cocktail shrimp.

He hit the door button and dodged.

Exquisitely graceful, exquisitely sharp, the spiral horn slammed into the closing door. The animal turned like white lightning in the confines of the cage, and again Svetz leapt for his life.

The point missed him by half an inch. It plunged past him and into the control board, through the plastic panel and into the wiring beneath.

Something sparkled and something sputtered.

The horse was taking careful aim, sighting along the spear in its forehead. Svetz did the only thing he could think of. He pulled the home-again lever.

*   *   *

The horse screamed as it went into free fall. The horn, intended for Svetz's navel, ripped past his ear and tore his breathing-balloon wide open.

Then gravity returned; but it was the peculiar gravity of an extension cage moving forward through time. Svetz and the horse were pulled against the padded walls. Svetz sighed in relief.

He sniffed again in disbelief. The smell was strong and strange, like nothing Svetz had ever smelled before. The animal's terrible horn must have damaged the air plant. Very likely he was breathing poison. If the cage didn't return in time . . .

But would it return at all? It might be going anywhere, anywhen, the way that ivory horn had smashed through anonymous wiring. They might come out at the end of time, when even the black infrasuns gave not enough heat to sustain life.

There might not even be a future to return to. He had left the flight stick. How would it be used? What would they make of it, with its control handle at one end and the brush-style static discharge at the other and the saddle in the middle? Perhaps the girl would try to use it. He could visualize her against the night sky, in the light of a full moon . . . and how would that change history?

The horse seemed on the verge of apoplexy. Its sides heaved, its eyes rolled wildly. Probably it was the cabin air, thick with carbon dioxide. Again, it might be the poison the horse had sucked from an open stream.

Gravity died. Svetz and the horse tumbled in free fall, and the horse queasily tried to gore him.

Gravity returned, and Svetz, who was ready for it, landed on top. Someone was already opening the door.

Svetz took the distance in one bound. The horse followed, screaming with rage, intent on murder. Two men went flying as it charged out into the Institute control center.

"It doesn't take anaesthetics!" Svetz shouted over his shoulder. The animal's agility was hampered here among the desks and lighted screens, and it was probably drunk on hyperventilation. It kept stumbling into desks and men. Svetz easily stayed ahead of the slashing horn.

A full panic was developing . . .

"We couldn't have done it without Zeera," Ra Chen told him much later. "Your idiot tanj horse had the whole Center terrorized. All of a sudden it went completely tame, walked up to Zeera and let her lead it away."

"Did you get it to the hospital in time?"

Ra Chen nodded gloomily. Gloom was his favorite expression and was no indication of his true feelings. "We found over fifty unknown varieties of bacteria in the beast's bloodstream. Yet it hardly looked sick! It looked healthy as a . . . healthy as a . . . it must have tremendous stamina. We managed to save not only the horse, but most of the bacteria too, for the Zoo."

Svetz was sitting up in a hospital bed, with his arm up to the elbow in a diagnostician. There was always the chance that he too had located some long-extinct bacterium He shifted uncomfortably, being careful not to move the wrong arm, and asked, "Did you ever find an anaesthetic that worked?"

"Nope. Sorry about that, Svetz. We still don't know why your needles didn't work. The tanj horse is simply immune to tranks of any kind.

"Incidentally, there was nothing wrong with your air plant. You were smelling the horse."

"I wish I'd known that. I thought I was dying."

"It's driving the interns crazy, that smell. And we can't seem to get it out of the Center." Ra Chen sat down on the edge of the bed. "What bothers me is the horn on his forehead. The horse in the picture book had no horns."

"No, sir."

"Then it must be a different species. It's not really a horse, Svetz. We'll have to send you back. It'll break our budget, Svetz."

"I disagree, sir—"

"Don't be so tanj polite."

"Then don't be so tanj stupid, sir." Svetz was *not* going back for another horse. "People who kept tame horses must have de-

veloped the habit of cutting off the horn when the animal was a
pup. Why not? We all saw how dangerous that horn is. Much too
dangerous for a domestic animal."

"Then why does our horse have a horn?"

"That's why I thought it was wild, the first time I saw it. I
suppose they didn't start cutting off horns until later in history."

Ra Chen nodded in gloomy satisfaction. "I thought so too. Our
problem is that the Secretary-General is barely bright enough to
notice that his horse has a horn, and the picture-book horse
doesn't. He's bound to blame me."

"Mmm." Svetz wasn't sure what was expected of him.

"I'll have to have the horn amputated."

"Somebody's bound to notice the scar," said Svetz.

"Tanj it, you're right. I've got enemies at court. They'd be only
too happy to claim I'd mutilated the Secretary-General's pet." Ra
Chen glared at Svetz. "All right, let's hear *your* idea."

Svetz was busy regretting. Why had he spoken? His vicious,
beautiful horse, tamely docked of its killer horn . . . He found the
thought repulsive. His impulse had betrayed him. What could they
do but remove the horn?

He had it. "Change the picture book, not the horse. A computer could duplicate the book in detail, but with a horn on
every horse. Use the Institute computer, then wipe the tape afterward."

Morosely thoughtful, Ra Chen said, "That might work. I know
someone who could switch the books." He looked up from under
bushy black brows. "Of course, you'd have to keep your mouth
shut."

"Yes, sir."

"Don't forget." Ra Chen got up. "When you get out of the diagnostician, you start a four-week vacation."

"I'm sending you back for one of these," Ra Chen told him four
weeks later. He opened the bestiary. "We picked up the book in a
public park around ten Post Atomic; left the kid who was holding
it playing with a corundum egg."

Svetz examined the picture. "That's *ugly*. That's really ugly.

You're trying to balance the horse, right? The horse was so beautiful, you've got to have one of these or the universe goes off balance."

Ra Chen closed his eyes in pain. "Just go get us the Gila monster, Svetz. The Secretary-General wants a Gila monster."

"How big is it?"

They both looked at the illustration. There was no way to tell.

"From the looks of it, we'd better use the *big* extension cage."

Svetz barely made it back that time. He was suffering from total exhaustion and extensive second-degree burns. The thing he brought back was thirty feet long, had vestigial batlike wings, breathed fire, and didn't look very much like the illustration; but it was as close as anything he'd found.

The Secretary-General loved it.

LEVIATHAN!

Two men stood on one side of a thick glass wall.

"You'll be airborne," Svetz's beefy red-faced boss was saying. "We made some improvements in the small extension cage while you were in the hospital. You can hover it, or fly it at up to fifty miles per hour, or let it fly itself; there's a constant-altitude setting. Your field of vision is total. We've made the shell of the extension cage completely transparent."

On the other side of the thick glass, something was trying to kill them. It was forty feet long from nose to tail and was equipped with vestigial batlike wings. Otherwise it was built something like a slender lizard. It screamed and scratched at the glass with murderous claws.

The sign on the glass read:

GILA MONSTER

Retrieved from the year 1230 Ante Atomic, approximately,
from the region of China, Earth. EXTINCT.

"You'll be well out of his reach," said Ra Chen.

"Yes, sir." Svetz stood with his arms folded about him, as if he had a chill. He was being sent after the biggest animal that had ever lived; and Svetz was afraid of animals.

"For Science's sake! What are you worried about, Svetz? It's only a big fish!"

"Yes, sir. You said that about the Gila monster. It's just an extinct lizard, you said."

"We only had a drawing in a children's book to go by. How could we know it would be so big?"

The Gila monster drew back from the glass. It inhaled hugely, took aim—yellow and orange flame spewed from its nostrils and played across the glass. Svetz squeaked and jumped for cover.

"He can't get through," said Ra Chen.

Svetz picked himself up. He was a slender, small-boned man with pale skin, light blue eyes, and very fine ash-blond hair. "How could we know it would breathe fire?" he mimicked. "That lizard almost *cremated* me. I spent four months in the hospital as it was. And what really burns me is, he looks less like the drawing every time I see him. Sometimes I wonder if I didn't get the wrong animal."

"What's the difference, Svetz? The Secretary-General loved him. That's what counts."

"Yes, sir. Speaking of the Secretary-General, what does he want with a sperm whale? He's got a horse, he's got a Gila monster—"

"That's a little complicated." Ra Chen grimaced. "Palace politics! It's *always* complicated. Right now, Svetz, somewhere in the United Nations Palace, a hundred plots are in various stages of development. And every last one of them involves getting the attention of the Secretary-General, and *holding* it. Keeping his attention isn't easy."

Svetz nodded. Everybody knew about the Secretary-General.

The family that had ruled the United Nations for seven hundred years was somewhat inbred.

The Secretary-General was twenty-eight years old. He was a happy person; he loved animals and flowers and pictures and people. Pictures of planets and multiple star systems made him clap his hands and coo with delight; and so the Institute for Space Research was mighty in the United Nations government. But he liked extinct animals too.

"Someone managed to convince the Secretary-General that he wants the largest animal on Earth. The idea may have been to take us down a peg or two," said Ra Chen. "Someone may think we're getting too big a share of the budget.

"By the time I got onto it, the Secretary-General wanted a brontosaur. We'd never have gotten him that. No extension cage will reach that far."

"Was it your idea to get him a sperm whale, sir?"

"Yah. It wasn't easy to persuade him. Sperm whales have been extinct for so long that we don't even have pictures. All I had to show him was a crystal sculpture from Archeology—dug out of the Steuben Glass Building—and a Bible and a dictionary. I managed to convince him that Leviathan and the sperm whale were one and the same."

"That's not strictly true." Svetz had read a computer-produced condensation of the Bible. The condensation had ruined the plot, in Svetz's opinion. "Leviathan could be anything big and destructive, even a horde of locusts."

"Thank Science you weren't there to help, Svetz! The issue was confused enough. Anyway, I promised the Secretary-General the largest animal that ever lived on Earth. All the literature says that that animal was a sperm whale. There were sperm whale herds all over the oceans as recently as the first century Ante Atomic. You shouldn't have any trouble finding one."

"In twenty minutes?"

Ra Chen looked startled. "What?"

"If I try to keep the big extension cage in the past for more than twenty minutes, I'll never be able to bring it home. The—"

"I know that."

"—uncertainty factor in the energy constants—"

"Svetz—"

"—blow the Institute right off the map."

"We thought of that, Svetz. You'll go back in the small extension cage. When you find a whale, you'll signal the big extension cage."

"Signal it how?"

"We've found a way to send a simple on-off pulse through time. Let's go back to the Institute and I'll show you."

Malevolent golden eyes watched them through the glass as they walked away.

The extension cage was the part of the time machine that did the moving. Within its transparent shell, Svetz seemed to ride a flying armchair equipped with an airplane passenger's lunch tray; except that the lunch tray was covered with lights and buttons and knobs and crawling green lines. He was somewhere off the east coast of North America, in or around the year 100 Ante Atomic or 1845 Anno Domini. The inertial calendar was not particularly accurate.

Svetz skimmed low over water the color of lead, beneath a sky the color of slate. But for the rise and fall of the sea, he might almost have been suspended in an enormous sphere painted half light, half dark. He let the extension cage fly itself, twenty meters above the water, while he watched the needle on the NAI, the Nervous Activities Indicator.

Hunting Leviathan.

His stomach was uneasy. Svetz had thought he was adjusting to the peculiar gravitational side effects of time travel. But apparently not.

At least he would not be here long.

On this trip he was not looking for a mere forty-foot Gila monster. Now he hunted the largest animal that had ever lived. A most conspicuous beast. And now he had a life-seeking instrument, the NAI . . .

The needle jerked hard over, and trembled.

Was it a whale? But the needle was trembling in apparent indecision. A cluster of sources, then. Svetz looked in the direction indicated.

A clipper ship, winged with white sail, long and slender and graceful as hell. Crowded, too, Svetz guessed. Many humans, closely packed, would affect the NAI in just that manner. A sperm whale—a single center of complex nervous activity—would attract the needle as violently, without making it jerk about like that.

The ship would interfere with reception. Svetz turned east and away; but not without regret. The ship was beautiful.

The uneasiness in Svetz's belly was getting worse, not better.

Endless gray-green water, rising and falling beneath Svetz's flying armchair.

Enlightenment came like something clicking in his head. *Seasick*. On automatic, the extension cage matched its motion to the surface over which it flew; and that surface was heaving in great dark swells.

No wonder his stomach was uneasy! Svetz grinned and reached for the manual controls.

The NAI needle suddenly jerked hard over. A bite! thought Svetz, and he looked off to the right. No sign of a ship. And submarines hadn't been invented yet. Had they? No, of course they hadn't.

The needle was rock-steady.

Svetz flipped the call button.

The source of the tremendous NAI signal was off to his right, and moving. Svetz turned to follow it. It would be minutes before the call signal reached the Institute for Temporal Research and brought the big extension cage with its weaponry for hooking Leviathan.

Many years ago, Ra Chen had dreamed of rescuing the Library at Alexandria from Caesar's fire. For this purpose he had built the big extension cage. Its door was a gaping iris, big enough to be loaded while the Library was actually burning. Its hold, at a guess, was at least twice large enough to hold all the scrolls in that ancient Library.

The big cage had cost a fortune in government money. It had failed to go back beyond 400 AA, or 1550 AD. The books burned at Alexandria were still lost to history, or at least to historians.

Such a boondoggle would have broken other men. Somehow Ra Chen had survived the blow to his reputation.

He had pointed out the changes to Svetz after they returned from the Zoo. "We've fitted the cage out with heavy duty stunners and antigravity beams. You'll operate them by remote control. Be careful not to let the stun beam touch you. It would kill even a sperm whale if you held it on him for more than a few seconds, and it'd kill a man instantly. Other than that you should have no problems."

It was at that moment that Svetz's stomach began to hurt.

"Our major change is the call button. It will actually send us a signal through time, so that we can send the big extension cage back to you. We can land it right beside you, no more than a few minutes off. That took considerable research, Svetz. The Treasury raised our budget for this year so that we could get that whale."

Svetz nodded.

"Just be sure you've got a whale before you call for the big extension cage."

Now, twelve hundred years earlier, Svetz followed an underwater source of nervous impulse. The signal was intensely powerful. It could not be anything smaller than an adult bull sperm whale.

A shadow formed in the air to his right. Svetz watched it take shape: a great gray-blue sphere floating beside him. Around the rim of the door were antigravity beamers and heavy-duty stun guns. The opposite side of the sphere wasn't there; it simply faded away.

To Svetz that was the most frightening thing about any time machine: the way it seemed to turn a corner that wasn't there.

Svetz was almost over the signal. Now he used the remote controls to swing the antigravity beamers around and down.

He had them locked on the source. He switched them on, and dials surged.

Leviathan was *heavy*. More massive than Svetz had expected. Svetz upped the power, and watched the NAI needle swing as Leviathan rose invisibly through the water.

Where the surface of the water bulged upward under the attack of the antigravity beams, a shadow formed. Leviathan rising . . .

Was there something wrong with the shape?

Then a trembling spherical bubble of water rose shivering from the ocean, and Leviathan was within it.

Partly within it. He was too big to fit, though he should not have been.

He was four times as massive as a sperm whale should have been, and a dozen times as long. He looked nothing like the crystal Steuben sculpture. Leviathan was a kind of serpent armored with red-bronze scales as big as a Viking's shield, armed with teeth like ivory spears. His triangular jaws gaped wide. As he floated toward Svetz he writhed, seeking with his bulging yellow eyes for whatever strange enemy had subjected him to this indignity.

Svetz was paralyzed with fear and indecision. Neither then nor later did he doubt that what he saw was the Biblical Leviathan. This had to be the largest beast that had ever roamed the sea; a beast large enough and fierce enough to be synonymous with anything big and destructive. Yet—if the crystal sculpture was anything like representational, this was not a sperm whale at all.

In any case, he was far too big for the extension cage.

Indecision stayed his hand—and then Svetz stopped thinking entirely, as the great slitted irises found him.

The beast was floating past him. Around its waist was a sphere of weightless water that shrank steadily as gobbets dripped away and rained back to the sea. The beast's nostrils flared—it was obviously an air-breather, though not a cetacean.

It stretched, reaching for Svetz with gaping jaws.

Teeth like scores of elephant's tusks all in a row. Polished and needle sharp. Svetz saw them close about him from above and below, while he sat frozen in fear.

At the last moment he shut his eyes tight.

When death did not come, Svetz opened his eyes.

The jaws had not entirely closed on Svetz and his armchair. Svetz heard them grinding faintly against—against the invisible surface of the extension cage, whose existence Svetz had forgotten entirely.

Svetz resumed breathing. He would return home with an empty entension cage, to face the wrath of Ra Chen . . . a fate better than death. Svetz moved his fingers to cut the antigravity beams from the big extension cage.

Metal whined against metal. Svetz whiffed hot oil, while red lights bloomed all over his lunch-tray control board. He hastily turned the beams on again.

The red lights blinked out one by reluctant one.

Through the transparent shell Svetz could hear the grinding of teeth. Leviathan was trying to chew his way into the extension cage.

His released weight had nearly torn the cage loose from the rest of the time machine. Svetz would have been stranded in the past, a hundred miles out to sea, in a broken extension cage that probably wouldn't float, with an angry sea monster waiting to snap him up. No, he couldn't turn off the antigravity beamers.

But the beamers were on the big extension cage, and he couldn't keep the big extension cage more than about fifteen minutes longer. When the big extension cage was gone, what would prevent Leviathan from pulling him to his doom?

"I'll stun him off," said Svetz.

There was dark red palate above him, and red gums and forking tongue beneath, and the long curved fangs all around. But between the two rows of teeth Svetz could see the big extension cage, and the battery of stunners around the door. By eye he rotated the stunners until they pointed straight toward Leviathan.

"I must be out of my mind," said Svetz, and he spun the stunners away from him. He couldn't fire the stunners at Leviathan without hitting himself.

And Leviathan wouldn't let go.

Trapped.

No, he thought with a burst of relief. He could escape with his life. The go-home lever would send his small extension cage out from between the jaws of Leviathan, back into the time stream, back to the Institute. His mission had failed, but that was hardly his fault. Why had Ra Chen been unable to uncover mention of a sea serpent bigger than a sperm whale?

"It's all his fault," said Svetz. And he reached for the go-home lever. But he stayed his hand.

"I can't just tell him so," he said. For Ra Chen terrified him.

The grinding of teeth came itchingly through the extension cage.

"Hate to just quit," said Svetz. "Think I'll try something . . ."

He could see the antigravity beamers by looking between the teeth. He could feel their influence, so nearly were they focussed on the extension cage itself. If he focussed them just on himself . . .

He felt the change; he felt both strong and light-headed, like a drunken ballet master. And if he now narrowed the focus . . .

The monster's teeth seemed to grind harder. Svetz looked between them, as best he could.

Leviathan was no longer floating. He was hanging straight down from the extension cage, hanging by his teeth. The antigravity beamers still balanced the pull of his mass; but now they did so by pulling straight up on the extension cage.

The monster was in obvious distress. Naturally. A water beast, he was supporting his own mass for the first time in his life. And by his teeth! His yellow eyes rolled frantically. His tail twitched slightly at the very tip. And still he clung . . .

"Let go," said Svetz. "Let go, you . . . monster."

The monster's teeth slid screeching down the transparent surface, and he fell.

Svetz cut the antigravity a fraction of a second late. He smelled burnt oil, and there were tiny red lights blinking off one by one on his control board.

Leviathan hit the water with a sound of thunder. His long, sinuous body rolled over and floated to the surface and lay as if dead. But his tail flicked once, and Svetz knew that he was alive.

"I could kill you," said Svetz. "Hold the stunners on you until you're dead. There's time enough . . ."

But he still had ten minutes to search for a sperm whale. It wasn't time enough. It didn't begin to be time enough, but if he used it all . . .

The sea serpent flicked its tail and began to swim away. Once he rolled to look at Svetz, and his jaws opened wide in fury. He finished his roll and was fleeing again.

"Just a minute," Svetz said thickly. "Just a science-perverting minute there . . ." And he swung the stunners to focus.

Gravity behaved strangely inside an extension cage. While the cage was moving forward in time, *down* was all directions outward from the center of the cage. Svetz was plastered against the curved wall. He waited for the trip to end.

Seasickness was nothing compared to the motion sickness of time travel.

Free fall, then normal gravity. Svetz moved unsteadily to the door.

Ra Chen was waiting to help him out. "Did you get it?"

"Leviathan? No sir." Svetz looked past his boss. "Where's the big extension cage?"

"We're bringing it back slowly, to minimize the gravitational side effects. But if you don't have the whale—"

"I said I don't have Leviathan."

"Well, just what *do* you have?" Ra Chen demanded.

Somewhat later he said, "It wasn't?"

Later yet he said, "You killed him? Why, Svetz? Pure spite?"

"No, sir. It was the most intelligent thing I did during the entire trip."

"But *why*? Never mind, Svetz, here's the big extension cage." A gray-blue shadow congealed in the hollow cradle of the time machine. "And there does seem to be something in it. Hi, you idiots, throw an antigravity beam inside the cage! Do you want the beast crushed?"

The cage had arrived. Ra Chen waved an arm in signal. The door opened.

Something tremendous hovered within the big extension cage.

It looked like a malevolent white mountain in there, peering back at its captors with a single tiny, angry eye. It was trying to get at Ra Chen, but it couldn't swim in air.

Its other eye was only a torn socket. One of its flippers was ripped along the trailing edge. Rips and ridges and puckers of scar tissue, and a forest of broken wood and broken steel, marked its tremendous expanse of albino skin. Lines trailed from many of the broken harpoons. High up on one flank, bound to the beast by broken and tangled lines, was the corpse of a bearded man with one leg.

"Hardly in mint condition, is he?" Ra Chen observed.

"Be careful, sir. He's a killer. I saw him ram a sailing ship and sink it clean before I could focus the stunners on him."

"What amazes me is that you found him at all in the time you had left. Svetz, I do not understand your luck. Or am I missing something?"

"It wasn't luck, sir," Svetz hurried to explain. "The sea serpent was just leaving the vicinity. I wanted to kill him, but I knew I didn't have the time. I was about to leave myself, when he turned back and bared his teeth.

"He was an obvious carnivore. Those teeth were built strictly for killing, sir. I should have noticed earlier. And I could think of only one animal big enough to feed a carnivore that size."

"Ah-h-h. Brilliant, Svetz."

"There was corroborative evidence. Our research never found any mention of giant sea serpents. The great geological surveys of the first century Post Atomic should have turned up something. Why didn't they?"

"Because the sea serpent quietly died out two centuries earlier, after whalers killed off his food supply."

Svetz colored. "Exactly. So I turned the stunners on Leviathan before he could swim away, and I kept the stunners on him until the NAI said he was dead. I reasoned that if Leviathan was here, there must be whales in the vicinity."

"And Leviathan's nervous output was masking the signal."

"Sure enough, it was. The moment he was dead the NAI registered another signal. I followed it to—" Svetz jerked his head. They were floating the whale out of the extension cage. "To him."

Days later, two men stood on one side of a thick glass wall.

"We took some clones from him, then passed him on to the Secretary-General's Vivarium," said Ra Chen. "Pity you had to settle for an albino." He waved aside Svetz's protest: "I know, I know, you were pressed for time."

Beyond the glass, the one-eyed whale glared at Svetz through murky seawater. Surgeons had removed most of the harpoons, but scars remained along his flanks; and Svetz, awed, wondered how long the beast had been at war with Man. Centuries? How long did sperm whales live?

Ra Chen lowered his voice. "We'd all be in trouble if the Secretary-General found out that there was once a bigger animal than his. You understand that, don't you, Svetz?"

"Yes sir."

"Good." Ra Chen's gaze swept across another glass wall, and a fire-breathing Gila monster. Further down, a horse looked back at him along the dangerous spiral horn in its forehead.

"Always we find the unexpected," said Ra Chen. "Sometimes I wonder . . ."

If you'd do your research better, Svetz thought . . .

"Did you know that time travel wasn't even a concept until the first century Ante Atomic? A writer invented it. From then until the fourth century Post Atomic, time travel was pure fantasy. It violates everything the scientists of the time thought were natural laws. Logic. Conservation of matter and energy. Momentum, reaction, any law of motion that makes time a part of the statement. Relativity.

"It strikes me," said Ra Chen, "that every time we push an extension cage past that particular four-century period, we shove it into a kind of fantasy world. That's why you keep finding giant sea serpents and fire-breathing—"

"That's nonsense," said Svetz. He was afraid of his boss, yes; but there were limits.

"You're right," Ra Chen said instantly. Almost with relief. "Take a month's vacation, Svetz, then back to work. The Secretary-General wants a bird."

"A bird?" Svetz smiled. A bird sounded harmless enough. "I suppose he found it in another children's book?"

"That's right. Ever hear of a bird called a *roc*?"

BIRD IN THE HAND

It's not a roc," said Ra Chen.

The bird looked stupidly back at them from behind a thick glass wall. Its wings were small and underdeveloped; its legs and feet were tremendous, ludicrous. It weighed three hundred pounds and stood nearly eight feet tall.

Other than that, it looked a lot like a baby chick.

"It kicked me," Svetz complained. A slender, small-boned man, he stood stiffly this day, with a slight list to port. "It kicked me in the side and broke four ribs. I barely made it back to the extension cage."

"It still isn't a roc. Sorry about that, Svetz. We did some research in the history section of the Beverly Hills Library while you were in the hospital. The roc was only a legend."

"But look at it!"

Svetz's beefy, red-faced boss nodded. "That's probably what

started the legend. Early explorers in Australia saw these—
ostriches wandering about. They said to themselves, 'If the chicks
are this size, what are the adults like?' Then they went home and
told stories about the adults."

"I got my ribs caved in for a flightless bird?"

"Cheer up, Svetz. It's not a total loss. The ostrich was extinct.
It makes a fine addition to the Secretary-General's Vivarium."

"But the Secretary-General wanted a roc. What are you going
to tell him?"

Ra Chen scowled. "It's worse than that. Do you know what the
Secretary-General wants now?"

People meeting Ra Chen for the first time thought he was constantly scowling, until they saw his *scowl*. Svetz had suspected Ra
Chen was worried. Now he knew it.

The Secretary-General was everybody's problem. A recessive
gene inherited from his powerful, inbred family had left him with
the intelligence of a six-year-old child. Another kind of inheritance
had made him overlord of the Earth and its colonies. His whim
was law throughout the explored universe.

Whatever the Secretary-General wanted now, it was vital that
he get it.

"Some idiot took him diving in Los Angeles," Ra Chen said.
"He wants to see the city before it sank."

"That doesn't sound too bad."

"It wouldn't be, if it had stopped there. Some of his Circle of
Advisors noticed his interest. They got him historical tapes on Los
Angeles. He loves them. He wants to join the first Watts Riot."

Svetz gulped. "That should raise some security problems."

"You'd think so, wouldn't you? The Secretary-General is almost
pure caucasian."

The ostrich cocked its head to one side, studying them. It still
looked like the tremendous chick of an even bigger bird. Svetz
could imagine that it had just cracked its way out of an egg the
size of a bungalow.

"I'm going to have a headache," he said. "Why do you tell me
these things? You *know* I don't like politics."

"Can you imagine what would happen if the Secretary-General

got himself killed with the help of the Institute for Temporal Research? There are enough factions already that would like to see us disbanded. Space, for instance; they'd *love* to swallow us up."

"But what can we do? We can't turn down a direct request from the Secretary-General!"

"We can distract him."

They had lowered their voices to conspiratorial whispers. Now they turned away from the ostrich and strolled casually down the line of glass cages.

"How?"

"I don't know yet. If I could only get to his nurse," Ra Chen said between his teeth. "I've tried hard enough. Maybe the Institute for Space Research has bought her. Then again, maybe she's loyal. She's been with him twenty-four years.

"How do I know what would catch his attention? I've only met the Secretary-General four times, all on formal occasions. But his attention span is low. He'd forget about Los Angeles if we could distract him."

The cage they were passing was labeled:

ELEPHANT
Retrieved from the year 700 Ante Atomic, approximately, from the region of India, Earth. EXTINCT.

The wrinkled gray beast watched them go with sleepy indifference. His air of inhuman age and wisdom was such that he must have recognized Svetz as his captor. But he didn't care.

Svetz had captured almost half of the animals in the Vivarium. And Svetz was afraid of animals. Especially big animals. Why did Ra Chen keep sending him after animals?

The thirty feet of lizard in the next cage (*GILA MONSTER*, the placard said) definitely recognized Svetz. It jetted orange-white flame at him, and flapped its tiny batlike wings in fury when the flame washed harmlessly across the glass. If it ever got loose—

But that was why the cages were airtight. The animals of Earth's past must be protected from the air of Earth's present.

Svetz remembered the cobalt-blue sky of Earth's past and was reassured. Today's afternoon sky was brilliant turquoise at the zenith, shading through pastel green and yellow to rich yellow-brown near the horizon. If the Chinese fire-breather ever got out, it would be too busy gasping for purer air to attack Svetz.

"What can we get him? I think he's tired of these animals. Svetz, what about a giraffe?"

"A what?"

"Or a dog, or a satyr . . . it's got to be unusual," Ra Chen muttered. "A teddy bear?"

Out of his fear of animals, Svetz ventured, "I wonder if you might not be on the wrong track, sir."

"Mph? Why?"

"The Secretary-General has enough animals to satisfy a thousand men. Worse than that, you're competing with Space when you bring back funny animals. They can do that too."

Ra Chen scratched behind his ear. "I never thought of that. You're right. But we've got to do *something*."

"There must be lots of things to do with a time machine."

They could have taken a displacement plate back to the Center. Ra Chen preferred to walk. It would give him a chance to think, he said.

Svetz walked with bowed head and blind eyes alongside his boss. Inspiration had come to him at similar times. But they had reached the red sandstone cube that was the Center, and the mental lightning had not struck.

A big hand closed on his upper arm. "Just a minute," Ra Chen said softly. "The Secretary-General's paying us a visit."

Svetz's heart lurched. "How do you know?"

"You should recognize that machine in the walkway. We brought it back last month from Los Angeles, from the day of the Great California Earthquake. It's an internal combustion automobile. It belongs to the Secretary-General."

"What'll we do?"

"Go in and show him around. Pray he doesn't insist on being taken back to Watts, August eleventh, twenty Post Atomic."

"Suppose he does?" If they boiled Ra Chen for treason, they would surely boil Svetz too.

"I'll have to send him back if he asks it. Oh, not with you, Svetz. With Zeera. She's black, and she speaks American. It might help."

"Not enough," said Svetz, but he was already calmer. Let Zeera take the risks.

They passed close by the Secretary-General's automobile. Svetz was intrigued by its odd, angular look, its complex control panels, the shiny chrome trim. Someone had removed the hood, so that the polished complexity of the motor was open to view.

"Wait," Svetz said suddenly. "Does he like it?"

"*Will* you come on?"

"Does the Secretary-General like his automobile?"

"Sure, Svetz. He loves it."

"Get him another car. California must have been full of automobiles on the day before the Great Quake."

Ra Chen stopped suddenly. "That could be it. It would hold him for a while, give us time . . ."

"Time for what?"

Ra Chen didn't hear. "A racing car . . . ? No, he'd kill himself. The Circle of Advisors would want to install a robot chauffeur-override. Maybe a dune buggy?"

"Why not ask *him*?"

"It's worth a try," said Ra Chen. They went up the steps.

In the Center there were three time machines, including the one with the big extension cage, plus a host of panels with flashing colored lights. The Secretary-General liked those. He smiled and chuckled as Ra Chen led him about. His guards hovered at his shoulders, their faces stiff, their fingernails clicking against their gunbutts.

Ra Chen introduced Svetz as "my best agent." Svetz was so overwhelmed by the honor that he could only stutter. But the Secretary-General didn't seem to notice.

Whether he had forgotten about seeing the Watts Riot was moot; but he did forget to ask on that occasion.

When Ra Chen asked about cars, the Secretary-General smiled all across his face and nodded so vigorously that Svetz worried about spinal injury. Faced by a vast array of choices, five or six decades with dozens of new models for every year, the Secretary-General put his finger in his mouth and considered well.

Then he made his choice.

" 'Why not ask him? Why not ask him?' " Ra Chen mimicked savagely. "Now we know. The first car! He wants the first car ever made!"

"I thought he'd ask for a *make* of car." Svetz rubbed his eyes hard. "How can we possibly find one car? A couple of decades to search through, and all of the North American and European continents!"

"It's not that bad. We'll use the books from the Beverly Hills Library. But it's bad enough, Svetz . . ."

The raid on the Beverly Hills Library had been launched in full daylight, using the big extension cage and a dozen guards armed with stunners, on June third, twenty-six Post Atomic. Giant time machines, crazy men wearing flying belts—on any other day it would have made every newspaper and television program in the country. But June the third was a kind of Happy Hunting Ground for the Institute for Temporal Research.

No Californian would report the raid, except to other Californians. If the story did get out, it would be swamped by more important news. The series of quakes would begin at sunset, and the ocean would rise like a great green wall . . .

Svetz and Ra Chen and Zeera Southworth spent half the night going through the history section of the Beverly Hills Library. Ra Chen knew enough white American to recognize titles; but in the end Zeera had to do all the reading.

Zeera Southworth was tall and slender and very dark, crowned with hair like a black powder explosion. She sat gracefully cross-legged on the floor, looking very angular, reading pertinent sections aloud while the others paced. They followed a twisting trail of references.

By two in the morning they were damp and furious.

"Nobody invented the automobile!" Ra Chen exploded. "It just happened!"

"We certainly have a wide range of choices," Zeera agreed. "I take it we won't want any of the steam automobiles. That would eliminate Gugnot and Trevethick and the later British steam coaches."

"We'll concentrate on internal combustion."

Svetz said, "Our best bets seem to be Lenoir of France and Marcus of Vienna. Except that Daimler and Benz have good claims, and Selden's patent held good in court—"

"Dammit, pick one!"

"Just a minute, sir." Zeera alone retained some semblance of calm. "This Ford might be the best we've got."

"Ford? Why? He invented nothing but a system of mass production."

Zeera held up the book. Svetz recognized it: a biography she had been reading earlier. "This book implies that Ford was responsible for everything: that he created the automobile industry singlehanded."

"But we know that isn't true," Svetz protested.

Ra Chen made a pushing motion with one hand. "Let's not be hasty. We take Ford's car, and we produce that book to authenticate it. Who'll know the difference?"

"But if someone does the same research we just—oh. Sure. He'll get the same answers. No answers. Ford's just as good a choice as anyone else."

"Better, if nobody looks further," Zeera said with satisfaction. "Too bad we can't take the Model T; it looks much more like an automobile. This thing he started with looks like a kiddy cart. It says he built it out of old pipes."

"Tough," said Ra Chen.

Late the next morning, Ra Chen delivered last-minute instructions.

"You can't just take the car," he told Zeera. "If you're interrupted, come back without it."

"Yes, sir. It would be less crucial if we took our duplicate from a later time, from the Smithsonian Institution, for instance."

"The automobile has to be new. Be reasonable, Zeera! We can't give the Secretary-General a second-hand automobile!"

"No sir."

"We'll land you about three in the morning. Use infrared and pills to change your vision. Don't show any visible light. Artificial light would probably scare them silly."

"Right."

"Were you shown—"

"I know how to use the duplicator." Zeera sounded faintly supercilious, as always. "I also know that it reverses the image."

"Never mind that. Bring back the reversed duplicate, and we'll just reverse it again."

"Of course." She seemed chagrined that she had not seen that for herself. "What about dialect?"

"You speak black and white American, but it's for a later period. Don't use slang. Stick to black unless you want to impress someone white. Then speak white, but speak slowly and carefully and use simple words. They'll think you're from another country. I hope."

Zeera nodded crisply. She stooped and entered the extension cage, turned and pulled the duplicator after her. Its bulk was small, but it weighed a ton or so without the lift field generator to float it. One end glowed white with glow-paint.

They watched the extension cage blur and vanish. It was still attached to the rest of the time machine, but attached along a direction that did not transmit light.

"Now then!" Ra Chen rubbed his hands together. "I don't expect she'll have any trouble getting Henry Ford's flightless flight stick. Our trouble may come when the Secretary-General sees what he's got."

Svetz nodded, remembering the gray-and-flat pictures in the history books. Ford's machine was ungainly, slipshod, ugly and undependable. A few small surreptitious additions would make it dependable enough to suit the Secretary-General. *Nothing* would make it beautiful.

"We need another distraction," said Ra Chen. "We've only bought ourselves more time to get it."

Zeera's small time machine gave off a sound of ripping cloth, subdued, monotonous, reassuring. A dozen workmen were readying the big extension cage. Zeera would need it to transport the duplicate automobile.

"There's something I'd like to try," Svetz ventured.

"Concerning what?"

"The roc."

Ra Chen grinned. "The ostrich? Svetz, don't you ever give up?"

Svetz looked stubborn. "Do you know anything about neoteny?"

"Never heard of it. Look, Svetz, we're going to be over budget because of the roc trip. Not your fault, of course, but another trip would cost us over a million commercials."

"I won't need the time machine."

"Oh?"

"But I could use the help of the Palace Veterinarian. Have you got enough pull to arrange that?"

The Palace Veterinarian was a stocky, blocky, busty woman with muscular legs and a thrusting jaw. A floating platform packed with equipment followed her between the rows of cages.

"I know most of these beasts," she told Svetz. "Once upon a time I was going to give then all names. An animal ought to have a name."

"They've got names."

"That's what I decided. *GILA MONSTER, ELEPHANT, OSTRICH*," she read. "You give Horace a name so you won't mix him up with Gilbert. But nobody would get *HORSE* mixed up with *ELEPHANT*. There's only one of each. Poor beasties." She stopped before the cage marked *OSTRICH*. "Is this your prize? I've been meaning to come see him."

The bird shifted its feet in indecision; it cocked its head to consider the couple on the other side of the glass. It seemed surprised at Svetz's return.

"He looks just like a newly hatched chick," she said. "Except for the legs and feet, of course. They seem to have developed to support the extra mass."

Svetz was edgy with the need to be in two places at once. His own suggestion had sparked Zeera's project. He ought to be at the Center. Yet—the ostrich had been his first failure.

He asked, "Does it look neotenous?"

"Neotenous? Of course. Neoteny is a common method of evolution. We have neotenous traits ourselves, you know. Bare skin, where all the other primates are covered with hair. When our ancestors started chasing their meat across the plains, they needed a better cooling system than most primates need. So they kept one aspect of immaturity, the bare skin. Probably the big head is another one.

"The axolotl is the classic example of neoteny—"

"Excuse me?"

"You know what a salamander was, don't you? It had gills and fins while immature. As an adult it grew lungs and shed the gills and lived on land. The axolotl was a viable offshoot that never lost the gills and fins. A gene shift, typical of neoteny."

"I never heard of either of them, axolotls or salamanders."

"They needed open streams and ponds to live, Svetz."

Svetz nodded. If they needed open water, then both species must be over a thousand years extinct.

"The problem is that we don't know when your bird lost its ability to fly. Some random neotenous development may have occurred far in the past, so that the bird's wings never developed. Then it may have evolved its present size to compensate."

"Oh. Then the ancestor—"

"May have been no bigger than a turkey. Shall we go in and find out?"

The glass irised open to admit them. Svetz stepped into the cage, felt the tug of the pressure curtain flowing over and around him. The ostrich backed warily away.

The vet opened a pouch on her floating platform, withdrew a stunner, and used it. The ostrich squawked in outrage and collapsed. No muss, no fuss.

The vet strode toward her patient—and stopped suddenly in the middle of the cage. She sniffed, sniffed again in horror. "Have I lost my sense of smell?"

Svetz produced two items like cellophane bags, handed her one. "Put this on."

"Why?"

"You might suffocate if you don't." He donned the other himself, by pulling it over his head, then pressing the rim against the skin of his neck. It stuck. When he finished he had a hermetic seal.

"This air is deadly," he explained. "It's the air of the Earth's past, reconstituted. Think of it as coming from fifteen hundred years ago. There's no civilization. Nothing's been burned yet. That's why you can't smell anything but ostrich.

"Out there—Well, you don't really need sulfur dioxide and carbon monoxide and nitric oxides to stay alive. You do need carbon dioxide. There's a nerve complex in the lymph glands under your left armpit, and it triggers the breathing reflex. It's activated by a certain concentration of CO_2 in the blood."

She had finished donning her filter helmet. "I take it the concentration is too low in here."

"Right. You'd forget to breathe. You're used to air that's four percent carbon dioxide. In here it's barely a tenth of that.

"The bird can breathe this bland stuff. In fact, it's die without it. What we've put into the air in the past fifteen hundred years, we've had fifteen hundred years to adapt to. The ostrich hasn't."

"I'll keep that in mind," she said shortly; so that Svetz wondered if he'd been lecturing someone who knew more than he did. She knelt beside the sleeping ostrich, and the platform floated lower for her convenience.

Svetz watched her as she ministered to the ostrich, taking tissue samples, testing blood pressure and heartbeat in reaction to small doses of hormones and drugs.

In a general way he knew what she was doing. There were techniques for reversing the most recent mutations in an animal's genetic makeup. One did not always get what one expected. Still— there was a *Homo habilis* several cages down, who had been in the Circle of Advisors until he called the Secretary-General a tyrannical fugghead.

While she was identifying the neotenous developments, she would also be trying to guess what she would have when they were eliminated. Then there were matters of metabolism. If Svetz was right, the bird's mass would increase rapidly. It must be fed intravenously, and even more rapidly.

In general—but the details of what she was doing were mysterious and dull.

Svetz found himself studying her filter helmet. Full inflation had rendered it almost invisible. A golden rim of it showed by diffraction against the yellow-brown sky.

Did Space really want to take over the Institute for Temporal Research? Then that golden halo was support for their claim. It was a semipermeable membrane. It would selectively pass gasses in both directions in such a way as to make an almost breathable atmosphere breathable.

It had been taken unchanged from a Space warehouse.

Other ITR equipment had come from the space industries. Flight sticks. Anaesthetic needle guns. The low-mass antigravity unit in the new extension cage.

But their basic argument was more subtle.

Once the ocean teemed with life, Svetz thought. *Now the continental shelf is as dead as the Moon: nothing but bubble cities. Once this whole continent was all forest and living desert and fresh water. We cut down the trees and shot the animals and poisoned the rivers and irrigated the deserts so that even the desert life died; and now there's nothing left but the food yeast and us.*

We've forgotten so much about the past that we can't separate legend from fact. We've wiped out most of the forms of life on Earth in the last fifteen hundred years, and changed the composition of the air to the extent that we'd be afraid to change it back.

I fear the unknown beasts of the past. I cannot breathe the air. I do not know the edible plants. I could not kill the animals for food. I do not know which would kill me.

The Earth's past is as alien to me as another planet.

Let Space have it!

The Palace Veterinarian was busy jabbing the pointed ends of color-coded tubing into various portions of the bird's anatomy. The tubes led back to machinery on the floating platform.

Svetz's pocket phone rang. He flipped it open.

"There's trouble," said Ra Chen's image. "Zeera's cage was on its way home. She must have pulled the go-home ever right after she called for the big extension cage."

"She left before the big cage could get there?"

Ra Chen nodded grimly. "Whatever happened must have happened fast. If she called for the big cage, then she had the automobile. A moment later she aborted the mission. Svetz, I'm worried."

"I'd hate to leave now, sir." Svetz turned to look at the ostrich. In that moment all of the bird's feathers fell out, leaving it plump and naked.

That decided him. "I can't leave now, sir. We'll have a full-grown roc here in another ten minutes."

"What? *Good!* But how?"

"The ostrich was a neotenous offshoot of the roc. We've produced a throwback."

"Good! Stick with it, Svetz. We'll handle it here." Ra Chen switched off.

The Palace Veterinarian said, "You shouldn't make promises you can't keep."

Svetz's heart leapt. "Trouble?"

"No. It's going beautifully so far."

"All the feathers fell out. Is that good?"

"Don't worry about it. See for yourself: already there's a coat of down. Your ostrich is reverting to chickhood," she said cheerfully. "Its ancestor's chickhood. If the ancestor really was no bigger than a turkey before it lost the ability to fly, it'll be even smaller as a chick."

"What'll happen then?"

"It'll drown in its own fat."

"We should have taken a clone."

"Too late. Look at it now: look at the legs. They aren't nearly as overdeveloped."

The bird was a big ball of pale yellow down. Its frame had shrunk, but its legs had shrunk much more. Standing, it would have been no more than four feet tall. The extra mass had turned to fat, so that the ostrich was nearly spherical; it bulged like a poolside toy, lying on its inflated side in a pool of feathers.

"Now it *really* looks like a chick," said Svetz.

"It does, Svetz. In fact, it is. That was a *big* chick. The adult is going to be tremendous." The Palace Veterinarian jumped to her feet. "Svetz, we've got to hurry. Is there a basic dole yeast source in this cage?"

"Sure. Why?"

"He'll starve at the rate he's growing, unless . . . Just show me, Svetz."

The animals of the Zoo ate dole yeast, like everyone else, but with special additives for each animal. A brain tap could induce the animal to imagine it was eating whatever it was used to eating when the time probe had picked it up.

Svetz showed her the yeast tap. She hooked the pipeline to one of the machines on her floating platform; she made adaptations, added another machine. . . .

The bird grew visibly. Its fat layer shrank, deflated. Its legs and wings stretched outward. The beak began to take a distinctive hooked form, sharp and wicked.

Svetz began to feel panic. Beneath its downy feathers the bird was little more than taut skin stretched over long bones.

The yeast was now feeding directly into two tanks on the floating platform, and from there into the colored tubes. Somehow the Palace Veterinarian was converting the yeast directly into sugar-plasma.

"It's working now," she said. "I wasn't sure it would. He'll be all right now, if the growth cycle slows down in time." She smiled up at him. "You were right all along. The ostrich was a neotenous roc."

At that moment the light changed.

Svetz wasn't sure what had disturbed him. But he looked up—and the sky was baby blue from the horizon to the zenith.

"What is it?" The woman beside him was bemused rather than frightened. "I never saw a color like that in my life!"

"I have."

"What is it?"

"Don't worry about it. But keep your filter helmet on, especially if you have to leave the cage. Can you remember that?"

"Of course." Her eyes narrowed. "You know something about this, Svetz. It's something to do with time, isn't it?"

"I think so." Svetz used the key beam then, to avoid further questions. The glass peeled back to let him out.

He turned for a last look through the glass.

The Palace Veterinarian looked frightened. She must have guessed too much for her own comfort. But she turned away to care for her patient.

The ostrich lay on its side, its eyes open now. It was tremendous, and still scrawny despite the volume of the intravenous feed. Its feathers were changing color. The bird would be black and green.

It was half as big as the elephant next door . . . whose air of gray wisdom was giving way to uneasiness as he watched the proceedings.

It looked nothing like an ostrich.

The sky was baby blue, the blue of the deep past, crossed with fluffy clouds of clean and shining white. Blue from the horizon to the zenith, without a trace of the additives that ought to be there.

Unconscious men and women lay everywhere. Svetz dared not stop to help. What he had to do was more important.

He slowed to a walk as he neared the Center. There was pain like a knife blade inserted between his partly healed ribs.

ITR crewmen had fallen in the walkway around the Center, presumably after staggering outside. And there was the Secretary-General's automobile sitting quietly in front. Behind it, flat on his back, was Ra Chen.

What did he think he was doing there?

Svetz heard the purr of the motor as he approached. So that was it. Ra Chen must have hoped that the exhaust would revive him. Damn clever; and it should have worked. Why hadn't it?

Svetz looked into the polished metal guts of the motor as he passed. The motor had changed . . . somehow. What ran it now? Steam? Electricity? A flywheel? In any event, the exhaust pipe Ra Chen had been searching for was no longer there.

Ra Chen was alive, his pulse rapid and frantic. But he wasn't breathing. Or . . . yes, he was. He was breathing perhaps twice a minute as carbon dioxide built up enough to activate the reflex.

Svetz went on into the Center.

More than a dozen men and women had collapsed across lighted control panels. Three more figures sprawled in an aisle. The Secretary-General lay in angular disorder, smiling foolishly up at the ceiling. His guards wore troubled sleeping expressions and held drawn guns.

The small extension cage had not returned.

Svetz looked into the empty gap in the time machine, and felt terror. What could he accomplish without Zeera to tell him what had gone wrong?

From 50 Ante Atomic to the present was a thirty minute trip. Ra Chen's call to the Zoo must have come less than thirty minutes ago. Weird, how an emergency could telescope time.

Unless that was a side effect of the paradox. Unless the paradox had chopped away Zeera's extension cage and left her stranded in the past, or cast off into an alternate world line, or . . .

There had never been a temporal paradox.

Math was no help. The mathematics of time travel was riddled with singularities.

Last year somebody had tried to do a topological analysis of the path of an extension cage. He had proved not only that time travel was impossible, but that you couldn't travel faster than light either. Ra Chen had leaked the news to Space on the off chance that their hyperdrive ships would stop working.

What to do? Start putting filter helmets on everyone? Great, but the helmets weren't kept at the Center; he'd have to go across town. Did he dare leave the Center?

Svetz forced himself to sit down.

*   *   *

Minutes later, he snapped alert at the *pop* of displaced air. The small extension cage had returned. Zeera was crawling out of the circular doorway.

"Get back in there," Svetz ordered. "Quick!"

"I don't take orders from you, Svetz." She brushed past him and looked about her. "The automobile's gone. Where's Ra Chen?" Zeera's face was blank with shock and exhaustion. Her voice was a monotone, ragged at the edges.

Svetz took her arm. "Zeera, we've—"

She jerked away. "We've got to *do* something. The automobile's gone. Didn't you hear me?"

"Did you hear *me*? Get back in the extension cage!"

"But we've got to decide what to *do*. Why can't I smell anything?" She sniffed at air that was scentless, empty, dead. She looked about her in bewilderment, realizing for the first time just how strange everything was.

Then the eyes rolled up in her head, and Svetz stepped forward to catch her.

He studied her sleeping face across the diameter of the extension cage. It was very different from her waking face. Softer, more vulnerable. And prettier. Zeera had quite a pretty face.

"You should relax more often," he said.

His ribs throbbed where the ostrich had kicked him. The pain seemed to beat like a heart.

Zeera opened her eyes. She asked, "Why are we in here?"

"The extension cage has its own air system," said Svetz. "You can't breathe the outside air."

"Why not?"

"You tell me."

Her eyes went wide. "The automobile! It's gone!"

"Why?"

"I don't know. Svetz, I *swear* I did everything right. But when I turned on the duplicator the automobile disappeared!"

"That. . . . doesn't sound at all good." Svetz strove to keep his voice level. "What did you—"

"I did it just the way they taught me! I hooked the glow-painted end to the frame, set the dials for an estimated mass plus a margin of error, read the dials off—"

"You must have hooked up the wrong end somehow. Wait a minute. Were you using the infrared flash?"

"Of course. It was dead of night."

"And you'd taken the pills so you'd be able to see infrared."

"Do you always think that slowly, Svetz?" Then her eyes changed. "I was seeing infrared. Of course. I hooked up the *hot* end."

"The duplicator end. That would duplicate empty space where there was an automobile. You'd get emptiness at both ends."

"Stupid," Zeera said bitterly. "Stupid."

She hooked her arms under her knees and relaxed against the curved side of the extension cage. Presently she said, "Henry Ford sold that automobile for two hundred dollars, according to the book. Later he had trouble getting financed."

"How much is two hundred dollars?"

"I think it depends on the year. Enough to ruin a man, apparently, if you take it away at the right time. Then someone else used assembly lines to make automobiles. And he must have liked steam or electricity."

"Steam, I'd guess. Steam cars came first."

"Why would that affect the air? We can breathe what comes out of an automobile exhaust pipe, but we don't need it to live. Except CO_2. A steam automobile would burn fuel, wouldn't it?"

"I wondered about that too," said Svetz. "It took me a while, but I got it. Some of what comes out of an exhaust pipe never goes away. It just stays in the air, like a curtain between us and the sun. It's been there for a thousand years, cutting off half our sunlight. And we made it didn't happen."

"Photosynthesis. *That's* where all the carbon dioxide went."

"Right."

"But if the air changed, why didn't we change with it? We evolved to be able to breathe a certain kind of air. Shouldn't the evolution have been cancelled too? For that matter, why do we remember?"

"I don't know. There's a lot we don't know about time travel."

"I'm not nagging, Svetz. I don't know either."

More silence.

"It's clear enough," Zeera said presently. "I'll have to go back and warn myself to get the duplicator on straight."

"That won't work. It *didn't* work. If you'd gotten the ends of the duplicator on straight we wouldn't be *in* this mess. Therefore you didn't."

"Logic and time travel don't go, remember?"

"Maybe we can go *around* you." Svetz hesitated, then plunged in. "Try this. Send me back to an hour before the earlier Zeera arrives. The automobile won't have disappeared yet. I'll duplicate it, duplicate the duplicate, take the reversed duplicate and the original past you in the big extension cage. That leaves you to destroy the duplicate. I reappear after you're gone, leave the original automobile for Ford, and come back here with the reverse duplicate. How's that?"

"It sounded great. Would you mind going through it again?"

"Let's see. I go back to—"

She was laughing at him. "Never mind. But it has to be me, Svetz. You couldn't find your way. You couldn't ask directions or read the street signs. You'll have to stay here and man the machinery."

Svetz was crawling out of the extension cage when there came a scream like the end of the world.

Momentarily he froze. Then he dashed around the swelling flank of the cage. Zeera followed, wearing the filter helmet she had worn during her attempt to duplicate Ford's automobile.

One wall of the Center was glass. It framed a crest of hill across from the Palace, and a double row of cages that made up the Zoo. One of the cages was breaking apart as they watched, smashing itself to pieces like—

—Like an egg hatching. And like a chick emerging, the roc stood up in the ruin of its cage.

The scream came again.

"What is it?" Zeera whispered.

"It was an ostrich. I'd hate to give it a name now."

The bird seemed to move in slow motion. There was so much of it! Green and black, beautiful and evil, big as eternity, and a crest of golden feathers had sprouted on its forehead. Its hooked beak descended toward a cage.

That cage ripped like tissue paper.

Zeera was shaking his arm. "Come on! If it came from the Zoo, we don't need to worry about it. It'll suffocate when we get the car back where it belongs."

"Oh. Right," said Svetz. They went to work moving the big extension cage a few hours further back in time.

When Svetz looked again, the bird was just taking to the air. Its wings flapped like sails, and their black shadows swept like clouds over the houses. As the roc rose fully into view, Svetz saw that something writhed and struggled in its tremendous talons.

Svetz recognized it . . . and realized just how big the roc really was.

"It's got *Elephant*," he said. An inexplicable sorrow gripped his heart. Inexplicable, for Svetz hated animals.

"What? Come *on,* Svetz!"

"Um? Oh, yes." He helped Zeera into the small extension cage and sent it on its way.

Despite its sleeping crew, the machinery of the Center was working perfectly. If anything got off, Svetz would have six men's work to do. Therefore he prowled among the control boards, alert for any discrepancy, making minor adjustments . . . And occasionally he looked out the picture window.

The roc had reached an enormous height. Any other bird would have been invisible long since. But the roc was all too apparent, hovering in the blue alien sky while it killed and ate *Elephant*.

Bloody bones fell in the walkway.

Time passed.

Twenty minutes for Zeera to get back.

More time to make two duplicates of the automobile. Load them into the big extension cage. Then to signal Svetz—

The signal came. She had the cars. Svetz played it safe, moved her forward six hours, almost to dawn on the crucial night. She might be caught by an early riser, but at least Ford would have his automobile back.

The roc had finished its bloody meal. *Elephant* was gone. And—Svetz watched until he was sure—the bird was dropping, riding down the sky on outstretched wings.

Svetz watched it grow bigger, and bigger yet, until it seemed to enfold the universe. It settled over the Center like a tornado cloud, in darkness, and wind. Like twin tornado funnels, two sets of curved talons touched down in the walkway.

The bird bent low. An inhuman face looked in at Svetz through the picture window. It nearly filled the window.

It knows me, Svetz thought. Even a bird's brain must be intelligent in a head that size.

The vast head rose out of sight above the roof.

I had the ostrich. I should have been satisfied, thought Svetz. *A coin in the hand is worth two in the street.* The ancient proverb could as easily be applied to birds.

The roof exploded downward around a tremendous hooked beak. Particles of concrete spattered against walls and floor. A yellow eye rolled and found Svetz, but the beak couldn't reach him. Not through *that* hole.

The head withdrew through the roof.

Three red lights. Svetz leapt for the board and began twisting dials. He made two lights turn green, then the third. It had not occurred to him to run. The bird would find him out wherever he hid . . .

There! Zeera had pulled the go-home lever. From here it was all automatic.

Crash!

Svetz was backed up against the big time machine, pinned by a yellow eye as big as himself. Half the roof was gone now. Still the curved beak couldn't reach him. But a great claw came seeking him through the shattered glass.

The light changed.

Svetz sagged. Behind the green and black feathers he could see that the sky had turned pale yellow-green, marked with yellow-brown streamers of cloud.

The bird sniffed incredulously, once, twice. Somehow the panic showed in its tremendous eye, before the great head rose through the roof. The roc stepped back from the Center for clearance; its dark wings swept down like night falling.

Svetz was beyond fear or common sense. He stepped out to watch it rise.

He had to hug an ornamental pillar. The wind of the wings was a hurricane. The bird looked down once, and recognized him, and looked away.

It was still well in view, rising and circling, when Zeera stepped out to join him. Presently Ra Chen was there to follow their eyes. Then half the Center maintenance team was gaping up in awe and astonishment.

The bird dwindled to a black shadow. Black against pastel green, climbing, climbing.

Suffocating.

One sniff had been enough. The bird's brain was as enormously proportioned as the rest of it. It had started climbing immediately, without waiting to snatch up Svetz for its dessert.

Climbing, climbing toward the edge of space. Reaching for clean air.

The Secretary-General stood beside Svetz, smiling in wonder, chuckling happily as he gazed upward.

Was the roc still climbing? No, the black shadow was growing larger, sliding down the sky. And the slow motion of the wings had stopped.

How was a roc to know that there was no clean air anywhere?

THERE'S A WOLF IN MY TIME MACHINE

The old extension cage had no fine controls; but that hardly mattered. It wasn't as if Svetz were chasing some particular extinct animal. Ra Chen had told him to take whatever came to hand.

Svetz guided the cage back to pre-Industrial America, somewhere in mid-continent, around 1000 Ante Atomic Era. Few humans, many animals. Perhaps he'd find a bison.

And when he pulled himself to the window, he looked out upon a vast white land.

Svetz had not planned to arrive in mid-winter.

Briefly he considered moving into the time stream again and using the interrupter circuit. Try another date, try his luck again. But the interrupter circuit was new, untried, and Svetz wasn't about to be the first man to test it.

Besides which, a trip into the past cost over a million commercials. Using the interrupter circuit would nearly double that. Ra Chen would be displeased.

Svetz began freezing to death the moment he opened the door. From the doorway the view was all white, with one white bounding shape far away.

Svetz shot it with a crystal of soluble anaesthetic.

He used the flight stick to reach the spot. Now that it was no longer moving, the beast was hard to find. It was just the color of the snow, but for its open red mouth and the black pads on its feet. Svetz tentatively identified it as an arctic wolf.

It would fit the Vivarium well enough. Svetz would have settled for anything that would let him leave this frozen wilderness. He felt uncommonly pleased with himself. A quick, easy mission.

Inside the cage, he rolled the sleeping beast into what might have been a clear plastic bag, and sealed it. He strapped the wolf against one curved wall of the extension cage. He relaxed into the curve of the opposite wall as the cage surged in a direction vertical to all directions.

Gravity shifted oddly.

A transparent sac covered Svetz's own head. Its lip was fixed to the skin of his neck. Now Svetz pulled it loose and dropped it. The air system was on; he would not need the filter sac.

The wolf would. It could not breathe Industrial Age air. Without the filter sac to remove the poisons, the wolf would choke to death. Wolves were extinct in Svetz's time.

Outside, time passed at a furious rate. Inside, time crawled. Nestled in the sphericalcurve of the extension cage, Svetz stared up at the wolf, who now seemed fitted into the curve of the ceiling.

Svetz had never met a wolf in the flesh. He had seen pictures in children's books . . . and even the children's books had been stolen from the deep past. Why should the wolf look so familiar?

It was a big beast, possibly as big as Hanville Svetz, who was a slender, small-boned man. Its sides heaved with its panting. Its tongue was long and red and its teeth were white and sharp.

Like the dogs, Svetz remembered. The dogs in the Vivarium, in the glass case labeled:

DOG
CONTEMPORARY

Alone of the beasts in the Vivarium, the dogs were not sealed in glass for their own protection. The others could not breathe the air outside. The dogs could.

In a very real sense, they were the work of one man. Lawrence Wash Porter had lived near the end of the Industrial Period, between 50 and 100 Post Atomic Era, when billions of human beings were dying of lung diseases while scant millions adapted. Porter had decided to save the dogs.

Why the dogs? His motives were obscure, but his methods smacked of genius. He had acquired members of each of the breeds of dog in the world, and bred them together, over many generations of dogs and most of his own lifetime.

There would never be another dog show. Not a purebred dog was left in the world. But hybrid vigor had produced a new breed. These, the ultimate mongrels, could breathe Industrial Age air, rich in oxides of carbon and nitrogen, scented with raw gasoline and sulfuric acid.

The dogs were behind glass because people were afraid of them. Too many species had died. The people of 1100 Post Atomic were not used to animals.

Wolves and dogs . . . could one have sired the other?

Svetz looked up at the sleeping wolf and wondered. He was both like and unlike the dogs. Dogs grinned out through the glass and wagged their tails when children waved. Dogs liked people. But the wolf, even in sleep . . .

Svetz shuddered. Of all the things he hated about his profession, this was the worst: the ride home, staring up at a strange and dangerous extinct animal. The first time he'd done it, a captured horse had seriously damaged the control panel. On his last mission an ostrich had kicked him and broken three ribs.

The wolf was stirring restlessly . . . and something about it had changed.

Something was changing now. The beast's snout was shorter,

wasn't it? Its forelegs lengthened peculiarly; its paws seemed to grow and spread. Svetz caught his breath.

Svetz caught his breath, and instantly forgot the wolf. Svetz was choking, dying. He snatched up his filter sac and threw himself at the controls.

Svetz stumbled out of the extension cage, took three steps and collapsed. Behind him, invisible contaminants poured into the open air.

The sun was setting in banks of orange cloud.

Svetz lay where he had fallen, retching, fighting for air. There was an outdoor carpet beneath him, green and damp, smelling of plants. Svetz did not recognize the smell, did not at once realize that the carpet was alive. He would not have cared at that point. He knew only that the cage's air system had tried to kill him. The way he felt, it had probably succeeded.

It had been a near thing. He had been passing 30 Post Atomic when the air went bad. He remembered clutching the interrupter switch, then waiting, waiting. The foul air stank in his nostrils and caught in his throat and tore at his larynx. He had waited through twenty years, feeling every second of them. At 50 Post Atomic he had pulled the interrupter switch and run choking from the cage.

50 PA. At least he had reached industrial times. He could breathe the air.

It was the horse, he thought without surprise. The horse had pushed its wickedly pointed horn through Svetz's control panel, three years ago. Maintenance was supposed to fix it. They *had* fixed it.

Something must have worn through.

The way he looked at me every time I passed his cage. I always knew the horse would get me, Svetz thought.

He noticed the filter sac still in his hand. Not that he'd be—

Svetz sat up suddenly.

There was green all about him. The damp green carpet beneath him was alive; it grew from the black ground. A rough, twisted pillar thrust from the ground, branched into an explosion of red and yellow papery things. More of the crumpled colored paper lay about the pillar's base. Something that was not an aircraft moved erratically overhead, a tiny thing that fluttered and warbled.

Living, all of it. A pre-Industrial wilderness.

Svetz pulled the filter sac over his head and hurriedly smoothed the edges around his neck to form a seal. Blind luck that he hadn't fainted yet. He waited for it to puff up around his head. A selectively permeable membrane, it would pass the right gasses in and out until the composition of the air was—was—

Svetz was choking, tearing at the sac.

He wadded it up and threw it, sobbing. First the air plant, now the filter sac! Had someone wrecked them both? The inertial calender too; he was at least a hundred years previous to 50 Post Atomic.

Someone had tried to kill him.

Svetz looked wildly about him. Uphill across a wide green carpet, he saw an angular vertical-sided formation painted in shades of faded green. It had to be artificial. There might be people there. He could—

No, he couldn't ask for help either. Who would believe him? How could they help him anyway? His only hope was the extension cage. And his time must be very short.

The extension cage rested a few yards away, the door a black circle on one curved side. The other side seemed to fade away into nothing. It was still attached to the rest of the time machine, in 1103 PA, along a direction eyes could not follow.

Svetz hesitated near the door. His only hope was to disable the air plant somehow. Hold his breath, then—

The smell of contaminants was gone.

Svetz sniffed at the air. Yes, gone. The air plant had exhausted itself, drained its contaminants into the open air. No need to wreck it now. Svetz was sick with relief.

He climbed in.

He remembered the wolf when he saw the filter sac, torn and empty. Then he saw the intruder towering over him, the coarse thick hair, the yellow eyes glaring, the taloned hands spread wide to kill.

*   *   *

The land was dark. In the east a few stars showed, though the west was still deep red. Perfumes tinged the air. A full moon was rising.

Svetz staggered uphill, bleeding.

The house on the hill was big and old. Big as a city block, and two floors high. It sprawled out in all directions, as though a mad architect had built to a whim that changed moment by moment. There were wrought iron railings on the upper windows, and wrought iron handles on the screens on both floors, all painted the same dusty shade of green. The screens were wood, painted a different shade of green. They were closed across every window. No light leaked through anywhere.

The door was built for someone twelve feet tall. The knob was huge. Svetz used both hands and put all his weight into it, and still would not turn. He moaned. He looked for the lens of a peeper camera and could not find it. How would anyone know he was here? He couldn't find a doorbell either.

Perhaps there was nobody inside. No telling what this building was. It was far too big to be a family dwelling, too spread out to be a hotel or apartment house. Might it be a warehouse or a factory? Making or storing what?

Svetz looked back toward the extension cage. Dimly he caught the glow of the interior lights. He also saw something moving on the living green that carpeted the hill.

Pale forms, more than one.

Moving this way?

Svetz pounded on the door with his fists. Nothing. He noticed a golden metal thing, very ornate, high on the door. He touched it, pulled at it, let it go. It clanked.

He took it in both hands and slammed the knob against its base again and again. Rhythmic clanking sounds. Someone should hear it.

Something zipped past his ear and hit the door hard. Svetz spun around, eyes wild, and dodged a rock the size of his fist. The white shapes were nearer now. Bipeds, walking hunched.

They looked too human—or not human enough.

The door opened.

She was young, perhaps sixteen. Her skin was very pale, and

her hair and brows were pure white, quite beautiful. Her garment covered her from neck to ankles, but left her arms bare. She seemed sleepy and angry as she pulled the door open—manually, and it was heavy, too. Then she saw Svetz.

"Help me," said Svetz.

Her eyes went wide. Her ears moved too. She said something Svetz had trouble interpreting, for she spoke in ancient American.

"What *are* you?"

Svetz couldn't blame her. Even in good condition his clothes would not fit the period. But his blouse was ripped to the navel, and so was his skin. Four vertical parallel lines of blood ran down his face and chest.

Zeera had been coaching him in the American speech. Now he said carefully, "I am a traveler. An animal, a monster, has taken my vehicle away from me."

Evidently the sense came through. "You poor man! What kind of animal?"

"Like a man, but hairy all over, with a horrible face—and claws—claws—"

"I see the mark they made."

"I don't know how he got in. I—" Svetz shuddered. No, he couldn't tell her that. It was insane, utterly insane, this conviction that Svetz's wolf had become a bloodthirsty humanoid monster. "He only hit me once. On the face. I could get him out with a weapon, I think. Have you a bazooka?"

"What a funny word! I don't think so. Come inside. Did the trolls bother you?" She took his arm and pulled him in and shut the door.

Trolls?

"You're a strange person," the girl said, looking him over. "You look strange, you smell strange, you move strangely. I did not know that there were people like you in the world. You must come from very far away."

"Very," said Svetz. He felt himself close to collapse. He was safe at last, safe inside. But why were the hairs on the back of his neck trying to stand upright?

He said, "My name is Svetz. What's yours?"

"Wrona." She smiled up at him, not afraid despite his strange-ness . . . and he must look strange to her, for she surely looked strange to Hanville Svetz. Her skin was sheet white, and her rich white hair would better have fit a centenarian. Her nose, very broad and flat, would have disfigured an ordinary girl. Somehow it fit Wrona's face well enough; but her face was most odd, and her ears were too large, almost pointed, and her eyes were too far apart, and her grin stretched *way* back . . . and Svetz liked it. Her grin was curiosity and enjoyment, and was not a bit too wide. The firm pressure of her hand was friendly, reassuring. Though her finger-nails were uncomfortably long and sharp.

"You should rest, Svetz," she said. "My parents will not be up for another hour, at least. Then they can decide how to help you. Come with me, I'll take you to a spare room."

He followed her through a room dominated by a great rectan-gular table and a double row of high-backed chairs. There was a large microwave oven at one end, and beside it a platter of . . . red things. Roughly conical they were, each about the size of a strong man's upper arm, each with a dot of white in the big end. Svetz had no idea what they were; but he didn't like their color. They seemed to be bleeding.

"Oh," Wrona exclaimed. "I should have asked. Are you hun-gry?"

Svetz was, suddenly. "Have you dole yeast?"

"Why, I don't know the word. Are those dole yeast? They are all we have."

"We'd better forget it." Svetz's stomach lurched at the thought of eating something that color. Even if it turned out to be a plant.

Wrona was half supporting him by the time they reached the room. It was rectangular and luxuriously large. The bed was wide enough, but only six inches off the floor, and without coverings. She helped him down to it. "There's a wash basin behind that door, if you find the strength. Best you rest, Svetz. In perhaps two hours I will call you."

Svetz eased himself back. The room seemed to rotate. He heard her go out.

How strange she was. How odd he must look to her. A good

thing she hadn't called anyone to tend him. A doctor would notice the differences.

Svetz had never dreamed that primitives would be so different from his own people. During the thousand years between now and the present, there must have been massive adaptation to changes in air and water, to DDT and other compounds in foods, to extinction of food plants and meat animals until only dole yeast was left, to higher noise levels, less room for exercise, greater dependence on medicines . . . Well, why shouldn't they be different? It was a wonder humanity had survived at all.

Wrona had not feared his strangeness, nor cringed from the scratches on his face and chest. She was only amused and interested. She had helped him without asking too many questions. He liked her for that.

He dozed.

Pain from deep scratches, stickiness in his clothes made his sleep restless. There were nightmares. Something big and shadowy, half man and half beast, reached far out to slash his face. Over and over. At some indeterminate time he woke completely, already trying to identify a musky, unfamiliar scent.

No use. He looked about him, at a strange room that seemed even stranger from floor level. High ceiling. One frosted globe, no brighter than a full moon, glowed so faintly that the room was all shadow. Wrought iron bars across the windows; black night beyond.

A wonder he'd wakened at all. The pre-Industrial air should have killed him hours ago.

It had been a futz of a day, he thought. And he shied from the memory of the thing in the extension cage. The snarling face, pointed ears, double row of pointed white teeth. The clawed hand reaching out, swiping down. The nightmare conviction that a wolf had turned into *that*.

It could not be. Animals did not change shape like that. Something must have gotten in while Svetz was fighting for air. Chased the wolf out, or killed it.

But there were legends of such things, weren't there? Two and three thousand years old and more, everywhere in the world, were the tales of men who could become beasts.

Svetz sat up. Pain gripped his chest, then relaxed. He stood up carefully and made his way to the bathroom.

The spiggots were not hard to solve. Svetz wet a cloth with warm water. He watched himself in the mirror, emerging from under the crusted blood. A pale, slender young man topped with thin blond hair ... and an odd distortion of chin and forehead. That must be the mirror, he decided. Primitive workmanship. It might have been worse. Hadn't the first mirrors been two-dimensional?

A shrill whistle sounded outside his door. Svetz went to look, and found Wrona. "Good, you're up," she said. "Father and Uncle Wrocky would like to see you."

Svetz stepped into the hall, and again noticed the elusive musky scent. He followed Wrona down the dark hallway. Like his room, it was lit only by a single white frosted globe. Why would Wrona's people keep the house so dark? They had electricity.

And why were they all sleeping at sunset? With breakfast laid out and waiting ...

Wrona opened a door, gestured him in.

Svetz hesitated a step beyond the threshold. The room was as dark as the hallway. The musky scent was stronger here. He jumped when a hand closed on his upper arm—it felt wrong, there was hair on the palm, the hard nails made a circlet of pressure points—and a gravelly male voice boomed, "Come in, Mister Svetz. My daughter tells me you're a traveler in need of help."

In the dim light Svetz made out a man and a woman seated on backless chairs. Both had hair as white as Wrona's, but the woman's hair bore a broad black stripe. A second man urged Svetz toward another backless chair. He too bore black markings: a single black eyebrow, a black crescent around one ear.

And Wrona was just behind him. Svetz looked around at them all, seeing how like they were, how different from Hanville Svetz.

The fear rose up in him like a strong drug. Svetz was a xenophobe.

They were all alike. Rich white hair and eyebrows, black markings. Narrow black fingernails. The broad flat noses and the wide,

wide mouths, the sharp white conical teeth, the high, pointed ears that moved, yellow eyes, hairy palms.

Svetz dropped heavily onto the padded footstool.

One of the males noticed: the larger one, who was still standing. "It must be the heavier gravity," he guessed. "It's true, isn't it, Svetz? You're from another world. Obviously you're not quite a man. You told Wrona you were a traveler, but you didn't say from how far away."

"Very far," Svetz said weakly. "From the future."

The smaller male was jolted. "The future? You're a time traveler?" His voice became a snarl. "You're saying that we will evolve into something like you!"

Svetz cringed. "No. Really."

"I hope not. What, then?"

"I think I must have gone sidewise in time. You're descended from wolves, aren't you? Not apes. Wolves."

"Yes, of course."

The seated male was looking him over. "Now that he mentions it, he does look much more like a troll than any man has a right to. No offense intended, Svetz."

Svetz, surrounded by wolf men, tried to relax. And failed. "What is a troll?"

Wrona perched on the edge of his stool. "You must have seen them on the lawn. We keep about thirty."

"Plains apes," the smaller male supplied. "Imported from Africa, sometime in the last century. They make good watchbeasts and meat animals. You have to be careful with them, though. They throw things."

"Introductions," the other said suddenly. "Excuse our manners, Svetz. I'm Flakee Wrocky. This is my brother Flakee Worrel, and Brenda, his wife. My niece you know."

"Pleased to meet you." Svetz said hollowly.

"You say you slipped sideways in time?"

"I think so. A futz of a long way, too," said Svetz. "Marooned. Gods protect me. It must have been the horse—"

Wrocky broke in. "Horse?"

"The horse. Three years ago, a horse damaged my extension

cage. It was supposed to be fixed. I suppose the repairs just wore through, and the cage slipped sideways in time instead of forward. Into a world where wolves evolved instead of *Homo habilis*. Gods know where I'm likely to wind up if I try to go back."

Then he remembered. "At least you can help me there. Some kind of monster has taken over my extension cage."

"Extension cage?"

"The part of the time machine that does the moving. You'll help me evict the monster?"

"Of course," said Worrel, at the same time the other was saying, "I don't think so. Bear with me, please, Worrel. Svetz, it would be a disservice to you if we chased the monster out of your extension cage. You would try to reach your own time, would you not?"

"Futz, yes!"

"But you would only get more and more lost. At least in our world you can eat the food and breathe the air. Yes, we grow food plants for the trolls; you can learn to eat them."

"You don't understand. I can't stay here. I'm a xenophobe!"

Wrocky frowned. His ears flicked forward enquiringly. "What?"

"I'm afraid of intelligent beings who aren't human. I can't help it. It's in my bones."

"Oh, I'm sure you'll get used to us, Svetz."

Svetz looked from one male to the other. It was obvious enough who was in charge. Wrocky's voice was much louder and deeper than Worrel's; he was bigger than the other man, and his white fur fell about his neck in a mane like a lion's. Worrel was making no attempt to assert himself. As for the women, neither had spoken a word since Svetz entered the room.

Wrocky was emphatically the boss. And Wrocky didn't want Svetz to leave.

"You don't understand," Svetz said desperately. "The air—" He stopped.

"What about the air?"

"It should have killed me by now. A dozen times over. In fact, why hasn't it?" Odd enough that he'd ever stopped wondering about that. "I must have adapted," Svetz said half to himself. "That's it. The cage passed too close to this line of history. My heredity changed. My lungs adapted to pre-Industrial air. Futz it! If I hadn't pulled the interrupter switch I'd have adapted back!"

"Then you can breathe our air," said Wrocky.

"I still don't understand it. Don't you have any industries?"

"Of course," Worrel said in surprise.

"Internal combustion cars and aircraft? Diesel trucks and ships? Chemical fertilizers, insect repellents—"

"No, none of that. Chemical fertilizers wash away, ruin the water. The only insect repellents I ever heard of smelled to high heaven. They never got beyond the experimental stage. Most of our vehicles are battery powered."

"There *was* a fad for internal combustion once," said Wrocky. "It didn't spread very far. They stank. The people inside didn't care, of course, because they were leaving the stink behind. At its peak there were over two hundred cars tootling around the city of Detroit, poisoning the air. Then one night the citizenry rose in a pack and tore all the cars to pieces. The owners too."

Worrel said, "I've always thought that men have more sensitive noses than trolls."

"Wrona noticed my smell long before I noticed hers. Wrocky, this is getting us nowhere. I've *got* to go home. I seem to have adapted to the air, but there are other things. Foods: I've never eaten anything but dole yeast; everything else died out long ago. Bacteria."

Wrocky shook his head. "Anywhere you go, Svetz, your broken time machine will only take you to more and more exotic environments. There must be a thousand ways the world could end. Suppose you stepped out into one of them? Or just passed near one?"

"But—"

"Here, on the other paw, you will be an honored guest. Think of all the things you can teach us! You, who were born into a culture that builds time traveling vehicles!"

So that was it. "Oh, no. You couldn't use what I know," said Svetz. "I'm no mechanic. I couldn't show you how to do anything. Besides, you'd hate the side effects. Too much of past civilizations was built on petrochemicals. And plastics. Burning plastics produces some of the strangest—"

"But even the most extensive oil reserves could not last forever. You must have developed other power sources by your own time." Wrocky's yellow eyes seemed to bore right through him. "Controlled hydrogen fusion?"

"But I can't tell you how it's done!" Svetz cried desperately. "I know nothing of plasma physics!"

"Plasma physics? What are plasma physics?"

"Using electromagnetic fields to manipulate ionized gasses. You *must* have plasma physics."

"No, but I'm sure you can give us some valuable hints. Already we have fusion bombs. And so do the Europeans . . . but we can discuss that later." Wrocky stood up. His black nails made pressure points on Svetz's arm. "Think it over, Svetz. Oh, and make yourself free of the house, but don't go outside without an escort. The trolls, you know."

Svetz left the room with his head whirling. The wolves would not let him leave.

"Svetz, I'm glad you're staying," Wrona chattered. "I like you. I'm sure you'll like it here. Let me show you the house."

Down the length of the hallway, one frosted globe burned dimly in the gloom, like a full moon transported indoors. Nocturnal, they were nocturnal.

Wolves.

"I'm a xenophobe," he said. "I can't help it. I was born that way."

"Oh, you'll learn to like us. You like me a little already, don't you, Svetz?" She reached up to scratch him behind the ear. A thrill of pleasure ran through him, unexpectedly sharp, so that he half closed his eyes.

"This way," she said.

"Where are we going?"

"I thought I'd show you some trolls. Svetz, are you really descended from trolls? I can't believe it!"

"I'll tell you when I see them," said Svetz. He remembered the *Homo habilis* in the Vivarium. It had been a man, an Advisor, until the Secretary-General ordered him regressed.

They went through the dining room, and Svetz saw unmistakable bones on the plates. He shivered. His forebears had eaten meat; the trolls were brute animals here, whatever they might be in Svetz's world—but Svetz shuddered. His thinking seemed turgid, his head felt thick. He had to get out of here.

"If you think Uncle Wrocky's tough, you should meet the European ambassador," said Wrona. "Perhaps you will."

"Does he come here?"

"Sometimes." Wrona growled low in her throat. "I don't like him. He's a different species, Svetz. Here it was the wolves that evolved into men; at least that's what our teacher tells us. In Europe it was something else."

"I don't think Uncle Wrocky will let me meet him. Or even tell him about me." Svetz rubbed at his eyes.

"You're lucky. Herr Dracula smiles a lot and says nasty things in a polite voice. It takes you a minute to—Svetz! What's wrong?"

Svetz groaned like a man in agony. "My eyes!" He felt higher. "My forehead! I don't have a forehead anymore!"

"I don't understand."

Svetz felt his face with his fingertips. His eyebrows were a caterpillar of hair on a thick, solid ridge of bone. From the brow ridge his forehead sloped back at forty-five degrees. And his chin, his chin was gone too. There was only a regular curve of jaw into neck.

"I'm regressing, I'm turning into a troll," said Svetz. "Wrona, if I turn into a troll, will they eat me?"

"I don't know. I'll stop them, Svetz!"

"No. Take me down to the extension cage. If you're not with me the trolls will kill me."

"All right. But, Svetz, what about the monster?"

"He should be easier to handle by now. It'll be all right. Just take me there. Please."

"All right, Svetz." She took his hand and led him.

The mirror hadn't lied. He'd been changing even then, adapting to this line of history. First his lungs had lost their adaptation to normal air. There had been no Industrial Age here. But there had been no *Homo sapiens* either . . .

Wrona opened the door. Svetz sniffed at the night. His sense of smell had become preternaturally acute. He smelled the trolls before he saw them, coming uphill toward him across the living green carpet. Svetz's fingers curled, wishing for a weapon.

Three of them. They formed a ring around Svetz and Wrona. One of them carried a length of white bone. They all walked upright on two legs, but they walked as if their feet hurt them. They were as hairless as men. Apes' heads mounted on men's bodies.

Homo habilis, the killer plains ape. Man's ancestor.

"Pay them no attention," Wrona said offhandedly. "They won't hurt us." She started down the hill. Svetz followed closely.

"He really shouldn't have that bone," she called back.

"We try to keep bones away from them. They use them as weapons. Sometimes they hurt each other. Once one of them got hold of the iron handle for the lawn sprinkler and killed a gardener with it."

"I'm not going to take it away from him."

"That glaring light, is that your extension cage?"

"Yes."

"I'm not sure about this, Svetz." She stopped suddenly. "Uncle Wrocky's right. You'll only get more lost. Here you'll at least be taken care of."

"No. Uncle Wrocky was wrong. See the dark side of the extension cage, how it fades away to nothing? It's still attached to the rest of the time machine. It'll just reel me in."

"Oh."

"No telling how long it's been veering across the time lines. Maybe ever since that futzy horse poked his futzy horn through the controls. Nobody ever noticed before. Why should they? Nobody ever stopped a time machine halfway before."

"Svetz, horses don't have horns."

"Mine does."

There was noise behind them. Wrona looked back into a darkness Svetz's eyes could not pierce. "Somebody must have noticed us! Come on, Svetz!"

She pulled him toward the lighted cage. They stopped just outside.

"My head feels thick," Svetz mumbled. "My tongue too."

"What are we going to do about the monster? I can't hear anything—"

"No monster. Just a man with amnesia, now. He was only dangerous in the transition stage."

She looked in. "Why, you're right! Sir, would you mind—Svetz, he doesn't seem to understand me."

"Sure not. Why should he? He thinks he's a white arctic wolf." Svetz stepped inside. The white-haired wolf man was backed into a corner, warily watching. He looked a lot like Wrona.

Svetz became aware that he had picked up a tree branch. His hand must have done it without telling his brain. He circled, holding the weapon ready. An unreasoning rage built up and up in him. Invader! The man had no business here in Svetz's territory.

The wolf man backed away, his slant eyes mad and frightened. Suddenly he was out the door and running, the trolls close behind.

"Your father can teach him, maybe," said Svetz.

Wrona was studying the controls. "How do you work it?"

"Let me see. I'm not sure I remember." Svetz rubbed at his drastically sloping forehead. "That one closes the door—"

Wrona pushed it. The door closed.

"Shouldn't you be outside?"

"I want to come with you," said Wrona.

"Oh." It was getting terribly difficult to think. Svetz looked over the control panel. Eeny, meeny—that one? Svetz pulled it.

Free fall. Wrona yipped. Gravity came, vectored radially outward from the center of the extension cage. It pulled them against the walls.

"When my lungs go back to normal, I'll probably go to sleep," said Svetz. "Don't worry about it." Was there something else he ought to tell Wrona? He tried to remember.

Oh, yes. "You can't go home again," said Svetz. "We'd never find this line of history again."

"I want to stay with you," said Wrona.

"All right."

*　　*　　*

Within a deep recess in the bulk of the time machine, a fog formed. It congealed abruptly—and Svetz's extension cage was back, hours late. The door popped open automatically. But Svetz didn't come out.

They had to pull him out by the shoulders, out of air that smelled of beast and honeysuckle.

"He'll be all right in a minute. Get a filter tent over that other thing," Ra Chen ordered. He stood over Svetz with his arms folded, waiting.

Svetz began breathing.

He opened his eyes.

"All right," said Ra Chen. "What happened?"

Svetz sat up. "Let me think. I went back to pre-Industrial America. It was all snowed in. I . . . shot a wolf."

"We've got it in a tent. Then what?"

"No. The wolf left. We chased him out." Svetz's eyes went wide. "Wrona!"

Wrona lay on her side in the filter tent. Her fur was thick and rich, white with black markings. She was built something like a wolf, but more compactly, with a big head and a short muzzle and a tightly curled tail. Her eyes were closed. She did not seem to be breathing.

Svetz knelt. "Help me get her out of there! Can't you tell the difference between a wolf and a dog?"

"No. Why would you bring back a dog, Svetz? We've got dozens of dogs."

Svetz wasn't listening. He pulled away the filter tent and bent over Wrona. "I think she's a dog. More dog than wolf, anyway. People tend to domesticate each other. She's adapted to our line of history. And our brand of air." Svetz looked up at his boss. "Sir, we'll have to junk the old extension cage. It's been veering sideways in time."

"Have you been eating gunchy pills on the job?"

"I'll tell you all about it—"

Wrona opened her eyes. She looked about her in rising panic until she found Svetz. She looked up at him, her golden eyes questioning.

"I'll take care of you. Don't worry," Svetz told her. He scratched her behind the ear, his fingertips deep in soft fur. To Ra Chen he said, "The Vivarium doesn't need any more dogs. She can stay with me."

"Are you crazy, Svetz? You, live with an animal? You hate animals!"

"She saved my life. I won't let anyone put her in a cage."

"Sure, keep it! Live with it! I don't suppose you plan to pay back the two million commercials she cost us? I thought not." Ra Chen made a disgusted sound. "All right, let's have your report. And keep that thing under control, will you?"

Wrona raised her nose and sniffed at the air. Then she howled. The sound echoed within the Institute, and heads turned in questioning and fear.

Puzzled, Svetz imitated the gesture, and understood.

The air was rich with petrochemicals and oxides of carbon and nitrogen and sulfur. Industrial air, the air Svetz had breathed all his life.

And Svetz hated it.

DEATH IN A CAGE

Svetz was coming home.

His narrow arms were folded on his chest. His back curved like a bow, to fit him into the curvature of the extension cage. He lay motionless, in stoic endurance, watching the inertial calendar.

Gravity behaved oddly in an extension cage. The pull was outward now as the cage moved into the future. −41, −40 . . . Svetz could not have reached the controls without considerable effort. They were overhead, at the center of the spherical shell. He did not need to reach them. The bulk of the time machine was fixed in timespace at the Institute for Temporal Research in 1102 Post Atomic. It would simply reel him in.

The small armored thing he'd captured was strapped to an opposite wall. It had not moved since Svetz shot it with an anaesthetic crystal.

The numbers on the inertial calendar rolled upward. +16, +17,

+18 . . . Gravity jumped and shivered like a car on a bumpy road. Svetz lay on his back and tried to ignore what his belly and his inner ear were telling him. In a couple of hours, internal time, he'd be home.

Something smoky began to obscure the control panel.

Svetz sniffed. The air was thick with oxides of nitrogen and sulfur, carbon monoxide and carbon dioxide and carbon tetrachloride, a mixture of industrial wastes that Svetz had been breathing since the day he was born. He sniffed and found nothing unusual.

But the haze was thickening.

It was not fanning out. It hung before the control panel, taking shape.

Svetz rubbed his eyes. It was still there, a shape like a cloaked and hooded man, distorting colors and outlines where they showed through. A vague stick-figure hand moulded itself around a lever, and pulled.

The interrupter circuit!

Svetz sat up. His head swam. He tried to stand, and overbalanced, and fell rolling.

The apparition braced its smoky feet against the control panel, heedless of the switches and dials. Its feet and ankles were terribly thin. It pantomimed frantic effort . . . but the lever marked EMERGENCY STOP did not move.

The figure turned to Svetz and screamed at him without sound. Svetz screamed back and threw his arms across his eyes. That face!

When Svetz dared look again, the thing was gone.

Svetz began to shake. The inertial calendar read +36, +37 . . .

"Ghosts, eh?" Svetz's beefy, red-faced boss scowled ferociously. At least he was taking it seriously. He might as easily have sent Svetz off for a psychiatric examination. "That's all we need. A haunted time machine. Well, have you got any idea what really happened?"

"There must be something wrong with the time machine. I think we ought to give up using it until we find out what."

"You do."

"Yes sir."

"Come here a minute." Ra Chen took Svetz's arm and walked away with him. He was twice Svetz's mass; his hand wrapped one and a half times around Svetz's bicep. He stopped them before the picture window that fronted the Institute for Temporal Research.

Spread below them, the shops and houses and crooked streets of the city of Capitol. On the hill across the valley, tremendous and daunting, the complex of buildings that was the United Nations Palace.

Ra Chen pointed downhill. "There."

There was a gap in the cityscape. A cluster of broken houses surrounded the broken corpse of a bird, a bird the size of a five-story building. It had been there for two weeks now. The stink reached them even here.

"Our worst failure to date. I forebear to point out to you, Svetz, that it was your idea to use regression treatments on an ostrich. Notice, however, that the futzy thing lies in full view of the Palace. We'll have to do something spectacular before the Advisors forget that gaff! And we'd better do it soon."

"Yes sir."

"We're in bad odor at the Palace, Svetz."

"Sir, I think that's the roc."

Ra Chen glared.

"We're already missing one time machine," he continued. "I had to yank it after we found out it was veering sidewise in time, across probability lines. The technical arm is still trying to find something wrong with it. Now you want me to yank the other one. Svetz, could you have imagined this—manifestation?"

"I've asked myself that."

"Well?"

"No, sir. It was real. Even if I could see through it."

"It's just such a lousy time to lose both time machines. Appropriations come up in three months."

The vets were removing his armadillo from the extension cage. Svetz watched them erect a gauzy filter tent over it to protect it from the air of 1102 Post Atomic.

"We ought to give up on funny animals," said Ra Chen. "The

Secretary-General already has more extinct animals than he knows what to do with. We ought to try something else."

"Yes, sir. But what?"

Ra Chen didn't answer. They watched as the medical team took clone samples from the armadillo, then moved away with it. It was awake, but doing very little to prove it. Tomorrow it would be in the Vivarium.

"This ghost, now," Ra Chen said suddenly. "Was it human, or just humanoid?"

"It—there was something wrong with the face. Something dreadful."

"But was it a man or an alien?"

"I couldn't tell. After all, it was thin as smoke! It was wearing a robe. I couldn't see anything but the face and hands—and they were dreadfully thin. It looked like a walking skeleton."

"A skeleton, huh? Maybe you were seeing through the flesh. Like a holo of a man in X-ray light."

"That sounds right."

"But why? Why would he be transparent?"

"Funny, I was just wondering the same thing."

"Don't be sarcastic, Svetz."

"Sorry, sir."

"We've both been assuming it was a sign of something wrong with the time machine. What if it wasn't? What if the thing was real?"

Svetz shook his head violently. "There are no such things as ghosts."

"We thought that about rocs. Why not? Think how long the ghost legend has been around. All over the world, in burial customs, folk tales, all the great religions. There are people who believe in ghosts even today. Not many, I admit—"

"But, sir, it's nonsense! Even if there were real ghosts, what*ever* they are, how would they get aboard an extension cage? And what could we do about it?"

"Capture it, of course. The Secretary-General would love it. He could even play with it; it sounded harmless enough—"

"But!"

"—Just ugly. As for how it got there, how should I know? I don't know anything about the theory of time travel. It should be possible to duplicate the conditions—"

"You say it's harmless. I saw it. I say it isn't!"

"We can look into that after we've got it. Svetz, we need a *coup*. We're going after that ghost."

"We? Me! And I won't!"

"Come," said Ra Chen. "Let us reason together."

Gravity behaved oddly in an extension cage. Going backward in time, the pull was inward, toward Svetz's navel. Its intensity fluctuated to no known laws.

"I must be getting used to this," Svetz thought.

He found that ominous. Svetz hated time travel. If he was getting used to the odd motion, he had probably given up hope of changing careers.

At least he didn't get sick anymore.

"How *did* he talk me into this?"

The extension cage slowed. Gravity dwindled, was gone, came back pointing down.

The inertial calendar read −704. 704 Ante Atomic, seven hundred years before the first nuclear explosion. Through the transparent hull of the extension cage Svetz could see a thousand shades of dark green, green in all directions: a place of obscenely proliferating life. It was the South American jungle where he had found the armadillo.

Svetz donned a filter sac and waited for it to inflate around his head. Then he cut the air system and opened the vents to flood the extension cage with outside air. The ghost had first appeared around 20 PA. If there was a ghost, and if it came, it would probably suffocate in Industrial Age air.

Svetz took a sonic stun gun from its place on the wall. Subsonics were less material than anaesthetic crystals, more likely to affect a ghost, he told himself.

He pulled the go-home lever.

And that was that. Svetz had no controls, only signals. The controls were in the future, with the bulk of the time machine in the Institute building. Now the technicians began bringing him home. They had readings from his last mission. They could make his cage behave as it had then.

Svetz had nothing to do but wait.

Time travel still cost over a million commercials a shot. If the cage simply brought him home now, he was going to feel like an idiot. But then, so would Ra Chen.

He was passing 17 Post Atomic when the haze began to form. Svetz stayed on his back, but he raised the handgun.

It was clearer now, more solid. A dark, voluminous cloak and hood showed behind the pale, translucent outline of a human skeleton. Details were blurred, mercifully perhaps, because the thing was moving too fast, screaming and pleading and gesticulating, all without a sound. It was frantic. It begged Svetz to stop the machine.

Svetz fired the stun weapon.

He kept the stud down until his own head buzzed from the echoes. The apparition screamed what must have been a string of curses, and thereafter ignored him. It wrapped the bones of its hands around the Emergency Stop, braced the bones of its feet against the control panel, and pulled.

The lever didn't move. It was as if fog clung to the control panel.

+46, +47, +48 . . .

Svetz began to relax. The thing was harmless.

He was willing to believe that it was man-shaped, though he could see no trace of the ghostly flesh that must surround the smoky bones. Perhaps he was watching some kind of probability phenomenon. As if the ghost-figure marked where a man might be if there were another man aboard Svetz's extension cage, and its transparency was a measure of just how improbable that was . . . Svetz's head began to ache. Certainly he could not be expected to capture a probability phenomenon.

The ghost slowly faded, then became clear. It shifted its grip. The white of bones gleamed faintly through dark cloak.

+132, +133, +134 . . .

The ghost came solid in an instant. It pulled the Emergency Stop down hard, turned and leapt.

It was still a skeleton.

Svetz screamed high and shrill, turned and tried to burrow into the hull. He felt the thing land on his back, light and dry and hard. He wailed again. He was in fetal position now, hugging his knees. Bony fingers tugged at his hand, and he screamed and let go of the stun gun. The fingers took it away.

For a long time nothing happened. Svetz waited for the end. Instead he heard slow footsteps, clickings . . .

And a hollow, grating voice that said, "All right, that's enough of that. Roll over."

Small bones prodded Svetz's ribs. He rolled over and opened his eyes.

It was as bad as he'd thought. Worse. The ghost-figure had turned solid, but it was still no more than a mobile skeleton. It stood now with its cloak flung back and a sonic stun gun in its finger bones. Its face was a skull. Far back in the black eye sockets, eyes watched him steadily.

"Stop staring," said the apparition.

It spoke Speech. It spoke Svetz's language. But the consonants came out mushy, because the thing's skull was lipless.

It chuckled hollowly. "You can see me, can't you? It means you're going to die. When people can see me, it's because they're going to die."

"No," Svetz whispered. His legs were trying to push him back through the wall of the extension cage.

"Stop staring! It's not my fault I'm this way. It was the radiation." The apparition shifted uncomfortably. "What's your name?"

"S-Svetz."

"Allow me to introduce myself. I am Doctor Nathaniel Reynolds, the world's first time traveler, and I've decided to hijack your time machine."

Svetz licked his lips. "I don't think so. The first time traveler—"

"I beat him to it. On another line of history, of course. A dead line. My own fault. Have you ever heard of the Cuban missile crisis? The date was nineteen fifty-eight AD, seventeen Post Atomic, your dating."

"No."

"You're sure? We called it the Short War."

Svetz shook his head.

"Doctor Reynolds" settled himself against the curved wall. He held Svetz's gun steadily on Svetz.

He was not as much a skeleton as Svetz had thought. There was skin over the bones, though the skin itself was the white of bleached bone. In Reynolds's neck there were trachea and gullet as well as the lumpy row of vertebrae.

The rib cage was something else again. Reynolds's ribs were naked bone. Behind the ribs was a narrow torso of flabby white flesh that pulsed like lungs. Torso and abdomen depended from the spine; but daylight showed between the exoskeletal ribs.

The nose and ears were mere holes.

The pelvic bones were sharp as ax blades.

Doctor Reynolds was both hairless and sexless.

He said, "I don't talk well. The only people who can see me and hear me are always about to die. Sometimes they're too sick to concentrate. Sometimes too busy. Sometimes too scared."

"Am I dying?"

Reynolds chuckled. "We'll decide that between us."

"What are you?"

"I'm a ghost. My own fault. But don't laugh. It could happen to you."

Svetz was not thinking of laughing.

"Let me tell you. I was born about a century after the Short War," said Doctor Reynolds. "By then it was obvious the human race was dying. Too many countries had dropped too many bombs in the Short War. Some were cobalt bombs. There was still too much radiation around. Too many mutations, mostly sick and mostly sterile, not to mention disgusting. I was one of the lucky ones."

Svetz said nothing.

"I'd have knocked your teeth out," said the hollow voice. "I really was one of the lucky ones. No brain damage. No gonads, but so what? With all the radiation around I wouldn't have bred true anyway. No organic damage that couldn't be fixed by available medicines. I had to take the pills every day, of course. Would you believe that I once had a pot belly?"

Svetz shook his head.

"A very small pot belly. I had to get rid of it. It hurt. My abdominal muscles couldn't carry the weight. Funny: I've never picked up fat anywhere else. Just the belly, and bones showing through the rest of me."

"How did you get to be a ghost?"

Reynolds laughed, a weak, hollow sound. "Deliberately, and by dint of great effort. There were thousands of us working on it. There wasn't any question that we were doomed. Our best brains, such as we were, were working on time travel. We called it Project Retake. You know what a retake is?"

"Doing a scene over for a sensory."

"That's what we were after. We weren't sure the past could be changed even if we did have time travel. But we had to try it. We did it, too. The time machine was just big enough for me and the scrambler system. They picked me because I only weigh about fifty pounds."

"What did you do?"

"Scrambled the guidance mechanisms of every guided missile in the Union of Soviet Socialist Republics, a week before the Cuban missile crisis. They had to back down and move the missiles out of Cuba. By the time they got their missiles fixed the crisis was over, and they still didn't know what had happened. It must have made them cautious for a while afterward.

"I monitored it all by radio. I made sure nobody saw me, of course. My appearance is a bit—"

"Right."

"So. Afterward I tried to go home. Not to my own present, but to the new one, the one I'd created. My time machine didn't work. We saved a lot of weight by leaving the power source fixed in the future. Now it was gone.

"I left the machine and went to give myself up. And found out I was gone too . . .

"Well, that's all over now," said Reynolds. He hefted the stunner. The bones of his hands were crossed by narrow strands of muscle. His fingernails were long and ragged. "We're going to put it back the way it was."

"Uh?"

"Using your time machine. Mine wouldn't do it, but yours will. We're going back to seventeen Post Atomic."

"We can't."

"I'll kill you if we don't."

Sventz believed him. When Nathaniel Reynolds gave himself a name, Svetz had stopped seeing him as a supernatural horror. But he was convinced that the bony physicist was mad.

He said, "You don't understand. This isn't a time machine, it's only the extension cage, the part that does the moving. The technicians have to haul me back to the present before they can send me back again."

"You're lying."

"No! Reynolds, there aren't any controls here—just on-off pulses to tell the technicians which way to move me. They can only move forward now."

"I almost believe you," Reynolds mused. "But I'll still kill you unless one of us thinks of something."

"You're crazy! You'd have to be crazy to want your bombed-out world back!"

The skeleton clacked his teeth. Svetz saw the red of his mouth, horribly incongruous in the white skull. "Svetz, you haven't asked me how long I've been a ghost."

"How long, then?"

"There's no way to measure. Svetz, I'm anchored to seventeen Post Atomic. I wait, I get eight months or so beyond the Cuban missile crisis, and then everything slows down and stops. I think it's been thousands of years. More.

"Can you imagine anything more horrible? It's a frozen world. People like statues. Pigeons nailed to the air. I'm frozen too. I don't get old, I don't get hungry. Sunlight goes right through me. See how white my skin is? And I can't die. I'm not real enough to die. I'd have gone crazy long ago if it weren't for the time machines."

Reynolds's eyes burned black within the pits of his skull. "The time machines. I see them going and coming, Svetz. Some from your line of history, some from others. Yours is the real future, the future I made. But I can ride the others too.

"Mostly I ride them into the past as far as they'll go. That way time passes normally for me, until seventeen Post Atomic rolls around again. I've been through the Middle Ages a dozen times.

"Funny thing, Svetz. I'm invisible to most people. But anyone can see me if he's about to die. Maybe because he's about to leave time entirely; it doesn't matter what line of history he's on, or I'm on." Reynolds laughed. "I think some of them die *because* they see mc. Heart failure."

Svetz shuddered. Reynolds was probably right.

Reynolds said, "Not funny, eh? I've been in the future too. Dozens of futures. Svetz, did you know that your time machines go sidewise in time?"

"We had one that did. It was damaged."

"They all do. They wobble. The self-powered ones get lost. The ones that are anchored to their own lines of history, like yours, they always get pulled back, no matter how far they slip across alternate probabilities.

"I've seen some strange futures. Svetz. Paradises. Alien invasions. One where elephants were civilized. I've been in *your* future," Reynolds said bitterly. "Long enough to learn Speech. Long enough to see what you've done to the world I made you."

"What do you mean?"

"What do I mean? Everything's dirty, everything's dead! You killed off everything but yourselves and that gray sludge you eat—"

"Dole yeast."

"Dole yeast. I know a short word that would fit it better. I've watched you ejecting that sludge from your mouths—"

"*What?*"

"I was going backward in time, of course, waiting to slide back to seventeen Post Atomic. The fun goes out of that awfully fast. I don't like hopping time machines into the future, not unless I can get a ride back.

"But I do it anyway. There's always the chance a time machine will wobble across my own line of history. Then I could get off, or even stop the machine. And it paid off, didn't it?"

"I don't understand."

"You haven't looked outside at all, have you, Svetz?"

For the first time, Svetz looked *past* Reynolds . . .

The extension cage rested on a plain of cracked black glass. Nothing grew. Far in the distance was a line of . . . Svetz abruptly realized that it was a rim wall. They were in something like a lunar crater.

"This is your world?"

"That's right. I'm home."

"I can't say I like it much."

Reynolds laughed his hollow, grating laugh. "It's cleaner than your world, Svetz. If I'd known you'd kill off everything on Earth, poison the land and the water and the air . . . well, never mind. We'll fix that."

"What do you mean? All you've got to do is step outside! You're home!"

"But it isn't real. I need you to make it real. This is the only time I've ever been able to affect a time machine. You're my only chance, Svetz."

"But I told you—"

"Svetz. This is a stun gun. It can't hurt anyone, but it can hold you still while I immobilize you. After that, well, I've spent considerable time in medieval torture chambers."

"Wait. Wait. What year did you leave from? What was the date when you left to stop the Short War?"

"Ah, twenty ninety-two. You wouldn't think to look at me that I was only twenty-two years old, would you? I haven't aged since—"

"What date Post Atomic?"

"Let's see. One forty-seven."

The inertial calendar read +134.

"All right. You can hitch a ride on your own time machine! It leaves thirteen years from now. We can't move back in time, but we can jump forward." Svetz reached for the go-home. In the same instant his arm became dead meat dropping limply back to his side.

Reynolds said, "But if we tried to go into the future, we'd likely slip sidewise, wouldn't we? And then the pattern of events would have been different, and I wouldn't exist anymore, would I?"

So it was certainly worth a try, thought Svetz. He said, "What are you going to do, wait thirteen years?"

"If I have to." Reynolds clacked his teeth. Apparently it was his only expression; it must make do for a smile, a scowl, a thoughtful look . . . "Hah! I can do better than that. Svetz, can you get me to Australia? Will this thing travel in space coordinates?"

"Yes."

"I'm going to change guns." Reynolds stood, examined the equipment lining the curved wall, selected a weapon. "A heavy needle gun. It wouldn't kill an elephant, maybe, but there's anaesthetic enough in here to kill a man."

"Yah," said Svetz. He felt very afraid.

"And now we'll go."

Australia. The eastern coast was a cityscape of streets and oblong buildings. "It's the only place on Earth that's even marginally habitable," said Reynolds. "It's mostly empty now." And he directed Svetz south along the coast.

He had not stopped talking during the entire flight. He sprawled motionless as a laboratory exhibit, the gun propped casually on one kneecap, while he poured out a steady monologue of reminiscence.

"Of course I have a poor opinion of mankind," he was saying in answer to one of his own questions. "Why not? If you'd seen people under stress as often as I have, in overcrowded hospitals, in torture chambers, on scaffolds and headsman's blocks, on battlefields—you'd know. People take stress badly. Especially on battlefields.

"Now, I may have a biased viewpoint. I suppose I should spend more time at square dances and New Year's Eve parties and palace balls, places where people laugh a lot, but, Svetz, who would I *talk* to? Nobody can see me or hear me unless he's about to die.

"And then they won't listen. Men bear suffering so badly! And they're so afraid to die. I've tried to tell them how lucky they are,

to be able to buy eternal peace at the price of a few hours of agony.
I've talked to millions of men and women and children, over tens
of thousands of years. The only ones who listen are the children,
sometimes. Svetz, are you afraid of death?"

"Yes."

"Idiot."

"Are you sure you know where we're going?"

"Oh, we'll find it, Svetz, don't worry. We're looking for the
school."

"A school? What for?"

"You'll see. There's only one school, Svetz. It's far too big for
the number of children . . . You know, sometimes the people I talk
to seem to recognize me. But then they always behave like idiots.
'Don't take me!' As if I had something to do with it. I've had men
offer me gold—how would I carry it? And what the women offer
me makes even less sense, if they'd only use their own senses."
Reynolds pointed. "There, that wide parkland."

Wide? It was vast, all green grass and the green heads of trees.
Svetz was reminded of the jungle where he'd found the armadillo.
But this greenery was neater, and there were white buildings show-
ing here and there.

"That's the zoo, that low building. All the real animals are dead,
but we have mechanical mockups. There, the athletic field; see the
white lines on the grass? Veer right. We want the lower grade
schoolyard."

There were children in the schoolyard, but not many, and they
weren't playing much. Many were distorted, their deformities obvious even at this altitude. One nine-year-old was terribly thin; he
looked like a small ambulatory skeleton.

"Hold her steady," said Reynolds. "Open the door."

"No!" Suddenly Svetz understood.

"Open the door." The bore of Reynolds's gun looked straight
into Svetz's eyes. Svetz opened the door.

When Reynolds turned to the door, Svetz jumped him.

His dead arm threw him off balance. Reynold's gun butt caught
him under the jaw. Svetz fell back with lights exploding in his head.

When his head cleared, Reynolds was braced in the doorway. Svetz struggled to his knees.

Reynolds fired into the playground.

Svetz staggered toward him with his good hand outstretched.

Reynolds fired again. Then he noticed Svetz and brought the gun around.

Svetz lurched forward to catch the muzzle.

Reynolds fought madly to turn the gun. He couldn't. Svetz, weak as a kitten and ready to die, was still too strong for him. When Reynolds suddenly kicked Svetz under the jaw, it was like being hit with foam plastic.

Six feet tall and a fifty-pound weakling. Svetz jerked the gun toward him, out of Reynolds's grip, and threw it behind him. Reynolds staggered helplessly after it. Svetz reached out and took him by the neck.

If he closed his fist, Reynolds would be dead. There was no muscle to protect his windpipe.

Svetz looked down.

The skeleton boy was sprawled beside a green bench, surrounded by boys and girls and small indeterminate beings. He looked dead. Svetz wasted some time trying to think of something to do. Then he moved two levers with his foot.

Gravity changed. Reynolds struggled furiously for a moment; and then Svetz's hand was empty. Something foggy seemed to be tugging at the Emergency Stop. Svetz watched it fade.

"But then he got away with it," said Ra Chen.

Svetz shrugged. "I did my best to stop him."

"You don't get it. He killed *himself*. He stopped himself from ever going back in time to stop the Short War."

Svetz nodded.

"Then—we aren't real! The Short War happened, and Reynolds's line of history happened, and ours didn't! So how can you be here at all?"

"The time machine pulled me home. An extension cage can't get lost, not if it's anchored to its own present."

Ra Chen's eyes were haunted. "But if Reynolds aborted our past, if we don't have a history anymore, then—"

"Metaphysics! What if we *aren't* real! What if we never *were* real! Sir, you feel real, don't you? So do I. We can always tell ourselves that Project Retake went ahead without Reynolds."

"But—"

"Or maybe the boy lived. He had no hair and practically no scalp. If Reynolds shot him in the head, the anaesthetic crystal would just ricochet off his skull, right? And knock him out."

"Um. I like that. If the kid was dead at age nine, Reynolds would have disappeared, right? Wrong, futz it!" Ra Chen snarled. "If he made himself unreal, he made you unreal too. Why shouldn't you go on seeing him?"

"Come here a minute." Svetz pulled at Ra Chen's arm, without effect; but after a moment Ra Chen followed him voluntarily.

Beyond the glass wall that fronted the ITR building, half a dozen broken buildings surrounded the broken corpse of a bird. The bird was several blocks long and several weeks dead.

"Now, don't you have enough to worry about besides whether you're real or not?"

"Futz, yes. We've got to do something about that roc," said Ra Chen. "There it lies, in full view of the United Nations Palace . . ."

AFTERWORD: SVETZ AND THE BEANSTALK

This book derives from events of more than thirty years ago. When I was still a novice, I had an insight that delighted me:

Time travel is fantasy.

But the only way to get fun out of it is to treat it as *Analog*–style science fiction. Keep it internally consistent. Lay out a set of rules and invite the reader to beat you to the consequences.

Hanville Svetz doesn't know that time travel is fantasy. He was born deep into a future polluted to match the sorriest predictions of Greenpeace. Most life-forms are extinct by Svetz's time. To Svetz the creatures of the past may be strange, dangerous, horrifying; anything but surprising. Svetz has the scientist's talent: he can wrap a theory around what he finds, rather than altering the evidence to fit a theory.

I dreamed up "The Flight of the Horse" one morning, spent the afternoon outlining it, and told it as a cocktail party story that night, without losing any listeners. You can't do that with every good story; but *when* you can do that, the story is *ready*.

I sold "Leviathan!" to *Playboy* magazine. It's the only time I've ever managed that. *Playboy* was a joy to work with. Editorial work was minimalist, all changes explicitly described, and the money was good too. I sent them "Bird in the Hand" too, but they sent it back.

"There's a Wolf in My Time Machine!" was set in an altered version of the Haunted House ride at Disneyland. The characters are alternate-timeline versions of the Keeshond show dogs I grew up with.

Time travel is fantasy! And the universe of fantasy is large . . . but after "Death in a Cage" I decided the joke was played out.

In the 1970s, Carl Sagan persuaded Kip Thorne, a world-class mathematician, to design him a time machine for a science fiction novel. Tipler got interested in the challenge, and other mathematicians joined in.

The time machines that emerged are solid science fiction, if you'll accept that the Ringworld is. That is, they require exotic materials and construction techniques, and the engineers need nearly godlike powers. But give them these, and all the laws of physics hold except what has never been proven: the law of cause and effect.

These time machines look less like a Delorian automobile than a freeway. You can't ride on a freeway except where it's been built! That is, we won't be seeing time travelers because the freeway hasn't been built in our time. Time travelers will already have god-like powers before they can travel in time . . . unless we should chance to find somebody's abandoned freeway. . . .

But in any era previous to the 1970s, time travel is fantasy.

Worlds don't disappear on me.

A notion was kicking around in my head . . . and on my computer disks, once Jerry Pournelle talked me into switching from a typewriter. For a quarter of a century I would occasionally stumble across "Beans": my file of disorganized notes comparing "Jack and the Beanstalk" to the orbital tower invented by Tsiolkovsky and later popularized in several stories including Arthur Clarke's *The Fountains of Paradise.*

I knew by then that I wouldn't ever lack for story ideas. "We are the masters of time," as Svetz says. "Svetz and the Beanstalk" could wait.

In 1990 a leaflet from Dangerous Visions, a bookstore in Van Nuys, alerted me that Terry Pratchett and Neal Gaiman would be in to autograph *Good Omens.* That sounded like fun. I'd barely discovered Neil Gaiman, but already I would buy anything by Terry Pratchett. I went to say Hi.

His flight had been delayed by six hours.

We went back to my place. I didn't know how that would work out, but Marilyn and I have one of the better art collections, and I have some computer games, or we could hike Mulholland. . . .

Nah. We started talking collaboration and spent our whole time that way. I tossed in the notion of a Beanstalk that's a plant. We carved out a loose novel structure from there.

And I've got those notes around somewhere, but I've never looked at them since.

We live eight time zones apart. He admitted to a tendency to blitz: to start writing and never quit. These things might make a collaboration awkward. Unless I could get the jump on him, he'd wind up handing me completed text!

But we were both involved in other projects. The Beanstalk would wait.

My first published story, set on Mercury, was obsolete before it hit print. When the world was told the truth about Venus's surface temperature, I was just behind it with "Becalmed in Hell." The astrophysicists kept changing Mars on me, and I wrote a string of stories to keep up.

Then I fell behind.

Now it's the nineties, and every hard science fiction writer has written a Mars story. *Red/Green/Blue Mars, Moving Mars, Mars Underground.* With competition like Robinson, Greg Bear, William

Hartmann, how was I going to find anything *new* to say? If I wanted to write about Mars, I would need another approach.

Then it all came together.

When a story is ready to be told, I write.

I started *Svetz and the Beanstalk* on a portable computer aboard a cruise ship docked at Ensenada, Mexico. We'd already seen the Blowhole. Marilyn went off to shop. I set up my laptop computer in the lounge that sells cappuccino, and began writing.

I saw nothing impossible about writing two Beanstalk stories, the second with Terry Pratchett. . . .

Except that I never leave anything out. It was my first insight as a writer. Never hold anything back from the reader. It was basic to Robert Heinlein's style too. Take one idea and explore *every* implication.

Yggdrasil (and a lot of Norsemen) was one of Terry's suggestions. A lot of that six-hour conversation must have worked its way into the novel.

Worried and embarrassed. I E-mailed Terry and told him what had happened. His opinion matches mine: ideas are cheap, it's the writing that makes them golden. He tells me he's ready to write a Beanstalk novel too. But, set on the Diskworld, it's likely to follow wildly different physics.

Then there's Suzanne Gibson. I met her through her husband, Warren James, who runs *Hour 25*, a local radio show, on Friday nights. When I was deep into Svetz and time travel and Mars, Suzanne volunteered to do some of my research.

The chapter heads all came from her. It seems as if every separate branch of humanity has its own tower to Heaven. I found some wonderful quotes from South America too, but I lost them.

So this is my take on Mars, and Yggdrasil, and (again, God help me) the space program.

What came before doesn't count. We always build from *now*.